Country

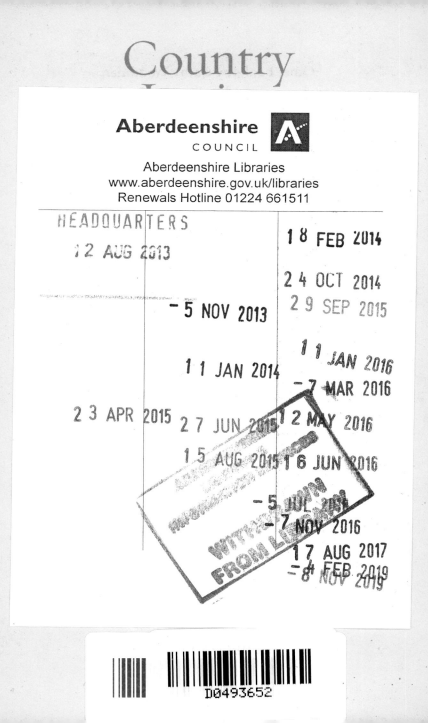

Other books by Cathy Woodman
Trust Me, I'm a Vet
Must Be Love
The Sweetest Thing
It's a Vet's Life
The Village Vet
Vets in Love

Cathy Woodman

Country Loving

arrow books

Published by Arrow Books 2013

2 4 6 8 10 9 7 5 3

First published in Great Britain in 2013 by Century

Arrow Books
Random House, 20 Vauxhall Bridge Road,
London SW1V 2SA

www.randomhouse.co.uk

Addresses for companies within The Random House Group Limited
can be found at: www.randomhouse.co.uk/offices.htm

The Random House Group Limited Reg. No. 954009

A CIP catalogue record for this book
is available from the British Library

ISBN 9780099584896

The Random House Group Limited supports the Forest Stewardship
Council® (FSC®), the leading international forest-certification organisation.
Our books carrying the FSC label are printed on FSC®-certified paper.
FSC is the only forest-certification scheme supported by the leading
environmental organisations, including Greenpeace.
Our paper procurement policy can be found at:
www.randomhouse.co.uk/environment

Typeset by SX Composing DTP, Rayleigh, Essex
Printed and bound by CPI Group (UK) Ltd, Croydon, CR0 4YY

To Tamsin and Will

Acknowledgements

I should like to thank Laura Longrigg at MBA Literary Agents, Gillian Holmes and the wonderful team at Random House for their continuing enthusiasm and support. I should also like to congratulate Grant Cowan on the beautiful cover illustrations, especially the one of the cute brown calf!

For their moral support and practical assistance while I've been writing this book, I'd like to thank Liz and Dave, Alex and Karen and their families, and my parents.

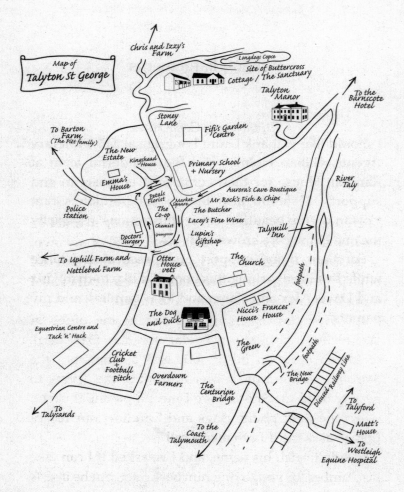

Map of
Talyton St George

Chris and Izzy's Farm

To Barton Farm
(The Pitt family)

Longdogs Copse

Site of Buttercross
Cottage / The Sanctuary

Talyton Manor

To the Barnscote Hotel

Stoney Lane

Fifi's Garden Centre

The New Estate

Kingshead House

Primary School + Nursery

Emma's House

Petals Florist

Market Square

The Co-op

chemist   greengrocer

Doctors' Surgery

Police station

Aurora's Cave Boutique

Mr Rock's Fish & Chips

The Butcher

Lacey's Fine Wines

Lupin's Giftshop

River Taly

Talymill Inn

To Uphill Farm and Nettlebed Farm

Otter House vets

The Church

footpath

The Dog and Duck

Nicci's House   Frances' House

Equestrian Centre and Tack 'n' Hack

The Green

footpath

Cricket Club + Football Pitch

Overdown Farmers

The New Bridge

Disused Railway Line

To Talysands

The Centurion Bridge

To Talyford

To the Coast Talymouth

Matt's House

To Westleigh Equine Hospital

Chapter One

Till the Cows Come Home

There are times when I'm afraid I'll wake up to find I've been dreaming. I have a great career, a flat of my own, at least two foreign holidays a year and a wonderful boyfriend who has asked me to marry him. All in all, I think I've done rather well for a farm girl.

It's Thursday morning and I'm in the office in Wimbledon with my calendar for the first week of March open on my mobile and a latte from the Starbucks around the corner in front of me, trying to get my head together before I meet a potential client, when the desk phone rings and Caroline, our receptionist, asks me if I can take a call.

'I didn't catch his name, and I've asked if I can take his number for you to ring him back later, but he insists on speaking to you straight away. I'm sorry, Stevie, I don't seem to be able to get through to him.'

I check the time. I have a few minutes.

'Thanks, Caroline. Put him through,' I say.

The caller is elderly and speaks with a strong Devon accent, the sound of his voice triggering a distant memory of ripening corn and blackberries.

'This is Stevie Dunsford's office?' he asks. 'Only I don't want to make a fool of myself. It's bad enough already that I'm doing this. I wouldn't normally snitch on anyone, let alone the boss.'

'You're speaking to her – Stevie, I mean.' Although I'm an accountant and good with numbers, two and two are definitely not making four at this moment.

'It's Cecil here,' he says, pronouncing his name to rhyme with thistle.

'Cecil? It's you.' I picture Cecil, an old man with a stoop – he's always seemed old to me – standing in the farmyard in his brown coat and boots, with his tweed cap shading his eyes as he chews on a piece of sweet hay and counts the black and white cows in from the field. 'Is everything all right?' It's a stupid question to ask, I think, because there has to be some kind of problem. He's never called me before, not like this, out of the blue. 'What's happened?'

I wait for Cecil to respond, a pulse thudding dully at my temple. He never was one for being quick on the uptake.

'It's Tom, your dad, he's up to his neck in the muck and the mire.'

'He's in trouble? What kind of trouble?'

'He's more than likely going to end up in prison,' Cecil responds.

'What on earth for?' I say, aghast because I was

assuming he'd been in some kind of accident on the farm. 'He can't go to prison at his time of life. He's seventy-five.'

'Someone reported him for neglect.'

'Who would do such a thing? How could anyone be so nasty?'

'I'm always telling Tom to keep his friends close and his enemies closer, but when has he ever listened to me?' Cecil says mournfully.

'Or anyone else for that matter,' I add.

'He hasn't always been a good neighbour.'

'What do you mean by that?'

'He and Guy from Uphill Farm next door have had a few fallings-out over the years and everything came to a head recently when Guy met your dad to discuss the state of the cows. They almost came to fisticuffs, and it ended with Guy contacting Animal Welfare.' Cecil pauses. 'Do you remember Jack Miller?'

I have a vague memory of meeting Jack at various events in Talyton St George when I used to live there.

'Anyway,' Cecil continues, 'he's the local Animal Welfare officer now and he's been out to the farm twice to inspect the cattle. He says if conditions don't improve before his next visit, he'll have no choice but to recommend Tom's charged with animal cruelty. He'll be fined, or locked up, and banned from keeping animals for life.'

'I don't understand.' Yes, my father is what many have described as an awkward old bugger, but he would never neglect the cows, and losing them from the farm would break his heart.' I'm growing angry now at the injustice of the accusation. 'It's impossible, Cecil. He loves those cows more than anything in the world.'

'Well, you know how it is, Stevie. It's been a right struggle keeping the farm going recently. Tom's hardly in the best of health. In fact, he's still very poorly.'

This is news to me.

'What's wrong with him?'

'I know you and your dad aren't on the best of terms, but I can't believe you've forgotten.'

I'm not usually lost for words, but I don't know what to say as Cecil says in an admonishing tone, 'Dr Mackie reckons it's going to be a long time till he's back on his feet proper-like. He might never come completely right.'

'Cecil, I'm afraid I don't know what you're talking about. The last time I spoke to my father he was as right as rain – his turn of phrase, not mine.'

'And when was that, my lover?' I'm seized by a mixture of guilt and regret when I work out exactly how long ago it was. 'More than three months?'

'Nearer six,' I confess.

'He hasn't told you then, his own flesh and blood?' Cecil continues. 'I had high hopes you two would put the past aside and move on. It was your mother's dearest wish.'

'Please just tell me what's going on,' I say with a touch of impatience. Any reminder of my mum is painful to me and I don't want to think about it.

'Tom's recovering from a stroke. He spent six weeks in hospital but he's home now.'

4

'I don't believe this. Why didn't he call me? Why didn't you let me know before?'

'Because he said he'd seen you. I've been running the farm by myself, so I didn't have any reason to doubt him when he said you'd made a couple of flying visits from London.' Cecil's voice softens. 'I was pretty sore when you didn't drop in to see me and Mary. We were such friends, Stevie.'

'How is my dad? How bad is it?'

'He tries to put a good face on it, but he's been forced to sleep downstairs in the house and he can't get much further than the front door on crutches or a stick. Mary cooks and cleans for him and the doctor comes in regular, so he's all right as far as it goes.'

'So he's housebound?'

'Pretty much.'

It's worse than I could have imagined. 'What about the milking?' I ask.

'I'm doing that. I've been milking cows twice a day for nigh on sixty years.' Cecil chuckles. 'I can do it in my sleep.'

'And the other work on the farm?'

'That will have to be done another time.'

'You need someone to give you a hand.' I glance out of the window. The sky is clearing. 'I'll talk to Dad.'

'It's no use,' Cecil says.

'I know how stubborn he is, but really, it's too much to expect you to run the show.' Cecil's older than my father by a few years.

'It's the money, Stevie. Tom can't afford to feed the cows, let alone take on another farmhand.'

'I don't see how he can afford not to.' I prefer to avoid any conflict with my father, I've had more than enough grief from him in the past, but hiding the fact he's been seriously ill from me, his daughter, and lying about it to Cecil, who's been the most loyal employee anyone could have, is beyond the pale. 'I'll call him after work.'

My solution to the problem isn't enough for Cecil.

'Stevie, you have to come and see it for yourself.'

'I'm very busy. I can't just drop everything.'

'You can drive down tomorrow and stay for the weekend. Mary will make up a bed and make sure you're fed.'

'I have plans for Saturday night,' I sigh. It's my flat-mate's thirtieth birthday and we're having a bit of a party. 'Won't it wait until next weekend?'

'No, because the next welfare inspection is tomorrow. We've had ten days to start turning it around and nothing's changed. Stevie, you have to come back to the farm otherwise everything your family has worked for over the years will be gone.'

My instant reaction is 'Why me?' Why should I have any compassion for my father after how he treated me, rejecting me for my brother?

I pick up the photo of Nick and me at the firm's Christmas party from my desk. (I met my boyfriend at work – Nick is one of the partners.) The girl who picked blackberries with Cecil would hardly recognise herself now: a tall, curvy woman of twenty-eight, wearing a short purple bodycon dress, with her rich brown hair pinned up, her brown eyes made up with false lashes and her nail extensions painted with black and silver crackle glaze.

'Have you spoken to Ray?' I ask.

'I think it would be better coming from you. You know Ray and I haven't always seen eye to eye.' Cecil hesitates. 'Please come home. Your dad's a very sick man, the cows are going without and, truth be told, I'm struggling. I'm not sure how much longer I can keep going. Some days my back's so bad I can hardly move.' For a man of few words, Cecil makes an impassioned speech. 'I know why you left the farm in the first place – I had many an argument with your dad over it, but he wouldn't bend, and why should he? I'm only the hired farmhand, when all's said and done. But you should have been the one who stayed, not that waste of space, Ray. I'm sorry, I shouldn't speak badly of your brother, but he never loved the place in the same way you did.

'I can't stand by and see them cows starve no more. It's breaking my heart to watch them like this. We need you, Stevie. Nettlebed Farm needs you. Please, I'm begging you to come home.'

I listen to Cecil's slow rasping breathing before the phone cuts out, then close my eyes, picturing the bony black and white cows waiting patiently outside the milking parlour, asking for nothing and giving everything. I can almost smell their sweet breath and hear the rhythmic pulse of the milking machine and it takes me back to when I was a teenager working alongside Cecil. We made a good team. He was always there for me. If nothing else, I owe it to him and the cows to see what I can do, but I don't owe my father anything.

I'm not going anywhere this weekend. I take a sip of coffee. My life is here in London and I've made plans for India's special birthday, but Cecil's call has disturbed my peace of mind because the very idea of Nettlebed Farm without cows is unthinkable.

'Do you remember that song by the Wurzels?' Nick says as he drives at speed along the motorway the following morning.

'The one you've been singing non-stop for the last twenty miles, you mean, about the combine harvester?' I say, amused. 'If you're not careful, I'll ask Mary to give you turnips for tea.'

'Dinner, you mean.' He sighs. 'I hate root vegetables.'

'I've told you before. In Devon, dinner is lunch and tea is dinner, if you get my drift, and we live on turnips and swedes in the country.'

'I remember now,' he says. 'It's like you came down from another planet, Stevie.'

'Thanks, Nick.' I fall silent for a while, recalling our last trip to the farm for my mum's funeral last year. They were the worst days of my life, but Nick was at my side, quietly supportive, and I'll always be grateful to him for that.

'Don't you think you ought to slow down a little?' I say eventually, clinging on to my seat.

'I thought there was some urgency about the situation.' Nick presses the accelerator down a touch, making the engine roar instead of merely purr. 'You said we needed to get there as soon as possible.'

'I'd like to get there in one piece.'

I glance towards my boyfriend, who's in his element behind the wheel of his car. He's well turned-out, the jeans and blue shirt understated but expensive. His eyes are blue-grey, his short brown hair is combed and waxed into place, his teeth are straight and white and his skin lightly tanned. It's his natural colour – it isn't long since we returned from the holiday of my dreams in Mauritius.

Nick flashes me a smile. 'I hope you aren't going to turn out to be a terrible nag, Stevie. You liked going fast when we first met. You said it gave you a thrill.'

I did because with the first flush of romance I'd felt immortal, but during our eighteen months together, my sense of self-preservation has gradually returned. I'm no longer so wrapped up in us being a couple, which, as I keep telling myself, is only to be expected.

Nick grows serious.

'I don't understand the rush, to be honest. Your dad's hardly been considerate of your feelings over the years and I really can't work out how a father can forget to tell his daughter he's had a stroke. What's that all about?'

I don't say anything. Glancing at the speed registering on the dashboard, I reckon it won't be long before we find out.

'I wish you'd let me drive for a while,' I say, changing the subject.

'This is my baby.' Nick drums his fingers against the steering wheel.

'One day what's yours will be mine, if we get married.'

9

'When, I hope. However, this is one of the "all my worldly goods" that we won't be sharing.'

'If you really loved me, you'd let me have a go,' I say archly. 'I've always wanted to drive an Aston Martin.'

'You know I love you,' he says.

'But you love your car more.'

'It isn't that. It's just that she's a bit livelier than what you're used to.'

'If I can drive a tractor, I can drive your car.'

'What are you suggesting, Stevie? She's nothing like a tractor.' Nick floors the accelerator and the car whisks into the fast lane, leaving the other traffic behind. 'Anyway, it's me who should be questioning you on your level of commitment.' His voice grows a little sulky, adding another grain to the slowly growing mound of doubt about where our future lies. 'I'm beginning to wonder what's taking you so long.'

'It's a big step,' I begin, not wanting to enter into this conversation. Nick is nine years older than me and has been married before. Sometimes I wonder if the age gap will become too much and if he's just too desperate to get married again. 'I want to be sure.'

'I'm sure,' he says, and I notice the creases form at the corner of his eye as he concentrates on the road ahead. I wish I could talk to him about my doubts and fears and my desire to stay as we are, without hurting his feelings. 'Stevie, when will you put me out of my misery and give me your answer?'

'Soon, I promise, but please don't keep pressuring me. I have a lot on my mind.' I pause, waiting for his response which doesn't come. 'Thank you.'

'What for?'

'For coming with me. I really appreciate it.' I'm not sure I can marry him. I'm not sure we'll last, but we're together, side by side, and that's enough for me for now. I reach out and touch his thigh.

'Not now, Stevie. I'm driving.' Nick flashes me a smile and pushes my hand away. 'I rather fancy a long weekend in sunny Devon, and it's always good to have an excuse to take the car for a spin,' he continues.

'I'm not sure it's going to be sunny,' I say, gazing at the hands of a man who's never worked outdoors and only ever works up a sweat at the gym. In fact, it's pouring, spray flying up from the cars ahead and rain streaking across the windscreen, but I don't think Nick hears me because he goes on, 'I want to prove I'll always be at your side when you need me.'

'Oh, Nick, that's so romantic.'

'Perhaps we can talk again about moving in together, like a trial run before getting hitched.'

'I suppose it would be a good idea to find out if we feel the same about each other when the dishes are piled up in the sink and the dirty socks are scattered across the bedroom floor.' I've had boyfriends before, but I've never lived with any of them.

'I always put my socks in the laundry bin,' Nick says, looking upset. 'I have one for whites and one for darks.'

I smile because that could be an issue. I'm not the tidiest person in the world.

'Forgive me if I sound like I'm complaining, Stevie. I'm not. I'm just observing when I say that I'm trying really hard here and I don't feel like I'm getting anything back. I've done the right thing, going down on one knee on the beach in the most amazing setting, with blue seas, coconut palms and cocktails, yet when I talk about moving in together, you reduce it to the level of the laundry arrangements. I thought you wanted the hearts and flowers.'

'I do . . .'

'Well, what's wrong then?'

'I can't really explain. I'm sorry if I come across as ungrateful when you're being so thoughtful and caring.' That seems to mollify him and it's a relief because I don't have to go on to tell him how I can't deal with the effort he purports to be making. I can't envisage marrying a man who has to try so hard. Surely love and romance should come more naturally. Is that too much to ask?

'We'll find a pub and stop for lunch as soon as we come off the motorway,' Nick says eventually.

'I'm not hungry, thank you. I'd prefer to keep going.' I have butterflies dancing in my stomach. Part of me wants to get to the farm to find out what's going on, while part of me wants to delay the moment for ever.

'It can't be easy going back,' Nick says, driving on. 'In fact, I'm amazed you even considered it, after what your father did.'

'I'm not going back for my father. I'm going back because of Cecil. He's always been very kind to me.' I'm fond of him, and I often wished he could have been my dad instead.

The motorway ends and we run into the back of

a queue of traffic that spreads out again across the plain where the ancient circle of stones, Stonehenge, stands in a grassy landscape with sheep grazing close together. Another hour later and, as we pass the sign reading 'Welcome to Devon', the rain clears and the sun comes out from behind the clouds.

'Are we nearly there yet?' Nick says, slipping on his Ray-Bans.

'There's some way to go yet,' I respond. It's another forty minutes before we reach the turning for Talyton St George, where the road narrows into a country lane with dense hedges on either side. We pass Talyton Manor before entering Talyton itself, where red, white and blue bunting flutters between the lampposts in Market Square.

Nothing much changes in this quiet country town, apart from the odd tweak in the window display in Aurora's Cave, where a mannequin is posing in a bikini. It's quite a shock to see it, because the sight of naked flesh – even plastic – was always considered an offence to the morals of the town's residents. The shutters are down at Mr Rock's fish-and-chip shop, and there's a sign on the butcher's shop door reading, 'Sorry Closed Early'. An elderly man, Nobby the church organist, is shuffling very slowly across the pedestrian crossing.

'Which way is it now?' Nick stops to wait for him to cross.

'Straight over at the next junction,' I say. 'What's happened to the sat nav?'

'She's crashed – there's no signal.'

'It isn't far now.'

'I thought you said it wasn't much further,' Nick grumbles as we drive along the lane out of town, which narrows down to single-track. A quarter of a mile or so along, a tractor comes bowling down the hill straight at us. Nick slams on the brakes and his face drains of colour as the tractor stops within a metre of the car's bumper.

'That was a close shave,' he breathes before opening the window and waving furiously at the tractor driver to reverse.

'That's Guy.'

'I don't give a monkey's who he is. He's in the way.'

'You'll have to reverse. There's a passing place further back.'

'I can't pull in there,' he says when we reach a gateway into a field. 'She'll catch her undercarriage. I'm not risking it.'

'In that case, you'll have to keep going back until we reach town again,' I say, wishing I'd brought my car.

'Who's this Guy person?' Nick asks once we're back on the road.

'He's our neighbour, the one who reported my father to Animal Welfare. He farms the land next door to ours.'

'Ours? Why do you keep calling it your farm? I thought it was the family farm.'

'I haven't really talked about it before, but part of it is mine.'

'Why on earth didn't you think to mention it? You're as bad as your father, keeping secrets.'

'I don't know. The subject has never really come up.'

I shrug. 'I don't like talking about the farm.'

'Do you have any say in how your father manages the land?' Nick asks.

'I have a part-share with my brother Ray, a financial interest – it's all to do with financial management and reducing inheritance tax. I don't think my father would accept it if I went in telling him what to do.'

'You might have to.'

'I hope not, because he's never listened to me before.'

We reach a fork in the road where the left-hand branch is signposted 'Uphill Farm and Uphill House', the sign itself leaning against a churn on a stone platform by the hedge. There is a board, too, with 'Potatoe's and Cider' chalked on it. Above that is a brand-new sign for 'Jennie's Cakes'.

'You said it was rural, but this really is the back of beyond,' Nick says as we keep right, turning the corner where the lane shrinks further, the overgrown hedgerows reaching out and caressing the wings of the car. There's grass growing up through the crazed surface of the tarmac in the middle of the road, and loose stones fly up now and again and ping against the paintwork, making Nick wince.

'Now left.' I can smell the scent of cow and fresh grass as we grow closer.

'Left? Where?'

'Just after the tree. There's a sign.' I look for the sign reading 'Nettlebed Farm', which is fixed to the trunk of the old oak, but it's obscured by a tangle of ivy. 'I'll have to open the gate.' When Nick pulls into the entrance to the farm, I slide out of the car to push and lift the rickety five-barred gate wide open. The March wind blusters through my hair, which I've left loose around my shoulders.

'Do you mean I have to drive up there?' Nick calls out of the window. 'It looks pretty bumpy.'

'That's nothing. You should see it when it's rained for a few days.' I give him a smile to cheer myself up. 'That's why we drive tractors around here.'

'I really can't imagine you handling a tractor, given that you struggle to park an Audi,' Nick adds with a cheeky grin, and I feel a surge of affection for him. If the truth be told, I'm so scared of what I'm going to find that I'm not sure I could have done this on my own. My father has always seemed immortal to me, and the survival of the family farm in perpetuity has never been in doubt before.

I close the gate behind him and jump back into the car. It's done now. I'm here and there's no going back. We follow the drive to the farmyard where we are greeted with a loud bang.

'What the hell was that?' Nick says with his hand on the gear stick, ready to reverse.

'Gunshot,' I say, my heart beating faster.

Chapter Two

Skinny Cows

Nick pulls into the farmyard between an Animal Welfare van and a police car. Ignoring his entreaties that I wait to see if it's safe, I get out and run across the yard in my Louboutin ankle boots, catching and scraping the heels in the cracks in the concrete and cobbles.

'Dad, stop!' I shout as I approach my father, who is standing in front of the tumbledown cob-and-thatch cowshed with a smoking shotgun aimed vaguely in the direction of a pale-faced policeman who gesticulates wildly as my dad loads it with another cartridge, fumbling with one arm in a grubby sling.

'Dad?' I am probably as shocked at the sight of him as he is of me. He's changed, aged. His dark grey hair has grown long and lank and has lost its lustrous sheen, and he looks as if he's wearing another man's clothes. He appears to have tried to shave and given up halfway through. The left side of his face has dropped, his eyelid droops and his mouth is twisted into a sardonic smile, a sharp contrast to the expression of anger and defeat in his hazel eyes.

'Stevie?' he mumbles.

'Give me the gun.' I step in close enough to grab it around the stock and barrel, but my father seems reluctant to relinquish it.

'If you don't put that gun down, Mr Dunsford,' the policeman says, 'I will have no choice but to place you under arrest for threatening behaviour.' He's a familiar face, patrolling the crime-free streets of Talyton St George, reuniting lost dogs with their owners.

'Dad, give me the gun,' I repeat.

'It's mine. I have a licence for it,' he says.

'Not a licence to kill though,' I say more gently, as a rush of adrenaline surges through my blood while I attempt to wrestle the gun from him. 'Come on, hand it over, then we can talk. Please, Dad. You're making things worse.'

Somehow, he finds the strength to wrench the gun from my grip and I can only hold my breath, scared stiff at what he'll do next, but he doesn't fire it again. He breaks the gun to make it safe and presents it to me.

'Thank you.' I find I'm trembling as I hand it over to the policeman. 'I'm Stevie, Stephanie, Mr Dunsford's daughter. Now you can tell me what's going on here.'

'All in good time.' The police constable – Kevin, he's called – turns to my father. 'Thomas Edwin Dunsford, I'll have to arrest you for a breach of the peace and take you down to the station.'

'That's ridiculous,' my father blusters. 'These people have come onto my farm without any by-your-leave. What is the world coming to when a landowner has no right to protect his property?'

'You've had plenty of warning,' the policeman says. He must be about my age but looks younger, his uniform ill-fitting around his shoulders and his trousers, which are spattered with mud, overlong. He pulls out his notebook and writes a couple of lines, the tip of his tongue sticking out.

'He's a very sick man,' I cut in. 'You can't arrest him.'

'I'll ask one of the local GPs to see him while he's in custody.'

'He's had a stroke recently.' I'm not making excuses for him, but I fear he'll have another one.

'Everyone has made allowances for Mr Dunsford's health, but it can't go on like this. Enough is enough.' The policeman turns to me. 'This is our second visit. On the last occasion Mr Dunsford made verbal threats to the Animal Welfare officer and the attending veterinary surgeon. This time he fired shots from his gun.'

'They're trying to take my cows away from me,' my father says, his cheeks flushed with resentment. 'What do you expect?'

'Dad, you could have killed someone.'

'I should have,' he goes on. 'That man, Guy Barnes, that neighbour of ours, he deserves to have some lead shot up his backside for what he's done.'

'You can't say that. Stop making it worse for yourself.' However, it seems it can't be any worse.

'If Jack Miller is unhappy with progress in remedying

the situation, I shall be arresting Mr Dunsford for offences under the Animal Welfare Act.'

'Look,' I say to PC Kevin, 'you're making a mistake. Please don't make him go to the police station.' There's a fine line between love and hate and I find that I can't stand by. 'Obviously, he isn't coping and what he needs is support.'

'It's no excuse in law. The courts will have to decide if it's a mitigating factor.'

'How's this going to look? The police arresting a sick and defenceless old man?'

'Hey, less of the old, Stevie,' Dad interrupts.

I glare at him to shut him up.

'Can we go inside the house and talk about this over a cup of tea?' I ask.

'Well, I don't know,' PC Kevin says hesitantly.

'I expect there'll be some cake,' I go on. 'Please, give me ten minutes to run through exactly what's been going on here, so I can give you the assurances you need to guarantee this kind of incident won't happen again, and the cows will be looked after.'

'I don't think it's that simple,' PC Kevin says.

He's beginning to infuriate me because, as far as I can see, it's pretty straightforward, but I hold my tongue and show him towards the farmhouse, picking up my father's crutch, which is lying on the ground in the mud and weeds. I give them to him and he struggles along at my side.

'No one mentioned you were coming,' he complains.

'No one told me you were ill.' My sense of anger and hurt dissipates slightly at the sight of the man in front of me, a shadow of his former self, physically at least.

'Why are you here?' he asks. 'To rub my nose in it?'

'Cecil contacted me.'

'The old buzzard!' My father hesitates when Nick joins us. 'Who is this?'

'Nick, my boyfriend,' I say. 'You must remember him. He came to Mum's funeral.'

'Oh yes.' My father nods as he stares at him, and I'm not convinced he has any recollection of him at all, but then it was a very stressful time and Nick tactfully stayed in the background.

'Hello, Tom,' Nick says. 'I thought it was supposed to be quiet living in the country.'

'We have our fair share of dramas,' PC Kevin says as a dog starts barking.

Nettlebed Farm is set in a dip in the hills. The farmhouse, which stands opposite the barn and collecting yard, isn't the most beautiful house in the world. Its tiled roof looks like an oversized hat and it is rendered grey so it looks like stone from a distance. It's a square building with three steps down to the porch and front door, where a shaggy tricolour creature, like a patchwork dog made up of pieces of many other dogs, is tied to a ring in the wall. Family history suggests that the ring was originally used by my great-grandmother to secure her hunter when she returned from a day out with the hounds. The dog redoubles his efforts at barking as we approach.

'Shut up, Bear,' I scold, and he stops instantly, gazing at me through one blue eye and one brown, and with one ear up and one ear down, before he starts snuffling and squeaking and wagging his tail, straining at the rope that restrains him. 'Good boy.'

'Be careful,' says PC Kevin. 'That dog's dangerous.'

'The dog isn't a danger to anyone,' I say, stepping down to unfasten the rope. His coat is matted and dirty. 'He's an old softie.'

'Stevie, I'm afraid Bear bit the vet,' Dad cuts in. 'He turned on him. Really nasty, it was, but it was the vet's fault for staring at him straight in the eyes. He can't be a proper vet. He's on death row.'

Bear is, or the vet, I want to ask. Bear must be twelve or thirteen now and, although I haven't seen him much over the years, I love that dog. I look to Nick for moral support, but he's staying well out of it. I know what he'll say later, that he saw how well I was handling the situation and didn't like to interfere. When I left the farm to work in London when I was eighteen, I wouldn't have said boo to a goose, but eventually I found the confidence that had been buried under layers of my father's overbearing attitude.

'We'll talk about that later. I'll lock him in the lean-to.' I run the dog around to the back of the house and make sure he's secured before entering the kitchen and letting Nick, my father and the policeman through the front. Cecil has now appeared too, in his flat cap and a faded set of blue overalls tied up with baling twine; he limps stiffly along behind them.

'Stevie, you came!' he exclaims. He pushes past, reaches out and grasps my arm. 'Thank goodness you're here. You speak to this ruddy policeman and make him see sense.'

22

'Cecil, that's what I'm doing. Oh, it's lovely to see you again.'

He gives me a hug and smiles, revealing a gap where his two front teeth should be.

'What happened?' I ask him.

'One of the heifers got me when she came out of the crush. She knocked me down and I lost my teeth on the railings. I tried a set of false ones, but they didn't agree with me. They belonged to my late father – I kept them in case, thinking they'd fit, but even though I filed them down, they were no use.'

'Cecil! Haven't you got a dentist?'

'I can't afford new teeth. It doesn't bother me – I mean, I'm hardly going to make it in Hollywood at my time of life – except I lost my whistle, so Mary bought me this.' He lifts a metal referee's whistle from a string around his neck. 'Cecil, she said, this is a whole lot cheaper than a new set of gnashers.'

'How is Mary?'

'You can ask her yourself. She's right behind me, come to put the kettle on.'

'Hello, Stevie.' Cecil's wife joins us. She's taller than Cecil, and the way she moves, slowly ambling along the hall, reminds me of an elderly cow. She wears a floral dress with a cardigan and apron, caramel stockings and flat brown moccasins. Her ankles are thick and her waist thicker, yet her wedding ring is so thin it's almost worn out. 'I've got a fruit cake in the Aga and a nice piece of mild cheese from the local dairy to go with it.'

'Well, that sounds remarkably good,' says PC Kevin.

23

'Go on through,' says Cecil. 'Stevie, I think it would be a good idea if you went and asked Jack and the vet if they'd like to join us as soon as they've finished.'

'I'll do that,' I say, taking the hint. It will be a whole lot easier talking to them without my dad weighing in with his side of the argument.

'Jack's in with the calves.'

'Thanks, Cecil.' I turn to Nick. 'Are you all right here?'

'I'll deal with it,' he says, and I leave him to negotiate between Kevin and my father over tea and cake.

I find Jack Miller emerging from the breezeblock building next to the old cowshed where my father rears the calves. I vaguely remember him from school – he was three or four years above me. He's always been the strong, silent type, tall and blond with brown eyes. He's wearing a shirt and tie, navy showerproof jacket, khaki cargo trousers and boots with odd laces, one black and one tan.

'If I'd had any idea what was going on here, I would have been back before now,' I say, my throat thick with regret as we walk to the far side of the yard, skirting a heap of rusting shovels, buckets, sickles, and an earth-encrusted plough that rises up from a huge clump of stinging nettles. 'I haven't visited my dad since my mother's funeral last year.' I give myself a mental shake. I don't want to be thought of as playing for the sympathy vote. 'Tell me what's going on.'

'I'll show you.' Jack stops to point to the cow standing in the crush in the collecting yard. Although she's terribly thin, her hips and ribs clearly visible under her skin behind the metal bars, I recognise Pollyanna, one of the oldest cows in the herd; she should have been moved on a long time ago. She doesn't like being restrained. She rolls her eyes and flicks her tail.

A man – the vet, I assume – is giving Pollyanna a pedicure. He has a rope looped around her pastern and tied to one of the rails, keeping one front foot clear of the ground. He runs a hoof knife around the horn of her claws, searching for any infection before he cleans up the foot, scrubbing in between her toes, and spraying antibiotic onto her skin.

'That looks better,' he says, looking up at Jack. 'She mustn't go back out in all this mud though.'

'Leave her here,' I say. 'I'll get the tractor out and scrape the yard.'

I'm ashamed to see that the yard can't have been cleared of muck for some time. When Cecil said he wasn't keeping up, it was an understatement.

'Who are you?' asks the vet, straightening up and untying the rope to release Pollyanna's foot. A pair of blue eyes peers through a mass of tangled curls of black hair. He's in his late twenties or early thirties, well built with a healthy complexion, broad shoulders and muscular arms, and dressed in blue overalls with an apron over the top.

'I'm sorry, you haven't been introduced,' Jack says. 'Leo, this is Stevie, Mr Dunsford's daughter. Stevie, this is Leo. He's the summer locum for Talyton Manor vets.'

'It doesn't seem much like summer yet,' I say, suddenly feeling awkward and exposed, aware that these men probably assume that I bear some of the responsibility for the state of the farm.

The vet's brow furrows slightly. 'Unsurprisingly, considering it's only March.'

I shrink back, unsure how to take him. He's charismatic rather than handsome, his lightly tanned complexion marked with a few small scars and glistening with perspiration. I glance away quickly, concentrating on the cows instead. There are seven, including Pollyanna, in the collecting yard, and they all look much the same, like portents of doom, their coats rough and staring and covered in muck, their bones with hardly an ounce of flesh on them.

The poor girls, I think. I could cry. They look as if they've never been fed.

'They're in a bad way,' says Leo as if he's reading my mind. 'As far as I'm concerned it's a clear case of neglect, and I'll be more than happy to act as an expert witness for the prosecution. It's absolutely appalling. I've never seen anything like it, not on this scale.'

'It happens,' says Jack. 'I've seen it before. Circumstances change. I'm not saying it's forgivable, just that sometimes in life –' Pollyanna lifts her tail and drops a spattering cowpat – 'shit happens.'

'There's really no excuse for it, no matter how you dress it up,' Leo interrupts, his eyes settling on my boots, which are entirely inappropriate for running round a farmyard. 'I'm surprised at you, Jack.'

Jack shrugs. 'Having been in this line of business for a while, both here and abroad, I've learned that a little humility and understanding goes a long way, particularly when you're working in a community. It's never just about the animals, no matter what you say. It's about people too, and I know Tom Dunsford wouldn't intentionally harm his cattle.'

'In my view, sins of omission are equally bad,' says Leo. He seems angry, his cheeks flaring with colour.

'I don't understand. Dad's always treated the cows like they're family.'

'I wouldn't treat my family like that,' Leo cuts in.

'Cecil told me what was going on and I came straight down from London.' I address this to Jack. 'Can't you give me a few days to sort things out?'

'We've already given him a week to start turning it around, but conditions are no better,' Jack says, folding his arms across his chest. 'The cows are underweight – on the verge of starving even – and they're suffering from a variety of conditions. There's an unacceptable level of lameness and foot problems in the herd and the accommodation is filthy.'

'A few days,' I say in desperation. 'That's all I'm asking for.'

'The welfare of the cows comes first,' says Leo, his tone like shattering glass.

'I'm not sure,' says Jack.

'Just over the weekend. Two days.'

'I don't see why you should negotiate,' Leo says.

'I'll do everything that needs doing,' I say, ignoring him. 'I'll clean the yard and the cubicles and make sure the cows are well fed. I'll get advice from Alex – he's our usual vet – about implementing a herd health pro-gramme . . . whatever it takes. Please . . .'

'I really don't—' Leo begins, but Jack overrides him.

'Two days, and I'll be back on Monday to check up on you, Stevie. You're to ring me in the meantime if you need more help or advice. I warn you though, if there's no improvement, Tom will be charged.'

'He'll be fined, imprisoned and banned from keeping animals for the rest of his life,' says Leo.

I stare at the muck on my Louboutins, sick to the pit of my stomach at Leo's summary of the situation. I'm really not warming to him.

'I shan't let it happen. My father's a sick man. Seeing the herd our family has built up over the years dispersed would kill him,' I say, looking up again and fixing my gaze on Leo's face. 'I know what I'm doing. I virtually ran the farm when I was eighteen,' I say, exaggerating a little because there is so much at stake.

'And what about the dog?' Leo says. 'He's out of control.'

'Leave the dog alone,' I say. Bear's in a bit of a state too. 'He isn't vicious. He's thirteen years old and he's never bitten anyone before.'

'And he never will again if I have my way,' says Leo. 'He got me in the groin. Luckily I was wearing more than one layer – he's still managed to break the skin, but it's only a flesh wound.'

'I'm so sorry. I don't know why he did it. Perhaps he took an instant dislike to you.' As I have. I don't say it. I bite my lip instead.

'Your father got himself wound up and was yelling at us, so the dog joined in,' Jack says.

'There's no excuse for it. I'm not risking my life – or

28

my balls – every time I come up to the farm. Not that I have any great desire to father children, but I'd rather keep them intact.'

'That's a bit of an exaggeration,' I say. 'It won't happen again.'

'It shouldn't, because a dog like that should be put down.'

I wait for Jack to give his opinion. I have everything crossed, fingers and toes. Bear was my mum's dog – I promised her I'd look after him and I'm wracked with guilt that it has turned out like this. I can't bear the thought of him being taken away and put to sleep. He's an old boy. He's never been any trouble before. Dad's right. It must have been the way the vet looked at him, or did Bear think they were all here to take my father away and turned on Leo in order to defend him?

'I'll make sure he's kept under control.' I find myself on the verge of bursting into tears once again. I swallow hard.

'It's up to you, Leo,' Jack says eventually. 'All I can say is that I think it's a one-off and I believe every animal deserves a second chance. But he's in a bit of a state too. He's on the skinny side, his coat is matted and his teeth need attention.'

I suppress a twinge of guilt, even though it isn't my fault that Bear's been neglected.

'I'll get him to a vet,' I say.

'Sooner rather than later,' Jack says.

'Don't go bringing him to me,' says Leo. 'I don't do dogs, especially ones that bite. You'd better take him to Otter House.'

'Thank you,' I say, upset at what feels like a personal attack. Love me, love my dog. I'm hot with embarrassment, desperately sad at the state of the cows and the dog and angry at Leo in particular. Does he have no consideration for anyone's feelings?

I can no longer quell the flow of tears that run down my cheeks.

'I'm sorry. You must think I'm such a fool,' I mutter as Leo and Jack look on. Jack fishes about in his pockets and apologises for not being in possession of a tissue.

'It isn't foolish to care about your animals,' Leo says gruffly, and I wonder if he's trying to apologise in an odd sort of way for upsetting me. I'm not having it though. It's too late. He's put my back up with his uncompromising views, whereas Jack – in my opinion – is a great guy, with compassion for both animals and their keepers.

'Stevie?' I turn at the sound of Nick's voice, finding him making his way gingerly across the farmyard, trying to avoid getting mud on his shoes. 'Is everything all right? You've been a while.'

I brush away my tears.

'It's only been five minutes,' I say, unsure why I feel mildly irritated, not grateful that he's come to find me.

'The tea's getting cold,' he says, taking a long hard look at Leo.

'This is Nick,' I say, hastily introducing him to Leo and Jack. 'Would you like to come inside for tea and cake?'

'I'll pop in and have a word with Kevin before I go,' Jack says.

'I won't stop,' Leo says. 'I have two more calls to make. Jack, let me know when you want me back here next week. If you need someone from the practice over the weekend, Alex is the duty vet.'

I begin to worry that, on top of everything else, these vet visits must be getting pretty expensive.

I look around at the yard and outbuildings, and the tatty mobile home my father bought a while back for a song. It appears as if a herd of wild bulls has torn right through Nettlebed Farm. There are potholes and weeds everywhere, the cob at the corner of the cowshed has fallen away, revealing the red earth at its heart, and the corrugated iron – meant to protect the occupants where the thatch has disintegrated – has slid from the top. My throat tightens with regret when I remember how it used to be, the stone trough by the brick building which houses the office once filled with bright spring flowers, now empty apart from compost and dead leaves. There's so much that needs doing I'm not sure where to start, and once I've got going, I haven't a clue where it will all end.

Chapter Three

Country Life

I can't stand back and let my father and Cecil flounder, something I try to explain to Nick when Jack, Kevin and I have finished negotiating over improving conditions for the cows and a deadline for Bear to see one of the vets at Otter House. We also agree that my father will sign over his shotgun to the police with immediate effect, and attend the station on Monday morning, where he will just receive a caution, on condition he gives up his gun licence without a fuss. The potential charges over the Animal Welfare offences go on hold for a limited time only.

'How do you think you're going to solve everything, Stevie?' Nick says as we sit around the massive oak table in the farmhouse kitchen with Mary, Cecil and my father.

'I don't want you interfering.' Dad slops half his tea onto his plate. 'I didn't ask you to come here.'

'Dad, we have a lot to talk about, but all I'll say for now is, if I hadn't turned up today, you would have been charged with neglecting the cows, and Animal Welfare would have begun whatever process it is to get them signed over.' I put it bluntly. It's the only language my father understands.

Dad splutters into his mug and chokes. Cecil thumps him on the back.

'That's enough,' Dad coughs. 'There's no need.'

'I'm sorry, Tom, but I don't want you dying on us now,' Cecil says dryly.

'Well, it seems Stevie thinks you don't need me any more,' Dad mutters.

'Stevie's doing you a favour,' Nick joins in, though I'd rather he didn't. I give him a warning glance.

'And what have you got to do with it?' Dad asks. 'I don't recall inviting you here into my house.'

'For goodness' sake, Dad, we're here to help.' I lean across the table. 'If you don't let us give you a hand to get you out of this mess, you'll lose the farm.'

'Lose it?' he says, staring at his good hand. His left hand remains in a sling, drooping and useless.

'If you lose the cows, you've lost the farm, unless you can think of another way to use the land and make your living.' I make to stand up. 'So, if you want it that way, Nick and I will head back to London and leave you to it. It's up to you.'

'Oh, I don't know,' he blusters. 'It seems a shame when you've just got here.'

'It seems a shame,' echoes Cecil. 'You've come all that way.'

33

'And I've got a leg of lamb in the Aga,' says Mary, joining the conversation for the first time. 'You must stay for a roast – I don't want it going to waste.' She smiles. 'I'd prefer not to have shepherd's pie for tea every day for the next week.'

I look at Nick. 'I reckon we'll stay then, just for a couple of days.' I get up properly this time.

'Where are you off to?' Nick asks me.

'I might as well get started. I'm going to scrape the yard. Who has the keys to the tractor?'

'They're in the cab,' says my father. 'We always leave them in the cab.'

'There's a bit of a problem,' Cecil says. 'Old Bertha broke down a couple of weeks ago.'

'Bertha?' says Nick.

'The tractor,' I explain.

'Why hasn't it been fixed?' I look towards my father, who merely shrugs as if he doesn't care.

'You mustn't have a go at him, Stevie,' Cecil murmurs quietly. 'Dr Mackie says he isn't to have any stress or he'll have another stroke.'

'I heard that, Cecil,' Dad cuts in. 'The stroke didn't do for my hearing.'

'We'll have to call out a mechanic. The cows must be trampling all that muck into the parlour.' I cover my face. It doesn't bear thinking about. I always liked to keep the parlour pristine. 'Have you got the number for the company that does the repairs?'

'It's in the office,' Dad says. 'You'll have to go and fetch it, Cecil.'

'It's all right. I'll find it on my mobile.' I check the

name and phone straight away, but it's no good. No cajoling or offers of paying extra will induce them to come out before Monday. 'I know, I'll go and see Guy. He'll lend us a tractor.'

'Ah no, my lover, I wouldn't do that,' Cecil says.

'Why not? We've helped him out before.'

'I forbid it.' My father thumps his fist weakly on the table. 'We are not fraternising with the enemy. I'm not going cap in hand to Guy Barnes.'

'I'm sure he won't mind.'

'About a month before they had the argument about the state of the cows, your dad had a bit of a falling out with Guy when he came round to have a word about the hedges.'

'A bit of a falling out?' I say suspiciously.

'Tom had his gun by his chair. It accidentally went off when Guy was here. He didn't appreciate it, like.'

'I'm not surprised.' I can see Nick's thinking that we're all mad and he's come to the funny farm. 'What choice do we have, though? The yard's a disgrace.' I think for a moment. 'Okay, there's only one thing for it. I'll do it myself with a shovel and broom. Any volunteers?' I gaze towards Nick.

'I'll help as long as I can borrow some boots and a coat.'

'There are some spares in the lean-to,' Mary says.

I lead Nick through from the kitchen into the lean-to, which was tacked on to the house to provide a utility area for muddy boots and the dog. Bear jumps down from his chair, a leather chesterfield; it is partially covered with a throw to hide where he chewed the stuffing out when he was a puppy. He comes up to me, squeaking with joy, his body curved to one side, wagging his tail.

'Stevie, be careful,' Nick warns, 'he's showing his teeth.'

'He's smiling.'

'Dogs don't smile. Don't be ridiculous.'

'Bear does.' I squat down to hug the dog, recoiling at the stench of his matted, greasy coat and a draught of bad breath. Perhaps close contact wasn't such a good idea. 'Bear, leave him alone,' I tell the dog as he tries to push his nose into Nick's crotch. 'And Nick, mind your head,' I add, noticing the pheasants and rabbit hanging from the washing line that runs from one side of the room to the other. 'Cleaning the yard is a pretty mucky business,' I go on doubtfully.

Nick picks up a pair of my father's boots from the lean-to, wrinkling his nose as he puts them on.

I take one of the waxed coats from the hooks on the back of the door, shaking out the spiders before handing it over to him. I find a pair of size sixes in the cupboard under the sink, alongside preserving jars filled with onions and plums, then take down one of my old green boiler suits from a hook on the wall and pull it on.

'What do you think?' I hold my hair up and give Nick a twirl. 'Sexy or what?'

'Or what, I should say,' he smiles.

'You're supposed to say: "Stevie, you look hot whatever you're wearing." Let's go.' I collect an apple – a pippin of some kind – from the wooden box, stored in newspaper from when it was picked and still good to eat in March. I stick it between my teeth. The fresh country air is making me hungry. Outside, Nick and I find a couple of broken brooms. I knock a brush and handle together and drive in a nail to hold them while Nick looks on in amazement.

'I didn't realise you were so practical,' he says as I hand him a broom and shovel. 'You aren't going to leave those cows wandering about in the yard,' he goes on when I let Pollyanna out of the crush to join the others.

'Don't worry, Nick, they won't charge you.'

'I might have to charge you for doing this,' he smiles. 'I don't come cheap.'

'Stop whingeing and get on with it,' I say, laughing.

He clambers between the rails and into the yard and starts scraping up the muck. 'Where am I putting this?'

'In the corner. I'll sort out a tractor ASAP – we'll move it then. It goes into the slurry pit and later we'll spread it on the fields.'

'I couldn't be a farmer,' Nick says after about fifteen minutes. He pauses, sweating and rubbing his back.

'It's better than a work-out down at the gym,' I say, getting into a rhythm.

The yard looks a little better when we've finished, but as soon as we let the cows through for milking, it's covered with muck again.

'That was a waste of time,' Nick observes.

'We can wash it down when the milking's done. I'll just grab the pressure hose and hey presto, it's done. I don't know what you want to do now, but I'm going to give Cecil a hand and find out what's been going on here.'

'I'll come with you.'

'Are you sure?'

'I've never milked a cow.'

I hesitate because I'm not sure Cecil will be willing to talk about the farm in front of a stranger, but Nick is determined to have a taste of country life so we join him in the parlour.

The cows, a black-and-white dairy breed, are waiting, queuing to get into the parlour for their afternoon feed.

'Do you mind if Nick joins us?' I yell through to Cecil, who's already in the well in the centre of the parlour between the two platforms on which the cows stand, five on each side so their udders are at Cecil's waist height.

'Not at all,' he calls back over the sounds of Radio Four, the hum of the milking machine and the mooing of the cows. 'It'll be nice to have some company – Tom hasn't been out here for a while now. The more the merrier.'

Nick and I pause on the balcony.

'This is udderly extraordinary,' says Nick.

'That isn't funny, Nick.'

'Do the cows like being milked?'

'They know when it's milking time,' Cecil says. 'They're always waiting. If one's missing, you know there's something wrong.'

'You can stay up here, Nick,' I say, before I join Cecil in the pit and pull the lever that slides the doors open to let the cows in each side. They wander in with purpose, as beautiful as ever I remember them, with their big ears, brown eyes with long lashes, dripping noses and cloven hooves, and their breath as sweet. However, their coats are dull and they have muddy knees and mucky tails that they flick against their bony backsides now and then.

If they were models, they would all be size zeros.

When there are ten inside, five to the left and five to the right, I pull the lever again to close the doors. Cecil makes sure that the cows move along to the end, filling the spaces. When they're all in place, he releases more levers to let the feed into the mangers in front of them. A few nuts rattle into each container.

'How much feed are you giving them?' I ask.

'I've had to cut back – Tom told me I had to make economies.'

'False economies, I should say.' I'm looking around at the milk running down the insides of the jars. I don't have to ask. I can see yields are way down.

'Food in equals milk out?' Nick enquires.

'Essentially, yes,' I say.

'How many cattle are there?' Nick asks. I look to Cecil for the answer.

'We have eighty-seven head on the farm, with about sixty in milk at one time. We calve them all year round.'

'They look like clones,' Nick says.

'They're closely related, many of them. Mothers and daughters, sisters and aunts.' Cecil bellows at the first cow to move forwards. 'Get up, Daisy Mae.'

'Can you tell them all apart?'

'Oh yes, I know them all, and if I should ever forget,

which I doubt, they have the yellow ear tags and their numbers freeze-marked onto their behinds.' Cecil picks up a hose and cleans the first cow's teats with a spray of sanitising solution before moving on to the next one.

'As we were, Cecil?' I ask, taking a paper towel from the dispenser and drying the first cow's udder. 'Daisy Mae must be one of the oldest cows – she's from the same generation as Pollyanna.' Her udder is enormous, covered with a down of white hair and a network of swollen milk veins. Her teats are like old man's fingers, almost touching the concrete floor and leaking milk.

'She's lost her figure,' Cecil says. 'I don't think she's going to make another year.'

'What will you do with her?' Nick says.

'She'll have to move on,' he says euphemistically. 'They don't last for long, seven lactations if you're lucky. 'Stevie, if you carry on and put the clusters on these, I'll start on the next lot.'

I slip the cluster, a claw-shaped contraption with four tubes or cups, one for each teat, onto Daisy Mae's teats, attaching her to the milking machine and waiting for the vacuum pump to suck the milk from her udder with its regular, rhythmic beat.

'Can I have a go?' Nick comes down from the balcony and waits beside me while I show him how to put the next cluster on Daisy Mae's neighbour.

'This is something to tell the guys at the office when we get back,' he says, keeping an eye on the chamber behind Daisy Mae, watching the milk pulsing into it.

'When are you intending to put the cows out?' I ask Cecil. 'They could do with fattening up on the spring grass.'

'I'd say tomorrow, but Tom's insisting they stay in till April Fools' Day as they've done other years, but the ground's dry enough for them to go out now, in my humble opinion, anyway.' Cecil shrugs.

I remove the clusters and flick the switch to let Daisy Mae's milk into the bulk tank through the pipe above us.

'Watch out,' Cecil says suddenly, but it's too late. One of the cows has raised her tail and spattered Nick with muck.

'Ugh, that is disgusting.' Nick steps back.

'Ever been in the shit before?' I say lightly.

'What goes in must come out one way or another,' Cecil chuckles. 'Now you have to keep your eyes on the other back ends.'

'How can this be hygienic?' Nick grumbles. 'I'll be having orange juice on my cereal in future.'

'At least you had a go,' I say.

We sweep and hose down the parlour after the last batch of cows before we take our bags from the car and freshen up for a roast dinner, Cecil and Mary having excused themselves, assuming I'd like to spend some quality time with my dad. I chat with Nick much of the time, my father preferring to concentrate on eating, not talking.

He pauses now and again to gesture with his good hand and tell us how he's looking forward to getting back to doing the milking and taking the dog up to the top of Steep Acres, the steepest field on the farm. My heart grows hollow at the realisation he won't be going far beyond these four walls in a hurry. It's painful to watch him struggle to cut up his meat and transfer morsels of food to his mouth without dropping them from the fork. I want to offer to cut it up for him and give him a spoon, but decide it's just too demeaning. He isn't happy about me turning up on the farm. I don't want him hating me for it.

I'd like to ask him why he didn't inform me of his stroke, but he's so preoccupied with feeding himself it doesn't seem right to distract him. It can wait, I think.

By the end of the meal, he's exhausted and needs to sleep. As he makes to stand up from the table, he drops his crutches.

'No, Stevie,' he snaps when I get up to assist. 'I can manage.'

'Yes, sure,' I say sarcastically, 'just like you can manage to run this farm.'

'Leave him be,' Nick says gently, resting his hand on mine. 'He says he doesn't need help.'

'But—'

'It's his choice. When he's ready he'll ask.'

'He's so stubborn.'

'Like you,' he says. 'Isn't that right, Tom? Like father, like daughter.'

The ghost of a smile crosses my father's lips as he uses one crutch and the edge of the table to support him on his way to bed.

Later, I'm lying in my old single bed unable to sleep.

Mary made up the double bed in my parents' room (Dad's been sleeping downstairs since he came home from hospital after his stroke) with fresh white linen and a patchwork quilt that my grandmother made, and aired the room. There was a small bunch of daffodils in a vase on the dressing table, a lovely, welcoming touch, but I couldn't sleep in my parents' room anyway, and as soon as I explained to Mary that Nick and I aren't married, she wondered aloud if Nick shouldn't have my brother's old room. I agreed and gave her a hand to make the other bedrooms ready.

In my old room, the furniture was covered with sheets. I wandered across the bare floorboards and onto the sheepskin rug to look at the trinkets on the bookcase. Everything was as I left it when I last visited the farm a year ago, almost to the day, for my mother's funeral. I picked up the faded photo of a grey pony and blew away the dust – reddish, brick-coloured dust that drifts from the fields in summer. I gave the frame a rub with the end of my sleeve and put it back on the shelf before helping Mary fold the sheets and put them away in the airing cupboard at the top of the stairs.

There's a knock on the door.

'Stevie, can I come in?'

'Nick, of course you can.'

'It's freezing in this house. Where's the thermostat?'

'There isn't one.' I switch the bedside light on to find Nick standing in the doorway with a blanket draped around his shoulders. 'There's no central heating.'

'Oh? Is there room for a small one?'

'Come on,' I say, shifting up against the wall for him to join me. I'm grateful for the company. 'I haven't been able to sleep for thinking.'

'Thinking about what?' Nick asks, looking down at me.

'The farm, of course.'

'Oh?' There is a long pause. 'Why didn't you introduce me to Jack and the vet as your boyfriend this afternoon? Are you ashamed of me, or have I reason to be jealous?'

I frown. 'What are you saying?'

'I thought I detected some tension when I appeared in the yard.'

'You did. Leo had just threatened to have Bear put to sleep and as good as blamed me for the state of the cows.'

'Leo?'

'The vet. He's called Leo.'

'So you're on first-name terms.'

'Nick, I don't know what you're getting at. You aren't really jealous, are you? Only I can assure you, you have absolutely no reason to be. Now, are you coming to bed, or not?'

Nick crawls under the quilt with me, cold and a little drunk on some scrumpy that Cecil made in the late autumn and stored in barrels in the barn. My brother Ray and I used to make and sell it to anyone who turned up with a vessel to put it in. We made a good income, but it was rough stuff, so sharp it stung your mouth. A glass of scrumpy was once the height of sophistication for me, but I prefer something much smoother now.

'Are you feeling warmer? I could warm you up even more if you like . . .'

I do like. Making love with Nick is familiar and comforting.

'I wish I'd kept a closer eye on the farm,' I say afterwards. 'I should have come down sooner, but I couldn't face it. After Mum's funeral I felt that the last tie holding me to the farm was gone, but seeing Cecil and Mary and Bear and the cows again . . .'

'You haven't mentioned . . .'

'My dad?' I smile wryly. 'I'm glad I've seen him, purely because I'd feel terribly guilty if he died and I hadn't seen him for months. Mum would have expected me to . . .' I bite my lip as Nick enfolds me in his arms, burying his face in my hair.

'Ugh,' Nick exclaims. 'You've showered and you still reek of cow.'

'It's one of the best smells in the world,' I sigh.

'That is debatable.' He hesitates. 'What shall we do tomorrow? We could go to the beach, or I could take you to the nearest city to look at engagement rings. We could have dinner, something light as opposed to that fat-laden meal we had this evening. Was she trying to kill us? I could feel my arteries clogging up as we were eating.'

'I thought it was delicious.' Lamb with fatty gravy, crispy roast potatoes, leeks in cheese sauce and carrots cooked in butter.

'So we'll go shopping?' Nick says.

'I'm sorry. I need to sort out a few things here.'

'Can't that wait until Monday? I mean, we're going

to have to be here then to take the dog to the vet and see that the tractor is fixed. Surely, you can take one day out?'

'Farming's full-time, twenty-four-seven, and although I'm not the farmer,' I continue, pre-empting Nick's next interruption, 'whether you like it or not, I am the farmer's daughter. And I know you're upset because I won't go and look at rings tomorrow.'

'I know. You can't deal with the marriage thing right now,' he says, his voice filled with regret.

It would be too easy, lying here in his arms, bathed in the afterglow of making love to say yes, I'll marry you, but in the stark light of the morning, I can't help thinking I'll feel it was a mistake. I sense that I've arrived at a crossroads like the one on the lane, where the signposts are blank and I don't know which way to go.

Chapter Four

Black and White

On Monday morning, I wake Nick, pretty sure that I look like a freak of nature, with my hair scraped back with a hairband, my nails engrained with muck, and wearing an ancient sweatshirt and jeans I found in the chest of drawers in my old room.

'Ugh, you stink,' he groans. 'What is it again?'

'Eau de cow-logne.'

'Very funny,' he says, chuckling lightly.

'You get used to it.'

'I don't think I ever could. It gets right up my nose.' He pauses as I plant a kiss on his cheek. 'Go and have a shower.'

'I'll have one later. I've a couple of errands to do before the tractor's fixed and then I'm going to scrape the yard and clean out the calves.' I bounce on the bed. 'Are you going to help?'

'I could really do with a lie in.'

'Spoilsport.' I tip my head to one side. 'I'll let you drive the tractor as soon as it's fixed. Come on, Nick.'

'I suppose I could get up,' he says. 'It is our last day on the farm, after all.'

'Ah, I meant to talk to you about that.' We've had a busy couple of days, cleaning the place up and making sure the cows have plenty of silage to eat from the racks in the barn. 'Jack from Animal Welfare comes back again this afternoon and I don't know what he's going to say.'

'Hopefully, he'll say it's looking good, he'll let the cows stay here on the farm, leave your father alone and we can get back to work, to our lives. I feel like an alien here.'

'Everyone admires your spaceship,' I point out.

'Yes, the car definitely turns heads,' Nick smiles.

'Anyway, going back to the subject of when we go home, I think I'll be staying on for a few more days, at least until the end of the week.'

'What for? We really should be getting back soon.'

'I know, but even if Jack says it's fine, I can't leave everything to Cecil and Dad. There's still far too much left for them to cope with.'

'Such as?'

'Checking all the bills have been paid and arranging for someone to do some general maintenance on the farm. I need to speak to my brother Ray and he isn't answering his phone. I've also got to take my father in for his appointment at the police station.'

'I thought we were going to spend some time

together, but I haven't seen much of you. You're always out milking the cows and doing the lady farmer thing.'

'I'm here to help out. I told you, it isn't a holiday.' I reach out and massage Nick's shoulder. 'If I can get things straight here, I can get back to normal very soon.' I hesitate. 'Why don't you go back home and I'll catch up as soon as I'm ready?'

'No, I'll stay a bit longer as it's only a couple more days.' He reaches out to the bedside cabinet for his mobile and checks it for emails and texts.

'Nick, that can wait. It's time for breakfast.'

He pulls himself up, the quilt falling away from his bony shoulder.

'How long have you been up?' he asks.

'Three hours,' I say, glancing at the clock. 'You've wasted half the day – it's a beautiful morning.'

'I didn't sleep a wink last night,' he groans. 'I thought it was meant to be peaceful in the country, but I could hear a cow bellowing and the dawn chorus.'

I kiss his cheek. 'Mary's got a full English ready – fried potatoes, bacon, eggs, mushrooms and black pudding.'

'A heart attack on a plate. I wish I'd brought my muesli.'

'Forget muesli. You need feeding up.'

'We could go to the pub for a late lunch.'

'I've got to take Bear to the vet's and see someone at Overdown Farmers about a delivery of cattle feed this morning. The silo's empty.'

'Silo? What's that?'

'The big silver tower.'

'The giant knob above the parlour,' Nick chuckles, having rediscovered his sense of humour at last.

'It's where the feed is stored. I climbed the ladder to have a look and it's empty.' The cows weren't happy this morning when I pulled the levers to feed them and nothing happened apart from the desultory clatter of a handful of pellets. They didn't have much for breakfast and skipping meals isn't conducive to their milk production. I'd like them to go out on the fields now and enjoy the spring grass, which is free, but according to my father the ground is still too wet after the winter.

After a hearty breakfast, I call Bear and slip his collar and lead on. He's hungry like the cows because he's been starved in case he needs an anaesthetic.

'You aren't putting that creature in my car. That would be sacrilege,' Nick says, keeping well clear of the dog as I take him out through the lean-to.

'That's a shame,' I say, teasing. 'I rather like the idea of him sitting in the passenger seat with his Ray-Bans on and the wind streaming through his hair.' I glance down at the tangles and teasels in Bear's matted coat.

We take Dad's Land Rover and travel to Otter House vets in Talyton St George with the windows wide open. As we park in the small car park at the side of the surgery, I feel a growing sense of shame and apprehension over the state of Bear's health. The receptionist is stern, the head nurse is decidedly disapproving, but Maz, the vet in lilac scrubs, who reminds me of Gwyneth Paltrow, is understanding when I explain the situation.

'He can stay for the day,' she says. 'We'll give him a bath and clip him out. Then we'll give him a general anaesthetic and remove the rotten teeth and clean up those that are left.' The nurse gives me a consent form to sign and, feeling really bad, like a traitor because he doesn't understand why I'm abandoning him, I leave Bear behind.

'He'll be cold – I'll buy him a coat,' I tell Nick when we're back in the Land Rover on the way to Overdown Farmers, the wholesalers.

'It's only a dog,' he says, and he waits impatiently for me to choose a dog coat and sort out an order for cattle feed, which is more complicated than I thought because it isn't that an order's been lost or not made in the first place. The feed hasn't been delivered because the bills haven't been paid for the past six months.

'I'm surprised you've let it go that long,' I say to Tony, the manager who's been here for years. He reminds me of the male rat in Beatrix Potter's *Tale of Samuel Whiskers* and I used to find his protruding eyes and whiskers rather alarming.

'I told your father on the phone I was worried about the welfare of the cows and I'd deliver enough feed to keep them going, but there is a limit. I'm not a charity.'

'I'll pay you now as long as you can deliver before milking today.'

'Oh, I don't know about that.'

'Please.'

'For you, Stevie,' he agrees eventually. 'It's a pity you didn't take on Nettlebed Farm. I always thought you would.'

'It wasn't to be,' I say, not wanting to rake up the past. I pay Tony by credit card, the bill much bigger than I anticipated, but at least I know the cows will be fed for a while. What about the next time, though? I try not to think about it.

Nick, having grown bored listening to the negotiations and small talk, is in one of the aisles trying on a waxed, wide-brimmed hat and a coat down to his knees.

'What do you think, Stevie? Aren't I the country gent?'

'I'm not sure it suits you.'

'Maybe not.' Smiling, he looks in a mirror that's buried under racks of walking socks, jackets and tweeds. 'I'm more the city slicker, whereas you appear to be able to carry off the country look rather well.'

I glance down at my hoodie, skinny jeans and long leather boots, and grin at him. 'I'm back where I belong, in my natural habitat.' I reach for his hand. 'Come on, let's go. Cecil's left a message on my voicemail to say the vet's on his way to see one of the cows.'

Before we leave the warehouse, I spot a familiar face.

'Hey, Stevie?' The man takes a step back, rattling the hangers on a display of fluorescent coats, and whistles through his teeth. 'It is you.'

'James?' I exclaim as he grabs me, gives me a bear hug and a big kiss on the cheek. When he releases me, I look him up and down. He hasn't changed much. About five foot ten with a round face, chubby red cheeks and a generous smile, he has a small paunch and big thighs, and wears a grey sweatshirt, jeans and tan workman's boots spattered and smeared with paint. His sandy hair is short and thick, and slicked down in the same style as when he used to take me out to Young Farmers' balls and discos. He still resembles a boy and, like Peter Pan, I wonder if he'll ever grow up.

'How are you?' I'm not sure what else to say as memories of the two of us fumbling in the dark come flooding into my head.

'Well, thank you,' he says, colour rising up his neck, and I wonder if he's remembering too. He was fun to be with and we had much in common, with farming and mutual friends, but it was a teenage fling, nothing more. Briefly, I wonder if he's married. I check for a ring on his finger. There is none, not that it means very much. I decide I'll ask my father, or Cecil – they'll know.

'I've come down to visit my dad.'

'I heard he had a stroke. It's a terrible business. It must have been such a shock to you.'

More of a shock than you'll ever know, I think.

'He's improving slowly,' I say.

'That's good news,' James says.

'Are you still working on the farm?' I ask.

He glances down at his clothes. 'No, I'm a jack-of-all-trades, an odd-job man. I'm always on the lookout for work. It's a long story. I'll tell you about it sometime.'

'Aren't you going to introduce us?' Nick cuts in. 'I'm Nick, Stevie's fiancé.'

'Oh? Congratulations. I'm James, by the way.' James shakes Nick's hand with great enthusiasm.

'We aren't engaged,' I say.

'Yet.' Nick slips his arm around my shoulder and brushes his lips against my hair.

'Why did you say that?' I say to him when we're back in the Land Rover on the way back to the farm.

'He seemed overly pleased to see you, like some giant puppy dog. I was afraid he was coming on to you, so I thought I'd help you out. How do you know him?'

'He was a Young Farmer. We went out for a while.'

The gearbox grates as I force the Land Rover into third gear and Nick continues, 'I'm glad I'm staying for a bit longer to keep an eye on you. I can see I need to make sure you aren't seduced by any of your exes.'

'Nick, how can you think that? I was hardly a loose woman, for goodness' sake.'

'Weren't you?' he asks seriously. 'We haven't really talked about the past. I mean, I know you went out with that guy Turner—'

'The slimy wine merchant,' I cut in. 'It lasted three dates.'

'And now this James has come out of the woodwork.'

'Nick, I don't think it's something a lady farmer talks about. Does it matter?'

'I don't suppose it does,' he says in a manner that suggests entirely the opposite. 'As long as you're mine, it doesn't matter. I don't give a toss how many boyfriends you've had before me. Where are we going now?'

'Back to the farm.'

Back at Nettlebed Farm, Nick and I join Cecil in the

cowshed where he has a cow – Domino, another of the older cows – haltered and tied to the ring in the crumbling wall. Leo, dressed in a short-sleeved green cotton gown and surgical gloves, is operating with his hands buried in the cow's flank.

Nick takes one look and excuses himself, saying he's going to have coffee.

'Aren't you coming with me, Stevie?' he asks.

'I'll stay. Are you squeamish?' I say lightly.

'Of course I'm not. I just don't see any point in hanging around when Cecil and Leo have everything under control.' I'm aware Nick is expecting me to go with him, but he knew I wanted to be back for the vet.

'I'll catch you later,' I say.

'Don't be too long.' He kisses my cheek before leaving and I turn my attention back to Domino and the surgery, hoping she and her unborn calf are going to make it.

As I watch Leo, I realise with a growing sense of astonishment that he's actually a very attractive man – seriously hot in fact. His cheeks are scarlet with exertion and his arms are rippling with muscle as he hauls at a pair of cloven hooves that appear through the incision he's made in Domino's side.

'It's stuck, so it had to be a Caesar,' Cecil says.

'It has to be done,' I say, trying not to think of the cost.

'I'm so glad you've come back to take the wheel and steer this ship back on the road, Stevie,' Cecil says, mixing his metaphors as he ties the string plait that acts as a belt to hold his trousers up.

'So am I.' I watch anxiously. 'How long's she been like this?'

'A while,' Cecil says noncommittally.

'Possibly a little too long,' Leo says as the calf begins to emerge still encased in its shiny membranes. I really don't like him for highlighting what sounds like a failure on our part. I wonder what time Cecil checked on the cattle last night and inwardly kick myself for not thinking to offer to give him a break and do it myself. Leo lays the calf out on the fresh straw where it lies ominously still.

'It's all yours,' he says to Cecil. 'I'll suture the old girl up while you deal with the calf. I don't think there's much hope for it.'

'It's all right. I'll take it,' I say, kneeling down beside it.

'Are you sure?' says Leo.

'She knows what to do. I taught her well,' Cecil says proudly. 'If anyone can bring it round, Stevie can.'

I wish I shared his confidence. I'm afraid I'm out of practice, but I soon remember what to do as I strip the membrane from the calf's nose and mouth and rub its chest with straw to stimulate it to breathe. I pause to listen, yet all I can hear is my heartbeat and Cecil's raspy breathing.

'We could hang it over the door and drain its lungs that way,' Cecil suggests.

'There's no need.' I can hear it now, a gurgle followed by an enormous, convulsive splutter and cough. The calf shakes its head and takes a few short, sharp breaths while I breathe a sigh of relief.

'Is it a heifer or bull calf?' Cecil asks.

'Heifer,' I say, checking.

'Good, good.' Cecil nods, takes his pipe from his breast pocket and lights up the tobacco with a match.

'Do you mind?' Leo says crossly. 'Firstly it's illegal to smoke in the workplace – yours and mine – and secondly I have no wish to go up in smoke. Look at all this straw everywhere.'

Cecil's been smoking a pipe around the farm for years and nothing has gone up in smoke as yet, apart from the vet who looks as if he has smoke coming out of his ears.

'I've talked to you about smoking before,' I say. 'You should have stopped years ago – for the sake of everyone's health, not just yours.'

'Look at me though,' Cecil protests. 'I'm almost eighty and it's never done me any harm.'

The vet finishes sewing up the cow's wound before cleaning up and tidying his kit away. He washes his hands in the sink in the dairy and says goodbye.

'Keep a close eye on Mum,' he says. 'I'm afraid you're going to have a problem with her. She's had a hard time.'

'Great,' I say with irony. That's just what the farm needs.

When he's gone, Cecil gives me his opinion of Leo.

'He's a funny one, that one. He doesn't come in for a nightcap like the other vets – he keeps himself to himself.'

Maybe that's what I find attractive about Leo, his self-contained assurance, I think, as Jack arrives in the Animal Welfare van at the same time as the driver from Overdown Farmers turns up with the feed lorry to fill the silo. I wonder briefly – as I did with James – whether or not Leo's attached, and feel a tiny stab of guilt for thinking about another man. If Nick was the One, I wouldn't be, would I? Or am I being unrealistic, having such high expectations of love and romance? I'm confused. Should love and relationships have to be worked at, or should they happen naturally, without forcing?

'Now Jack is always happy to stop and talk,' says Cecil, and I smile to myself, wondering exactly how happy he is about that when Cecil, lonely for company because farming can be a solitary occupation, ambushes him in the yard.

'Hello, Cecil. I can see that it's all systems go here. I'm impressed so far.' Jack's expression is businesslike, bordering on stern, which I suppose he has to be considering the situation. When he picks up a clipboard, pen and camera, my palms begin to prick with sweat. I turn away, take a deep breath and count to ten to calm my growing anxiety. The fate of Nettlebed Farm lies in Jack's hands. I notice the grey swathes of cloud gathering across the hilltops to the southwest. If Jack insists on moving the cows from my father's care and prosecuting him for neglect, it won't be because of my lack of effort. I have tried so hard that I ache all over from the physical toil, something I'm not used to, having spent years working in an office with the occasional visit to the gym. I'm exhausted from the early starts with Cecil and I'm stressed out worrying about the future.

'Where's the dog?' Jack asks, acknowledging me with a nod.

'At the vet's,' I say. 'I'm collecting him later.'

'Good.' Jack ticks a box on a sheet of paper and looks around the yard, not giving anything away in his expression, before heading to the barn to look at the cows.

'I'll let them out,' Cecil says. 'You'll be able to see them better and it's time for milking anyway.'

'Thanks, Cecil,' Jack responds. 'I see there's plenty of silage in the racks this time.'

'Stevie's been keeping it topped up. She's handy with a wheelbarrow and fork.' Cecil enters the collecting yard and opens the gates from the barn. Several of the cows walk out immediately, making straight for the parlour, while the rest follow on afterwards.

'What do you think of the cows?' I say, impatient for Jack's verdict.

'They don't appear to be in such a hurry to get their feed at milking,' he observes.

'I'm going to start cleaning out the cubicles later,' I say. 'The tractor's been fixed today.'

'Hey, Stevie,' says Jack. 'What you're doing is admirable, but don't kill yourself trying to do everything at once. You've met the targets I set you the other day.'

'So you aren't going to take the cows away?'

'No, I'm not, and I'm glad I don't have to – Tessa, my fiancée who works for Talyton Animal Rescue, hasn't got room for all those cows at the Sanctuary.' Jack smiles. 'Let's review the targets and set some new ones for the end of this week. I'll be back on Friday, unless

59

you want to discuss anything before that. I know it can feel like I'm the Big Bad Wolf, but I'm not. I want to support your father, not make his life a misery.'

'He isn't the easiest person in the world to work with,' I point out.

'He isn't the worst I've had to deal with,' Jack says wryly.

'Is there anything else I need to do?' I ask once we've run through Jack's expectations for the end of the week.

'I don't think so. I'll leave you in peace. I expect Cecil appreciates all this help.'

'Ah, I can't give him a hand with the milking tonight. I've got to go and collect the dog.'

'You do realise that I'll have to make sure everything's in place to maintain the welfare of the animals on the farm once you head off back to London?'

'Of course I do.' I hope Jack isn't going to ask me how I can guarantee this because I haven't come to any conclusion yet. 'I'll see you soon, on Friday at dinnertime.'

'Lunchtime,' I confirm.

'That's right. I'll be here at midday.'

'Thanks, Jack.' I wait for him to leave before I go and fetch the dog. He is recovering from his experience at the vet's; at least the stench has gone and I don't have to drive with the windows open on the way back to the farm. However, when I take Bear into the sitting room in his new coat, my father scowls, unimpressed.

'What have you done to the dog? He looks bloody ridiculous in that. Stevie, you're turning out to be a real soft townie.'

'I didn't do it to improve his looks. I've done it for his health. He's had ten teeth removed.'

'Poor bugger – he must be in agony.'

'He's on painkillers and he'll feel a lot better without a mouthful of rotten teeth.'

'He looks a right wuss now, like a fancy show dog prancing about at Crufts.'

'Dad, it was part of the agreement I made with Jack Miller to get you out of the hole you've dug with Animal Welfare. If I were you, I'd be just a teensy bit grateful.' He isn't, of course, and I wasn't expecting him to be, and I'm angry at him for that as well as everything else. I know I shouldn't be stressing him out because he's ill, but I can't hold back.

'By the way, I've paid the outstanding bill at Overdown Farmers. You can't keep using them as a bank. Tony said he tried to keep the deliveries going for the sake of the animals, but it came to a point where they couldn't ignore it any longer. They have to pay their suppliers.'

'Stop preaching at me! You didn't have to pay it. I didn't ask you to go poking your nose in where it's not wanted.'

'Well, somebody has to.'

'I can't help it. I've been ill.' Dad bangs the end of a crutch against the floor. 'I've been in hospital.' A tear drips from the end of his nose; although I've never seen my father cry before, I can't help thinking they're only crocodile tears. 'What do you expect?'

'A thank you and some respect. I'm your daughter.

It isn't too much to ask.' Unable to continue the conversation without saying something I'll regret, I head back out into the kitchen, feed Bear a small meal of cold chicken from the fridge and put his blanket through the wash. Bear sits quietly beside the Aga, hardly able to keep his eyes open, and as he nods off, I realise someone is missing and that someone is Nick.

'Dad,' I call, 'have you seen Nick?'

'Last time I saw him, he said he was going for a walk.'

'That's odd.' I check my mobile. There are three missed calls. I switched it to silent when I went into the vet's to collect Bear. I listen to the voicemails. They're all from Nick and getting increasingly desperate.

I'm in the barn. Can you come and find me?

Stevie, where are you? I thought you'd be back from the vet's by now. What's keeping you?

I'm stuck. You've got to help me get the hell out of here.

I slip back into my wellies and run straight out across the yard to the barn where the cows are indoors resting and chewing the cud. I stand at the gate.

'Nick, where are you?'

'Over here.' He sounds petrified. 'Stevie, help me. I'm trapped.'

I climb the gate and walk along the first aisle of cubicles. They are pens open at one end and separated by rails; the cows can walk in and out of them at will and feed on silage or lie down. Nick is in the far corner where the walls of the barn are too high to climb, perched on an upside-down metal bucket scoop surrounded by several nosy cows, one of whom is licking his boot.

'They won't let me go.'

'Wave your arms and yell at them. Grow a pair, man. They'll soon move.' I start laughing as he waves and says shoo so quietly I can hardly hear him. 'What are you scared of? They won't eat you. They're vegetarian.'

'It isn't funny. I've read stories about people being trampled to death.'

'They're curious about you, that's all,' I say, strolling across and moving them away. 'There you go.'

'Thanks,' he says grudgingly. 'I was afraid no one would find me before it was too late.'

I lean up for a kiss. 'What were you doing anyway?'

'I came looking for you. I had a message from work and I really need to get back to the office by tomorrow lunchtime. Is that okay with you?'

'That's fine.'

'I thought we'd make an early start,' he says, heading rapidly for the exit.

'We . . . ? Nick, I can't go back tomorrow. You can see how it is. I've hardly started.'

Back outside in the farmyard, I am reminded of how much the farm has been neglected. The house has sash windows that have seen better days. My father used to repair and paint them every year, but the blue paint has peeled away to leave rotten wood exposed to the elements. A pane of glass in the front door has broken and been covered with tape.

'Stevie, it isn't your responsibility.' Nick runs his hands through his hair as if he's losing patience with me. 'The farm belongs to your father. You have a life, a job, a flat, friends . . . me . . . of your own in London. You don't need to take on this place as well.'

'It isn't for ever. I want to do what I can, at the very least leave the farm in a manageable state for Cecil and Dad, and I do have a stake in it, remember?'

'You don't have to spend your money on it, though. What have you paid for so far? Feed for the cows and the vet's bill for the dog. It isn't right.'

'I have savings. I have a good income. I'm doing it because I want to.'

'But there's our future to think about . . .'

I know what he's hinting at, the Big Wedding, the one I haven't agreed to yet.

'Look, Nick, the more you push me, the less I'm able to decide. I don't know why, but it's annoying.'

'I don't want you to forget, darling.'

'As if.' I try to lighten the mood with some gentle teasing. 'It's your memory you should be concerned about, old man.'

'Stevie, I'm not that much older than you,' Nick says, 'and talking of old men, maybe it's time you thought of alternative ways of raising money to keep the farm going. Cecil's well overdue for retirement. If he and Mary moved out of the cottage, your father could tidy it up and rent it out.'

'Oh no, that isn't going to happen. My father would never agree to make Cecil and Mary homeless. And nor would I – that would be very cold and callous and I couldn't have it on my conscience. They've lived at Nettlebed Farm for ever. Where would they go?'

'I don't know.' Nick shrugs. 'It isn't your problem.'

I stare at him. I'm not sure I like him very much at the moment.

'I think it's a rotten idea. Who would look after the cows?' I go on.

'Your father can hire a younger person and give them a room in the farmhouse – it's big enough. Come on, Stevie, you can do the maths. It's a no-brainer.'

'You're right that something drastic needs to be done to bring the farm back into profit, but I have to disagree with your suggestion of how to go about it,' I say crossly. 'I don't want to discuss it any further.'

Unlike the cows, the situation isn't black and white.

Chapter Five

Chicken Run

Nick goes back to London the day after Jack's visit to Nettlebed Farm and texts me several times a day for the next couple of days, asking me when I'm coming home. Jack continues to monitor the welfare of the animals on the farm, and he is quietly optimistic that he won't have to take further action, although he's still worried about what will happen when I leave.

There isn't much sign of that being possible at the moment, I think, as almost a week passes and people at work start to hassle me about deadlines and cancelled appointments. Cecil and I do the milking together, which means he has a little spare time. He fills it with other tasks such as repairing the chicken run, because I mentioned in passing that it would be good to have hens around the place again like we used to. I contact Ruthie, who runs Hen Welfare, to arrange for Cecil to pick up a dozen hens and Ray calls me back at last, although he is singularly unhelpful, suggesting we should sell up. When I point out that Dad and I would outvote him, he says he's happy to remain a sleeping partner in Nettlebed Farm, but he doesn't want to get involved in maintaining the dairy herd.

The morning after speaking to my brother, I'm washing down the parlour, with Bear watching me from the top of the steps, keeping out of the way of the end of the hose. My thoughts return to Nick, how much I'm missing him and what it would be like to be married. We have similar tastes in music and food, and we have work in common, so there's no reason not to be married, but neither can I find a reason that we should be. If we did tie the knot, we could afford a really good house close to Wimbledon Common, where we could walk the dog, one like Bear, which we'd have when we had our children, a boy and a girl, and I was working part-time, or not at all. I smile to myself. I could become a yummy mummy.

I check the temperature on the bulk tank, wash my hands and go inside for a cooked breakfast. While I'm waiting for my coffee to cool down, I call India.

'Hi, how are you?' I ask, picturing her with the espresso she has to have to give her a kick-start in the mornings. She's a night owl, whereas I'm an early bird.

'I'm missing my happy flatmate, of course. When are you coming home?'

'Soon, I hope. Well, as soon as I can. Another week should do it.'

'I really can't imagine you working on the farm in jeans and wellies.' India chuckles. 'You missed a great party for Eddie's flat-warming on Saturday. Aren't you bored witless stuck out in the middle of nowhere?'

'It's giving me time to think about me and Nick, and what I want out of life.'

'You sound like you're about ninety,' India sighs.

'Nick wants an answer and it isn't fair to keep him hanging on.'

'I know.'

'Have you seen him?'

'I saw him at the party and when he dropped in to pick up his spare phone charger. He said he left it here the last time he stayed over with you.'

'Oh? He didn't mention it.'

'He didn't stop for long. Stevie, he's missing you like mad. He didn't stop talking about you.'

It doesn't feel right though, I muse. India's my best friend – she's supposed to gossip with me, not with Nick.

'He adores you,' India goes on, 'which is why I can't understand why you're taking so long to decide.'

'You won't say anything to him, will you?' I ask, hesitant to reveal my innermost thoughts because India, although well-meaning, is also well known to suffer from bouts of 'foot-in-mouth syndrome', letting slip secrets to the wrong people.

I gaze out of the kitchen window towards the ash tree that, although upended by the wind over the winter, is springing into leaf in the garden. 'I'm not sure I can commit to Nick at the moment.' Like the tree, I feel strangely uprooted.

'You are coming back?' India says.

'Yes, of course. There's nothing to keep me here, is there?'

'I don't know, hun, that's why I'm asking.' She pauses. 'I'd better go – I'm late for work.'

'You're always late for work,' I laugh.

'I miss you,' she says.

'Miss you too.' I cut the call and begin tidying up. I'm on a mission when Dad turns up half-dressed for breakfast.

'Did that dog sleep upstairs with you last night?' he asks.

'No,' I say, outright denial seeming like the best option. Bear had looked at me with his head cocked to one side when I was about to shut him in the lean-to, and I thought, why not? I let him up on condition he slept on a blanket on the floor, but I woke in the small hours with him lying across my feet.

'He isn't a pet, Stevie. He's a working dog and he needs to know his place – like someone else not so far away from here.'

'Like me, you mean?'

'You've waltzed in here and taken over, and you speak to me as if I'm as mad as a sack full of ferrets. I'm not stupid.'

It's true. I probably would treat him differently if he was well. I take a quick guilt-trip around the kitchen to pour the tea from the pot. One of the mugs is chipped.

'I'm going to throw this away, Dad.'

'Where do you think I'm going to get another one? I'm not made of money, you know.'

'I know that, but it's broken.'

'It can be mended.'

'I imagine it can, but by whom? It's finished. Dad, you can't keep all this rubbish.'

'That mug with the sunflowers reminds me of your mother,' he says gruffly. 'It was her favourite.'

'I'm sorry.' I place the mug on the windowsill, the sudden wave of sorrow at the mention of my mum reminding me to temper my enthusiasm for tidying up.

'I can see what you're doing, clearing the house so you can sell up as soon as I pop my clogs.'

'It's nothing of the sort. I'm trying to make the house habitable. It's unhygienic – there are mouse droppings in the cupboard under the sink. It can't go on.' My mother wasn't house-proud, but she would never have let the place get into such a state.

'We should do something in Mum's memory,' I suggest. 'We could go to the church together and take some flowers.'

'I don't want to go and spend time at the grave. I'll be there with her long enough.'

'Dad, that's a terrible thing to say.'

'It's true.'

'Oh, for goodness' sake, snap out of it.' Annoyed at myself for saying what I did – because my father can't help being a grumpy old man – I go outside towards the cowshed to mix up the milk replacer for the calves. They are kept in what we call the 'nursery' next door, a breezeblock building with a stable door and deep straw bedding. The calves are hungry, as always, with the exception of the smallest, Domino's heifer calf – Cecil has named her Pearl. She hangs back in the far corner, her head down and her belly tucked up, while the others crowd me, nudging at my legs and the buckets, eager to be fed. Making my way through the group, I fill the feeder. The calves latch on to the rubber teats and drink, sucking noisily.

'Come on, Pearl.' I push her across to the feeder with my arms around her chest and hindquarters, but she isn't interested. Her nose is dry and her eyes are dull. I check her temperature, which is sky high, and her navel, which is swollen and sticky.

'Well, Pearl, I'll have to call the vet,' I tell her. 'If I believed in the paranormal, I'd think something was out to get us with the run of bad luck we're having.'

It's Leo who calls in to see the calf. He gives me a lecture on the importance of good stockmanship and hygiene in preventing navel ill before stopping abruptly and looking me straight in the eye.

'What's that phrase,' he says, 'the one about teaching your grandmother to suck eggs? I'm sorry for going on at you – you must be getting rather a complex. I saw Jack earlier today when he brought a badger in for euthanasia. He said you had everything under control.'

'I'm doing what I can.'

'What about the dog? Have you got that under control as well?'

'Bear's locked indoors, but you don't need to worry about him biting you – Maz at Otter House has pulled most of his teeth out.'

'Poor dog,' he says, surprising me with his sympathy for Bear as he injects the calf and hands me some needles and a bottle of penicillin.

'I can remember what to do,' I say, before he can give me another lecture on how to use them. 'I used to do all the injections on the farm.'

'I'll be back in five days' time to see her. In the meantime, she'll need some TLC.'

'Do you need to see her again?' I don't want Leo to think I'm not putting the welfare of the cattle first, but I'm finding it hard to justify the cost of another visit. 'Alex doesn't normally have to come back.'

'We work in different ways and I'd rather check up on her.' Leo's gaze lingers on my face for just a fraction too long, making me wonder if he's really intent on checking up on me.

'I could let you know how the calf is on the phone to save you a trip. Nettlebed Farm's a bit out of the way.'

'It certainly is.' Leo counts out some syringes for me from his box. 'I'm staying with the Pitts at Barton Farm.'

'I know them: Stewart, his wife Lynsey and their family.'

'That's right. There are supposed to be seven children, but it feels like seventy. The house never sleeps. There's always something going on, some crisis or other. Last night the little one, Frances, fell down the stairs and had to be rushed to A and E with concussion. The night before that, two of the brothers got into a scrap and I was enlisted to mop up the blood and close a head wound with butterfly strips.'

'You aren't keen on children then?' I smile.

'They're a necessary part of life, but preferably not mine. Friends say it's different when you have your own, but I have no immediate plans.'

Our fingers touch as Leo hands over the syringes. I pull sharply away as if his skin is on fire and a rush of blood sweeps up my neck at the thought of a quick roll in the hay with him. I put it down to an indefinable animal instinct, a pheromone-mediated urge beyond my control. I'm with Nick, so why am I wondering what it would be like to be up close and personal with someone else, least of all this man who, although in a better frame of mind than when I first met him, doesn't exactly come across as a warm-hearted character?

'I'll see you in a few days' time,' he says, a spark of amusement in his eyes.

'If I'm still here.'

Leo frowns.

'It's all right. You don't have to pretend to be disappointed,' I say brightly. 'I'll be going back to London. I have a flat and a job there.' Maybe it's because Leo has already met Nick briefly that I decide not to bother to mention the boyfriend. 'I'm an accountant.'

'The role of lady farmer suits you,' Leo says. 'I can't imagine you working in an office.'

'I don't mind, but I'm going to find it hard to go back to working indoors after this.' I pause. Leo doesn't seem to be in any hurry to leave and I wonder about offering him coffee, but I can't really spare the time.

'The cow, Domino. How is she?' Leo asks.

'I'll show you if you like.' We cross the farmyard together and stop at the barn. 'That's her.' I point to the one lying down in the first cubicle. She flicks a lazy fly from her ear and chews on the cud.

'She looks better already,' Leo says, sounding surprised.

'Actually, there's another one you could look at today while you're here, if you don't mind.' I noticed her limping slightly this morning, and feel a twinge of remorse that I'd forgotten about her until Leo's presence jogged my memory.

He's already lifting the catch on the gate and pushing it open.

'I'll get her in the crush,' I say, marshalling the patient out of the barn. 'This is Honeydew the third.'

'Out of Honeydew the second, I assume,' Leo says lightly.

'Yes, and I'm very afraid that there won't be a fourth generation of Honeydews the way the farm is going. I can fix the immediate problems by throwing some money at them, but it's the long term I'm worried about.' It's been keeping me awake at night. 'There's so much to put right when you look at the buildings and the land. The farm needs more investment than my father can make from dairy farming.'

'Perhaps you should think of something else to do with the land.'

'Diversify, you mean? I can't see Nettlebed Farm without cattle.'

Leo tips his head to one side. 'You'd be mad not to consider the alternatives.'

Honeydew limps into the crush quite happily while Leo puts on a waterproof gown and I fetch a bucket of hot water from the dairy. She's a good girl, obliging Leo by picking up her back foot.

'What is it?' I say when he's scrubbed it clean.

'It's a mild case of slurry heel.'

My heart sinks because – again – it's something that could have been avoided if the yard had been kept clean.

'Hey, don't feel bad about it,' Leo says, as if he's reading my mind. 'We're seeing a lot of it because it's the end of the winter and the cows have been housed for months.'

'We're going to turn them out for the first time before the weekend. I can't wait to see their faces.'

'They'll go mad. I love seeing them gambolling about,' Leo says. 'I'd suggest that when they come back indoors for next winter, that you set up a weekly foot bath. Prevention's always better than cure.'

'Thank you, Leo.'

'It's no problem, Stevie.' He clears his throat. 'I hope you don't go rushing back to the big bad city too soon.'

'It isn't all that bad,' I say, smiling. 'I like the people and the buzz you get from living in London.'

'You sound as though you're missing it.'

'I am a little,' I admit. 'In fact, I'd be torn if I had to decide between my life in the city and life on the farm.'

When Leo leaves, I go back and separate Pearl from the rest of her friends, penning her off a small section in the shed so she can still see them. I shake out some fresh straw, giving her a clean bed and bottle-feeding her so I know what she's taking. She's reluctant at first, and soon there's more milk down my overalls than down her throat.

'Now, Pearl, I won't cry and make a fuss over spilt milk as long as you promise me you'll get better.' I go and clean the bottle before returning to the yard where Cecil is drawing up in the Land Rover.

'I've got them,' he mutters, struggling out of the vehicle with his cap over his eyes and his pipe in his mouth. 'A cockerel and a baker's dozen from Ruthie at Hen Welfare.'

I move round and open the tailgate, finding two open-sided plastic crates of light-brown hens and a cardboard box containing the cockerel, which is making a noisy protest over being confined.

'The cock's from a local smallholding, surplus to requirements, while the hens are ex-battery, but they've got a lot of eggs left in them, according to Ruthie,' Cecil observes. 'Mind you, they do look a bit scrawny.'

Cecil and I carry the crates to the run, placing them inside on the ground. We lift the lids and wait for the hens to hop out to investigate their new surroundings.

'There are fourteen hens,' I say, counting them.

'Ah, Ruthie gave us one for luck. Actually, she has so many she doesn't know what to do with them all, so I said we could take an extra.'

I pick one out, holding her wings close to her body. She's very light and she's lost almost all her feathers. Her skin is pale, rough and pimply, and she has a red, rubbery comb on the top of her head and wattles under her beak. I let her go on the ground and she stands blinking at me with one orange eye before deciding it's safe to stretch her wings.

Three more hop onto the edge of the crate and survey the scene, tilting their heads and cawing softly, before joining the hen on the ground where she's tapping at the straw with her beak. She scratches at it with her feet and reverses to see if she's unearthed some hidden treasure, a worm or a morsel of layers mash.

'I've got some treats.' Cecil sticks his hand in his pocket and pulls out a handful of mealworms, live ones, scattering them for the hens, at which more emerge from the crates. There is a lot of noisy squabbling before they settle down, continuing their search for mealworms, while the cockerel, a proud and elegant specimen, decides to join them, stalking among his new girlfriends.

'Thank you, Cecil.'

'It's a pleasure to have chickens on the farm again,' he says. 'I'm looking forward to a fresh brown egg for breakfast, not a shop-bought one.'

'Don't you buy eggs from Jennie and Guy next door at Uphill Farm?'

'Your father wouldn't countenance it.' Cecil pauses. 'I'm going indoors for a sandwich.'

'I'll catch you later.' Having fed the chickens some layers mash and filled up their water, I head for the brick-built outbuilding between the barn and the nursery to check the cows' records. They should all be on the desktop computer, but as I suspected it's been untouched since my brother left the farm seven years ago. I can't even persuade it to switch on.

The details of the dry cows – the ones waiting to calve down, the fertility rates and the medical notes have been scrawled into a dog-eared desk diary or added as notes on scraps of paper. It upsets me because the office used to be so organised. I could have told you instantly how many cows were barren or how many due to calve within the next months.

The accounts are in a muddle too. Receipts stamped with muddy footprints lie across the floor, and box files overflowing with paperwork and piles of unopened mail, bills mainly, I suspect, are piled up on the desk.

I decide to tackle my father, finding him indoors in the sitting room where he's in his chair, dressed in his tweed jacket, with Bear at his feet and a gun aimed towards the garden. A gun? How has he got hold of a gun?

'What are you doing?' I exclaim, but my words are lost in an explosion of rifle fire as he takes a pot shot through the open French windows at a fat wood-pigeon that has dared to waddle its way across the lawn. 'Dad!' I shout as the pigeon takes flight, lumbering into the air like a wide-bellied cargo plane.

'What the—?' My father turns towards me, holding the gun pointing right between my eyes, which I find somewhat unnerving. 'What do you think you're doing, creeping up on us like that?'

'Put the gun down,' I say wearily.

'I'd have got it, if you hadn't come in and spooked it.'

'Put it down!'

He lays the gun across his lap and stares out at the lawn. Some of the other pigeons haven't been so lucky – there are three lying lifeless in the grass.

'It seems a shame to kill them,' I observe.

'They're a nuisance,' he says firmly, 'and I fancy a pigeon pie. Mary says she'll make it. Go and get them, Stevie. I can't persuade Bear to fetch them, bloody useless dog,' he adds, fondling Bear's head.

'What do you expect? He isn't a retriever. And I'm not going to fetch the birds. Get them yourself. And before you say anything, it isn't because I'm squeamish. I think it's time you did a little more for yourself to help with your rehab.'

'You aren't a doctor. What do you know about strokes?'

'A bit.' I've gleaned some information from the internet.

'You can't know what it's like, unless you've been through it yourself,' he growls. 'It's like dying a little.' His voice trembles and my instinct to comfort him takes over. I move closer and touch his shoulder. He freezes. 'I might as well be dead. I can't do much. I can't look after myself, let alone the farm. And no one wants to know me any more.'

'That isn't true,' I say, but my reassurances only wind him up further.

'Where is everyone then? Tell me!'

'Perhaps they don't want to disturb you.' I take my hand away, aware that the contact is unwelcome.

'Ray never shows his face.'

'I expect he's busy,' I say, not wishing to enter into a conversation about my father and Ray's rather volatile history.

'Too busy for an old man with half a body who can't go out shooting any more and has to wait for the birds to come to him.' He pauses. 'I can't shave myself properly, let alone do the milking.' I worry that he's depressed, but he looks up at me with a wicked gleam in his eye that suggests he's milking the situation – so to speak – for all it's worth. 'Stevie,' he goes on, 'will you please get those pigeons and take them in for Mary? I'd hate to think of the foxes getting them for their tea.'

'Oh, all right. I'll do it just this once, because there won't be a next time – you aren't supposed to be in possession of a gun. In case you've forgotten, which I'm sure you haven't, your licence has been revoked. Wait there. I'll be back.' I collect the birds, picking them up gingerly, and take them through to the kitchen where Mary is rolling out pastry. 'They're all yours.' I put them beside the sink. 'Don't worry about me. I'll do myself an omelette tonight.'

'You never were that fond of pigeon pie,' she says, smiling.

'Do you think Dad's all right? He seems very down,' I say.

'Dr Mackie says it's quite normal for someone to have depression after a stroke. He's got some antidepressants.'

'I heard that,' Dad calls through. 'There's no need to talk about me as if I'm not here. As for the happy pills, I don't like drugs so I stopped taking them.'

80

'That explains a lot,' Mary says lightly. 'That's why you're even more of a grumpy old beggar than normal. Take them and be happy, Tom.'

I'm surprised at her talking to her boss like that. There was a time when she looked up to him with respect, afraid to cross him in any way. I guess that being his carer has blurred the boundaries of their relationship.

I push the kitchen door up so my father can't hear.

'Thank you for all you've done for Dad,' I say as I eat a piece of the pastry trimmings Mary offers me, remembering how I used to love eating them uncooked as a girl. 'He wouldn't have managed without you.'

'Tom isn't always the easiest of patients, but we've made some compromises and I like looking after him,' she adds fiercely. 'He was lost after Pippa died. We all were.' Mary looks down, wringing a damp cloth. 'I reckon that's why he had that stroke.'

I feel a pang of guilt for not being there for him, for being so wrapped up in my own grief for my mum that I didn't consider my dad's feelings.

'You mustn't blame yourself, Stevie. He doesn't deserve you after how he treated you over the farm. If you'd been our daughter and we'd owned the farm, we'd have—' Mary breaks off, mid-sentence, as if worried she's said too much. She and Cecil never had children. 'Never mind,' she goes on eventually. 'It's a pity Nick had to go home so soon. He's a handsome young man, just like James Bond with that beautiful car.' She drops the cloth into the washing-up bowl in the butler sink. 'He's a bit weedy though – he could do with feeding up.'

'He'll be at the gym now,' I observe. 'He worries about his figure.'

'Oh, I'm not sure I like that,' Mary says. 'It has to be a real man for me.'

'Mary,' I say in mock surprise.

'You can tell by Nick's hands that he hasn't done a proper day's work in his life. They're so clean and smooth, like a baby's bottom.' She pauses. 'I always thought you'd marry one of us, a country lad, someone rough and ready with a warm heart . . . not that I'm saying Nick doesn't have a warm heart when he's with you, like—'

'It's all right, Mary,' I say, stalling her.

'I'm sorry for wittering on like this. Tom and Cecil don't do a lot of talking.'

'Neither does Nick – he prefers to text.' I return to the sitting room and close the double doors.

'Where's the gun?' I say, turning to my father who merely shrugs in response. 'I thought you'd had to leave it with the police.' I pause, watching the sly look on his face. 'You did leave it?'

'I certainly did.'

'But you had another one somewhere in the house. For goodness' sake, Dad, if anyone finds out, you'll be arrested and charged this time for unlawful possession of a firearm.'

'No one is going to find out unless you tell them,' he says. 'You wouldn't grass on your poor old father, would you, especially when he's so sick?'

'Not so sick you can't get up and hide a gun, I notice. Where is it? It can't stay here.'

'It's locked away in the cabinet.' He waves towards the hallway where the gun cabinet is set into the alcove under the stairs. 'That dim-witted police constable will never think of looking there. It's too bloody obvious. And if you insist on handing that one in, I have others tucked away.'

'You're going to have to show me where they all are.' I wonder if he's calling my bluff. I wouldn't put it past him. 'Give me the key.' I hold out my hand. 'If you don't, I will report you to the police and you'll be sent down for some time.'

'Oh, Stevie, you are an old shrew,' he grumbles, but he gives me the key from his jacket pocket. I take it and slip it into my purse. I'll decide what to do about the gun situation later. 'I'm going to go through the files from the office tonight.'

'There's no need—' Dad begins, but I cut him off.

'There's every need. When did you last have the books made up?'

'How can I remember something like that? This year? Last year?'

'When did you last pay a tax bill?'

'I really don't know. Your mother –' his voice softens – 'Pippa used to deal with the accountant. What was his name?' He grinds his fist against his forehead.

'Never mind, I'll deal with it.'

'I can't believe you took up accounting.'

'You can criticise all you like, but it's kept a roof over my head and I've done well out of it. I agree it isn't the most exciting job in the world, but it's a good career.'

'It's like being an estate agent or a banker,' Dad

insists. 'You must be about as popular as a fart in a phone box.'

'I beg your pardon?' I can't help it. I start to laugh. 'Where did you get that one from?'

'It's been around a long time – Andy, the AI man, told it to me.' (Andy is the artificial inseminator – we don't keep a bull on the farm any more.) Dad starts laughing too, but his good humour doesn't last for long.

After a meal and a couple of glasses of scrumpy, I turn my attention to the files, sitting down with Bear and the paperwork at the kitchen table. Dad shuffles in with his stick and slippers, wearing his green plaid robe over his pyjamas.

'I don't need your help,' I tell him firmly. 'Please go away.'

'This is my home, Stevie, my farm and my business, not yours,' he begins.

'I don't think you're in any position to tell me what I can and can't do. I've bailed you out – temporarily, at least. You owe it to me to let me find out about the state of your finances before someone sends the bailiffs in.'

'Bailiffs,' he blusters. 'Don't talk nonsense.'

'You haven't a clue, have you? I bet you're completely in the dark about what money you have and what you owe.'

As Dad starts to deny it, the lights go out.

'A power cut? That's all I need,' I sigh, switching on the flashlight on my mobile and shining it around the kitchen. 'Where do you keep the candles?'

'I don't know. Pippa used to look after the candles . . .'

I check the drawers of the oak dresser, finding a stash of matches. Mary lends me three stubby candles, one an advent candle burned down to day twenty-two, which I take back to light the kitchen. Dad says he's going to bed – I think he's scared now of what I'm going to find.

I open all the post, throwing away the advertising and keeping the letters and invoices from various people and businesses, such as Talyton Manor vets, the company that delivers the oil for the Aga and, worst of all, an enormous bill from the Inland Revenue demanding immediate payment.

I trawl through the paperwork, dividing it into piles and subdividing those into year and then month. I try to cross-reference the documents and receipts – some of which appear to have been chewed by rats – with the ledger entries my father has made, until I have to give up and start again with a fresh sheet of paper. I sit there inputting data until my eyes ache and the figures blur into one.

I can't believe that someone who used to be so careful with his money – some would say 'tight' – has left his financial affairs to chance, and all but abandoned them really.

I take a break to call Nick. I call it a break, but we talk about the farm accounts and how I'm going to approach the enormous task of sorting them out. It's good to have someone who understands. Occasionally, I hear the sound of talking and the chinking of glasses in the background.

'Are you out and about?' I ask him.

'I've got a couple of friends round – Jeff and Annette. You met them at Christmas.'

I remember them, Jeff with the wandering hands and the saintly Annette whose self-professed role in life was to make her husband happy. She was writing a book about it. She said she'd give me a signed copy as a wedding present. I reckon that's what started Nick on his pursuit of marriage in the first place.

'I shouldn't interrupt then, if you have visitors. Why didn't you say?'

'Don't go just yet, Stevie,' he says quickly. 'I'm glad to get away for a few minutes – I wouldn't recommend Annette's book if it ever makes the bookshelves. She's carping on at Jeff all the time. I don't know how he stands it.'

I feel as if I'm on the fringe of Nick's life, not at the centre. He has these old friends he's known for years, far longer than he's been going out with me. I don't know them. I'm sure they're nice enough, but they aren't my kind of people.

I try to divert him by talking about the farm, telling him about Leo and the calf.

'Not Leo again,' Nick sighs. 'I'm beginning to think you fancy him.'

'Nick, that's a ridiculous thing to say, and you know it.'

'Do I?' he says wryly, and I find myself altering what I was going to say from 'Leo's advised us to set up a foot bath for the herd' to 'We're going to set up a foot bath for the herd.'

'A foot spa for cows? Now I've heard everything. That's cheered me up.' He chuckles. 'When are you coming home? Have you decided yet? It's been almost two weeks since I last saw you.'

'I wondered if you wanted to come down on Sunday. I'm nowhere near finished, but—'

'I'll drive down on Sunday morning. We'll go out for lunch, my treat.'

'Let me know when you're on your way,' I say. 'I hope you enjoy the rest of the evening.'

'Don't work too hard, darling. Miss you.'

'Goodnight, Nick.'

When I close the final file at midnight, I wander into the sitting room to check the light switches are off in case the power returns overnight. I think I hear a low thud and the soft whisper of a female voice. My heart misses a beat.

'Mum,' I mouth, but it isn't her, of course. My rational mind says there are no ghosts, but there is a small part of me that wants to believe in a soul that remains once the body has gone. It was the flutter of the curtain in a draught as I opened the door, the shadow of the standard lamp, its fringes like a shawl, the flicker of the flames in the grate and the scent of rose petals that combined to create the illusion of my mother's presence. I wish she was here.

She was quiet, gentle and painfully shy, and, in many ways, the best mum in the world.

She was ten years younger than my dad and used to tell me how at nineteen she felt she was going to be left on the shelf, because no one noticed her until she caught my dad's eye at the annual Country Show when she was showing her father's prize bull. She said she was wearing a white coat and wellington boots and a yellow rose in her long, dark-brown hair. The first time Dad spoke to her, he said he admired the way she handled cattle, and it took her three dates before she plucked up the courage to ask him his name. He gave her yellow roses every year after they married as an anniversary gift.

It must have been hard for her moving onto the farm with her new husband and mother-in-law, and my father was often contrary – if Mum said the grass was green, he would insist it was blue.

I remember I have to feed Pearl. I slip into my wellies and walk across the shadowy yard under the light of the moon and the stars. Some might think it spooky, but to me there's nothing to be afraid of. I take a deep breath of fresh country air and smile to myself. The chickens are tucked up in their coop inside the run and the cows are in the barn. I am home.

The electricity is back when I turn the light on in the nursery. I grab a bottle of milk I made up earlier, shake it and take it in to the calves, being mugged on the way through to Pearl's pen. 'You've had enough,' I tell them, chuckling. 'Go to bed.'

Pearl is less enthusiastic than the others, but she accepts the teat, chewing on it a couple of times as if she's forgotten what to do before she drains the bottle. She lets the teat drop out of her mouth and gives me a gentle nudge as if to say thanks, before returning to the corner of her pen and lying down front end first in the straw. I sit down on a spare bale of straw and watch her for a while as she falls asleep, hoping she's going to make it. She seems cold so I fetch an old sweater of my father's that I find in the lean-to and, with the aid of a pair of scissors, create a woolly coat for her.

It's peaceful in the nursery. Out here I can hear myself think. I have a lot on my mind, what with Nick and the farm. I do miss my boyfriend when we're apart, but not in an all-consuming, can't-live-without-him way. Is that enough? I don't think so. I would rather remain single than commit totally to someone I could live without, but how can I tell Nick I can't marry him? How can I let him down gently?

Grieving for the end of my relationship – because, although I'm being pragmatic, I'm not heartless – I blow my nose on a piece of tissue that I find in my pocket and let my thoughts run on.

If I'm no longer committed to Nick, what is there to keep me in London? There's India and my other friends. Leaving them and my flat would be a terrible wrench, and my job is special to me – I'd miss everyone at work.

'Hey, Stevie, what are you doing out here at this time of night?' Cecil's voice cuts into my consciousness, making me jump.

'Cecil, I might say the same of you.'

'I saw the light,' he says simply.

I smile to myself. So have I – seen the light, I mean. If I went back to London, I could continue with my career, keep seeing my friends and I could marry Nick.

If I stayed here in Devon, I could fight to turn the family business round as a tribute to my mother's memory, because the fate of Nettlebed Farm lies in my hands.

Chapter Six

Home Is Where the Herd Is

My first thought when I wake at dawn the next day to the sound of the cockerel is how I'm going to tell Nick what I plan to do. I hate to hurt anyone's feelings, especially those of a man who's stuck by me through my mum's death and some tough times at work when a client was pressuring me to falsify their accounts. I suppose it worked both ways, though, because I was there for Nick when he was admitted to hospital with bleeding from a gastric ulcer, and afterwards during a prolonged convalescence. We've been through a lot together and I'm very fond of him, but I cannot marry him.

The cockerel crows three more times before I manage to drag myself out of bed. I throw on some clothes and grab a coffee on the way out through the kitchen, then walk across the yard in the pale dawn light to the nursery, wondering if Pearl has made it through the night. I switch the light on and check Pearl's pen. She's lying on her side with her limbs sprawled out. My heart stops. It doesn't look good.

I make my way over to her, pushing aside the other calves, which are hungry for milk. I can't see her breathing through Dad's sweater.

'Pearl?' I reach down and touch her ear. It flicks, making me start. She opens her eye and stretches. 'Are you having me on?' I say lightly as she rolls onto her brisket and yawns. 'You'll never make it into the herd if you can't get up in the mornings.'

I feed all the calves and inject Pearl with her antibiotic. It's Thursday and she has three more days of treatment, maybe more, if Leo decides she needs it.

'Good morning, Stevie. Did you sleep in there?' Cecil asks, popping his head around the door into the nursery.

'No, but I would have done if I'd thought it would help.'

'What's this?' he says, staring at Pearl. 'It's a bit odd, isn't it, dressing her up like that? I never thought I'd see the day.'

'She was cold.'

'Isn't that Tom's favourite jumper?'

'I found it in the lean-to.'

'He'll have your guts for garters if he finds out. He wears that one all winter.'

'I'll have to hope he doesn't find out then,' I say, walking back towards the collecting yard with Cecil. He's struggling this morning, puffing as he limps across the yard, pressing his fist into his lower back. 'Are you all right?'

'It's my lumbago giving me gip,' he says.

'Have you taken something for it?'

'Like Tom, I don't believe in taking drugs,' he grumbles.

'I'll do the milking this morning. You can have a break. Go on, put your feet up.'

'I can't do that. I'm here and I'm going to get on with it. It's no good, Stevie. If I sit around doing nothing but whittling, I shall seize up like the tin man.'

'You never get a break. You can't have had a holiday for years.'

'Mary and I went to her cousin's for a long weekend in the New Year and we visited my great-niece for her wedding last August.' He holds the gate open for me. 'What about you, Stevie?'

'Nick and I went to Mauritius.' I'm sure I've mentioned it, but Cecil appears to have forgotten.

'Those islands that are sinking underwater?'

'It's the sea level that's rising,' I point out. 'It's all down to global warming.'

'I don't believe in science and scientists. No one will convince me on a frosty winter's morning that the world is growing hotter.'

'I'm afraid we're partly to blame, keeping cows. They produce an awful lot of gas from the fermenting grass in their stomachs.'

'That's just daft, Stevie.'

I've tried to explain the effect of methane on the ozone layer to Cecil before, but he won't have it. 'Go back indoors. I can manage.'

'You're here to see your dad, not work yourself to

the bone. I bet you can't wait to get back to your office in London.'

'What would you think if I said I wasn't going back to London?'

'I'd wonder if you were right in the head. Come on, maid, let's get on with it. These girls don't milk themselves, more's the pity.'

We start the milking and settle into the familiar rhythms of the process.

Piskie aims a kick at me as I slip the clusters onto her teats.

'Hey, what's up with you?' I ask her.

'She isn't a kicker,' says Cecil above the sound of the machine.

'I'll keep the milk back,' I decide. I didn't suspect a problem when I cleaned her udder, except she was slightly more fidgety than usual. 'We'll keep her in the yard today. I'll call Leo.'

When I'm hosing down the parlour later, Cecil chats from the balcony, acting in a supervisory capacity, which suggests his back must really be sore, because usually he won't let me do it.

'By the way, Cecil, I don't think I've thanked you for looking after my dad while he's been ill.'

'Oh, it's Mary who's borne the brunt of it. She feeds him and, before you came back, she'd take him a flask of cocoa last thing of an evening. He can't do much, but he's better than he was when it first happened. I thought he was a goner.'

'I don't know how to thank you both,' I say, but actually, when I think about it, I do. Keeping the farm on its feet so they can keep a roof over their heads until the end of their days would be the best reward for their loyalty to my father and his family.

I envy Cecil and Mary. They seem content. I watch how they behave, noticing the little things, how they always have a smile or a touch for each other, and put each other first. I have never heard them undermining each other, or sniping.

'My Mary is a star. She does everything for me, which makes me want to do the same in return. I reckon that's the secret to a long and happy marriage. You know, you shouldn't marry that boyfriend of yours,' Cecil adds. 'He told me he asked you to marry him.' For once, Cecil doesn't let me get a word in edge-ways. 'He's too full of himself, worrying about his money and his appearance, and the cows really don't like him.'

'I'm not sure I should let my life be ruled by the cows' opinions,' I say, amused.

'They might look stupid on occasions, like when they're all trying to push through the gate at the same time, but they're good judges of character. You must turn him down because you deserve better.'

'Thanks for the advice, but I've already decided I'm not going to marry Nick, and when I said I was staying here on the farm, I meant it. I'm needed here.'

'Have you spoken to Tom and Ray about this? I'm sure they'll have an opinion.'

'I'll speak to Dad later. I'm not sure I need to talk to Ray. He's made it clear he has his own life and he isn't interested in what's going on here.' As long as he receives his inheritance when my father dies, I think, and it occurs to me that in the long term, I might have to buy my brother out from his share in the farm.

'Are you really going to milk cows for the rest of your life, Stevie? I know you're more than capable of doing it, but would it be right? You've got more brains than the rest of us put together. Wouldn't you be wasting your talents staying here?'

'Don't worry about that. Saving the farm will stretch my brain beyond anything I've done before.'

'It's hard manual work that will save the farm, not brainpower,' says Cecil.

'We need to make some changes.'

Cecil's face falls and to my horror, his eyes fill with tears. 'I suppose it had to come. We can move out . . .'

'You and Mary can stay in the cottage for ever. That won't change.'

He sniffs. 'I'm afraid you'll change your mind and we'll have to find a little place in Talyton, because it's obvious you can make money renting the cottage, or taking on a younger man than me.'

'It won't happen, Cecil. I promise.' I reach out and touch his arm. 'You and Mary are part of the family. No, what I'm thinking about are other ways of making money from the farm. The cows, much as I adore them, aren't paying their way at the moment, and we could do with another source of income.'

'What, like converting the barns into offices?' Cecil frowns. 'I think that's been done too many times around here and there's no demand for another farm shop. It would be heartbreaking not to have any animals here.'

'That's what I've been thinking. I was wondering about opening a petting farm for children to come and learn about farming and the environment, and have fun too.' I pause. 'What do you think?'

A smile crosses Cecil's craggy face. 'I think you should run that past your father. I'd like to see his face when you do.'

'I'm planning to speak to him this morning.'

'He isn't very good in the mornings.'

'I know.' I bite my lip as Cecil tips his head to one side and goes on. 'He isn't very good in the evenings either, so I'll wish you the best of luck.'

'Okay, I'm going in for breakfast,' I say, turning off the tap. 'Are you coming?'

'Mary has something waiting for me at the cottage. It's our anniversary.'

'Oh, I didn't know. Congratulations.'

'I'll pick a few flowers from the hedgerow and tie them up with a piece of ribbon, and tonight we'll have fish and chips at the seaside.'

'Take the rest of the day off, I insist. Call it a present from me and Dad. Go and enjoy it.'

'Maybe I shall, Stevie. Maybe I shall.'

I smile, thinking of my parents' marriage as I watch him go. Mum said her marriage had been a happy one on the whole, although she regretted how she gave way to my father's wishes and opinions and didn't stand up for me when he told me I couldn't stay to work on the farm when I left college. My father chose my brother over me because he was the male heir. The family farm always passed down the male line and he wasn't going to change the natural order for me, his elder child, because I happened to be born a girl.

I was capable, reliable and would have done anything to keep the family farm running smoothly. I could milk a cow by hand, drive a tractor, show a heifer and lay a hedge. The problem was my brother Ray could do all that too and he carried a Y chromosome.

Mum didn't believe I'd leave the farm when my father told me I couldn't work with him and Ray. She thought I'd stay, find some kind of job locally and wait – as she had – for a young farmer to ask me to marry him and take on the role of a farmer's wife. But I was devastated by my father's rejection, so I left to seek my fortune in London, far away from Nettlebed Farm. Looking back, that was pretty brave for a eighteen-year-old girl, and possibly foolhardy, but I didn't think I had anything to lose.

Mum and I didn't see each other for four years, although we kept in regular contact by phone, and after all Dad's machinations to install my brother as his successor, Ray married and walked out on the farm.

I return to the house where I find my father burning toast. I cut fresh slices from the loaf and start again.

'I've given Cecil the day off,' I begin.

'What did you go and do that for?' My father's good hand tightens on his stick as he shuffles his way back to his chair at the table. 'How do you think the work's going to get done?'

'I'll do it. It's his wedding anniversary.'

'I never took a day off for mine,' Dad grumbles. 'I worked all day every day, seven days a week—'

'So you've said, many times,' I cut in, and I wonder if he ever regrets it and whether being a workaholic contributed to the state of his health. 'Anyway, I don't want to discuss it. Jack Miller is dropping by later.'

'I don't see why he has to keep poking his nose in,' Dad starts.

'You're on probation. He's coming to check on our progress.' I think we've made a lot of headway, but I'm still worried. 'I thought we'd turn the cows out tomorrow after morning milking. The forecast is for dry and sunny weather and the grass looks amazing.'

'I don't like letting them out till April Fools' Day.'

'There's no reason to delay. It'll save us money, the cows will pick up quickly on the spring grass and we'll be able to give the cubicles a deep clean. You'd be an April fool not to go ahead, Dad,' I warn.

'It isn't up to you, Stevie.'

'I will have my say, whether you like it or not. I have an interest in the business.'

'I wish you'd never come back.' Saliva trickles down Dad's chin. I pass him a tissue but he pushes it away. 'Go back to London.'

'I've decided to stay on for good. You need me.'

'I've never needed anybody. I've always stood on my own two feet.'

I butter a piece of toast and put it in front of him. Bear sits at his feet, his muzzle resting on Dad's lap. He whines. Dad smiles and breaks off a corner of the crust and feeds it to him.

'I don't want the cows going out tomorrow,' he says.

'You'll be telling me we'll run out of grass next.'

'It's none of your business how I run this farm,' he goes on, not listening to me.

'Dad, I'm not prepared to put up with any more of your nonsense,' I tell him, hurt that he shows no gratitude or appreciation at all, or any awareness that I am about to give up everything to be back here. 'I won't be bullied. I've told you before, if I walk out on you now, you'll end up losing everything – the cows, your home, even your freedom if you get taken to court. Is that what you want?'

He sits there, mute.

'I didn't think so. I'm here to keep the farm running smoothly so it's here when you get better.'

'*If* I get better, Stevie. I'm no fool. This is it.' He lifts his limp hand with his good one and drops it with a thud on the table. 'This is about as good as I'm going to get.'

'I'm sorry.' Like his body, my father's life has shrunk, confining him to the house and farmyard, and keeping him dependent on other people.

'Sometimes I wish I'd died,' he adds gruffly.

'Dad, please don't. You seem to have grown stronger in the last couple of weeks.'

'That's because I have someone to fight with,' he says eventually, a small uneven smile on his lips.

'So it isn't all bad, me being here?'

'Well, you've done wonders for Cecil – you've cheered him up no end – and you've paid some of the bills, though you didn't have to do that because I had them in hand.'

'Sure,' I say dryly. 'Anyway, let's put the past aside

and think about the future. As I've said, I've decided to stay.'

'It isn't a job for a girl. There's never been a lady farmer at Nettlebed Farm.'

'Times change and I'm more than capable of running the farm. I've proved that.'

'You're too feisty, too flighty. Stevie, I forbid it.'

'But I'm determined.' My heart is pounding as I recall the night we argued and I left the farm for London. This time I will stand my ground, older and wiser.

I lean close to my father and rest my hands on the table.

'You can't make me leave because I have an interest in the farm. If you insist on making my life a misery, as you did when I was eighteen, I will have no hesitation in making a takeover bid. I'm sure with Ray's help and a good solicitor I can make a sound case for obtaining power of attorney, and then you'll have no say at all in what happens.'

'You can't do that,' he says, his eyes flashing with anger. 'You wouldn't . . .'

I stand straight, cross my arms across my chest and wait for him to work it out. He breaks off another corner of toast and gives it to the dog before looking back to me.

'Stay, if you must, bed and board, but you won't be able to take a wage from the business.'

'Not until we start making money again,' I agree. 'We need to talk about other ways of making the farm pay.'

'Diversification?' He chokes on the word.

'There's little profit in milk. We should consider cutting down on the herd or getting rid of them altogether.'

'No, Stevie.' Dad's face is dark with pain. 'Over my dead body! There have always been cows at Nettlebed Farm and there always will be.'

'I thought we could look at ways to continue keeping animals on the farm, so I was thinking of some kind of visitor attraction – a petting farm for children,' I say tentatively. 'With tourists in the summer and school visits, we could make a comfortable income. We could keep a few of the cows, the old favourites, and some of the heifers. We could open a tearoom.'

'You're mad! Where are you going to get the money from? You'll need planning permission. The neighbours won't like it.'

'I thought you'd appreciate winding Guy up.'

'It won't just be Guy, will it? The whole town will want its say. There'll be uproar.'

'I thought you'd relish the thought of a fight,' I say, 'or are you going to roll over and give up? I can call a couple of estate agents and see what they'll value the farm at. We can put Nettlebed Farm on the market, sell up and find you a retirement flat or a room in the nursing home, if you prefer.' For a moment I wonder if he's going to have another stroke. He is apoplectic and so am I. I can't bear to look at him any longer. 'Oh, do what you like, you stubborn old bugger,' I tell him before I storm out and hide in the nursery with the calves, where I sink down against the wall and burst into tears of sorrow and frustration. As I sit there in the straw, the calves form a semicircle around me, gazing at me as if to say, where's our milk?

'You've had breakfast,' I tell them.

A soft, enquiring yap announces Bear's arrival. He jumps the hurdle into the pen, making the calves scatter and take refuge in the far corner, but Bear isn't interested in them. He sits down at my side and licks the tears from my cheeks. Although it sounds mean, I'm glad he's chosen to find me rather than stay with my dad.

'Stevie? Stevie, I was afraid you'd gone.' It's the following afternoon and I'm taking a break before starting on the milking. My father is knocking at my bedroom door. 'Can we talk? I've been thinking about what you said this morning and I don't want to sell up.'

'And?'

'And what?'

'An apology would be nice,' I tell him.

'I'm sorry. Will you let me in?' There's a pause. 'I'm feeling a bit dizzy.'

I jump up from the bed and open the door.

'Come and sit down,' I say, guiding him to the armchair in the corner. 'You shouldn't be climbing the stairs.'

He sits down and lays his crutches across his lap, looking around the room at the same time. 'I haven't been up here for a while. Why don't you have mine and your mother's room? Mary made it up for you.'

'I know, but it didn't feel right.'

'Well, you should have it now since you're the lady of

the house.' I stare at him as he continues. 'You're probably wondering if I'm quite right in the head, but I've been sitting in the kitchen all alone, what with Mary and Cecil out celebrating and you doing a disappearing act, and I've realised that's what my life will be like if you should go back to London. I'll have nothing.' He pauses, his lip trembling. 'I'm too late, aren't I? Please tell me I've not left it too late.'

'Oh, Dad.' I've never seen him like this, so weak and helpless. I kneel beside him and hold his hands. 'You're going to make me cry too.'

'I miss Pippa. She's left a hole in my heart that'll never mend.'

'I'm sorry. I miss her too.'

'I know . . .' After a long pause, my father sits up straight, pulls a handkerchief from his pocket and blows his nose. 'It must be time for the milking.'

'You'll have to do it,' I say lightly, testing him. 'There is no one else.'

'Stevie, I've said sorry. There's nothing I'd like more than for you to stay on. I'm not so sure about the petting farm idea, but I'm willing to consider it if you show me some idea of how you think it can work. As for the cows, Jack Miller came by this afternoon—'

'I missed him?' I interrupt. He was supposed to turn up yesterday, but he got held up rescuing a dog from a storm drain.

'You must have been asleep.' Dad grins. 'You've gone soft, living in the city. You can't stand the pace.'

'Very funny,' I say wryly. 'What did Jack say?'

'He says you're doing a marvellous job and the cows

are looking much better. And when I suggested we put them out tomorrow, he agreed that it was the best thing we could do to put some weight on them.'

Amused, I decide to play along with it being my father's idea, and the next morning I drive him to the chosen field so he can watch the cows being turned out to grass for the first time after six long months indoors. Cecil brings them along the lane with Bear.

I could watch them for hours, gambolling around in the morning sunshine, kicking up their heels, rubbing their heads against the ground, having a good scratch against the trunks of the oak trees, and pulling at the grass which is lush and long and up to their knees. Eventually they begin to settle down, some continuing to graze, some resting and chewing the cud.

'They're the most beautiful girls in the county of Devon,' my father says proudly. 'Stevie, there's one particularly nice heifer amongst the dry cows. I'd like you to enter her for the Country Show.'

'Oh no, Dad. The thought of being towed around the show ring by one of your heifers in front of everyone is just too embarrassing.'

'Your mother used to love it and you had some success too as a junior handler.'

'It isn't my thing. Let's forget the show this year.'

'Forget it? We've attended the show every year so far – except for when it was cancelled for foot and mouth and the year it rained for forty days and forty nights before . . . and last year, of course,' he continues sadly. 'If you're going to be the lady farmer, you have to act like one. It's up to you to represent Nettlebed Farm.'

I suppose it could be a good marketing opportunity, I think, and a chance to meet all the locals.

'I reckon that heifer will win. She's a beauty.'

'All right, I'll think about it.'

'I'll see if I can find the show halter for her – it's probably in the office somewhere.' My father changes the subject. 'What does your boyfriend think about you staying on at the farm?'

'Um, he doesn't know yet,' I say. 'I know, I should have told him first, but this is something I have to do face to face, not over the phone.'

In the evening, I call him.

'There's been a change of plan,' I say. 'Don't worry about driving down this weekend. I'll come up to London tomorrow.'

'You're coming home? Oh, Stevie, thank goodness for that. Jeff and Annette have asked us round for dinner and I thought I'd have to go alone. I can't wait for life to get back to normal.'

'Please don't get too excited. I'm coming to collect my car and a few bits and pieces.'

'You're staying longer? How much longer?'

'Nick, I don't want to talk about it on the phone. We'll discuss it when I see you.'

'You'll talk and I'll listen, you mean,' he says. 'You've hardly been in touch over the past few days, and when you have it's all been very matter-of-fact. Can I safely assume that this conversation isn't going to be about planning the wedding?'

'Don't make this more difficult than it already is.'

'I see,' he says after a pause. 'You're dumping me,

aren't you? Go on, admit it. It's only fair you're straight with me. I should have known you didn't want to get married. If you'd loved me, you'd have let me know your answer straight away.'

'I wasn't sure.' It's my favourite phrase, yet I stumble over the words because, if I'm honest, Nick is right. If I'd been head over heels in love with him, I'd have fallen into his arms and screamed yes, yes, yes . . . Did I think I was helping by letting him down gently? I'm embarrassed to admit I've been a coward and I resolve to be straight in all my dealings with the opposite sex in future.

'My life's taken a new turn.'

'Is it the vet? Leo?' Nick says, his tone acidic.

'What are you talking about?' I recall his complaint that I fancied Leo and dismiss it. 'I can't expect you to live on the farm. You'd hate it.'

'I can commute.'

'That's completely impractical.'

'It isn't entirely. I could spend weekends with you and the week in London. People do.'

'But it isn't a good way to start married life.'

'I reckon you planned this all along. That you'd come back to the farm.'

'Nick, please don't.'

'I can't help feeling bitter when you've been leading me on for the past eighteen months.'

'I haven't been leading you on. I didn't know this was going to happen. I didn't plan it. The last thing I'd wish on anyone is a stroke. And all this about me looking at men is ridiculous. I don't fancy Leo, or anyone else for that matter. I really wouldn't want to

107

marry you when you're so jealous. It's your insecurity that's the problem here.' Among your other flaws, I could add, but don't, as I recall how easily he talked about evicting Cecil and Mary from the cottage.

'You won't end up with Leo. You'll marry someone like James and live in that dump for the rest of your life, shopping at the Co-op and buying your clothes at Overdown Farmers. Your children will grow up talking like yokels and chewing on straw like Cecil. Well, go on and enjoy the simple things in life. A man like James is certainly that – simple.'

'This is about the farm. The farm needs me,' I tell him.

'It's a farm. It doesn't need you in particular. You could employ a manager for a while. And I can't imagine how you'll stick sitting with your dad every night with him dribbling—'

'Nick, that's a horrid thing to say.'

'I'm sorry. I didn't think you had any respect left for him. That's what you say when you're talking about your past.'

'Yes, but he's still a human being. And he's my dad.' I pause, trying to swallow the lump that forms in my throat at the thought of how my father has suffered. 'I wanted to be angry with him, but how can I?'

'What are you going to do about your job?'

'I'm resigning.'

'That's crazy – you won't get another position like that.' Nick softens a little. 'Can't we see how it goes? Take a sabbatical and give it a few months. You might well change your mind. You'll miss everyone at work, India and me,' he adds hopefully.

'I want a clean break,' I say. I want to make it hard for me to go back, impossible even, because I know – Nick's right again – that there will be times when I crave my old life.

'Are you going to sell the flat?' he asks.

'I thought I'd hang on to it for a while at least.'

'So you're keeping it as some kind of insurance? If it doesn't work out for you down on the farm, you have somewhere to come back to.'

'It's because of India, and it's a good investment for the future. Nick, listen. This is hard for me—'

'Hard for you?' he cuts in acidly. 'You've kept stringing me along and all the time you were plotting to move away.'

'It wasn't like that.'

'Oh, what was it like then?'

'You know what happened. I didn't want or expect you to propose to me.'

'You didn't say at the time.'

'How could I? You were so happy and excited.'

'God, you're a strange woman.' Nick clears his throat and I imagine the muscle in his cheek tensing and relaxing repeatedly before he goes on, 'Maybe it's for the best. I wouldn't want to see you at work every day, reminding me of what could have been.'

'I'm so sorry, Nick. We aren't right for each other.'

'But we have the same careers, interests and . . . some of the same friends.'

'Is that a basis for marriage, sharing a few mates who fancy having a party?' I hesitate. 'Do you realise that not once have you said you want to marry me because you love me and you want us to spend the rest of our lives together?

'I think you're being very unfair, Stevie. Of course I love you. I might not have said it, but I've done everything within my power to show it.'

'I'm sorry.' I feel a little ashamed when I realise that when I thought he was trying too hard, he believed he was proving how much he loved me.

'I wish I'd given you a ring. When I proposed to you, I should have had the ring with me.'

'Do you think I can be bribed with a bit of sparkly gold or silver?'

'It might have helped make it seem more real.'

'I didn't set out to hurt you. What we had was special and I'll remember our time together fondly.'

'Well, you can say that, can't you, seeing as you're the guilty party?'

'Guilty party? You mean for breaking it off with you?'

'There's someone else. There has to be.' It's the only way Nick can begin to accept it. 'There has to be a better reason than you just don't love me enough. Who is it?'

'Nick! There is no one else.' What else can I say? 'I don't love you anymore.'

There's a long pause. 'So that's it then,' he says sadly. 'I can't make you love me, Stevie. That's something I'll always regret.'

The line goes dead. It's done. My heart is heavy with grief and regret at the pain I've caused him, but there's relief too. It's time for me to move on, but not until after I've had a reminder of the past from India. She calls me at midnight when I'm lying in bed with the moon casting its rays across my pillow.

'I know it's late, but I hope you don't mind me disturbing you when you'll have to be up at the crack of dawn to milk cows or whatever it is you do down on the farm.' India sounds a little drunk. 'Nick's just turned up. Why didn't you speak to him face to face? He doesn't deserve to be dumped long-distance by mobile.'

'I wanted to see him, but he guessed why I'd asked him to meet me. What else could I do? He doesn't need to see me now. It would be like rubbing salt into a wound.'

'You really could have let it ride for a couple more weeks and told him when you came back.'

'India, she isn't coming back.' I overhear Nick in the background.

'Why didn't you tell me?' From the sound of her voice, India is incandescent.

'I thought you'd have guessed by now,' I say lamely.

'How could I have guessed? I'm not a bloody psychic.' Without waiting for me to respond, she continues, 'What am I going to do without you? Where am I going to live? Have you thought about that?'

'India, you'll always be my best friend and you're welcome to stay in the flat for as long as you want. I'm going to keep it as an investment,' I say, 'and somewhere to stay when I come and visit. It's a couple of hours' drive away, that's all.'

'So you're not kicking me out on the streets?'

'Absolutely not. I promise you.'

There's a long pause before India speaks again.

'You could have just broken it off with Nick. You don't have to do a complete disappearing act because you feel guilty. It is rather extreme.'

'It's down to a combination of circumstances,' I point out. 'I found out my dad was ill and the farm was in trouble at the same time as I realised that I had to finish with Nick. I can't marry him and I'm not committed enough to make a long-distance relationship work. Nick isn't a country person – he's scared of cows, he hates mud and he uses moisturiser.'

'He's pretty cut up about the whole thing. He thinks you led him on.'

'I can see why and I feel really bad about it. I am fond of him.'

'Fond?'

'I like him a lot. It's just that I can't see myself spending the rest of my life with him – with anyone, for that matter.'

'That's because he isn't the One,' India says, lowering her voice. 'I told you so in the first place, but it's typical of you to allow yourself to be swept off your feet with the romance of a new relationship, just like it happens in all the chick flicks.'

I'm not sure it was like that, I muse. I fancied Nick and I'd hoped the fireworks would begin when I got to know him better, but waiting for passion to sweep me off my feet was like the long cold wait for the display on the Green in Talyton St George to start on Bonfire Night, except in this case it had never come.

Chapter Seven

April Fools' Day

It's late morning and Cecil and I have finished the milking, eaten breakfast – a full English – and I'm taking advantage of half an hour's peace and quiet to update the paperwork in the office. I'm looking out over the farmyard where the new hens with their feathery knickerbockers are being blustered around by the wind while they scratch about and peck for tasty snacks. One looks up and caws. When she spots another hen with a worm dangling from her beak, she rushes in and snatches it. There's a squabble as the two hens argue over the worm like the ladies of the WI fighting over a prized article at a jumble sale. The fight is settled when the top hen in the pecking order intervenes and eats the worm, leaving her subordinates with nothing.

My mind drifts and I find myself wondering how Nick is. I'd like to contact him, but I don't want to encourage him into thinking there's any chance of reconciliation. I miss the little things like him texting *Gdnite xx* or calling to say hello halfway through the day. I had hoped we could be friends, but it isn't going to happen. He's closed the door on me, shutting me out of his life, and I don't think we'll ever be in touch again. There's no reason why our paths should cross in the future.

Suddenly, the hens scatter across the yard with much squawking and the cockerel takes refuge on the bonnet of the Land Rover as Guy from Uphill Farm screams up on his quad bike, yelling and shaking his fist.

'Tom, Cecil, get yourselves out here now!' he yells in a West Country accent as thick as clotted cream. 'Your ruddy cows are on the loose!'

I join Guy in the yard with Bear at my side. His expression is unfriendly. His forehead is furrowed and his grey-blue eyes glint with irritation.

'Is this some kind of April Fool?' I ask coolly.

'Of course it isn't.' He swears and runs his fingers through his wavy light-brown hair. 'Your dry cows and heifers are out and about. I wouldn't normally care less, but they've gone straight through the fence onto my land. They've trampled the grass I was going to cut for silage and now they've moved on to the maize field. That's my winter rations, that is.'

'I'm sorry, Guy.'

'Is that all you can say? How am I going to get my cattle through the winter?' He hesitates before going on, 'Where's Tom?'

'He's indoors.' I plant myself in front of the quad bike, folding my arms across my chest, determined not to be intimidated. 'You'll have to deal with me.'

'Stevie?' Guy's attitude falters slightly. 'I didn't recognise you at first. The last time I saw you was at your mother's funeral. I knew you were back, of course. Everybody around here knows Cecil sent out an SOS.'

I recall Guy as a brusque young man, shy and quiet. He's approaching forty now, but he's well preserved. He's married to a woman five years older than him with three children who moved down from London, which was a surprise to everyone because we expected him to marry Ruthie who runs Hen Welfare, or not at all.

He glances around the yard. 'I reckon it's too late to save Nettlebed Farm.'

'That's your opinion,' I say rather bluntly, upset by his point of view.

'This place is really run-down. The hedges are over-grown, the gates are falling down – and don't get me started on the weeds.'

'I'm back now and I'm dealing with it. Where did you say the heifers were?'

'They're eating my maize.'

I whistle for Bear and jump into the Land Rover – the keys are in the ignition – and start it up. The exhaust belches a cloud of black smoke, showing it isn't only the hedges and gates that need some TLC. Revving the engine to keep it from cutting out, I follow Guy back out of the drive and along the lane, only to find the escapees have tired of eating maize and decided to head along the public highway to pastures new. The thirteen heifers and dry cows are in a bolshy mood, bellowing as if they're egging each other on.

I swear under my breath because it's too late to cut them off. They're well on their way to Talyton St George. The song 'Here Come the Girls' pops into my brain, but it's no light-hearted matter. It's market day and we're going to need reinforcements.

I pull back, tooting the horn at Guy because by following them, we're only making them run faster. We stop the vehicles and jump out. Guy opens a gate.

'I'm going to try heading them off,' Guy calls over his shoulder as he drives the quad bike into the field. 'Hang back – don't scare them.'

'There's no need for him to tell me how to handle cows,' I say to Bear; he's sitting upright on the passenger seat, quivering with excitement over his unexpected adventure. The heifers slow down and start to eat the long grass at the side of the lane as they wander along, and I begin to breathe more easily, taking a moment to call Cecil who doesn't answer his phone.

However, Guy doesn't make it to the next gateway in time to head them off. When he does emerge on the quad bike, he's just behind me, waving for me to let him pass. I pull into the lay-by at the bottom of town. There the Land Rover stalls and, after a couple of attempts to get it going again, I abandon it and make my way on foot with Bear at my heels. Guy parks the quad bike outside the doctor's surgery and we chase along the road, following the black and white rumps and the cow pats that the girls leave behind them.

I'm hoping they'll go right at the junction and head

away from the town past Otter House, but they trot straight over against the flow of the traffic in the one-way system.

'They're going to end up in Market Square,' Guy observes as the cars stop or pull over to let the cows go by. One driver jumps out and waves his arms, but the heifers take no notice.

'They're on a mission, my lover,' says an elderly woman who stands in the doorway of one of the terraced houses, sheltering with a friend. 'Hasn't anyone told them they've forgotten their shopping bags?'

'I'm sorry for frightening you,' I say, beginning to gasp with the exertion.

'Oh, it's fine. I haven't had so much excitement since I married my fourth husband.'

I run on with Guy. PC Kevin joins us, radioing for back-up as the heifers gambol on into Market Square where they snatch the flowers from the buckets outside the florist's and turn over a couple of the stalls – Jennie's Cakes and the plant stall – in front of horrified market traders and shoppers. I can hardly bear to watch as cupcakes, seed packets and rose bushes go flying across the square. This is going to be an expensive day out.

A woman with a child in a buggy begins to scream as the heifers head straight for her.

'Stop them!' I yell as I quicken my pace, but I'm no Olympic sprinter and with a sick sensation in my stomach I realise I can't get there in time and neither can Guy. The woman is crying and the heifers are almost upon her as she struggles to push the buggy out of their way but, just in time, a man dashes out of the butcher's and smacks the first heifer over the head with a leg of lamb. As the man snatches the child from the buggy, the heifer stops, takes a sideways step, turns and charges back through Market Square with the rest of her friends.

Although Bear is barking at them and Guy and I are standing our ground, they keep coming, panicking at all the noise and the unfamiliar surroundings, and even for an experienced lady farmer, the sight of a herd of heifers galloping and bucking towards me is too much. I duck back and press myself against the nearest lamppost, letting them go by, furious with them for behaving like a mob, and with my father and Cecil for not feeding them properly before.

I glance back to where the have-a-go hero is standing with the child bawling in his arms. It's Leo, the vet. Noticing me, he hands the child back to its mum as if it's a hot potato and comes jogging over to offer assistance.

'Thanks for that,' I say as we follow the heifers, which have taken the left-hand turn up towards the church. They appear unstoppable, but just before they reach the entrance to the churchyard, Wendy, the dog fosterer for Talyton Animal Rescue, who fostered Bear before we took him on as a puppy, appears at the top of the hill ahead with five dogs. She sits back on her heels as the dogs start barking and straining on their leads. The heifers stop dead, deciding not to approach Wendy's pack of unruly hounds.

I set Bear up just below the entrance to the churchyard with PC Kevin, Guy and Leo lined up across the road.

'Ho, girls,' I call. They turn again with Wendy and her dogs following along behind them. When they see the line of people blocking their way, with Leo waving a baguette in the air this time, they decide the best option is to divert into the churchyard where they settle down amongst the gravestones and drop their heads to eat the grass. I close the gates behind them, leaning back against the railings with relief.

'Thank goodness,' I sigh. 'Thank you, everyone.' I feel so ashamed and embarrassed at what's happened. 'I'll pay for any damage the girls have caused.'

'I should hope so,' Guy says. 'They've torn Jennie's stall to pieces and scared her half to death.'

'Is she all right?' I ask.

'She's in shock,' he says, checking a text on his mobile. 'I'm going back to find her to make sure she's okay. She's pregnant, and if anything happens to our baby, I'll . . .'

Jennie is Guy's wife. Why did the heifers choose to upend Jennie's stall out of all the stalls in Market Square today?

'I'm sorry,' I repeat, realising this incident has done nothing to improve neighbourly relations.

'It's too late for that.' Guy storms off back towards the square.

'It's great that we've caught them,' says Leo, moving up to my side as if he's decided I'm in need of his protection, 'but how are we going to get them home?'

'First things first,' says Kevin. 'Here comes the vicar.'

I look along the path towards the church, which is like a cathedral in miniature, built from sandstone and decorated with vampire-like gargoyles that have dark stains dribbling from their mouths. The vicar is coming towards us in his robes.

'The blessing of the animals is next week,' he says, smiling, 'and although the church welcomes all creatures great and small, I was expecting people to attend with their pets, not farm livestock.' He nods towards the gate where a crowd is gathering to watch.

'I think you're being papped, Stevie,' Leo says.

I turn to find a woman taking pictures through the railings.

'Who is that?' I ask.

'That's Allie, roving reporter for the local rag,' says the vicar. He tweaks his dog collar and runs one hand through his short grey hair. 'I expect she'll want an interview.'

'Well, she won't be getting one with me,' Leo says, but it's Leo she wants to put in the *Chronicle* as front-page news. He tells her it will have to wait until later. 'We need to get these cows back to Nettlebed Farm,' he says firmly. 'Stevie, what do you suggest?'

'I could see if I can borrow a lorry, or we could drive them back – they look much quieter now.' They're enjoying the floral tributes left on some of the graves, which seems very disrespectful. I wish I was back in my office in Wimbledon, anywhere but here.

'If Kevin can hold the traffic, we can move them back to the farm,' Leo suggests.

'You're the expert, Leo,' Kevin says.

Eventually, we drive them home with Leo at the front in his four-by-four, and Bear and me bringing up the rear in the Land Rover, which I manage to start this time. Back at the farm, I let the heifers into the collecting yard where they stand and bellow as if they're complaining about their day out being cut short.

Leo checks up on them to make sure none of them are hurt, while Kevin takes down details of the incident and gives me a stern telling-off about allowing livestock to stray onto the highway. He doesn't need to tell me we've had a lucky escape. I know all too well what the consequences could have been and I shudder as I think how close the child in the buggy was to being injured, or worse. I worry too about what Guy said about Jennie being pregnant. I'd never forgive myself if Jennie loses her baby because we didn't get around to fixing the fences.

Kevin leaves and I wait for Leo to finish in the yard.

'No injuries,' says Leo at the gate. 'They've had a lucky escape.'

'Well, they won't be escaping again,' I say glumly. 'Thank you, Leo. I'm very grateful. You're a hero, rescuing that little kid.'

'It's what anyone would have done.'

'But not with such panache – and with a leg of lamb.' I relax into a smile. 'I'm sorry about your dinner – I'll buy you another one.'

'Oh no, that wasn't my dinner. I was picking up some bacon for Lynsey. I grabbed the lamb as I went out the door.' Leo grins. 'I think you owe Mr Dyer, the butcher.'

'I'll add him to the list,' I say ruefully.

'Where did Guy run off to? He's a grumpy git.'

'Are you allowed to speak about your clients like that?'

'It's a statement of fact. I'm only going on what I've seen of him today. Alex is his regular vet. I haven't had the privilege of being allowed to visit Uphill Farm yet.'

'At least he helped,' I say, going to fetch a couple of wedges of silage in the wheelbarrow from the big bale that's open in the farmyard. 'He didn't have to do that.'

'I suppose not.' Leo follows me, helping me lift the silage onto the barrow and offering to wheel it back for me, 'but he is your neighbour and I thought the farming community around here prided itself on being close-knit and supportive.'

'There's no love lost between Guy and my father.' I take the barrow myself as Leo's mobile rings. He takes the call then excuses himself, saying he has an emergency visit on a farm the other side of Talyford.

'Cheer up, Stevie,' he says as he leaves. 'I'll see you again soon, no doubt.'

'Thanks again, Leo.' It's inevitable that he'll be back at Nettlebed Farm in the near future and I'm glad. I'm starting to like him. He does have a sense of humour after all, and he's warm and friendly, in contrast with the impression he gave when I first met him. He's a hero. Not only does he save sick animals, he rescues small children too.

I throw the silage over the rails for the heifers and take a moment to watch them pulling at it, tugging out long strands like pieces of spaghetti. 'You are very bad girls.' The sight of them makes me feel let down and emotional. I've just split with Nick, I've got Guy on my back – and probably half the town – and I can see my money's not going to last for long at the rate I'm spending it. 'Perhaps I should head back to London and leave you to it after all.'

One of the heifers stops chewing and looks straight at me, the gentle and innocent look in her soft brown eyes melting my heart.

'I won't,' I say, before glancing around me. People think I'm crazy already without finding me talking to myself.

I call Bear and head up to the fields to check the fences. The barbed wire is down and several of the wooden posts, which are rotten at the base, have snapped. The big aluminium-coated trough in the corner of the field is empty. I open up the compartment at the side and fiddle with the ballcock until the water comes pouring in. It is no wonder the cows made a break for it. They weren't just hungry. They were thirsty too. I feel really guilty for not noticing they were out of water. Cecil and I used to drive around the farm every day to check the troughs and fences.

I can fix the water, but not the fences. I miss out on lunch and grab a hunk of bread, some cheese and a tomato before meeting with Cecil to get the cows in for milking.

'Where have you been?' I say. 'I tried ringing you.'

'Oh? Did you?' He fumbles for his mobile, which he pulls out of his pocket. 'So you did, Stevie.'

'Let me have a look.' I take it from him and check the sound. 'You've switched it to silent.'

'I'm not good with these newfangled machines,' he says. 'Mary said I needed one in case I got into trouble when I was working on my own on the farm.'

'It wasn't much use today, was it? Do you even know the heifers were out?'

'I can't say I do.' He frowns, his brow forming deep leathery folds.

'They went all the way into town,' I say, 'and now we need someone to fix the fence urgently, otherwise they'll have to stay in.'

'Can't they go across the drive?' Cecil asks.

'I was keeping that for silage.'

'The grass will grow again.'

'Isn't there too much grass out there? They'll get bloat.'

'We could run a piece of electric fence across the middle.'

After milking I decide to let them out as Cecil suggests. Cecil and I hunt out a length of electric tape and some plastic posts that have seen better days. In fact, I'm not sure why my father kept them, since half of them have spikes missing so we can't get them into the ground. Finally, we discover the battery for the energiser is out of charge, which puts our plans on hold.

'They'll be all right overnight, my lover,' Cecil says.

'I hope so. I really don't want to have to call the vet out again.' I stick the battery – it's an old car battery – into the wheelbarrow and take it back to the house where I put it in the lean-to to charge before I find James's number to see if he'd like some work, knocking a few posts in. My dad isn't impressed when

I tell him what I've done. He says James will over-charge and won't do a good job. When I ask him to suggest someone else to do it, he can't.

Much later, I settle down to watch television. It's been quite a day and I want to tell Nick . . . but we are no longer an item. It's lonely without him. I didn't realise I'd miss him this much. I look towards my father who's nodding off in his chair, snoring with his mouth half open and his jaw slack. How am I going to get anywhere with making changes when he's such a stubborn and obstructive old bugger?

I leave it overnight before I go and see Jennie to apolo-gise and find out the cost of the damage to the market stall. I have no doubt that Guy will contact me with his bill sooner rather than later. I grab my coat from the lean-to, telling a disgruntled Bear he has to stay behind.

As I walk down the drive, I check on the heifers and dry cows. The fact that they're lying down makes me panic, but they're all fine. Their bellies are full, but they aren't bloated with gas. The sooner they go back into their original field the better. I head up the lane and take the turning to Uphill Farm. Uphill House – also known as Jennie's Folly – is a beautiful longhouse, dating back to the sixteenth century. It has diamond-leaded windows set deep into thick walls of cob that are painted the palest pink, and a roof of golden thatch. The new farmhouse where Guy used to live is a good thirty metres or so further along the drive and on the opposite side.

I walk through the picket gate and along the path to the porch, which is surrounded by wisteria, climbing rosebushes and honeysuckle, waiting to burst into flower. I knock on the door. I wasn't particularly looking forward to meeting Jennie, but my heart sinks further when Guy opens it and a small grey dog comes flying out.

'Lucky, get inside!' Guy growls. 'What are you doing here, Stevie?'

'I've come to see you and Jennie.'

'Don't bother. I'll be sending you the bill for yesterday's debacle through my solicitor.' He is pushing the door closed when a woman's voice rings out from behind him.

'Guy, don't be so silly.'

'I don't want you having any more stress.'

'I'm pregnant. I'm not ill.'

Guy turns. 'I'm sorry, love, but I'm worried sick about you and the baby.'

'I know you are, and it's lovely, but sometimes I feel like I'm suffocating under all this attention. Now, move out of the way and let Stevie in. It is Stevie, isn't it?'

'Hello, Jennie,' I say, hovering on the doorstep as she addresses her husband again, suggesting he has another go at halter-breaking their wild heifer because it's another hour before dinner's ready. I smile to myself as Guy turns from tiger to pussycat, kissing Jennie on the cheek and offering to carve when he returns.

'Come in, Stevie,' Jennie says as Guy disappears into the house.

'I've dropped by to apologise about yesterday.'

'Ah yes, the day the Wild West came to Talyton St George. It was quite a show.'

'I'd like to pay for the damage the cows did to your stall.'

'Thank you. That sounds very reasonable.'

'Have you any idea of a figure?'

'I'll have to work it out. I'll need to replace the table and banner. I didn't lose much in the way of stock – the cakes were almost sold out already.' She pauses. 'Listen to me. What am I doing, making you stand there? Come and sit down. The kettle's just boiled.'

'Well, if you're sure.'

'Of course I am. I'm sorry about Guy. He can be rather abrupt at times.'

'At least he came to let me know the heifers were out and he did help round them up.' I follow Jennie through the dark-panelled hallway. She's in her forties, according to Mary, and although pregnant, wearing an apron over her bump, she's quite petite. Her hair is brunette with a trace of grey.

'I hear they went to church.' Jennie giggles. 'That must have been quite a sight.'

'The pictures will be in the *Chronicle* tomorrow.'

'Take a seat.' Jennie shows me into a dream country kitchen with views to the front and rear gardens, which are laid with lawns and flowerbeds. In the stone alcove, which used to house the open fire, is a recon-ditioned Aga. To the right, there is a bread oven. There are blue and white plates on the oak dresser and red tiles on the floor. 'I should apologise for my husband too. He's been a right old bear about this.'

'I guess I'd be pretty miffed in the same situation.'

'Have some cake – it's coffee and walnut.'

'Thank you.' It's delicious, a soft sponge with crunchy nuts and a butter-cream icing that melts in the mouth.

Jennie clears her throat. 'Guy and I – both of us – are a little apprehensive about your plans for Nettlebed Farm. I know we shouldn't listen to gossip, but we've heard a rumour you're planning to diversify and get rid of the dairy herd.'

'Where did that come from?' I almost choke on a mouthful of crumbs.

'Mary happened to mention it when we were queuing at the butcher's. Please don't blame her for spreading gossip. She likes to chat and she's over the moon that you've decided to stay here in Talyton. She wanted to share the news.'

'What did she say?'

'That you're going to build a theme park. In my opinion, it would have been nice if you'd consulted us, your neighbours. I moved here for peace and quiet, not to live next door to a rollercoaster filled with screaming thrill-seekers.'

I should have talked to Jennie and Guy before the news leaked out, as I knew it would, one way or another.

'We're going to have a small-scale petting farm with a tearoom, that's all. I don't want to live beside a rollercoaster either. Yes, there'll be some development on the farm, but it's going to be eco-friendly and blend in with the landscape. There'll be more traffic in the lane at certain times of day, but, on the other hand, it will boost the local economy and provide much-needed employment for the young people in the area.' I pause. 'I'm actually very excited about it.'

'And the cows?'

'We're going to downsize the herd to a smaller, more manageable number, so we won't be dependent on milk for our income. You know what it's like.'

'We make a premium on ours with Uphill Farm being certified organic. That's one of the reasons Guy gets annoyed about the weeds – we aren't allowed to use chemicals to control them, otherwise we lose our organic status.' Jennie smiles. 'That's enough farming talk, except –' she pours me a second mug of tea and stirs in the milk – 'if you're opening a tearoom, I'd be interested in supplying the cakes.'

'Well, yes, that's a great idea.'

'When I moved here, I thought I'd have a tearoom one day, but the baking business took over and I didn't have time for anything else. I've been very fortunate. I've gone from single mum with three kids, an almost derelict house and no money, to successful business-woman, married to a farmer and with a fourth child on the way.'

'I don't know how you've coped.'

'Neither do I.' Jennie gazes into the distance, apparently lost in thought. 'It was tough, especially with Adam, my son. He hated it here at first. He missed his father and friends. How about you?'

'I love being back. It feels like home,' I say. 'I expect you know that I've finished with my boyfriend.'

'The one with the Aston Martin? Adam was so impressed. He thought James Bond had come to Talyton.'

'No, I did not, Mother.' A lanky teenage boy wanders into the kitchen, rolling his eyes at Jennie. He's about seventeen and at least six foot tall. He has short brown hair, grey eyes, pale stubble and a smattering of teenage spots. He wears a Superdry top and chinos and his feet are bare. 'Is it dinnertime yet?'

'This is Adam. Adam, this is Stevie from next door. And the food won't be ready for another hour or so.'

Adam moves to the fridge and helps himself to a yoghurt.

'Don't ruin your appetite,' Jennie warns.

'I won't. I could eat a horse.'

'Please don't start winding Sophie up about that again. Your sister had nightmares about you eating Bracken.' Jennie turns to me. 'Sophie's my youngest. Bracken's her pony. She and Georgia are out riding.' She points to a photo on the dresser of two girls side by side, one of about eleven and the other thirteen or fourteen. 'Georgia's the tomboy in the jeans with her hair tied back in a ponytail. Sophie with the blonde curls is the girlie one.'

'The spoilt brat, you mean. If that baby is another girl, I'll leave home,' Adam says, frowning at his mother.

'I'll be hoping for a girl then,' Jennie says lightly, teasing him, 'so you'll think about moving out . . . Not really.' She reaches up and ruffles his hair. 'But it would be nice if you could make a decision about what you want to do in the future.'

'I've said I want to work on the farm with Guy.'

'You don't have to though. You could go to uni.'

'And do what?'

'Anything. Adam, you could do anything you like. You're so lucky.'

'I like it here.' He leans across the draining board, gazes out of the window and starts laughing. 'It looks like Guy's having cow trouble.'

Jennie and I get up to see what's going on. Guy is being towed across the lawn by a roan-and-white heifer with a halter caught up around her ears. The heifer bucks and tosses her head, pulling the rope from his hands before trotting away through the middle of the vegetable patch, bringing down bean sticks and netting, and the last we see of Guy is him chasing off after her, red-faced and flustered.

'Are you entering the show this year?' Jennie asks.

'Looking at the competition, I think we have a good chance,' I say, smiling, 'but Dad's choice of heifer isn't even halter-broken yet. I don't know.'

'Oh, go on. It will be fun.'

'Fun? You'd think it was a matter of life and death the way my dad goes on. I'm not sure I'll have time to prepare anyway. I'm researching local architects and builders for the project at the moment.' I worry that the plan will not come to fruition, especially if Mary's led everyone to believe we're turning Nettlebed Farm into a mega version of Alton Towers. We'll have environmental activists and hippy campaigners with nothing better to do camped out at the end of the drive if we're not careful.

'I'd better go,' I say eventually. 'Thank you for the tea and cake, and the chat.'

'We must catch up again soon.'

I didn't think we would become friends because of Guy and what happened yesterday, and because I didn't think Jennie and I would have much in common, but we have plenty to talk about.

'Good luck with the new venture. If you need any help or advice, you know where I am,' Jennie says. 'And don't forget Jennie's Cakes are the best when you're looking to stock your tearoom.'

I walk home, taking a short-cut across the fields, hoping Guy doesn't have a go at me for trespassing. I walk down the long, gently sloping field back to the farm, where I stand in the yard and look back across the drive and try to visualise how Nettlebed Farm could be.

There's plenty of room for a car park, landscaped with trees and shrubs, and a building of some kind. It needs a centre, a focus where visitors can meet, eat and shop. I see it now, an eco-friendly building made from wood and glass, with a patio outside with tables and chairs with parasols for sunny summer days. The accommodation for some of the animals can be in the next field over, and we can create a nature walk taking in the pond with the added attraction of a few ducks. From the pond, it would be easy to divert a path into the copse to create a woodland area with flowers and a few pigs.

Slow down, Stevie, I tell myself. You're getting carried away.

Chapter Eight

Mad Cows and Englishwomen

'Thanks for doing this,' I say when James turns up on the balcony in the parlour on a Tuesday morning, a couple of weeks after the great escape.

'It's a pleasure,' he says with a big smile on his face and his hands in his coat pockets. 'Hello, Cecil.'

'Good morning, young man,' Cecil calls back.

'I'll show you where they got out,' I say.

'You go, Stevie,' Cecil says, shooing me out.

'I've got the gear in the van,' James says as I accompany him to the yard.

'Do you want to dump it in the back of the Land Rover?' I ask. 'I don't want you getting stuck. It's pretty muddy.'

'I won't get stuck. I'm sure I've driven through worse.'

'You haven't seen it yet,' I smile. 'We've had an awful lot of rain.'

I take the Land Rover and James follows in the van, driving past the house and the cottage up the track and into the field. I keep the Land Rover in a low gear and let it eat up the muddy ground on the way up the hill. When I reach the broken section of fence, I pull in alongside it, glancing in my mirror to check James is with me. He isn't. He's in his van, which is stuck in the gateway. I turn round and take the Land Rover back down, parking in front of the stranded vehicle.

I jump out and watch James revving the engine, sending up a spray of mud and digging the wheels deeper into the ruts. He leans out of the window.

'Don't say "I told you so",' he says with a rueful grin.

'Let's load the Land Rover with your stuff and then I'll go and get the tractor to tow you out.' James doesn't argue this time. He jumps out, the mud coming up to the top of his work-boots. His feet squelch each time he takes a lumbering step as we fill the back of the Land Rover with fence posts and equipment.

'Have you got the keys handy?' James asks.

'They're in the ignition.'

'Hey, stop laughing at me, Stevie Dunsford. I don't need you to remind me I'm a complete prat.'

'I'll see you in a few minutes,' I say, and I walk back to the farmyard to collect a flask of sugary coffee and Bertha, who obliges by starting first time. When I get back, I leave her behind the van and walk up the hill to join James, who is already hard at work, hammering a second new post into the ground. He's hung his coat over the first post and sweat drips from his brow, in spite of the cold, blustery wind that blows from the east.

'What can I do?' I ask.

'You don't have to do anything. I believe you're the lady farmer and I'm the tradesman,' James says lightly.

'I can clear the barbed wire away, I suppose. I hate the stuff.'

'I've got some wire cutters in the holdall over there.'

I fetch them and spend half an hour rolling up the barbed wire that's been torn away from the fence where the cows broke through into Guy's field. I wish I could mend fences with Guy, so to speak, but I can't see that happening.

When I've finished, I pour James a coffee. He doesn't stop working, but he does talk almost non-stop.

'So how are things at Wellhouse Farm?' I ask him, curious as to why he's working as an odd-job man, not on the family farm.

'Ah, no one's told you then. I'm surprised,' he says, and his expression changes to one of deep sadness. 'I don't like to talk about it.'

'It can't be that bad. You can't be in such dire straits as my dad.'

'We lost it.' He leans back against one of the old fence posts that's leaning at an angle and snaps it before chucking it in the back of the Land Rover. 'We sold up.'

'I'm sorry. What happened? James, you don't have to say . . .'

'It's all right. I don't mind speaking to you. When we were in Young Farmers', do you remember my sister used to hang around with that creepy bloke, Andrew?'

'I think so. There were a few old farmers who couldn't bring themselves to leave the club.'

'They were the stupid, immature ones who never grew up,' James says wryly. 'Andrew was the one with the milkmaid tattoo on his arm and a fag in his mouth, the one who drove around in a Mercedes with an air horn. He was a right tosser.'

'I remember now. He used to help my uncle Robert with the harvest and ploughing.' I shudder. 'He made my skin crawl.'

'Sue liked him. She made him her mission and, when she finally got her claws into him, he became quite the reformed character, cleaned himself up and quit smoking.'

'What did your parents think of him?' From what I recall, he wasn't universally liked by girls' parents.

'My dad called him the weasel. Mum adored him, though. She thought the sun shone out of his—' James shuts up abruptly. 'I'm sorry.'

'What for?

'For not speaking proper-like in front of you.'

'You never used to worry. I haven't changed.'

James gazes at me for a moment. 'You seem different. You've lost the accent, for a start, and you're much more confident – whereas I'm still the same, apart from carrying a few extra pounds – awkward and uncouth.'

'You haven't finished telling me about your sister.'

'Before we knew it, she and Andrew were engaged. Sue had the big white wedding and a reception for one hundred and fifty at the Barnscote, with a horse and carriage and a marquee and everything. It cost my parents an arm and a leg.

'Anyway, to cut a long story short, Dad set them up with a house and a farm-machinery business, but within three years, Andrew had remortgaged the house, gone through my sister's savings and petitioned for divorce. The bastard went for everything he could get.'

'Including the farm? I don't see how he could make a claim against it.'

'Not only had my father taken out loans against the farm to provide for Sue and her husband, he'd also planned ahead against death duties by handing over a financial interest in the farm to each of us. What with having to pay off the debts and settle the solicitor's bills, he was forced into selling up.' James swings a hammer down hard onto the top of another post. There's a loud crack and it shears straight through. 'Bugger,' he says, bashing it to smithereens before fetching another one. 'I thought my parents would have fought harder for it, but they couldn't see any way out. My father lost heart really.'

'It's shocking to see what effect a single bad apple can have. What a rotten thing to happen.'

'I told Sue she should have a pre-nup, but she was completely besotted with the weasel and convinced their marriage was going to last for ever.'

'Where is your sister now?' I ask.

'She's a survivor. She married again and moved away to the other side of Exeter. She has a couple of kids, a boy and a girl.'

'And your parents?'

'Mum and Dad live in a tiny house on the new estate in Talyton. I rent one of the houses opposite the church.' He pauses. 'I have some money put by to buy a place of my own one day. I do a bit of painting and decorating and any odd jobs that need doing. I've made the best of it and, all in all, I can say I'm a happy man.'

'Are you married?' I ask.

He shakes his head. 'I live alone, but I don't let on that I'm single to my clients. Some of them are right goers.' He chuckles. 'I sometimes think I should take on an apprentice to fend off their advances.'

'Don't you miss the farm?'

'I know I used to grumble about the hours and the muck, but I'd love to work in farming again, although I'd find it hard to work for someone else. I was the boss's son and used to making decisions. Of course, if we'd diversified like you're planning to do, we might have managed to hold on to a few acres.'

James's family reared pigs for fattening. I remember the rows of pig sheds, the smell and the ear-splitting squealing of hundreds of hungry piglets. It made me appreciate the cows.

'If I were you,' James says, 'I'd see if I could apply for a grant to convert the outbuildings to office space and retail instead of setting up a petting farm. Haven't you ever heard the phrase, never work with animals and children?'

'It's too late. I've set my heart on it.'

'I wish you luck. Some people – not me – are up in arms over the idea. Apparently, you're single-handedly bringing gridlock to Talyton St George.'

'I thought that happened already.'

'It does in the summer, but it doesn't stop them.'

'What else are they complaining about?'

'You're altering the character of the area, moving from traditional farming to some way-out-there enterprise.'

'That's ridiculous. This way, we'll still have animals on the farm, and continue to take care of the countryside.'

'Are you working to a deadline?' James asks.

'I want it up and running by next spring. It's the perfect time of year. There'll be newborn lambs, cute baby bunnies and fluffy chicks.'

James grins. 'What about an Easter egg hunt?'

'That's a great suggestion. Thanks.'

'I shouldn't worry about the locals. They don't like change, but they'll come round in the end. They usually do.' James is struggling to get the next post into the ground. He fetches a shovel from the Land Rover and starts digging about in the soil. 'I didn't understand why you took off to London when you finished college.'

'You must know what happened, that my father handed the farm over to my brother. I was expected to go and marry a farmer.' I look at him. 'I think my dad wanted me to marry you.'

'Hey, don't laugh so loud about that. There was a time when I thought you might.'

'I was eighteen. I wasn't ready to settle down and you were very serious. You brought me a red rose on the first date and chocolates on the second. It was quite scary.'

'I sometimes wonder what would have happened if you had stayed.' James rubs his chin, deep in thought.

'James, I liked you, as a friend.'

'I used to hate it that you were so popular with the men.'

'Are you saying I'm a bit of a slapper?' I say lightly.

'I'm just saying that men like you, and so do women, but not in the same way I hasten to add.' James is blushing.

'I think you'd better stop.' It's my turn to be amused. 'I think it's called digging yourself into a hole.'

'Well, I'm glad we ran into each other again.'

'So am I. You know, I might have a proposition for you if you're looking for work.'

'How can I refuse?' he says, nodding down the hill towards the gateway. 'I don't suppose you'll tow the van out until I say yes.'

'You're right,' I tease.

Later, I attach James's van to the tractor and drag it out onto firmer ground before leaving him to finish the fencing.

'Where are you off to?' he says, sounding envious.

'I'm going to start halter-breaking the heifer Dad's chosen as our entry for the Country Show.'

'Best of luck. We used to take a couple of pigs every year.' James looks wistful. 'I used to love giving them a bath.'

'Isn't that a bit weird?'

'It's probably why I haven't got a girlfriend,' he says in a mocking, self-deprecatory way. 'Have fun. I'll catch you later.'

'Mind you don't get stuck again.' I give him a wave and take the tractor back to the farmyard. Then I head into the house to see my father, who's supposed to be showing me the heifer with the most potential to win a hotly contested class.

'What are you doing back?' my father asks. He's watching *This Morning*.

'We're going to look at the heifer, remember?' I move over and grab the remote control to switch the television off in case he can't hear what I'm saying.

'Which heifer?' he asks.

'Magnificent Millicent, or whatever you say she's called – the one who's going to take supreme champion at the show.'

'Oh yes, I see. Good idea.' He looks around at the photos on the wall that show various winning cattle from Nettlebed Farm, his eyes eventually settling on the walnut cabinet in the corner where he keeps the cups and shields and a few fading rosettes.

'You aren't properly dressed,' I say, noticing he's still wearing his pyjama top with green cords and no socks.

'I must have nodded off,' he says sheepishly. 'I'll find my coat and boots.'

'I'll get them. Go and put some socks on. It isn't terribly warm out there.'

'For goodness' sake, Stevie, you sound like your mother.'

'Hurry up,' I insist. 'By the way, did you find the halter?'

'It's on Bear's chair in the lean-to. It's a bit grubby,

141

but I think it will clean up well with a wash and some whitener.'

'Are you offering?' I ask. 'No, I thought not. So that's another job for me – as if I need anything else to do.' I collect the boots, coat and halter, and soon Dad and I are walking slowly across the drive with Bear to the field where the heifers and dry cows have their heads down grazing.

'That's Milly.' My father points in the general direction of the small herd. 'The black-and-white one,' he goes on, deadpan.

'Dad.' I groan, but I can't help chuckling. The Country Show appears to have sparked his interest. I haven't seen him this animated since I arrived back on the farm. 'She's nicely put together.'

'She has a winning dairyness about her,' he says.

'What do you mean by that?'

'It's what the judge always says about our cattle. Aren't you going to go and catch her?' he asks.

'These girls are pretty wild,' I say, remembering how they behaved on their trip into town. 'I'd rather round them all up and catch her in a confined space, not try to lasso her out in the middle of the field.' I whistle Bear to help me move the cows across the drive and into the collecting yard, making sure the gate onto the lane is firmly shut so there can be no repeat of their great escape. They are fairly amenable to the possibility of some extra food, but they become quite fractious when they discover their freedom has been curtailed once more.

My father closes the gate behind them and Bear

sits guarding it. Brandishing his crutches, Dad and I separate Milly from the others, cornering her so I can approach her with the halter behind my back. She is highly suspicious, fidgeting and pawing at the concrete.

'She might be the most beautiful heifer we have, Dad, but has she the temperament for this?'

'She'll get used to it.' Dad scratches her head from a safe distance with the end of one of his crutches. 'Go on, Stevie, slip that halter over her head.'

I step in close to Milly's shoulder and give her withers a good scratch, moving up her neck to her ears. When she appears completely chilled, I lean over and slip the halter up over her nose and back of her head, at which she takes umbrage, tosses her head in the air and kicks up her heels.

'Mind yourself, Dad,' I yell, as Milly trots away at speed, yanking the rope through my hands and leaving my palms stinging with rope burns. I watch the heifer dragging the end of the rope through the muck as she pushes her friends aside so she can hide behind them.

'Now you're going to have to get that off,' Dad chuckles.

'I'm tempted to leave it on.' Not for the first time in my life, I am reminded where the term 'silly cow' must have originated. 'I'll wait until she calms down. Are you sure about this, Dad?' I ask while we watch the cows milling about. 'I can give her a couple of baths and groom her, but she's pretty skinny. She'll need more flesh than that on her to have any chance of catching the judge's eye.'

'There's plenty of time yet. The show isn't until the third weekend in June. That's eight or nine weeks away.'

'Do you know who's judging?'

Dad names Roger Jones who was born into the dairy industry – rumour has it that his mother gave birth to him in a cowshed – and he's a Holstein classifier, so Dad reckons he'll favour our black-and-white cows over Guy's roan-and-white shorthorns.

'I've put the entry in already so you can't back out, Stevie,' Dad continues.

'Thanks for checking with me first.'

'Oh, it's all right, I knew you wouldn't mind.'

Magnificent Millicent and I don't hit it off the first time we meet, and our relationship doesn't improve much over the following couple of weeks. I have to entice her into the crush with a bucket of feed in front of her and Bear, or Cecil with a stick, behind, but suddenly we click and she holds her head still, albeit showing the whites of her eyes, for me to slip the halter on and knot the rope at the side of her face.

The next time she lets me put it on without a fuss, I take her for a walk, making the most of the half an hour I have before one of the vets from Talyton Manor calls. He's coming to look at one of the other cows; her water bag has broken but she has made no further headway in giving birth to her calf, which is now a couple of days overdue.

At first Milly isn't keen on leaving her friends in the collecting yard, but I manage to persuade her to walk – with her neck outstretched as she drags back on the rope – down the drive towards the lane, tickling her now and then with a stick of ash I've pulled from the hedge.

As we reach the gate, a vehicle draws up, and my heart skips a beat when I realise it's Leo. He jumps out and opens the gate as I apologise for not opening it for him.

'Don't worry,' he says. 'I'm glad the mad lady farmer isn't thinking of taking her pet heifer into town after what happened the last time.'

I lead Milly onto the verge and ask her to stand like a celebrity on a red carpet – with one hind leg slightly behind the other to show off her figure – so Leo can drive past safely.

'Nice heifer,' he says, stopping beside us.

His wicked grin makes me blush and Milly takes advantage of my loss of concentration, diving off into the hedge to tear out great mouthfuls of vegetation.

'I should stick with walking the dog in future,' Leo says.

'Are you laughing at me?'

'It is quite comical,' he says, tipping his head to one side. 'Where's this cow I'm supposed to be looking at?'

'She's in the cowshed. I'll be with you in a minute.'

'I won't hold my breath. Is Cecil about?'

'You'll find him in the dairy cleaning out the bulk tank.' I tug at Milly's rope, but she refuses to budge.

'Ask her to moooove.' Leo laughs at his own joke, before continuing, 'I think you're going to need more practice if you're planning to show her. You know, you have a lot of competition – half the dairy farms I've visited in the past week have been training their animals for this Country Show.'

'It's very important. It's the one of the highlights of Talyton's year.'

'Each to their own,' Leo shrugs as he drives away.

Ten minutes later, I'm still trying to extract Milly from the hedge. Eventually, thoroughly irritated and overheated, I throw the rope down.

'You are one stubborn cow,' I tell her. 'You can stay there for the rest of the day. You can stay there all night if you want to. I don't care.' I stamp my foot, but she takes no notice and I walk away in despair. She'll never be any good in the show ring.

However, within a few seconds she's right behind me, afraid perhaps that she's going to be left on her own.

'Did you miss me?' I ask her when she catches up. 'I didn't think so,' I add as she trots past and rejoins her friends, running up and down along the railings, bellowing to be allowed back into the collecting yard. I whip the halter off and let her in.

Thanks to Milly, I'm not in the best of moods when I catch up with Leo and Cecil in the cowshed.

'I hear that heifer's been running rings round you, my lover,' Cecil observes, his face more creased than ever with delight.

Leo glances up from where he's examining the rear end of the cow, Honeydew the third, who is lying on her side in the straw.

'I'd give up, if I were you,' he says brightly.

146

'I don't give up that easily.' I move closer to Leo. 'What's up?'

'The calf's in the birth canal but it's rather large – I'm not sure it's going to come out without help.'

'Does that mean another Caesarean?'

'I'll try the ropes first.' Leo opens the plastic box he's brought along with him and takes out a pair of white ropes, which he ties around the calf's fetlocks. 'Let's have a go.' He takes the ropes and pulls, leaning right back and pushing his foot against the cow's rump. Honeydew strains and lets out a groan of pain that makes me wince.

'It makes your toes curl, doesn't it, Stevie?' Cecil says.

I have to agree with him. 'There's no way I'll ever choose to fall pregnant, now I've seen the agony some of the cows go through.'

I can hardly watch as the cow strains again and again and Leo pulls on the calving ropes. He pauses to wipe his brow, readjusts the ropes and repeats the exercise several more times. The cow strains and Leo pulls until I can see sweat dripping from the end of his nose.

'It isn't budging,' he says eventually.

'Can't you stop?' I beg. 'I'd prefer to pay for her to have a caesarean.'

'Who's the vet here? I decide,' Leo says.

'Look at her.' Honeydew's body is trembling and her eyes are dark with anxiety because she's scared. 'She's suffering.'

'Let him be, Stevie,' Cecil says gently.

'But this isn't right! I've seen lots of difficult calvings

before and you can't keep pulling like that with nothing happening.'

'I think I've seen a few more than you have,' Leo says with a hint of irritation. 'I'm going to have one last try.' He takes up the slack in the ropes once more. I glare at him and he looks away, keeping his eyes focused on the calf's limbs which, as the cow strains one more time, emerge to the level of the shanks.

'It's coming now,' Cecil says.

'It's too slow,' I say. 'It'll be dead—'

'Will you shut up!' Leo snaps. His face is red with annoyance, the sinews in his arms and neck taut with effort.

'I'll shut up when you stop being so pig-headed and change your mind about a natural delivery. This is cruel.' Honeydew the third was the last heifer my mum showed at the Country Show. She was supreme champion and her favourite cow.

'Stevie, hush,' says Cecil. 'Leo knows what he's doing.'

'Does he?' I say rather curtly.

'Here it comes.' Leo falls back into the straw as Honeydew groans again and the calf emerges tail end first with an accompanying rush of fluid. Cecil dives in to help (I say 'dives', but he's struggling to get about today), hauling the calf with Leo so it's fully born. Ashamed at my lack of confidence in Leo's judgement, I stand back while the two men work on the calf, trying to revive it.

'I reckon she's got water in the lungs,' Cecil opines as Leo picks the calf up with ease and holds it by the

148

back legs over his shoulder so the fluid can drain from its nostrils. It's a big calf, a monster, more black than white, and it's no wonder Honeydew had so much difficulty giving birth to it.

I turn my attention to the cow, which is exhausted, lying flat out with her head resting on the ground.

'It's got a heartbeat,' I overhear Leo say. 'I'm not giving up on it yet. Come on, breathe.'

'There we go,' says Cecil as the calf utters a tiny cough. 'It's breathing now.'

'Leo, please can you look at mum?' I ask urgently. 'She's bleeding. Look.'

'Are you sure you trust me to do that?' Leo is being sarcastic. 'It's all right, I can see.'

'I'm sorry about earlier,' I say, as Leo and I study the blood that is pooling at the rear end of the cow and staining the straw.

'That doesn't look too good.' Leo slips a fresh glove over his right arm and kneels down to examine her. 'It was a traumatic birth. Maybe you were right and I should have gone for a Caesarean delivery.'

'No, you were right, I was being unreasonable. It was the correct decision at the time.'

'How do you work that one out?' Leo is still fishing around with his arm inside the cow.

'The calf coming backwards like that – it would have died before you got the epidural in.'

'Probably,' Leo agrees.

'Can you feel anything? A tear?'

'Nope.' Leo withdraws his arm, which is covered with blood. 'I'm going to give her a shot of something

149

to encourage the womb to contract right down and a bottle of calcium into a vein. She's showing signs of milk fever.'

'Do you think she's going to get up?'

'Let's wait and see, shall we?' Leo speaks to me more gently. 'Is she always this impatient, Cecil?'

'Stevie's her father's daughter,' Cecil says, pressing his fist into the small of his back as if he's in pain, coming out in sympathy with the cow. 'Mary and I often say so. That's why they don't always get on – they're too alike.'

'I hope I'm nothing like him,' I say, more cheerfully now I know Honeydew and her calf both seem to be safe. 'Cecil, go and put your feet up for a while. I'll finish up here.'

'Well, thank you. I'll do that.' I'm surprised he acquiesced so quickly, I think as he shuffles away. He must be sore again.

'Tea would be lovely, thanks,' Leo says, as he stands running the calcium into the cow's jugular vein.

'I'm sorry, I should have offered before.' I relax a little. 'That must have been thirsty work. How do you take it?'

'However it comes,' he says, amused, and I wonder if he's referring merely to the tea.

'Milk and sugar?'

'Milk, no sugar, thanks.'

I wonder about inviting Leo into the house, but decide against it because my father will only want to join in and I like the idea of having him to myself. I fetch tea and we settle on bales of straw to watch the calf and its mother. I steal a sneaky glance in Leo's direction just at the same time as he steals a glance in mine. Caught out! He flashes me a grin as if to say, 'I saw that.'

'You know my reasons for coming back to Talyton St George . . .' I begin. Well, how about yours? Why did you choose to come to work here? It's so quiet and . . . well, a bit of a backwater in many ways.'

'I saw the ad in the *Vet News* and I thought, 'Why not have a few months in the West Country?' I admit it's been a culture shock, having to take life more slowly, but it's a pleasant change.'

'You miss things when you rush about.'

'Like what?' he asks.

'Oh, never mind.'

'Go on.' He frowns, his forehead lined under his thick black curls, and I wonder what it would be like to run my fingers through the hair on his head and tangle them in the dark curls on his chest, which are visible where the top buttons have come undone on his shirt. 'Tell me.'

'Okay, now I know this sounds silly, but this morning after the rain, I saw a snail leaving its shiny trail down the wall from the eaves of the cowshed, and a pair of blackbirds building their nest in the honeysuckle.'

'It isn't silly,' Leo says. 'No, it's the people who drive me mad – not you, I hasten to add. I'm not talking about you.'

'I'm glad to hear it. You know, you can always move on if you dislike Talyton that much. I suppose that's another good reason for being a locum vet – as well as being able to leave if you upset someone or make a mistake.'

'That's a bit harsh,' he says, and I apologise for overstepping the mark. I don't know what's got into me today. I pick pieces of straw from my fleece top. I'm a bit scratchy.

'Perhaps it's because the reality of being the lady farmer has suddenly hit me,' I say. 'It's quite daunting.'

'You've made plenty of improvements and the cows are looking much better, apart from this one.' He looks towards the cow – she's still down and the calf is up on its feet, nuzzling her mother's shoulder for milk.

'That's the wrong end,' Leo says wryly, standing up. 'We need to make sure this calf gets the first milk if we can.'

Honeydew struggles to her feet with a little encouragement and the calf suckles.

'Where were you working before you came here, Leo?' I ask, keen to know more about him. There's an attraction between us which is most definitely mutual.

'I finished at a practice in South Wales last month.' He smiles. 'I was there for most of the lambing season. Before that, I did a stint in Norfolk and prior to that . . . well, I'm beginning to lose track.' Leo falls silent as if he doesn't want to talk about it, and I let it go for now, although I'm curious as to why he doesn't seem to want to settle in one place.

'I'll get some more straw,' I say, and I fetch a barrow of straw to add to the bed, tie up the gate across the shed and check the water. The buckets are empty so I get the hose and fill them up.

'I'm glad I'm not a farmer,' Leo says above the sound of the water. 'There's always something not right in a farmer's life – the weather; too much rain, too little rain.'

'It isn't all bad.' I smile as I watch the cow and calf. They've both made it, thanks to our amazing farm vet. 'How are things up at Barton Farm?'

'About the same.' Leo shrugs. 'Can you promise me you won't say anything?'

'Depends on what it is.'

'Well, I don't want to offend Lynsey and Stewart, but I'm looking for somewhere else to stay for the rest of the summer. If you hear of anything, would you let me know?'

'Yes, of course. Have you tried the small ads in the newsagent's window or the *Chronicle*?'

'I've had a look but they want long-term tenants. I'm waiting for a call back about a holiday let.' He takes a last mouthful of tea. 'I'd better go. I'll see you around, Stevie. Good luck with the heifer – and your plans for Nettlebed Farm.'

'How do you know about those?' I ask.

'It's common knowledge. You're supposed to be establishing a zoo and wildlife park, according to the gossips in the baker's, or a theme park if you listen to that mad woman from the garden centre.'

'Fifi Green? Do you know her?'

'She introduced herself when I moved here – she came to Barton Farm one evening with leaflets about the church, art club and useful local contacts – and I dropped in to the garden centre for a cream tea.' Leo picks up his box of equipment. 'Anyway, which is it to be: the zoo or Nettlebed Towers?'

'Neither, because it's going to be a petting farm.'

Leo smiles again. 'I know we talked of diversification, but I reckon you would do better sticking with the cows, Stevie. Have you thought about the health and safety issues that arise when you put animals and children together? You'll have to put in measures to reduce the risk of bites and the transfer of diseases. It'll be a complete nightmare.'

As when James tried to put me off, I refuse to be deterred. I smile back. 'You'll be able to help me then, seeing how you know so much about it.'

Chapter Nine

Third Time Lucky

It's the beginning of May and the hawthorn is in blossom. It's time for the afternoon milking and I'm getting the cows in with Bear. I pull a piece of hazel from the hedge and use it as a tickling stick to make sure the stragglers keep moving.

'Come on, Domino, old girl. Your milk will go off before you get to the parlour,' I sing out to her. She's always last, but today she's slower than ever, holding up the traffic on the lane. 'I'm sorry,' I mouth to the first motorist in the queue and a cyclist who wobbles precariously to avoid a cowpat. Bear nips at Domino's heels; she stamps one foot and turns to stare at him with a pathetic expression on her face, as if to say, 'Don't hassle me; can't you see I'm ill?'

Driving her on, I wait until we're safely in the farm-yard before I take a closer look at her.

'Domino's off her food again and her milk was down

155

this morning,' Cecil says, joining me. 'Maybe I should have kept her in, but I thought I'd give whatever it is a chance to pass over.'

Domino stands in the yard away from the others, looking really sorry for herself. Her back is arched, her eyes sunken and her skin seems to be sticking to her bones, as if she hasn't been drinking either.

'What do you think, Cecil?' I ask.

'I reckon she's got a twist in her stomach. Look at the way she's blown out at the side.'

'So it's a job for the vet.' More money, I think. The farm is like a dripping tap, constantly leaking cash. I'm beginning to wonder if I'm making the right decision holding on to the flat.

'We could have a go at running her up Steep Acres. Tom and I have done that a fair few times before.'

'Does it work?'

'Once in a blue moon,' Cecil responds. 'Or we could put her in the trailer and take her for a bumpy ride – that's supposed to sort it out.'

'We could have a go,' I say, looking at Domino and wondering how on earth we can make her run in her condition.

'We'll just chase her up the field. It won't take us five minutes. If it doesn't work, you can call the vet out.'

'I'm not sure she's going to run anywhere, least of all uphill,' I say doubtfully, 'and what about you, Cecil? You shouldn't be running with your bad back.'

'You and Bear can do the chasing,' Cecil says with a twinkle in his eye. 'I'll hold the gate for you, my lover.'

Looking up at the ground that rises steeply to the

ridge, the earth stepped out in terrace fashion, I use my stick of hazel to chase Domino up the field, she won't move faster than a slow amble and I end up hot and bothered while she looks just the same.

Guy is driving his tractor on the other side of the fence. He toots the horn and leans out of the cab. 'I've seen it all now,' he yells, 'my crazy neighbours are training a cow for the next Olympics.'

Before I can explain that I'm testing one of Cecil's theories, the tractor is roaring away straight up the hill towards the ridge. I walk back in the opposite direction with Domino and Bear, calling Talyton Manor vets on my mobile and hoping Leo will come.

'Hi Leo, it's—'

'Stevie,' he says, 'I recognised the number. What's up – or should I say, what's down, seeing as it's probably another cow, knowing your luck?'

'It's Domino, the cow who had the Caesarean.'

'I hope she isn't worrying about her bikini line,' Leo says flippantly. 'I thought my stitches were amazing. I'm sorry, Stevie. What's wrong with her?'

'I don't know. That's why I'm ringing you,' I say, equally flippantly. 'She isn't right again.'

'Is it urgent?'

'I don't think it will wait until tomorrow. I'd prefer someone to see her fairly soon.'

'Okay, I'll be over in twenty minutes.'

'Thanks,' I say, but he's already hung up. Whether it's down to the running or something I ate for breakfast, a dodgy mushroom perhaps, but I throw up in the long grass alongside the parlour. I ask Cecil to carry on with the milking and check there's some of Jennie's lemon drizzle cake – which I bought from the bakery – left, in case Leo should make an exception and stay for tea. Then I shut Bear in the lean-to where he howls to be let out.

'What are you doing back?' Dad asks from his chair when I pop my head around the door to the sitting room. He's watching an episode of *Friends*.

'I've had to call the vet out.'

'You've what?'

'I've had to call the vet for Domino,' I repeat.

'I beg your pardon. Stevie, you really need to learn how to make yourself heard.'

'Turn the telly down and you'll be able to hear me, you silly old fool,' I shout at the top of my voice in annoyance.

'Hey, I heard that. What kind of a daughter are you?'

'It doesn't matter because I'm the only one you've got. I don't see your precious son here. Where is Ray? How often has he been to see you?'

'Don't you have a dig at Ray. He has three farms and a haulage firm to oversee.'

'Good for him,' I say snappily. 'He's chosen his wife's family business over Nettlebed Farm after all you did for him.'

'That's just sour grapes on your part.'

'I'm here. Ray isn't.'

'What's wrong with Domino?' Dad says, changing the subject. He doesn't like to talk about his son, it seems. Does he feel guilty for putting Ray before me when it came to the farm, or is he still harbouring

158

resentment for the way Ray cast him and the farm aside when he married Gabrielle?'

'I'll be sure when the vet comes.'

'Well, I hope it's one who knows what he's talking about. Is it Old Fox-Gifford?'

'It's the locum, Leo,' I say, concerned. 'Old Fox-Gifford's been dead for a while, Dad. His son runs the practice.'

'Alex?' Dad rubs his chin with his good hand. 'I remember now. Of course I remember.'

I worry about his memory. Is he tired? Did the stroke irreversibly damage some essential parts of his brain? Is he going senile? I'm not sure I could cope with that. I worry too that he doesn't offer to come out and interfere.

Still feeling queasy, I head back outdoors where Leo is parking his four-by-four in the yard as the door into the parlour slides open, letting five of the queuing cows inside to be milked.

'Hello.' Leo leans out of the window. 'Where's the dog?'

'Safely locked away,' I say as Bear starts howling all over again.

Apparently reassured, Leo jumps out. He's wearing a grey T-shirt, navy work trousers and green wellies.

'Where's the patient?' he asks, pulling a set of over-alls and stethoscope from the back of the vehicle.

'I've left her tied up in the cowshed. She isn't happy.'

Leo follows me to where Domino stands looking forlornly in the direction of the other cows. I stand at her head while Leo examines her from nose to tail. He

159

taps at her belly, and listens with his stethoscope at the same time.

'Do you want to have a listen?' he asks. 'Can you hear the 'ping'?'

Holding the bell of the stethoscope against Domino's belly, he hands me the other end and I listen, aware of his proximity and his masculine scent of musk and antibiotic.

'Well?' he says, tapping the cow again.

I nod. I've heard it before, but I don't say so. I rather like getting up close and personal to Leo.

'It's characteristic of a displaced—'

'Twisted stomach, as Cecil says,' I cut in, stepping back and handing over the stethoscope.

'I don't know why you called me out,' he says good-humouredly. 'Who needs a vet when Cecil can treat it with one of the traditional methods?'

'We've had a go at running her up the hill. It didn't work – all it did was prove how unfit I am.'

Leo looks me up and down. 'You look pretty fit to me, Stevie.'

I don't know where to put myself. 'Are you coming on to me?' I say, blushing.

'I'm paying you a compliment.' He arches one eyebrow. 'I'm not expecting anything in return, although it would be nice.'

'Thank you,' I say, not giving anything away as to the state of my feelings.

'Getting back to the matter in hand . . .' Leo hangs his stethoscope around his neck. 'What do you want me to do? It's your call.'

'You mean we should cull her?' I look at Domino and my eyes begin to prick with tears. 'I'm not sure that's an option after all she's been through.'

'Hasn't she been through enough recently? Besides, she's one of the older members of the herd, so she probably hasn't got much productive life left.'

'I know, but it seems a shame to give up on her now. I'd like to give her another chance.'

'Are you absolutely sure?'

My mind is made up. 'If you don't want to do it, I'll call someone else out.'

'There's no need to do that.' He thinks I'm over-reacting, but I would do anything for our cows.

'Will you operate?' I've seen enough cases like these before to know that surgery is an option.

'I'll try casting her first. It might save you some money.' He looks me straight in the eyes, making me feel uncomfortable. 'I'm afraid you're getting a bit of a reputation with the practice.'

What does he mean, I wonder as I scratch Domino's bony back, urging her silently to get better. Exactly what rumours are circulating around town?

'Alex says I'm to warn you we can't keep coming out like this if you don't pay your bill in full with interest by the end of the month,' Leo says, looking embarrassed.

'I'm sorry.' Does he know we haven't paid a single vet's bill for six months? 'I'll sort it out this week, I promise.'

Leo fetches a length of rope from his vehicle.

'Let's give this a go,' he says. 'I'm going to cast her

and roll her onto her back to see if that fixes it. If I drench her with some calcium, it might just work. If it doesn't, then you really should put some serious consideration into culling her. She isn't going to produce her quota of milk this lactation or have another calf within a year, which means you're losing out all the time.'

'Life isn't all about money,' I say hotly.

'Ah, but it's what makes the world go round.'

'That's love, isn't it? It's love that makes the world go round.'

'You could be right there.' Leo smiles. 'You must think I'm a right mercenary git.'

'Well, aren't you?' I challenge him. 'You're a vet. You must be rolling in it.'

'That's a misconception, like the myth about poor farmers.'

'You've probably got an amazing house.'

'I don't own a house,' he says.

'Where do you live then?'

'Wherever,' he shrugs. 'I like being a free spirit.' He throws me the end of the rope. 'Let's get her down. There's a nice soft landing for her here.'

I help Leo rope Domino up and cast her onto her side. From there we roll her onto her back, straighten her hind legs and turn her onto her brisket. Domino is not happy, but I take it as a good sign that there is a hint of rebellion, not defeat in her expression.

'I'm sorry, this is most undignified,' I tell her when we repeat the process for a second time. Domino struggles up onto her feet and I watch, holding my breath, but it's still there, the balloon of gas and the ping sound.

'That's a bugger,' Leo says, which makes me smile in spite of the situation.

'Indeed,' I agree. 'Let's go ahead with the surgery.'

'If you're certain.'

'I'll fetch some hot water.' I bring a couple of plastic buckets full from the dairy while Leo spreads a green cotton drape across a straw bale and lines up the equipment he needs: needles and syringes, bottles of local anaesthetic and antibiotic, more drapes, a kidney dish containing surgical scrub, a pack of instruments. He operates, making a long cut into Domino's belly, so he can reposition her stomach and anchor it to the inside of her flank with big stitches to keep it in place in future.

'That's a neat job,' I say, watching Leo sewing Domino up.

'Thanks.'

'Did you always want to be a vet?'

'Not always. I come from a farming family. We farmed five hundred acres in Lincolnshire. It was largely arable, a mixture of winter wheat, spring barley and sugar beet, but we also had a small pig unit and beef for fattening.'

'You didn't want to stay at home and work on the farm then?'

'My parents sold up. I made it clear I didn't want to work all hours like they did, dawn to dusk seven days a week, fifty-two weeks a year.' He smiles ruefully. 'I ended up working all hours as a vet instead.'

'Did your mum and dad regret giving up?'

'I think the change in lifestyle finished them off. They died within a year, Mum from breast cancer and my father from a broken heart.'

'I'm sorry . . . That's so sad.'

'At least they're together. They were very close.' Leo gazes at me, screwing up his eyes as the bright sunlight enters the cowshed between the slats.

'Have you any other family? Brothers and sisters?'

'An older sister,' he says. 'What about you? Why did you leave Devon in the first place?'

'I wanted to stay here on the farm. In fact, I worked like mad when I was younger because I wanted it so badly, but my father chose my brother over me because I was a girl.'

'That's very short-sighted – and misogynistic, if you ask me.'

'I packed some things, took my father's Volvo and drove up to London. My grandmother used to read me the story of Dick Whittington – it's all right, I didn't believe it; but there must have been part of me that remembered London was a good place to seek your fortune. I was eighteen and didn't have much money on me.'

'That was a brave thing to do.'

'I was lucky. I met India in a café – she's my best friend – and she let me stay on her sofa. I did some waitressing and clearing tables so I could pay my way, but it wasn't long before I realised I didn't want to do that for the rest of my life, so I looked for a position where I could do my accountancy exams. I ended up working for a firm in Wimbledon.'

'You must have earned a fortune. Why on earth have you given it up for this?'

'I earned good money, but I love being here working outdoors with the cows. On the whole they're a lot easier to work with than some of my clients – less demanding.' I smile. 'I cut ties with my father, and kept in touch with my mum by phone. Cecil and Mary maintained contact through birthday and Christmas cards.

'It wasn't until my mum was diagnosed . . .' I pause to collect myself before continuing. 'That's when I first came back to the farm. I was lucky I didn't leave it too late.' I fall silent, remembering my mother.

'I imagine you'd still be in London if it hadn't been for your father's ill health.'

'I hadn't been back since my mum passed away. I'm not sure I would have ever returned if it hadn't been for Cecil contacting me with his SOS.'

'I suppose you miss your boyfriend?' Leo asks tentatively. 'I'm sorry,' he goes on, reading my expression. 'I shouldn't have asked. It's none of my business.'

'Oh, it's okay.' I shrug. 'We decided to call it a day. I couldn't deal with a long-distance relationship and he wasn't exactly a country man, although he wanted to look the part.' I think of Nick and my heart twists with unexpected pain. 'It's one of those things.' I'm suddenly homesick for London, my lovely flat and India, on top of my moment of weakness over my ex. 'How about you? Are you taken?'

'Taken?'

'Have you a girlfriend?' I feel myself blushing.

'Not at the moment.' Gazing at me, he washes his

165

hands and wipes them on some paper towels I grabbed from the parlour. 'I have had various girlfriends, and a fiancée – not at the same time, I hasten to add. I can go the distance if the lady is worth it, but I've been living the single life for a while now.'

'What happened to the fiancée?'

'Oh, it didn't work out,' he says dismissively. 'Stevie, have you seen my stethoscope?'

'It's around your neck,' I say, grinning as Leo chuckles at his mistake.

'You asked if I knew of somewhere you could stay for the summer,' I begin. 'It isn't much, but you're welcome to have the mobile home on the yard. You'd have it to yourself and be completely independent. There's a microwave, fridge, hob and oven – I can check to see if they work.' My enthusiasm for the idea fizzles out as I watch Leo's expression. Have I overstepped the mark suggesting he stays here at Nettlebed Farm? Is he worried about my motives? Because, if I'm really honest with myself, he should be.

'Your father's okay with this?' Leo asks. 'Only he's a bit handy with a gun.'

'He's had his gun licence revoked.' I start to worry that I haven't run this offer past my father. 'It'll be fine. I don't know why he bought the mobile home if he wasn't expecting anyone to live in it.'

'Why did he buy it then?'

'It was cheap. He likes a bargain, even if it's something that's no use to him.' I start to backtrack. 'Look, Leo, it's pretty ancient and, in fact, I'm not sure it's habitable.'

'I really don't want to stay at the Pitts' all summer. I don't mind half an hour on the Xbox, but no more. I find it a bit exhausting with all the kids after a long day at work. And I like my own company.'

'I suppose I prefer to be around people, so sometimes it's a bit too quiet for me on the farm,' I say. 'Cecil isn't exactly chatty and there's no one to talk to when you're out on the hill with the muck-spreader, although I do often text India. And there's Jennie next door – she's friendly, but I don't have much time to go round for coffee. There's a huge amount to catch up with on the farm – Dad and Cecil can't help it, but they've really let it go.'

'You're making me feel guilty, but I have to be polite and respectful to my clients all day, and sometimes in the middle of the night too.'

'You seemed to have some difficulty with that when I first met you.'

'Did I? Oh yes, I was rather wound up that day. I thought Alex should have turned up with Jack, not me. And I'm never happy when I see animals suffering unnecessarily.'

'I know . . .' I still feel guilty.

'It isn't your fault. I realise that now.' Leo smiles. 'And I like visiting Nettlebed Farm – it holds a special attraction for me . . . You're different. And you make a great mug of tea,' he grins cheekily.

'Is that a hint that you'd like one?' I say archly.

'If you're making one, I wouldn't say no.' And, I think, if he asked me to kiss him I wouldn't say no either. I don't know where this is coming from. I'm not normally like this. Is it because I'm missing the closeness with Nick and looking for solace? 'Can I have a look inside the mobile home?' he goes on.

'I'll have to find the key first. Why don't you drop by tomorrow?' I hesitate. Does that sound too keen? 'Or maybe you're on call. I'm free most days, every day in fact, pretty well.' Suddenly, I'm embarrassed at revealing my availability. So what! Being single doesn't have to mean I'm sad.

'Tomorrow would be perfect.' Leo smiles and my heart flips. Spending time in his company makes me happy.

'Thank you for going ahead with the surgery. I know you weren't keen on the idea.'

'That's okay. Your instincts were right – she's made it so far, and I reckon if we're lucky, she'll make a good recovery. Whether she'll ever have another calf is another matter.'

'I'll retire her,' I say.

'Can you afford to do that?'

'There's plenty of grass around. I wouldn't do it for all of the cows, but this one's special.'

'You'll have to start up a retirement home for dairy cattle. What would Cecil and your father think of that?'

'I can guess. My father's already had a lot to say about the plan for a petting farm.' As soon as I utter the word 'petting', it takes on a new significance, and my face is burning at the idea of some heavy petting with Leo.

Leo gives me a telling grin. 'I'll see you tomorrow, Stevie,' he says in a caressing voice, as if he can hardly wait to see me again, and I watch him leave, my heart pounding with desire and the hope that our deepening friendship might soon grow into something more. I know he's only the locum, but who knows? Maybe he'll stay on.

I decide to go and ask my father for the key to the mobile home, so I can give it a quick once-over before Leo returns. I find Dad in the kitchen, sitting at the table with a packet of lemon creams and a scrapbook of yellowing newspaper clippings.

'Hello, Stevie. What are you doing indoors?'

'Cecil's finished milking and the vet's just left.'

'He was here a ruddy long time. I dread to think how much that call-out cost.'

I thought he might have come out to see what was going on because Domino is one of his favourites too. We all love her. I wonder if he was too scared that we might lose her.

'Aren't you going to ask how Domino is?'

'It doesn't worry me,' he mutters.

'So you aren't looking at her picture for any particular reason?' I say, looking over his shoulder.

'I just happened upon it,' he says, closing the scrapbook. 'It opened at the year when she took Show Champion. Don't you remember?'

I shake my head. 'Dad, it was eight years ago. I wasn't here.'

He frowns as if he's forgotten I was ever absent from the farm, which doesn't bode well for the prospect of finding the key to the mobile home. However, he is convinced that it's on a key ring which is taped to the back of one of the drawers in the desk in the office.

'What do you want it for anyway?'

'Leo is looking for somewhere to stay. I thought as it was standing empty—'

'You should have asked me first,' my father says. 'I'm planning to use that as a holiday let for the summer.'

'I think that's rather optimistic – who would want to stay there for a holiday?'

'A family who wants to live on a working farm for a week.'

'Dad, you're deluded. It's a wreck.'

'So why would some rich vet want to stay in it?' he counters, and he does have a point.

'He's looking for some peace and quiet.'

'He'll pay rent?'

'I expect so.' I begin to falter. 'I haven't got that far yet.'

'I'm afraid you'll get a reputation.'

'Oh, for goodness' sake, there's nothing seedy about the arrangement. I'm not going out with Leo.'

'You're too old to be having fun. You should be settling down, getting married and thinking about starting a family.' My father hesitates. 'James is a pleasant enough young man.'

'He's pretty easygoing and he's a hard worker,' I say, thinking of the job he made of the new fence, 'but he is rather dull. I'm sorry, but he is.' I suppose by criticising James, a man of the land, I'm also criticising my father. 'We don't have a lot in common anymore.'

'I married your mother when she turned twenty.'

'Yet you didn't start a family until she was in her thirties,' I point out. 'I'm twenty-eight, so I don't understand the rush.'

'She wanted a baby sooner, but it didn't happen for a long while. In fact, she'd all but given up hope when she found she was pregnant with you.'

'Well, marriage and babies aren't a priority for me. Please don't start matchmaking on my behalf.'

'Well, maybe it isn't such a bad idea having a vet on the premises. If you keep in with Leo, we're bound to get a discount. He can't charge for diesel if he's living right here.'

'Dad, you are not to mention it. Leo's coming here because he doesn't want a load of hassle. If you even hint at a discount, I'll be furious with you. Do I make myself clear?'

'As clear as mud.'

'Please don't pretend you don't understand,' I say wearily. 'It's simple. While Leo's staying, the mobile home is out of bounds.' I change the subject. 'I'm going to find this key.'

To my amazement, the key is in the office where Dad said it would be, and I enter the mobile home armed with bleach, cloths, a pair of yellow marigolds and a lot of optimism, which fizzles away as I pick at the mould under the window.

It's damp, cold and miserable. The bathroom facilities bear a pervading stench of stagnant water, which makes me feel nauseous. A mouse has nibbled its way through the foam in one of the cushions on the sofa. The mattress on the bed is damp. The fridge is okay because it's been left with the door propped open, and it makes a whirring sound when I switch it on. The hob works too, proving there's some gas left in the canister that stands outside. I open the cupboard under the sink, finding a dog bowl and some fearsome-looking veterinary instruments, evidence of the mobile home's history. It moved from Talysands Holiday Park to the farm via Otter House vets, who used it as a temporary surgery after what became known as the Great Flood, when the river Taly burst its banks a couple of years ago.

I'm more than a little apprehensive at what Leo will think. I should have had a closer look before offering it to him. I call him on his mobile number and leave a message on his voicemail.

'I think you should have a look first,' I say. 'Don't pack your things just yet.'

As I'm cleaning, my mind runs round in circles. I wonder if it's the glamour of Leo being a vet that's especially attractive, but he doesn't look all that glamorous when he turns up on the farm with mud on his boots and cow dung smeared across his shirt. Nick was eminently available and a good-looking, ordinary man wanting to settle down and start a family, yet I rejected him; whereas Leo, who is charismatic, enigmatic and not intending to hang around for long, turns me into a lustful, weak-kneed . . . Stop right there, I tell myself. It's nothing, just a reaction to moving back to the farm. I'm still missing my friends and colleagues, and the hustle and bustle of the city. This feeling will pass.

India agrees with me when I speak to her on the

172

phone, having taken a quick break outside to clear my nostrils of the stench of bleach.

'It's a whim, a passing phase,' India says. 'I know what you're like Stevie. You have these enthusiasms and they never last.'

'Excuse me, I went out with Nick for eighteen months,' I protest.

'Exactly, and it's really sad that you think a year and a half is a long-term relationship.'

'Well, it is,' I say, amused until I realise India is being serious.

'Nick came into the restaurant with a client the other day – he's still completely devastated. He thought he was going to spend the rest of his life with you.'

'India, don't keep making me feel guilty.' I feel bad enough without her help. I know it was for the best. 'If I'd accepted Nick's proposal, we would never have made it to the altar.'

'You shouldn't have dragged it out the way you did. You should have put him out of his misery before you went on holiday together.'

'I didn't know for certain that it wasn't going to work—'

'Until you'd had two weeks in paradise at Nick's expense.'

'I paid my share,' I say, hurt at her suggestion that I'd taken advantage of him.

'That isn't what he says.'

'You seem to know a lot about Nick all of a sudden.'

'He always gives me a good tip. And we've shared a couple of bottles of wine recently.'

I wonder if Nick's going out with India on the rebound. He always said how much he hated being on his own.

'I hope you don't mind him crying on your shoulder,' I say. 'You two aren't . . .?'

'Oh no, he isn't my type – and anyway, he's far too wrapped up in you and what happened.'

'Sometimes I wonder if I'll ever settle for anyone.'

'You're too fussy, Stevie. That's your trouble. No one will ever be good enough for you.'

'You make it sound as though there's a queue of men waiting to knock down my door,' I say dryly.

'You never have any trouble attracting them.'

Do I detect a hint of bitterness in India's voice? She's the pretty one with model looks, not me, yet it's true, I have more male friends and acquaintances than she does. I don't go out looking for them. They seem to find me.

'Leo's different,' I say.

'OMG, men are all different when you first meet them. When you get to know them, they're all pretty much the same.'

'India! How can you say that?'

'Oh, I don't know. I'm tired. I've had a chaotic week. You know how it is.'

'I do,' I say, smiling.

'How are the plans for the farm going?' she asks, changing the subject.

'You must come and stay sometime soon so I can show you. Keep in touch. I've got to go.' I still have loads to do.

Chapter Ten

Animal Farm

Leo tells me to stop apologising for the mobile home when he drops by the following day because it's just what he's been looking for.

'You haven't been inside yet,' I say as I unlock the door and inhale a draught of bleach-laden air. 'It's going to be pretty hot in here in the summer.'

'It's perfect, Stevie,' he says, as if I'm offering him the run of Buckingham Palace. Leo squeezes past me in the tiny hallway, brushing his arm against mine. I catch his scent of aftershave and penicillin and my unruly heart misses a beat because, although my motives for inviting this almost irresistible man to live effectively next door are purely altruistic . . . Fingers of heat creep up the back of my neck at the thought I might give away my feelings for him, because he is very attractive and I'm a lonely lady farmer . . .

'I'll wait for you to have a look around,' I say, taking

a seat at the table in the open-plan kitchen diner living area, which has chintz curtains to match the sofa covers, a scuffed lino floor and cheap veneered units.

'It's small, but it has everything I need and more,' Leo says cheerfully. 'What are the neighbours like?' he laughs. He moves across to the sink to look out of the window. I get up to join him so we're standing close together, side by side.

'I'm sorry about the view,' I say, looking out at the weeds dying in the stone trough and the tumbledown walls of the cowshed.

'I'd say I have a pretty good view from here,' he says, glancing out of the corner of his eye, and I start to feel a little giddy and weak at the knees.

Suddenly, though, Leo jumps back and moves behind me, hanging on to me by the shoulders, making my heart beat even faster than it already was.

'What's wrong?' I ask.

'There's a spider in the sink.'

'I forgot to mention you'd have to share.' Leo doesn't seem to get the joke. 'Where is it?' I can feel his body pressed against mine as he peers past me. 'I can't see one.'

'It's beside the plughole. You can't miss it – it's enormous,' Leo gasps.

A spider crawls out from underneath one of the rubber gloves I left in the sink. 'I'd say that was a medium.'

'It's massive.'

I start to laugh as I pick the spider up, caging it in my

hands. I turn and hold it up to him, but he backs right into the cupboard behind us, his face pale, and keeping me at arm's length. I try to duck closer.

'No, Stevie,' he says sharply, and I realise he's serious. 'Take it away. Please!'

'I'll put it outside in the barn. It's only a spider.'

He stands well clear as I pass him, folding his arms across his chest and grimacing, and when I return inside, he's waiting to grab me and give me a hug.

'Thank you for saving my life,' he says, his hands around my back, pulling me close.

'I didn't realise you could be so melodramatic.'

'I'm not talking about the eight-legged monster. I mean with the caravan. I don't think I could have stayed with the Pitts another night. I had to play Top Trumps for three hours after work.'

'Now I've looked at the place, it isn't all that great. Couldn't you have stayed with Alex Fox-Gifford? I thought there would be plenty of room at Talyton Manor.'

'I don't think it's a good idea to fraternise with the boss, although I'm tempted to get to know my land-lady a whole lot better.' Leo touches his lips to my forehead before gazing hungrily into my eyes and, for a moment, I think he's going to kiss me on the lips, but we're interrupted by the sound of Cecil's voice.

'Is everything all right in there? I thought I heard someone in trouble.'

'Everything's fine,' I call back, moving away from Leo and looking out of the door of the mobile home. Leo is behind me. 'Leo was in a bit of bother.'

'It's nothing,' Leo says quickly.

'That's all right then,' Cecil says before he walks away with his metal bucket of scraps to feed the hens.

'I didn't think—' I begin.

'I'd never live it down if that got out.' Leo grins. 'A large animal vet who's scared of spiders. I have a phobia of them. I used to have a recurring nightmare when I was a child about spiders getting trapped in my hair.'

'That is quite weird.'

'It's one of the reasons I didn't become a zoo vet,' Leo explains. 'You did release it far enough away for it not to find its way back?'

'You'll have to wait and see,' I grin, but then hesitate as I see his expression. 'You really do have it bad.'

'I can't stand them.'

'There could be mice,' I say, testing him.

'I don't mind warm furry things.' He gives me another cheeky grin. 'Why don't I take you out for a meal at the weekend? I'll make sure you're home early. I know you have to get up in the morning.'

'A date, you mean?' My heart is doing somersaults.

'It can be whatever you like,' he says, blushing. 'Alex recommends the Barnscote Hotel or the new Indian on the seafront at Talymouth. Are you free on Saturday night?'

'Yes. Yes, I am. Thanks, Leo.'

'If it's okay with you, I'll bring my things over this evening after work.'

Unable to stop smiling, I give him the key.

'Thank you, Stevie,' he says, and if I wasn't completely besotted with him before, I am now.

'So you're going out with Leo?' Cecil says, when I mention that I want to finish the milking in good time on the following Saturday afternoon. 'He's a catch.'

I'm in the parlour with him, having turned on the milking machine in the dairy.

'We're going out for a meal, that's all. Come on, let's call the girls in and get this party started.'

Cecil stares at me as if he thinks I'm slightly touched. He takes his cap off to scratch his head and puts it back on again at an angle.

'It's a figure of speech,' I explain.

The milking goes smoothly and Cecil offers to hose down the parlour at the end so I can go and shower and change. I choose one of my London outfits, nothing too over the top – a strappy lilac top with a diamante detail across the front, a smart jacket, navy trousers and heels – and I'm ready when Leo knocks at the front door of the farmhouse. Bear runs up barking.

'Go away,' I tell him as I open the door to greet Leo, who looks me up and down, pursing his lips in what I hope is admiration.

'Stevie, you look . . .'

'Different?' I say, wondering if I should have worn my jeans.

'No . . . Well, yes. That's quite some transformation.' Leo smiles and leans forward to kiss me briefly on the cheek. 'You scrub up well.'

'Thank you.' I glance down at my chipped nails –
I've done my best.

'Shall we go?' Leo says. I hear my father's stick
tapping along the hallway towards us.

'What time will you be back, Stevie?' he calls.

'It doesn't matter, Dad. I can let myself in.'

'I'll make sure she's home by midnight, like
Cinderella,' Leo says, amused.

'You'd better, young lad.'

'Dad, leave it,' I say. 'You are so embarrassing. Come
on, Leo. Let's go.'

It's a relief to get away from the farm for a while.
With Leo, I can almost forget about my father, the
money and the project. I can change out of my wellies,
dress up and be normal, except I find myself talking
about the show and the cows and the project on the
way to Talymouth.

'Tell me if I talk too much,' I say, and Leo is grinning
as he parks the four-by-four in a space a few metres
from the Taj Mahal, which looks out over the seafront.

Inside, Leo orders vindaloo and a beer, while I order
korma and red wine, and I wonder briefly if we're
incompatible, but we have plenty to talk about, including his plans for when he's finished working for Alex
Fox-Gifford.

'Do you have any idea where you'll end up next?' I
ask. 'I mean, do you plan in advance or do you go with
the flow?'

'I have a long-term plan to emigrate.'

'To go abroad?'

'I believe that's part of it,' Leo says, amused. 'I have

180

Life can be a bitch, I know that, but to deny your loving nature and your desire to have a family because of one cruel accident of fate seems rather extreme to me.

'I'm afraid that if I get close to any child . . .' Leo's voice falters before returning more strongly. 'You know what I'm getting at. There isn't a day that goes by without me wondering what he would be doing if he'd had the opportunity to grow up like an ordinary boy.'

'What about your sister? How does she cope?' I ask.

'We've coped in different ways. She's gone on to have another baby.'

'That's nice,' I say hesitantly.

'It feels like as soon as she replaced Jonas with another child, she forgot about him.'

'I'm sure that isn't the case.'

Leo shrugs. 'Maybe not, but that's how it feels. I've been a bit of a coward. I didn't like to see my sister because it reminded me of what we all went through, and now I hardly see her at all.' I wait for him to continue. 'Let's change the subject,' he says, closing his wallet. 'Does your brother have any kids?'

'He has a stepdaughter and a girl of his own.' After Leo's experience, I can't bring myself to mention that I've seen very little of them, so we go on to talk about less intense subjects – where we've travelled and what food we enjoy. At the end of dinner, Leo suggests that, as it's relatively warm for early May, we grab a couple of coats from his four-by-four and take a walk on the beach. But then he remembers I'm wearing heels.

'No, it'll be fine. I'll take them off,' I say. 'Let's walk. It'll be fun.'

When we reach the sand at the base of the steps, I slip out of my shoes and carry them, walking hand in hand with Leo down to the sea where the silvery reflection of the moon is dancing on the water. The soft sand slides between my toes as we hesitate.

'Shall we?' Leo asks in a low voice.

'Yes, but you'll have to take your shoes off too.'

Leo uses my arm to balance himself as he kicks off his shoes without untying the laces. As he straightens, he moves his hand around my back and holds on to the curve of my waist. 'Are you ready?' he says.

I take a step forwards, placing my foot on the cold, wet sand and waiting for the next wave to roll in and break across my toes.

'It's freezing!' I scream. I would run away, but Leo is hanging on to me, laughing at my reaction.

'It's tropical, Stevie.'

'You are joking?' I turn to him. His eyes flash in the dark.

He pulls me close and somehow I'm in his arms and up to my ankles in the waves, and although my feet are cold, the rest of my body is shot through with heat and my heart is pounding with desire as he presses his lips very gently against mine.

'I'm not joking now though,' he murmurs, and he doesn't stop kissing me – nor I him – apart from on the brief trip back to the farm, where he escorts me to the top of the steps down to the front door and takes me in his arms, tangling his fingers in my hair at the nape of my neck and kissing me again.

A light comes on and my heart sinks. I push Leo gently away.

'That'll be my father spying on us.'

'Does it matter?' Leo pulls me back. Giggling, I let him. 'You don't want to . . .' He glances towards the mobile home, but seems to change his mind when he hears the click of the lock on the front door as my father opens it, exposing us to the glare of a storm lantern.

'I thought I heard intruders,' he says, but I know he's lying. Bear would have barked. He's being nosy, checking up on me.

'Thanks for a wonderful evening, Stevie,' Leo says. 'Goodnight.'

'Goodnight, Leo,' I say regretfully, as he takes a step back, putting some space between us. 'Thank you for that, Dad,' I add as Leo strides away across the farmyard. 'I'm almost thirty and you're still trying to ruin my love life.'

'Where are you going now in those clothes?' he says.

'To check on the calves.' I glance down at my feet. 'I'll just throw on a coat and change my shoes.'

'Shouldn't you be going to bed?'

I want to say, 'Yes, with Leo,' to wind him up, but it's too close to the truth. If Leo had asked me, would I have stopped at a kiss?

It's the beginning of June and Leo has been ensconced in the caravan for three weeks. He's made some improvements – there's a boot rack outside for his wellies, a clotheshorse for his waterproofs and a pot of yellow tulips. I'm half expecting him to put up a white picket fence like the ones at the caravan park in Talysands. We have spent a couple of evenings sitting chatting, drinking tea and kissing, but he hasn't suggested a second date and, even if he asked me, I'm not sure how I'd respond. I'm torn between wanting to take things further and holding back because, in spite of what he said in the restaurant about being open to altering his plans, it doesn't seem very likely and I'm naturally wary of making any kind of commitment, emotional or physical, to someone who cannot commit to me. I'm assuming Leo has guessed why I'm hesitant, which is why he's been a gentleman and backed off.

I wonder too when I'm sitting in the house with the windows open, drawing up my plans for the farm, listening to him singing ballads along to his guitar, if he's withdrawn a little because he's embarrassed about having revealed more than he intended of his emotions over the loss of his nephew, and sometimes I tell myself I'm reading too much into it. Perhaps nothing has changed because we've both been rushed off our feet, Leo working for the practice and me consumed by the challenge of taking on the farm.

In fact, I've just spent three long days chugging up and down the fields with Bertha, cutting and turning grass for hay, having decided to take an early crop with the expectation of making a second cut in July when the grass has grown back again. I was driving until midnight last night, and up to milk the cows, before going out with the tractor again today.

It's gone seven in the evening, I'm half asleep in front of the television with my father, and I'm so shattered I'm thinking of having a long bath and an early night when I hear a car bumping along the drive, which is odd because we aren't expecting anyone as far as I know. It's been a hot day, but it's cooling down quickly, so I throw a jumper over my vest and glance at my watch before going outside with Bear for a quick stroll. Leo's four-by-four is parked alongside the Land Rover, and the caravan door is jammed open with a broom handle. He has music on – he isn't playing so I assume it must be on the radio – and he's singing along with it. I toy with the idea of going up to say hi, but hesitate as two cars turn into the yard.

I smile to myself on discovering that I'm affronted by the presence of strangers on the farm – I must be spending too much time with my dad.

'I'm afraid you must've taken a wrong turning somewhere,' I tell the driver of the first car as she opens her window.

'This is Nettlebed Farm?' she says, frowning.

'It is.'

'We're looking for Leo. He invited us.'

'Oh? I'm sorry, my mistake. Yes, he lives in the mobile home over there. You can park on the yard, anywhere you like.' I back off quickly, not wanting to appear nosy, but I do watch from the side of the house as the occupants of the cars emerge. There are two men and three women – friends of Leo's, I assume, and my jealous mind goes into overdrive.

'Hello.' Leo comes striding over towards his visitors from the mobile home, freshly showered and dressed in shorts, T-shirt and battered canvas shoes. As he greets them, his eye catches mine, making me cringe with embarrassment at being caught out spying on him. He calls me over to introduce me to three of his contemporaries from vet school, and a married couple he met while working for them as a locum on his travels, describing me as the farmer, not the farmer's daughter, which is sweet of him, but deep down I wish he would talk of me as his girlfriend.

'Stevie saved my sanity, offering me this place to stay for the summer.'

'I hope you have a lovely evening,' I say valiantly.

'I'm sorry, Stevie,' Leo says in an aside to me as his guests enter the caravan. 'I should have asked you before if I could have a party. I realise it's a bit of an imposition.'

'It's no problem,' I say, a little grudgingly, because if there's a party, I'd have liked to have been invited too. 'Isn't it going to be a little overcrowded?'

'It could be a bit of a game of seeing how many vets you can get into a mobile home,' he grins. 'I thought I'd take them down to the beach – we'll have a barbecue by the sea and swim.'

'Are they staying over?' Immediately, I wish I hadn't said that. 'I shouldn't have asked. It's up to you. Only, if you like, I could make up a couple of beds in the house if you need them.'

'It's all right, thanks. You've done enough for me already.' He pauses. 'Would you like to join us? You're very welcome.'

I hesitate. 'I've got a lot to do. No, I'm sure you have a lot to catch up on.'

'Too much work and all that . . .' He tips his head to one side and my heart misses a beat. 'Join us for a drink later?'

'Thank you, Leo.' I head inside, feeling a pang of regret for the parties I'm missing. India is out tonight – she texted me a photo of her glammed up in a dress she bought in a sale.

Later, I look out of the bedroom window and catch sight of Leo and his friends, sitting outside on picnic chairs, drinking wine, laughing and joking. I decide I will feel too much like an outsider if I join them, so I fall into bed with Bear jumping up to lie across my feet. I can't sleep, though, because I'm consumed with envy, which is ridiculous because Leo is perfectly free to do as he likes. I lie there listening to his low voice talking to the women and I wonder if they'll stay over and if one of them will sleep in his bed.

The sound of Leo's guitar slides through the summer darkness, the melody pulling on my heartstrings. Tonight I wonder if I made the right decision in abandoning my old life and moving back to Devon. I have my dad, Cecil and Mary, and I have India and other friends in London, so why do I feel so alone?

Chapter Eleven

Making Hay While the Sun Shines

The next morning, I'm up early to milk the cows, creeping across the yard in order not to wake the occupants of the mobile home. Cecil joins me in the parlour after I've got the cows in, and there is much slow speculation about Leo's guests.

'I did offer to put them up in the house, but Leo declined,' I say.

'I reckon we should get them in for a hearty breakfast, looking at the number of empty bottles on the step outside. A good fry-up will set them right for the rest of the day.'

I'm not sure how Leo's feeling, but one of the cows, Wily – so-called because she's very smart, according to Cecil – is definitely under the weather. I check the volume of milk in the jar once the cluster is off. Her yield is well down.

'She hasn't cleared up her grub,' Cecil observes.

'I'll ask Leo to have a look at her.'

'I don't think you should – he'll have a sore head.'

It does seem unlikely that he's on duty this weekend when he's entertaining friends.

'I'll call the practice and find out who's available. Actually, Cecil, can you do that? only as soon as I've finished here, I'm going to take the tractor up to the seven acres to turn the hay crop so we can bale it before it rains.'

'The weather's going to break soon,' Cecil confirms. 'You get going, my lover. I can finish off here.'

'Thank you. I don't know what I'd do without you.' Stripping off my overalls, I jog back across the yard, past the tractor and the mobile home where the occupants appear to be sleeping peacefully. I duck inside the kitchen and grab two thick slices of bread and some bacon that Mary's left warming on the plate before going back outside and climbing into the tractor.

Unfortunately, Bertha won't start. I try reasoning with her and treating her gently, but it isn't long before I'm out of the cab, yelling insults and aiming an angry kick at one of her tyres, which hurts my toes far more than it hurts her.

'Hey, what's going on?' I turn at the sound of Leo's plaintive voice. He's hanging out of the window of the caravan, wearing the T-shirt he was dressed in yesterday. His complexion is pale and shadowy with dark stubble and his curly hair scruffy. 'Can't you keep the noise down?'

'Have you got a headache?' I enquire rather sharply.

'What do you think? It was a night to remember –

or maybe not.' He rubs at his temple and swears. 'I haven't done that for ages – got that wasted, I mean.'

'It's all right for some. Some of us have to work at the weekend.'

'Have you got a problem with the tractor?'

'She won't bloody well start.'

'Is there anything I can do to help?'

'I'll go and see if I can borrow Guy's while I get the engineer out to fix it. We *really* need a new one.'

'I'll see you later,' Leo says. 'Perhaps I could buy you dinner.'

'I'll be working late by the looks of it.' I leave Leo to his friends and take the Land Rover round to Uphill Farm. I knock at the door of Jennie's Folly, but there's no one at home, and then I remember that it's Saturday, which is market day, and she'll be there with her stall, selling cakes. I walk up to the farmyard at Uphill Farm, the sun warm on my back. The bakery is closed and there's no sign of Guy or his tractor – not that I have any great expectation that he'll lend it to me, unless Jennie can twist his arm.

I decide to call Jennie to see if she knows her husband's whereabouts. I can hear the shouts of the market traders in the background as they try to sell the last of their produce: tomato plants, three for a pound, and pigs' ears on special offer to treat your canine friend.

'I'm sorry for bothering you,' I begin.

'That's okay. I'm finished. How are you?'

'Fine, thanks. I'm looking for Guy. It's a bit of a cheek, but I'm looking to borrow a tractor.' Unfortunately, according to Jennie, Guy is using his tractor to help a friend make hay elsewhere. 'It was a long shot, anyway. I can't see any reason why Guy would be willing to lend us a tractor. We've hardly been good neighbours.'

'Isn't there anyone else you could ask?' Jennie asks. 'Your father must have some contacts.'

'Dad's fallen out with just about everyone he knows. There's my brother and a couple of uncles, but they'll be using their machinery. It's the time of year when everyone's busy . . . and anyway, I want to get the hay turned again today so I can bale it before it rains.'

'I'll stick with baking cakes,' Jennie says. 'Making hay is always such hard work. Guy's out all hours this time of year.'

'There's only one thing for it. I'll have to do it the traditional way, by hand.'

'That'll take you hours.'

'It'll be good for me.'

'I could ask Adam and the girls to help you out later this afternoon. The girls will do it for a bag of carrots for the ponies, but Adam has this inflated idea of his own worth – you'll have to watch out he doesn't sting you.'

'Thanks, but don't worry. How are you anyway?'

'Very well, thank you, although I'm beginning to feel rather tired, even though I still have a couple of months to go. I knew it would be harder now I'm an older mum, but I didn't realise how exhausting it would be. I'm shattered.'

'I don't envy you. I'll catch up with you soon.'

I return to the yard and load a couple of forks into

the back of the Land Rover. My dad comes shuffling out to offer his services but I decline.

'It's good of you to offer, but it's too hot for you today, Dad. I don't want you collapsing on me.'

'You make me feel ruddy useless,' he grumbles. 'I can use a pitchfork. One year I turned forty acres single-handed.'

'That must have been a long time ago. I'm going to get this cut turned by the end of the day. If you'd looked after Bertha properly, I wouldn't have to do it myself.'

'I could do with a new one, but tractors don't grow on trees, Stevie.' He shakes his head sadly. 'I'll never be able to afford it.'

'If the petting farm works out, we might have the money for a tractor,' I say, dreaming of a big shiny red one with air con and somewhere to plug in an iPhone.

'Pah,' he snorts. 'You'll be paying off the loan for that for ever. The next generation of Dunsfords – and the one after that, most likely – will be mired in debt, thanks to you.'

'Everyone's entitled to their opinion,' I say quietly. 'I'm not going to discuss it again. I'd like you to be with me on this, but if you can't, I understand. I'm trying to save Nettlebed Farm for you, for us and for future generations.'

'If there are any future generations to save it for. I can't see you breeding the way you carry on.'

'What do you mean by that?' The skin on the back of my neck prickles with antagonism.

'The way you carry on with men and never settle for one.'

'That's rubbish,' I say hotly. 'I haven't been carrying on with anyone.'

'There was that townie, Nick.'

'I didn't settle for Nick because we weren't right for each other. Could you see him living here in the country?'

Dad smiles ruefully. 'No, but he was loaded, wasn't he? He could have sold that car of his and saved Nettlebed Farm just like that. You didn't have your head screwed on properly when you turned him down.'

'I am not marrying for money. That's crazy.'

'Stupider things have happened. Your brother Ray married into money.'

'I notice he hasn't brought any of his good fortune this way.'

'Why should he?' Dad says sharply. 'We're not a bloody charity. Anyway, I'd never accept money from that turncoat brother of yours. He had everything, and he buggered off, leaving me and your mother to run the farm ourselves.'

'Things could have been so very different if you'd let me stay all those years ago,' I say. 'I'd have taken care of the farm.'

'We had to make a choice between you and Ray. The land couldn't support us and two families if you should both marry. And we were worried that you'd marry some young man in haste and repent at leisure. I've seen what happens when there's a divorce. Farms are sold to pay solicitors and settlements.'

'It doesn't have to be that way. There are such things as pre-nups.'

'Would you have agreed to sign one? No, of course you wouldn't. You would have said it was unnecessary because you were in love. The trouble with you, as I've been saying, is you're always falling in and out of love, Stevie.'

'Hardly,' I protest again.

'What about Leo, an outright foreigner –' by that he means someone who isn't a local, not someone born in another country – 'and a man who's been pretty unpleasant about the whole welfare issue, telling me I don't have a clue how to look after my cattle and recommending I'm prosecuted for animal cruelty? You've virtually moved him in.'

'He needed somewhere to stay and I thought we could do with the rent,' I say weakly.

'I haven't seen any of his money yet.'

'That's because it's gone straight back into paying the bills.' I'm being economical with the truth when it comes to the economics of Leo renting the mobile home. The fact is, I can't bring myself to charge him when I feel as if it should be me paying him to stay there.

'You didn't like it when those people came to see him last night, did you?' Dad taunts me. 'It's all right, Stevie, I know you've got the hots for him, though goodness knows why.'

'Hang on a moment, Leo's been good to us. He's great with the cows.'

Dad merely grunts, turns and walks away, his shoulders stooped.

'Why don't you go and have a bit of a sort-out in the office,' I call after him, but if he hears me he takes no notice and heads back inside the house. If he weren't so infuriating, I would feel sorry for him. It must drive him mad, sitting indoors all day when he used to spend all his time outside, working with the cows or on the fields from dawn till dusk.

A tiny brown wren hops onto the wall beside me. As I move, she flits away again.

Up at the field, I stop the Land Rover in the gateway and grab a pitchfork. I pick up a handful of cut grass from the end of one of the rows that run from one side of the field to the other, and sniff it. It smells sweet, but it's too green to bale yet. Once it's baled we let it mature for a few weeks in the end of the barn, sell some to horse owners and keep some back for the cows. Haymaking is one of those activities that can't be rushed.

Within two hours of turning hay with the fork, I'm burning up, even though I'm stripped down to a cap, vest, shorts and trainers. I pause, looking at the blue haze on the horizon. All the muscles in my arms and legs ache and sweat trickles down my chest and back. A horsefly bites my arm. I flick it away and start again.

It's hard labour, yet soothing. I stop counting the rows of grass. I stop thinking about Leo, Nick and my plans for the farm, losing myself in the rhythm of forking the grass into the air and letting it fall. I work from the hedge on the west side to the copse on the east, and back, listening to the almost human cries of a

197

pair of buzzards as they soar and circle overhead, and the chirriping sounds of the crickets at my feet.

'Hi there, Stevie.'

'Leo?' I turn at the sound of his voice.

'Cecil told me where you were. I thought I'd wander up and find you – I've brought lunch and a cold drink.'

'You didn't have to.' My forehead tightens.

'I know that, but I did.'

'Have your visitors gone already?' I lean on the end of the fork.

'They're busy people.' Leo walks up close and hands me a basket filled with bread and cheese and a jar of home-made chutney. 'Mary packed it for us. I thought we could have something to eat and then I'd give you a hand, although having seen how big this field is, I might have changed my mind.' He's sweating a little already, his face shiny and the roots of his hair damp with perspiration.

'I'm not sure you'll be that much use anyway. You look pretty wrecked.'

'Thanks for your honesty.'

'But if you want some fresh air,' I say, flirting with him, 'you're more than welcome to take over for a while.'

'Lunch first.' Leo takes the basket back, his fingers brushing mine. 'Shall we sit in the shade?'

'Can't you stand the heat?' I tease. I look towards the old oak tree by the gateway. 'There's a piece of tarpaulin in the back of the Land Rover – we can sit on that.' I fetch it and lay it out under the tree, which is wider than it is tall, its spreading branches in full leaf and sprouting small acorns. I sit down and Leo hands me a water bottle filled with iced squash.

Leo sits down too, opens the chutney and spreads the bread, cheese and tomatoes out on a tea towel, making a picnic. There are butterflies – fritillaries of some kind – dancing around the tree. One lands on the tea towel.

'They're beautiful, aren't they?' Leo says.

'They are . . .' I watch for a while, but I can't stop for long. I pick up a piece of bread and a hunk of cheese. I'm starving, but Leo can hardly take a bite.

'You look as if you need the hair of the dog,' I say, amused.

'I haven't had a hangover for ages.' He smiles wryly and I feel a hot rush of sympathy for his condition, although it was entirely self-inflicted.

'Have I offended my landlady in some way?' he asks.

'No,' I say a little too quickly.

'I'm sorry about last night – I didn't think. It's your home. The last thing you want is a load of strangers wandering about.'

'We're going to have to get used to it when we open up the farm to visitors.'

'Are you sure nothing's happened to upset you?'

'Perfectly sure.'

'Cecil told me he was calling the vet out.'

'I assumed you weren't on duty.'

'And you're right, but I've had a look at the cow. What's her name again?'

'Wily. You didn't have to.'

'I didn't have a choice.' He smiles. 'Alex is duty vet today – he rang to see if I could check on her because he's been caught up with an emergency. She's got a slight fever, milk drop and mild bellyache. You know how they grunt sometimes if they aren't right.'

'Poor cow,' I say. 'What can we do?'

'I've given her a shot of antibiotic and painkiller. Now, we'll have to wait and see. I have a hunch, although I can't be sure, that she might have hardware disease.'

'The wire, you mean?'

'That's it. If I was a betting man, I'd put money on her having swallowed some metal object that's beginning to migrate through the stomach wall. I hope you don't mind, but I dosed her with a magnet. Cecil says you don't use them routinely.'

'It's pretty serious, isn't it?'

'If I've got it right and you've caught it in time, the magnet will draw the wire or whatever it is back into the reticulum and keep it there.'

The reticulum is one of the chambers of the cow's stomach. It seems odd to think Wily will spend the rest of her life carrying a magnet around inside her. 'It gives new meaning to the term "animal magnetism",' I say, with a rueful smile.

Leo's appearance is pretty magnetic, drawing my gaze and keeping my attention focused on his shorts and strong, muscular limbs.

'What if it's gone too far?' I ask.

'She'll have to go,' Leo says gently. 'I wouldn't recommend surgery.'

I'm angry now. I blame my father for the rubbish that's been left lying around the farm.

'What about the other cows? Shouldn't they all have magnets too?'

'Prevention's always better than cure.'

'We've never used them before.' I bite my lip. It's another expense I hadn't counted on. 'Please tell me I can administer the magnets myself?'

'You can, but I'll give you a hand. It's all right, I won't tell Alex I'm moonlighting.' Leo raises his hands. 'And don't say, "You don't have to." I know I don't have to. I *want* to.'

'Come on then.' Smiling, I get up and offer my hand to help pull him up. 'No more slacking.' I feel the sensation of the hairs on his arm against my skin, sending a frisson of longing through my loins. So what if there are other women in Leo's life? I'm here now and they are not.

Leo and I work along the rows side by side.

'I've never done this before,' he says, stopping to wipe the back of his hand across his forehead.

'And you a farmer's son,' I comment. I'm glad it's hot – it excuses the flush his presence brings to my cheeks.

'I don't remember making hay. I drove the combine to harvest the wheat.'

'Keep going,' I say.

'You're a hard taskmaster, Stevie.'

By seven, we're almost there, right at the furthest corner of the field where the stream runs along the base of the hedge, widening into a small pool edged with hawthorn and brambles and dammed off by a bank of stones that my brother and I built over one long summer when we were about twelve and fourteen.

I put my pitchfork down and gaze at the water. It's pretty clear – I can see the mud at the bottom – and it's very tempting.

'I'm going for a paddle,' I tell Leo. I take off my trainers and walk to the edge, sliding my toes into the cool, soft mud, and creating swirling red clouds in the pool.

'How deep is it?' Leo asks.

'I remember it being chest deep in the middle, but it might have silted up over the years.'

'I'll test it.' Leo strips off his T-shirt, revealing a well-toned torso with a six-pack. He turns away to slip out of his shorts. 'You don't mind?'

I cover my face. 'I won't look,' I say, peeking between my fingers. I'm ashamed to say that I can't help but notice he has a well-muscled back and tight buttocks. I catch my breath as I watch him run into the water and dive beneath, popping up in the middle of the pool, shaking his head and scattering silver droplets through the air. 'It's deep enough,' he calls. 'Come on in. Don't be shy. I won't bite . . . unless you ask me to.'

'Are you flirting with me now?'

'Maybe.' He ducks under the water again and surfaces to splash water at me. I scream and laugh and pretend to run away, but the temptation to join him is overwhelming.

'Don't look,' I call, stripping down to my bra and pants. A little self-conscious of my body, although I'm looking pretty fit from working on the farm, I wade into the pool; we splash about, racing and diving, until I'm gasping for breath.

'I think it's time I went back,' I say.

'Do you have to?' Leo reaches out for my hand underwater and links his fingers through mine.

'Dad will be wondering where I am. I expect he'll send out a search party soon.' I pause. 'Why don't you come with me? My tea will be waiting for me in the Aga. There's bound to be enough for two.'

'Why don't I take you out again?'

'Because Mary doesn't like wasting food,' I say with mock sternness. 'Come on, eat with me.'

'Thanks, Stevie. Um, are you going to get out first, or shall I? I wouldn't like to offend your sensibilities.'

'Well, I've seen it all before. Not you, I mean, just naked men in general,' I blunder on. Now I've made it sound as if I spend all my time in the company of naked men. 'I'll keep my eyes closed this time.'

'This time? You mean you peeked when I was undressing just now?' He chuckles and pulls me close, holding my waist and kissing me full on the lips, and I'm drowning with desire at the look of lust in his eyes. I slip my arms around his neck as he deepens the kiss.

'Oh, Leo . . .' I breathe, and I don't know how long we embrace, oblivious to the approach of a tractor until it is right alongside the pool, its engine throbbing and the driver hanging out of the cab.

'Oh no, it's Guy,' I groan.

'It's all right. Don't mind me,' he says with a huge

grin on his face. 'Jennie said you were in a bit of a fix, but I see you've managed without me. I was going to lend you the tractor – as a favour to my wife, not you, in case you were under any illusions.'

'Thank you, Guy,' I say, keeping my shoulders under water.

'So you've finished in time to go skinny-dipping, I see. Well, I'm off indoors for my tea,' he says before driving away.

'Ohmigod,' I say. 'This is embarrassing.'

'I think it's a lot of fun.' Leo keeps me close. 'My hangover's almost gone.'

'I'm afraid there's going to be a hangover for me from this incident – I can't imagine Guy will keep it quiet.' Reluctantly, I take a step back. 'I really should be getting back.'

Leo and I wade out of the water together and get dressed, Leo hiding discreetly behind a tree while I slip into my clothes further along the hedge. We walk down the field in the dusk side by side, holding hands.

'Is there any particular reason why you don't want anyone else to know about –' Leo hesitates before continuing – 'us?'

'You know how this place is,' I say lightly, 'the gossips will have us married off by next May Day.'

Leo stops before we reach the gateway. I turn to face him.

'Does it matter?' he asks, reaching out and stroking my hair away from my face. 'I don't care if you don't.'

'I don't,' I murmur, desire pulsing in my throat. At this moment, I don't care about anything except Leo, as he moves in for another electrifying kiss and my blood surges with the heat of passion.

Chapter Twelve

Summer Loving

Leo's been my boyfriend for almost three weeks now – twenty days to be precise, because I'm still count-ing – not only the days but my lucky stars too, because he's wonderful, in my opinion anyway. He's considerate, kind and sexy, although we haven't actually slept togeth-er yet. I know Leo wants to and so do I, but I'm not ready. I can't quite get my head around the idea that he is more than likely to leave at the end of the summer.

I put him out of my thoughts while I'm milking the cows with Jennie's son Adam. I've borrowed him so Cecil can go to the dentist to have his teeth fixed. While we're getting the cows in, Adam confides in me about how he's worried about another baby in the family.

'It should never have happened,' he says, clapping his hands behind Domino's rump to make her move up the lane and out of the hedge where she's found a clump of dandelions.

One of the cars queued up behind us sounds its horn. Adam turns and gives the driver a rude gesture with two fingers.

'Adam!' I say. 'Is that necessary?'

'They have no idea about living in the country,' he grumbles. 'What if they scare the cows and create a stampede? What if they do that behind my sisters and their ponies? They'll cause an accident. Idiots!'

He's right, of course.

'Anyway, this baby,' he goes on. 'It's really annoying. Someone in my group in the sixth form –' I notice he never describes himself as being at school – 'his mum's just had a baby girl and she's driving them mad with her screaming. He says he hasn't had a good night's sleep for three months. He looks half dead and keeps falling asleep in double chemistry. Mind you, I do that anyway, it's so boring.'

'Your mum's used to looking after babies,' I point out.

'What if she's forgotten?'

I whistle Bear back to heel as Adam continues. 'This is all very embarrassing. Mum said it was an accident, but she and Guy must have known what they were doing. Ugh, they're both too old to be doing that kind of thing.'

'Having sex, you mean?' I ask, amused at the way the colour rises up his neck. 'Adam, maybe it wasn't so much of an accident as your mum made out. It's natural when you marry someone to want to have a child with them.'

'But she should be going through the menopause by now.'

'She isn't quite ready for that,' I chuckle. 'She isn't that old.'

'What if the baby makes her sick?'

'She'll be fine.' I try to reassure him.

'She's an older mother,' Adam insists. 'I looked it up on the internet. It isn't right.'

'There could be some benefits to having a baby in the family.'

'I can't see any. I expect I'll get dragged in as the babysitter like I used to with Sophie.'

'You'll have to make sure you get paid.'

He smiles and I smile back, relieved he's feeling a bit better about the whole idea. It must be a bit of a shock when your mother suddenly announces she's having a baby when you're sixteen or seventeen.

'What do Sophie and Georgia think?' I ask.

'Sophie's really excited – well, she's still a baby herself, the way she acts. Georgia isn't sure – she says the only good thing about it is we'll be able to have another pony. She's told Guy to look out for a miniature Shetland for the baby to ride. I don't want another pony – they take up so much time and energy and it's all the girls ever talk about.'

When I come back across the yard, having finished the milking with Adam, paid him generously and turfed the cows back out to graze, I find my dad outside the mobile home, chatting with Leo who's leaning out of the window.

'Young Alex Fox-Gifford can't be working you hard

enough,' Dad says, leaning on his stick. 'It's gone ten o'clock.'

'Dad, leave him alone. How many times?' As I draw close, I go on, 'Haven't you got Dr Mackie coming out in half an hour?'

'Indeed I have. Stevie, I'm being sociable, talking to our tenant.'

'Please go inside now,' I tell him sharply, and he gives me one of his looks before relenting and shuffling back into the house. I apologise to Leo who isn't dressed. At least, he's wearing nothing on his top half, revealing his lightly tanned muscular chest with a generous inverted triangle of hair.

'It's good to see my father getting out and about at last, but I've noticed how he's spending rather a lot of time out here all of a sudden. It's hardly the peace and quiet you were seeking.'

'I expect the novelty will soon wear off.'

'I didn't hear you come back last night,' I say, 'and your car wasn't here when I got up this morning.'

'That's because I didn't get home until about an hour ago.' Leo yawns. 'I don't know why, but it felt like half of Talyton's cows had decided to calve at the same time. Would you like a coffee?'

'Oh, I don't know . . . I feel bad now, chasing my father off.'

'Come in, Stevie.' Leo moves round and opens the door.

How can I refuse him, I think, smiling. I step inside and sit on the sofa in the living area.

'This looks nice. What have you done to it?' I ask.

'I bought a couple of throws from the garden centre to brighten it up. I was passing by the other day and I thought I'd have a quick look around,' Leo says. 'Would you like coffee or tea?'

'Coffee, please.'

'Biscuits?' He pulls a packet of chocolate fingers out of one of the cupboards. 'I've run out of cereal.'

'I love chocolate fingers,' I say, taking two to stave off the pangs of hunger that are so strong I feel sick. 'What are you going to do on your day off?'

'This isn't a day off. I start after lunch. Alex gave me the morning free because I've just had two nights in a row on call when I didn't get to bed. I thought I'd chill for a while. How about you?'

'I'm going into Exeter – I have an appointment at two to see an architect about the plans for the visitor centre.'

'So it's serious now, your idea for diversification?'

'Of course it's serious.'

'So you aren't merely playing at being the lady farmer?' Leo scratches at the stubble on his cheek. 'I thought—'

'You thought wrong,' I interrupt. 'I'm not playing. I'm here for good and I'm going to save Nettlebed Farm one way or another. I'm determined.' Why do I feel I have to prove myself to Leo, I wonder?

'Have another finger,' he says quickly, and I take three this time. Milking cows is hungry work. 'Has the heifer taken you for a walk recently? I haven't seen you out with her.'

'A few times,' I say, smiling. 'She is calming down – she

isn't keen on the exercise, but she'll stand for hours to be brushed.'

'Will she be ready for the show?'

I nod. 'Will you be there? Has Alex asked you to judge the pet show?'

'Alex is going to make the most of the hospitality in the members' enclosure and I'm duty vet – I don't mind because the extra cash is always useful. One of the vets from Otter House deals with the pets. It's a bit of a poisoned chalice, I believe. I've been told there's usually at least one appeal to the show committee.'

We are interrupted by an enormous bang that makes both Leo and me leap up from our seats.

'What the hell is that?'

'It's a gun, a .22, I'd guess,' I say as we try to leave the mobile home via the narrow doorway at the same time.

'After you,' Leo says. 'No, wait.' He grabs me by the shoulders. 'It might be dangerous.'

'It'll be my dad.' I go first, running around the side of the house and in via the lean-to with Leo hot on my heels. I push the living-room door open and there on his armchair, pushed up to the window with his back to us, is my father taking a pot shot at some poor bewildered pheasant that has had the audacity to stroll across the lawn in the bright sunshine.

The shot misses.

'Damn and blast it!' Dad exclaims.

'Dad! Dad! It's me, Stevie.' I reach to touch his shoulder – not a good idea it turns out, because Dad slowly turns to see what is going on, discharging the gun towards the ceiling. Pellets and plaster come showering down.

'Put that gun down,' I yell, furious with him for breaking the law yet again. 'Do you want to go to prison? Because if you do, I won't waste my breath trying to stop you this time. Put it down!'

He breaks the gun and rests it awkwardly across his lap.

'I don't know what's wrong with me. I was always an excellent shot.'

'I expect the pheasant's relieved,' Leo says, reminding me of his presence as I pick up the rifle.

'Where did you get this one from?' I ask.

'I happened upon it.'

'Where was it?'

'Lying around.'

'Dad, where?' I stamp my foot.

'Under the floorboards on the landing,' he mumbles, looking down at his feet. 'I thought I'd check it was still there – and then I picked it up, and it's a lovely rifle and I couldn't resist having one more shot with it before I handed it in to the police. I'm not allowed to keep a gun any longer,' he adds in an aside to Leo. 'I don't know why.'

'Probably because you appear to have a knack of firing indiscriminately,' Leo suggests, looking up at the hole in the ceiling. 'I'll catch you later, Stevie,' he adds, kissing me full on the lips before he leaves.

On my way into Exeter, I drop the rifle and the gun from the cabinet in at the police station and leave them for PC Kevin to deal with. I meet with the architect, but it isn't until later that I can concentrate properly on our mutual vision for the visitor attraction, which unfortunately doesn't coincide with my father's. Dad is sitting in his chair with the television on mute, the pictures flickering in the falling dusk. I switch on the standard lamp so I can see what I'm doing.

'Children don't want petting farms and real animals nowadays,' Dad says. 'They want computers and suchlike – video games and virtual pets.'

'So we fill a niche, going back to nature and learning about the countryside in a fun way.' I pause. 'Dad, do you even know what having fun is?'

'You mean you're going to turn Nettlebed Farm into one giant playground? Over my dead body.'

'Well, don't go and die before you've had a chance to see it,' I say ironically, 'because it's going ahead whether you like it or not.'

'If the planners agree to the change of use and the extra traffic.'

'If they don't agree first time round, I'll keep trying until they do. I've spoken to a couple of people on the council, contacted the planning department to see how to submit an application and been to see the architect about the visitor centre.'

My father snorts with disapproval as I continue. 'The design will be for a timber-clad building with lots of glass to sit in the dip in the field across the drive.'

'I don't know why you don't just go with some breezeblock and corrugated iron for half the price.'

'It's got to look inviting and I want to make a statement.'

'In fact, why do you need a building at all?'

'I've been doing some research – I visited a similar farm in Dorset, I've done some informal market research in Talyton and I've spoken to Jennie. We need cover for when it rains, a tearoom, nappy-changing facilities and somewhere to warm a bottle of milk, eat sandwiches and allow children to let off steam. As well as the animals, we need a couple of fun activities – maybe tractor rides and an adventure play area. Oh, and a gift shop because everyone likes a souvenir.'

'Aren't you rushing into this too fast, Stevie?'

'You won't put me off by stalling me. This project has to be off the ground as soon as possible. I'm planning to open by Easter.' I can see it now: chicks and lambs and an Easter egg hunt.

'What about the finance? I can't afford it.'

'I've got some money behind me.' If necessary, I'll remortgage or sell my flat, but I don't tell my father about that possibility.

'A builder? Who's going to turn this dream into reality?'

'I thought I'd ask DJ Appleyard. I've seen his truck around town.'

'You want to watch him,' says Dad. 'I wouldn't touch him with a bargepole. He's known as the builder who starts and doesn't finish.'

'I don't have much choice. I've rung around and he's the only builder in the area who has a gap in his schedule.'

'Then you should be wondering why.'

214

'He's between jobs. He has a team on standby ready to start as soon as I get the go-ahead.'

'Has he given you a quote?'

'We haven't got that far yet. I've got to wait for the architect.'

'So you've commissioned him already?'

'Her. Yes.'

'A female architect? A woman?' My father shakes his head in disapproval. 'What is this country coming to?'

'It's nothing new,' I point out.

'It is to me.'

'I'm not going to argue with you. I'm going upstairs to change.'

Dad calls for me as I return.

'What is it?' I say, fastening the press-studs on my overalls in preparation for doing the milking.

'If you want to make yourself useful, you can get rid of that awful woman.' He hovers in the hall, leaning on his crutches behind one of the curtains so he can look out of the window without being seen.

'Which woman?'

'Fifi Green. She's just parked in the yard. Everyone says she means well, but I can't stand her. I lost any respect I had for her when I found out she'd been carrying on with all and sundry in spite of her being a married woman. I don't want to sit listening to her opinions.'

'I can imagine.' Two opinionated people together – it doesn't bear thinking about. 'I can't stop, I've got to go and get the cows in.'

'Cecil can do that.'

I follow my father's gaze out onto the farmyard where a woman in her sixties, dressed up in a royal-blue suit and heels, is making her way gingerly towards the house, avoiding the puddles and mud. She holds a coordinating handbag in one hand and clutches a spotty blue-and-white chiffon scarf across her nose, as if to protect her from some particularly foul stench.

I recognise her. She's lived in Talyton St George for as long as I can remember, running the Garden Centre on Stoney Lane with her husband, creating a goldmine selling a range of goods from plants and greenhouses to wall art and slippers. If anyone has made a success of diversification it's Fifi Green, at times lady mayoress, local busybody and chairperson of the WI and Talyton Animal Rescue.

The dog barks from the lean-to before she reaches the front door and gives it an authoritative rap with her knuckles. The doorbell doesn't work.

'What shall we do?' Dad asks in a whisper.

'Pretend we aren't here?' I say dryly. 'For goodness' sake, she isn't going to eat you.'

'Rumour has it she'll have you for breakfast and now me being a widower . . . Your mum would have seen her off.'

'You can't be serious.'

'There was a time – at one of the Fox-Giffords' New Year parties up at the manor – when Fifi grabbed me and took advantage under the mistletoe.'

'When you say "took advantage", what exactly do you mean?' I ask, prepared to be suitably outraged by the woman's exploits.

'She kissed me.'

'Oh, Dad, that's what everyone does when they've had a bit to drink.'

'It was in front of your mother.' He shakes his head. 'I tell you, I took her straight home.'

I smile because my mother was less of a prude than my dad imagined. My father is not good with women. He doesn't understand them, so it's no wonder he ran a mile if Fifi really did come on to him. A little impatient, I open the door. We don't have many visitors to the farm and it's better to have her on our side if possible.

'Hello, Fifi,' I say. 'Come in.'

'Hello, Stevie.' She wipes her feet on the mat inside the door. 'I'm not stopping for long.'

'Stay as long as you like. Would you like tea?'

'Yes, please. Is Tom, your father, at home?'

'Of course.' I turn to include him, but he's disappeared into the living room, the clacking of his crutches against the woodblock floor evidence of his rapid escape.

'Come on in.' I show her through, where her gaze immediately falls on the holes in the ceiling. 'There was a bit of an accident.' I smile, but Fifi doesn't smile back. She turns to my father.

'Don't get up on my account,' Fifi says, goading him as he sits there, hardly acknowledging her presence. 'Tom, how are you?'

'Not so bad,' he grunts. 'Yourself?'

'Very well, thank you.'

'I'll go and get tea,' I say.

I make three cups of basic tea-bag tea and cut three

217

slices of Jennie's cider cake – she dropped it round to the farm as a free sample to remind me about her desire to supply the tearoom. I return to find Fifi chatting and my father gazing pointedly at the clock on the mantelpiece. I pass the tea and cake around before settling down on the sofa. It crosses my mind that it's the same sofa – loud with blue swirls – that James and I used to cuddle up on when he came round to the farm to see me.

'We don't have many callers,' I say, trying to break the ice. It's true. There's Jack, James, Leo, the tanker driver, the AI man, the mechanic and the guy who delivers the feed, but no one who comes into the house to socialise.

'But I hear you are hoping to encourage many more visitors to Nettlebed Farm,' Fifi says, as Bear comes trotting across the carpet and stops right beside her to give himself a good shake. Fifi grimaces.

'Bear, come here,' I say.

'I've spoken to the planning department and raised the issue at the recent council meeting—'

'I'm sure you have,' I cut in.

Fifi stares at me, her lips pursed. 'I have a duty to ensure this area maintains its identity as a tranquil country retreat for us, the local people, to enjoy as we always have done.' She warms to her theme. 'It's entirely wrong to encourage the plebs. I'm sure you realise this enterprise is completely inappropriate.'

'Hardly,' I say. 'We're in the middle of a popular tourist spot. It would be mad not to take advantage of it.'

'You won't make much money out of stroking animals. Why would people want to pay for that when they can go to the Sanctuary and see animals for free?'

'Grockles don't get up in the morning and say, "let's have a day out at the rescue centre,"' Dad says, joining in.

'Whatever you say, I shall be voting against your planning application.'

'Fifi, you have to understand there is no other way for the farm to survive. We're facing financial ruin. This is the only way out for us.'

'Have you considered how much extra traffic there'll be to clog up the lanes? It will be a nightmare travelling anywhere, and I can't begin to imagine how much it will affect the environment. We'll all have asthma from the fumes.'

'I wasn't aware you had any concern for the environment, Fifi. Look at the car you drive.'

'That's a great big huge gas-guzzler if ever I saw one,' Dad says.

'I need a four-by-four to get about,' Fifi argues.

'That's never been off-road.' Dad leans forward, spilling half his tea. 'It's far too clean and shiny.'

'We can address the traffic issues,' I say hastily. 'Firstly, this is a small-scale venture. We aren't expecting hundreds of visitors every day. Secondly, we're planning to create extra lay-bys along the lane where drivers can pull in to let other vehicles pass, and thirdly, we're improving access to the farm by altering the entrance to the drive.'

'That's all very well,' Fifi says dismissively. 'What about all the other nuisance?'

'What nuisance? I don't think you understand what we're planning. This attraction is a petting farm where parents and carers can bring their children to meet the animals, play in the fresh air and learn about the countryside at the same time as having fun.'

'What about the diseases?' Fifi looks aghast as Bear sits in the middle of the carpet, licking his private parts. 'As you know, I love animals, but only in their place.'

'I've looked into the health and safety aspects of setting up this kind of business . . .' Thanks to Leo, I think. 'Fifi, I'm not stupid.'

'You really haven't thought this through.'

'You're wrong there,' Dad says. 'Stevie's thought of little else since she came back.'

'She hasn't thought about the effect on other local businesses. People will go bankrupt because of you. Can you really have that on your conscience?'

'There's one other farm that's diversified into a similar enterprise, but they've concentrated more on building an adventure play area than the animals. I really can't see there's a problem.'

'There's none so blind who cannot see.' Fifi sips at her tea and wrinkles her nose. 'This town cannot possibly support another tearoom.'

'You mean you're worried about your profits at the garden centre. It won't affect you. The tearoom is for our visitors,' I say adamantly.

'There are only so many cream teas you can eat while

220

on holiday,' Fifi argues. She's like an old battleship that won't alter its course.

'I will fight for this,' I say.

'You're a fool, Stevie. You both are if you think it will work.' Fifi gets up to leave.

I look at Dad and he smiles. 'Stick to your guns, girl.'

'And by the way, you're wasting your time thinking you can run a tearoom when you can't make a decent cup of tea. What is it? It tastes more like some supermarket brand than a good Lapsang Souchong.'

'Oh no,' I say. 'It was Assam, fair trade, organic and handpicked.'

'Oh? Oh, was it really?'

Dad raises one eyebrow, his good one. I give him a shake of my head in warning. Don't say anything, but he has a nervous tic and I start to think he's having another stroke.

'I'm surprised you didn't pick that up when your palate is so discerning,' I say, turning back to Fifi.

'I must have a touch of hay fever,' she sniffs. 'It dulls the senses.'

I notice my dad slumped over in his seat.

'Are you all right?' I say, standing up. 'Shall I call the doctor?'

'Not yet,' he says with a gasp.

'Fifi, I think you'd better go,' I say quickly.

'Oh dear,' she says. 'I hope I haven't—'

'Dr Mackie says I mustn't have any stress whatsoever,' my father goes on, catching his breath and rolling his eyes.

'Goodbye, Tom. Goodbye, Stevie.'

When she has gone, my father grimaces and guffaws with glee.

'Dad, were you putting it on?' I ask, both amused and annoyed.

'You really got her there with the tea, Stevie. Assam my ass! Interfering woman. I can't stand her.'

'I thought you might be on her side,' I say, goading him.

'If Fifi doesn't want the petting farm to go ahead, I'm all for it.'

'I'm worried though.' I bite my lip. 'Fifi has a lot of influence where it matters. She won't be the only one to object.'

'Don't give up too soon, Stevie. I'm on your side – blood is thicker than water, after all. It's a good thing you've come back and shaken us up. Why should we give up on our project because people like Fifi are out to guard their own interests? I can't see what they're fussing about anyway. Where's the harm in a little more traffic? If it upsets those smug gits on the council, then I'm ready for a fight.'

My father's decision to fight with me, not against, is one less obstacle to overcome, and I smile to myself as he goes on with a wicked gleam in his eye. 'Let the Battle of the Cream Teas commence.'

'Just one thing though,' I say. 'This war between you and Guy?'

'It isn't all-out war, it's merely a skirmish,' Dad says.

'It seems pretty serious. You haven't done anything in particular to upset him?'

'Nothing at all. Look at me, Stevie. I'm a sick old man.'

'Let's have less of the self-pity,' I cut in.

'If he was a true neighbour, he would have come round to see if I was all right. He'd have offered to cut down them there weeds himself instead of making a right royal row about it.'

'So there's nothing else you've forgotten to mention?'

'I don't think so.' My father taps his temple. 'I promise you, I haven't lost my marbles.'

'I can't help wondering if you've conveniently mislaid them though.'

'Is there another cup of Assam in the pot?' he says, changing the subject.

'I'll go and see.' After tea and milking, I spend some time bonding with Milly before I give her a bath. I change into a waterproof top and trousers, collect up whitening shampoo, conditioner and a couple of sponges from the office and tie her outside in the collecting yard so I can run a hosepipe from the hot tap in the dairy. It doesn't seem fair to use cold water. I don't want to make her hate me before the show.

I fill up a couple of buckets and get started, rinsing, lathering and scrubbing the muddy bits, including her knees, with a soft brush. Milly likes the sensation of the brush, but hates the water dripping from her flanks. She fidgets and stamps her feet.

'I've seen it all now,' Leo says, joining me. 'You should put that on YouTube.'

'What? A clip of the lady farmer bathing her cow?'

'You're wet,' he grins, as Milly whisks her tail.

223

I take the hose, check the temperature of the water and rinse out the suds from the heifer's coat.

'What was the point of that?' Leo teases. 'Now she's clean and you're dirty.'

I flick the end of the hose at him, wetting his boots.

'Hey, what's that for?' He chuckles.

'For making fun of what is a serious endeavour,' I say brightly. 'Tomorrow is Milly's big day.' I use a sweat-scraper to remove the excess moisture from her coat and take an elastic band from my pocket. 'I've just got to plait the switch at the end of her tail and I'm almost done.'

'Why on earth do you want to do that?'

'To make it look curly for the show.'

'What's to stop her getting mucky again overnight?' Leo asks.

'I have a blanket for her, an old pony rug – Jennie lent it to me. I've also made her up a pen with the deepest bed of clean straw you've ever seen, so here's hoping.'

'If I can't get away to watch you tomorrow, I'll be thinking of you.' Leo pauses, reluctant to leave. 'Would you like to come over for a nightcap when you've finished?'

'I'd love to. I'll be with you soon.' I make sure Milly is tucked up for the night before quickly washing my hands and changing into a clean shirt and jeans. I head across to the mobile home where the door is open and the lights are on.

I knock as I spring up the steps. 'Leo, I'm here.' I move along the hallway to the living area. 'Leo?' I pause, catching the sound of snoring, and there he is, still fully dressed and wearing his boots, sprawled across the sofa. My heart melting with tenderness for him – and pride because he works so very hard – I grab his duvet from the bedroom and spread it gently over him, tucking it around his shoulders before I press my lips to his cheek. The snoring stops for a moment and he utters a sigh.

I'm tempted to wake him.

'Leo?' I whisper, but the snoring starts again, so I leave him to sleep.

Chapter Thirteen

Let the Cow See the Bull

It's a very early start, even for me, on the morning of the show. I wake feeling sick with excitement and I wonder how many other farmers are feeling the same. I help Cecil milk the cows; they are a little disgruntled at being kept indoors overnight because we thought we'd get through them quicker if we didn't have to get them in from the field. Wily kicks out harder and with a better aim than usual, and the ones who are slow to let their milk down are slower than ever.

'I think it was a mistake,' I tell Cecil as we let them out across the drive into the field where they trot away, bucking, as if they've never seen grass before.

'It had to be done, otherwise you wouldn't have time to give Milly a brush before the class.' Cecil shuts the gate behind the herd and ties it up with a piece of rope. 'I expect you'll see Ray at the show today. That'll be the first time since you've been back, won't it?'

'I've spoken to him on the phone. To be honest, I'm looking forward to seeing him again, but I'm also slightly apprehensive. I went to his wedding, I saw him at Mum's funeral and we exchange Christmas cards and that's about it. I wonder if we'll feel like strangers.'

'You'll be fine,' Cecil says. 'For all that happened, you never did seem to bear any resentment towards your brother.'

'I resented the fact that he was a boy while I was *only* a girl, but he was always on my side,' I point out. 'He came to blows with Dad.'

'I recall the fight. It was on the day you left the farm, and I had to break it up, if I remember rightly.' Cecil touches the bridge of his nose. 'Tom broke my hooter.'

We return to the farmyard where Leo appears to be sleeping still, to bathe the heifer and load her and her show kit into the trailer.

I check and recheck the gear we need: feed, hay, buckets; paperwork, including Milly's passport without which she can't travel; a leather head-collar and lead strap. Also Milly has her show box with her brushes, curry comb and spare towels, while I have a set of clean clothes including a white shirt, tie and dark trousers and clean shoes.

'Are you ready yet?' Cecil asks.

'I'm ready,' I reply. 'I'll fetch Dad and Mary.' They're coming with us while Bear stays at home as guard dog. I wonder about waking Leo, and decide against it. I don't think he'll have to be at the show until later.

Half an hour later, I'm driving the Land Rover and

trailer into the showground, heading to the exhibitors' parking. At the show, Milly has a pen of her own in the cattle barn, into which Cecil throws down a bale of fresh straw. My father, leaning on his crutches, supervises, while Mary is sent to buy coffee and bacon butties.

'Watch out,' says my father. 'Here comes Guy Barnes with his shorthorns.'

Guy turns up with his wild-eyed heifer and a dairy cow with her calf at foot. Georgia is with him too.

'Hello,' I say. 'How are you?'

'Reassured now I know that Uphill Farm's going to take best heifer in show today,' Guy says cheerfully. 'I don't know why you bothered to bring her really. I mean, she isn't a bad specimen. She's looking better than when I saw her last, but she isn't going to beat Jessie J here.'

I know it's just gamesmanship on his part, but I can see my father is bristling with annoyance. Milly is in proportion, with a good top-line and shapely udder, and so is Jessie J.

'You aren't going to park your cattle next door?' Dad grumbles.

'Why, are you worried we're going to show you up?' Guy says, entering the pen beside ours.

'Dad, I've left the brass polish in the Land Rover. Would you mind?' I ask, aware it will take him a while to fetch it and keep him from starting a row with Guy.

'Have you got the key, Stevie?' he says.

'It isn't locked.' I watch him go before turning to Guy and Georgia. 'Hi, Georgia, I thought you'd be riding your horse.'

'We're showjumping later and Sophie's doing the mounted games with her pony. Well, she's reserve actually because Bracken isn't very fast.'

'Good luck. I'd better be getting on.' I text Leo in case he's forgotten to get up before I slip the leather head-collar on in place of the rope halter and apply a little hairspray along the hair on Milly's back. The scent of beauty products almost overwhelms the sweet aroma of cow.

'Let's make you even more beautiful,' I tell her, looking through the lotions and potions in the show box – ones my mum used to use, like Vaseline and an ancient pot of Oil of Olay. 'Because you're worth it,' I say to Milly as I dab a tiny smear of it onto her shoulder to see if it adds a miracle shine. 'I'm not sure quite what to do with it,' I say to Cecil. 'Can you remember?'

'I wasn't privy to your mother's titivating,' he says. 'Are you sure that isn't her make-up for when she went into the ring?'

'Oh!' I laugh out loud, releasing the tension. 'I hadn't thought of that. I assumed it was for the cow.'

Mary brings coffee and she and Cecil drift off to find my father, leaving me to continue to get ready.

Jack Miller appears to say hello as I'm giving Milly's coat a final brush.

'Are you here for work or pleasure?' I ask him.

'I'm working. How are you?'

'Well, thank you.' I drop the brush back into the show box.

'That heifer's looking good,' Jack says.

'So she should be. I've been working on her for a couple of months now.'

'I'm glad to see it.' Jack moves closer. 'I'm pleased we didn't have to prosecute your father in the end. It was lucky you came back when you did.'

'Better late than never, I suppose.' I'll never forget the shame and embarrassment of seeing the cows in such a state and having to hear Leo's opinion of my father's lack of care.

'I hear through the grapevine that you're planning to create a petting zoo at Nettlebed Farm.'

'You heard right, except it's going to be more of a farm than a zoo, with sheep, goats, chickens, rabbits and guinea pigs, and maybe a donkey.'

'There's a lot of opposition to your plans,' Jack observes, glancing towards Guy, who's speaking with a man wearing a trilby and cricket whites. 'That's one of the local councillors. Guy's been lobbying everyone, trying to influence the outcome of your planning application.'

'I'm waiting for a decision, but there are all sorts of delays.' I take out the plait at end of Milly's tail so the hair looks crimped. 'Guy won't win. I will fight for it. And you needn't worry about the animals – we'll have the highest standards of welfare.'

'Of course that will come under scrutiny because of the farm's recent history. Considering the circumstances, I think it would be wise to involve Animal Welfare right from the beginning. That way, there'll be no comeback,' Jack smiles. 'And it should help your cause with the locals.'

'Thanks, Jack. That's very thoughtful of you.'

'I figure it's the best chance you have of saving the farm. It could also be good for Talyton Animal Rescue – which my fiancée Tessa and I are heavily involved with – if you sourced some of the animals from there. We have so many rescues and abandoned animals of all shapes and sizes that we don't know what to do with them. The Sanctuary is filled to overflowing and we're getting to the point where we can't take any more. The last thing we want to do is to turn animals away.' He pauses. 'If you want rabbits, we have plenty.'

'Do you have a donkey?' I say lightly.

'You would need to take on a pair,' he says. 'We don't like to re-home them singly.'

'If we get the planning permission for the project, I'd love to choose rescue animals.' We could offer a donation and it would be good publicity for both the Sanctuary and Nettlebed Farm. 'The only thing is, they would have to be good to handle.'

'Many of them are,' Jack says. 'Tessa is extremely careful about matching animals to their prospective owners because she doesn't want them coming back if at all possible. Anyway, I'd better let you get on. Good luck, Stevie. Let the best heifer win!'

'Thank you.' I get changed and I'm ready to go. Guy is ready too and we lead the heifers out of the barn and along the grassy walkway to the main arena, where a team flying birds of prey in a display have lost one of their star performers, a Harris hawk.

'He's gone,' says Cecil who's come along to check I'm okay. 'I think he got stage fright.'

It's true that the crowd in the grandstand and around the perimeter of the arena is large and noisy. In fact, the applause as we enter the ring unnerves Milly, and she tries to trot after Guy and Jessie J, rolling her eyes and holding her head high, tugging at the strap in my hand.

'Steady there,' I tell her. I keep half an eye out for Leo and Ray, and cast a glance across to the members' area, catching sight of my father sitting in a chair with Mary beside him, but I'm too busy hanging on to Milly to worry about the rest of the audience. I walk clockwise around the ring, leading her from her left-hand side to show her off.

The judge, in a baggy tweed suit, shirt and tie, wearing a badge and sporting a carnation in his button-hole, stands in the centre of the arena with a steward, who calls us into a line according to the judge's instructions. To my delight, Milly is called in first ahead of Jessie J. Guy frowns at me. I ignore him.

'I remember your mother,' says the judge.

'I believe that's favouritism,' Guy mutters, and I think he isn't doing himself any favours, criticising the judge.

'Whichever animal wins, it will be fair and square,' says the judge. 'Are you casting aspersions? Only I'm an honourable man.'

Guy falls silent, but his face is flushed and his fingers tense on his heifer's strap.

I lead Milly forwards and persuade her to stand properly with one hind foot in front of the other for the judge to study her closely, comparing her conform-ation with his interpretation of the breed standards.

Milly fidgets at first, but she soon settles down. Jessie J is a reformed character too, and I sense the result is too close to call as we're sent to walk around the ring again while the judge makes his final decision.

As I walk, breathing the scent of bruised grass and fresh dung, my heart beats faster. Will we win? I didn't realise how much I wanted it until now.

'Stevie. Stevie!' Guy is shouting at me. 'They're calling you. Dopey cow,' he adds in a low voice when I realise Milly is being called in first in the final line-up. I try to remain cool, calm and professional when I'd rather be screaming and yelling with happiness. I've done it. I've done it for Nettlebed Farm and my father, but most of all I've done it for Mum.

My eyes fill with tears as I stand beside Milly and scratch at her withers.

'Congratulations,' mutters Guy as Jessie J is pulled in second.

'Thank you.' I shake Guy's hand and thank the judge when he awards me the winner's rosette and silver shield.

'You handle that heifer just like your mother used to,' he says. 'I'll see you later.'

I frown just as the photographer who's with Ally Jackson from the *Chronicle* takes a picture of me and the winning heifer.

'I'm judging the championship,' he explains, and I smile to myself as I realise that, as one of the first two in the class, I'm going to have to brave the ring all over again.

Milly is in her element in the championship class,

flirting with the top bulls in the show. They look pretty cool with their hair slicked up into quiffs with gel as they lumber around the arena with rings through their noses and two handlers each. Once again, Milly is the winner, the Supreme Champion in Show. This time, after she's been awarded her rosette and sash and perpetual challenge trophy, she stands for her photo to be taken, but loses the plot when a group of ring stewards turn up with a tractor and trailer, bringing the poles and wings to make a course of showjumps for the next event in the main arena.

As I lead her around on her lap of honour, the loudspeakers crackle into life and blast out some celebratory marching music, sending the cattle wild. Milly decides she's had enough and gallops from one end to the other, towing me along on the end of the lead strap and starting a stampede of cattle towards the exit. The commentator appeals for calm as the crowd hold their breath. It's a warm, sunny day anyway, and the sweat is trickling down the back of my neck as I run as fast as I can, trying to keep up.

'Milly, come back,' I yell when I have to let go and watch her disappearing off into the distance back towards the cattle barn.

'Well, she didn't win a prize for her manners,' Guy says, still gamely hanging on to Jessie J. 'And she can run faster than you, Stevie.' He hesitates. 'If I wasn't such a busy man, I might just have gone and lodged an appeal.'

'What would you want to do that for? You're a poor loser, Guy.'

'I reckon your father's had a hand in nobbling the judge. I'm sure that was fixed.'

'I wish you and Dad would settle this feud,' I say, hurrying along beside him. It's tedious.'

'He started it,' Guy says. 'He has no regard for anyone else.'

'There's no need to carry it on though. He's a sick man and he's getting on a bit. Can't you let it go?'

'I don't see why I should.'

'Is it you who's been spreading the gossip about our plans for the farm?'

'It's common knowledge,' Guy responds. 'Everyone I've spoken to, including the local councillor, is against it.'

'I saw you talking to him. What did you offer him to vote against us?' I ask lightly.

"I should get after that heifer of yours, if I were you," Guy says, sounding amused, and I turn my attention back to Milly. She and her fellow escapees have headed off into the horsebox parking, where they're frightening some of the kids and their ponies. I grab Milly and tell her off, but she's more interested in the grass now.

'Hi there, Stevie. Let me give you a hand.' I look up to find my brother Ray beside me, with his familiar lopsided smile. He looks heavier than before in his rugby shirt and cords. He's shaved his head and grown a small beard, giving him the appearance of an old goat. 'I've been looking out for you.' He kisses me on both cheeks. 'It's great to see you at last. I should have tried to meet up with you before, but I've been working flat out.'

'Same here.' I smile back. I've been slightly miffed that my brother hasn't shown much interest in saving Nettlebed Farm, but now we have a chance to catch up and chat about my plans. 'Did you watch any of the cattle classes?'

'I wasn't watching, but I heard the results. Congratulations.' He gazes down at his brogues and adds in a gravelly voice, 'It reminds me of how Mum . . .'

'I know.' I reach out and touch his hand.

'Let me help you get the heifer back to her pen,' he says, collecting himself.

'Thanks. I can manage her now. She didn't like the noise in the arena,' I say, but Ray clips a lead rope to the head-collar on the other side of Milly's head.

'Let's go, sis,' he says.

'Ray, where are you going?' calls a woman's voice from one of the lorries. 'We need you right here.'

'I'll be back in two secs,' he calls back.

'You're still under the thumb, I see.'

'Gabrielle likes to think she wears the trousers . . . How is it going?' Ray asks as we walk Milly back to the cattle barn. 'How's Dad?'

'You should ask him yourself. He's in the members' enclosure with Mary.'

'You know we don't get along.'

'Mum would knock your heads together if she knew you hadn't spoken since the funeral.'

'Well, she doesn't . . .'

'In here,' I say, directing Milly back into her pen.

'I'd better get back.' Ray wipes his palms on his

cords. 'The boss will be waiting for me. Why don't you come along too? The girls would like to see you again. They're competing in the next class in ring two.'

'Why not?' I wish I knew my nieces – Ray's daughter and stepdaughter – better. They're riding their show ponies and are dressed up in jackets and matching hats with ribbons in their hair. The ponies have diamond patterns brushed into the hair on their gleaming rumps and their hooves are shiny with oil.

'Here's Auntie Stevie,' says Ray.

'It's the auntie with the boy's name,' says the older girl, who is a most precocious nine year old.

'I'm sorry,' says Ray. 'Please apologise, Alisiana.'

'I'm sorry you have such a funny name,' she says seriously, which makes me laugh.

'It doesn't matter. It's short for Stephanie.'

'Mummy doesn't like us to shorten our names,' the other girl, the equally precocious five-year-old Christiane, points out. 'She says it's common and if you've been given a beautiful name, you should use it.'

'Are you two taking my name in vain?' interrupts Gabrielle, the girls' mother. Several years older than Ray, she's dressed in a tweed suit and a hat with a purple ribbon, which matches the ones in the girls' hair, and carries a short showing cane. 'Hello, Stevie. It's lovely to see you again.'

She's being polite, I think.

'Ray, go and get their numbers,' she orders as she dabs a little Vaseline around one of the pony's nostrils. 'And don't forget to bring the goats'-hair brush this time. And have you got the lead rein, the leather one?'

'If there's a prize for the best turned-out mother, she'll win it,' Ray says to me as he runs off to do his errands, trotting along on tiptoe, pointing his feet. It's comical.

'Ray, I do believe you're evolving into a show pony,' I laugh when he returns.

'What makes you say that, sis?'

'You're beginning to move like one.'

'I am not.'

'You are.'

'Not!' Ray grins as he reaches out to ruffle my hair with a grooming brush. I duck away. 'The trouble is you have too much imagination.' He grows serious. 'I think you've been letting it run away with you with this project.'

'I have to do something,' I say.

'Forget about keeping animals, Stevie – they cost a fortune in care and maintenance. I should know.' He looks towards the ponies. 'You should develop the farm buildings – extend the cottage and the house, transform the cowshed and nursery, and sell off a couple of acres with each dwelling. You could get back to London and our father could afford a suite in a nursing home.'

'Ray, how could you?' I say, pained by his insensitivity. 'Dad would hate it. It would probably kill him.'

'What's come over you?' Ray asks. 'I didn't think you'd be all that bothered about what happened to him. He hasn't exactly treated you well in the past.'

'If you saw him you'd understand. He's half the man he was.'

'Is he sorry? Has he ever apologised to you?' Ray stares at me through narrowed eyes. '. . . I thought not.'

'Someone has to look after him,' I say stubbornly. 'I'm doing it because it's what Mum would have expected. And he is my father . . .'

'He is father to me in the biological sense only.' Ray's tone is bitter like orange peel. 'I've disowned him pretty much, as he's disowned me and my family. I could take it if it weren't for Christiane, but he refuses to even acknowledge his own granddaughter, the old bastard.' Ray pauses for a moment before his lips curve into a half-smile. 'Mary and Cecil would say that we're all alike, you, me and him.'

'I know. Ray, I'm going to go ahead with the petting farm, whatever your opinion, but it would be wonderful if I knew I could count on your support.' I feel as though he owes me something for being given the farm while I was rejected, but it seems he can't even bring himself to do that.

'I wish you nothing but the best, Stevie, but it'll never work. You're on a hiding to nothing.'

'Thanks a lot,' I say. Ray picks up on my sarcasm.

'I'm sorry, but I'm not going to pretend. As I said on the phone, I'll remain a sleeping partner, keeping my share of the farm. However, I shan't be investing in your project. Shall we go and watch the girls?' he says, abruptly changing the subject, but making it clear I'm on my own when it comes to taking the plans for Nettlebed Farm forward.

I'll prove it to him though. I'll show all the cynics and doubters that my idea is a winner, I think as I watch the class with Ray, who's delighted when his daughters take first and second place. It seems effortless. The girls appear to do nothing but hang on in the saddle as their proud steeds perform figures of eight and flying changes in front of the judge. As soon as the class is over, my brother heads for the beer tent.

'Gabrielle will be wanting champagne,' Ray says. 'Would you like to join us?'

'No, thank you. I'm going to have a look around.' I'm also hoping I'll run into Leo.

'I'm sorry for not being on your side when it comes to your plans, Stevie,' my brother repeats. 'It's nothing personal. It's just business.'

'Okay,' I say, biting my lip. It feels personal . . .

'It's been good to catch up with my big sister. We must spend some more time together soon.'

'We must,' I agree, but I'm not sure either of us means it.

'Call me,' he says, before he disappears inside the tent.

I buy candyfloss and doughnuts, and take a stroll through the WI marquee where the atmosphere, laden with the scent of rose petals and lavender, is tense as the ladies – and a couple of gentlemen, I notice – await the results of the Victoria sponge competition. Jennie is judging, tasting a piece of one of the cakes. Giving her a quick smile, I duck out again. I check out the fancy hens, the sheepshearing and farriery before returning to the main arena to

240

wait for the Pony Club mounted games to begin. It's always good for a laugh.

'Hi, Stevie.'

I turn to find Leo at my side, pinching my bum. Grinning, I lean up and kiss him on the lips.

'I came to find you last night, but you were asleep,' I say.

'You should have woken me,' he says with a wicked twinkle in his eye. 'We could have had some fun.'

'It was tempting, but you looked so peaceful . . .' I look him up and down. He looks cool in a shirt and tie. I offer him a doughnut.

'Thanks,' he says, taking one. 'I saw you in the arena with the heifer.'

'You didn't see her gallop off, did you? I was so embarrassed.'

'I missed that. I saw you having your photo taken with Milly. Congratulations.'

'Thank you. Have you been busy?'

'I've dealt with an overheated guinea pig, a fancy chicken with a limp and a pony that got kicked on the lorry.'

'How did you treat the guinea pig?' I ask.

'With wet flannels and a prescription for extra vitamin C. He didn't half squeak, which I thought was a good sign. I don't normally see guinea pigs.' Leo pauses to lick sugar from the corner of his mouth. 'I think he overheated because he was left in his carrier in the sun while waiting for the Pet Show to start. He had to pull out, which is a shame because he had a good chance – he had a hairstyle a lot like mine.' Leo grins. 'I'm blagging it. What do I know about showing small furry animals?'

'What happened to the pony?'

'It's one of your neighbour's ponies, Bracken.'

'Poor Sophie won't be able to ride in the mounted games.'

'She won't because Bracken's still sedated. I had to stitch her up. It'll be a while before she can be ridden again.' Leo pauses, cocking his head to one side. 'Did I hear my name?'

'I don't know. Did you?' I listen for the tannoy announcement.

'Yes, that's me, Vet on Call,' Leo says, tapping the badge pinned to his tie. 'Can we catch up later, darling?' He fans his fingers across the small of my back and pulls me close for a kiss.

'How about tonight?'

'I'm not sure. Justin, Alex's assistant, is away for a few days, so it's just me and Alex juggling the on-call. I'm off tomorrow. I could take you out for lunch and then I'll help you with the afternoon milking to give Cecil a break.'

'Help or hinder?' I say with a sigh of happiness as he releases me to go and attend to a sheep at the shearing display that has met with the equivalent of either a razor cut or shaving rash.

'A bit of both, I hope.' He chuckles as he walks away, and I wonder how long the milking will take with Leo involved when we can hardly keep our hands off each other.

It's late when we return to Nettlebed Farm, and Cecil

worried about me. I'm afraid Leo will break my heart too, which is why I've been holding back. I desperately want him to make love to me – I can hardly think about anything else – but I know that if I give myself to him completely, I'll be utterly committed to him and the idea of him leaving would be unbearable.

June drifts into July and Leo and I get to know each other better. We can chat about anything and every-thing – apart from his nephew and his plans. Although I give him plenty of opportunity to talk about Jonas if he wants to, it's clear it's an area of his life that he keeps locked away in his heart, and when it comes to Leo moving away, I can't bring myself to discuss it with him for fear it will be bad news for our relationship, or that he'll think I'm trying to put pressure on him to stay. For the moment, I want to enjoy being together, to be happy, not filled with angst about the future.

As well as spending time with Leo, I organise the public meeting, sending out invitations to everyone I can think of and advertising it in the newsagent's window. I order sherry from Mr Lacey of Lacey's Fine Wines and cupcakes from Jennie, having checked I won't be offending Mary by not asking her to make her special-occasion fruit cake.

I obtain a copy of the plans for the Shed, the new building, from the architect, and put them up on a board in the living room, along with details of the planning application, the animals we're intending to have and the accommodation James is building for them in anticipation. I pay Adam to tidy the farmyard and cut the nettles, and rent a man with a hedge-cutter too, and I have some hardcore put down in the gateways in case it rains before the tour I've arranged for our guests.

On the night before the meeting, I check on the calves, including Pearl; she is flourishing and growing into a real beauty, a potential Supreme Champion for next year's show. I look again at the notes I've prepared; I know if anyone can speak about this project – my baby – with passion, it's me. I drop by at the caravan to ask Leo's opinion – and have a cuddle and a smooch if I'm lucky, I smile to myself. I knock on the door, noticing as I wait for him to answer that the yellow rose that rambles up the wall of the cowshed is in full bloom.

'Hi,' I say when Leo appears, his hair ruffled and his eyes bleary with sleep. 'I'm sorry, I've disturbed you. I should have let sleeping vets lie.'

'Oh no, come in.' He yawns. 'I wanted to come along to the meeting tomorrow to provide moral support, but I can't make it – Alex has got me out TB testing all day. I'm sorry.'

'You will be,' I say, walking up the steps to receive a kiss. 'You're going to miss out on the free cake.'

'Save me some,' he chuckles.

'That could be difficult – there are lots of people coming.' I take a seat in the living area, moving a couple of newspapers and some of Leo's clothes out of the way first, while he makes hot chocolate.

'Can I read you my speech?' I ask as he hands me a mug.

'Okay. Go for it.'

I pull my notes from my jeans pocket.

'How shall I address everyone, if they come? Should I be casual and chatty, or formal?'

'Formal I think, then you can relax and do the chatty stuff later. You have to show you're professional about this.'

'I'm not sure this is going to work.' I sink back into the squashy cushions. 'What made me imagine it would?'

'It could be like convincing the members of the Flat Earth Society that the globe is spherical,' Leo agrees, sitting down next to me and looking over my shoulder at my notes. 'At least they won't be able to complain they haven't been consulted. Hey, Stevie, are you listening?' Leo slides his arm around my back and gives me a squeeze.

'Yes. Yes, I am,' I say, but I wasn't really concentrating.

'I would welcome them and give them the guided tour before letting them loose on the sherry and cakes while they study the plans. I wouldn't alienate them by making them stop and listen to a speech.'

'Do you think so?'

'Let the sherry and cake do their magic.'

'Are you serious or pulling my leg again?' I ask him as his lips curve into a smile.

'I'll leave that to you to decide.'

Being close to him, watching the rise and fall of his chest and breathing his scent of mint and chocolate makes me begin to lose the power of rational thought.

He strokes my thigh, sending a quiver of longing up my spine, at the same time as his mobile vibrates in his pocket.

'I'm sorry, I have to take this – I'm on call.' Frowning, Leo answers it and arranges to visit a sick pig near Talysands, making me feel as sick as a pig myself. 'I haven't a clue where it is. I'll have to programme the sat nav.' He turns back to me. 'Come over tomorrow night and tell me all about it –' he arches one eyebrow – 'and don't forget my cake.' He pauses. 'Or you could wait here for me.' He lowers his voice to a seductive whisper and adds, 'I wouldn't mind coming back to find you in my bed, Stevie.'

'Go and see to that pig,' I say lightly. 'I'll see you tomorrow.'

'Good luck with the meeting,' Leo adds.

The next day, I complete the preparations, vacuuming the floors and opening up the double doors onto the garden before the guests start arriving from one o'clock onwards, carefully timed to fit between the morning and afternoon milking. Plenty of people turn up, but no one wants to join the farm tour, so I show them straight into the living room where they pounce on the cupcakes and begin knocking back the sherry. Fifi Green is here with her husband, along with some of the shopkeepers from Talyton St George and local farmers, including the Pitts from Barton Farm and Chris, who keeps sheep.

'If you're trying to sweeten us up, it won't work,' Guy says when he arrives with Jennie.

'Guy, don't start.' Jennie hangs on to his arm as if

she's trying to hold him back. 'Remember this is a business opportunity for me. Go and look at the plans or something while I have a chat with Stevie.'

'Why do I get the feeling this was a bad idea?' I say as I fetch a glass of orange juice for Jennie.

'It's inevitable you'll have ups and downs when you're setting up a business,' Jennie says. 'My first order for a wedding cake was almost a disaster, thanks to Lucky, our dog, who snaffled it down at the last minute. I spent the night before baking and decorating cupcakes. It was a great success in the end, but it gave me my first grey hairs. Hang in there, Stevie. You'll get through it.'

My father is talking to Guy. He bangs his stick on the floor. 'You don't like it because my daughter is going to make a success of this farm. You're scared we're going to make pots of cash out of this venture.'

'Dad! It isn't all about money,' I interrupt.

'Oh, don't dress it up, Stevie,' Guy responds. 'I don't believe all your environmental awareness crap. We all know the bottom line is money.'

'Have you gazed into your own navel recently?' I ask Guy.

'You have fingers in plenty of other pies: dairy, renting out your farmhouse and converting the bakery,' Dad says.

'And we didn't object to any of that,' I point out.

'Yes, you did.' Guy stands with his arms folded. 'You had a right go about it, didn't you, Tom?'

'Dad, how could you?' I feel let down. How can he act like the innocent when he's as bad as the neighbours?

Why didn't he mention it to me? I'd never have let him speak to Guy if I'd known.

'You've never liked anything I've done on the farm,' Guy complains. 'You've been the neighbour from hell over the years. You were the one who moved that ruddy fence.'

'What fence?' My father blusters in such a way that proves he knows perfectly well which fence Guy is referring to.

'The one you moved in the middle of the night,' Guy says.

'You had those contractors build it three feet over on our side of the boundary,' my father counters.

'So you did move the fence,' Guy says with a smirk of triumph. 'I knew it. We all knew it.'

'Dad!' I exclaim.

'I put it back in its rightful place,' he insists.

'You stole a strip of my land.' Guy is incandescent with anger. 'If it weren't for Jennie, I'd have come round and torn a strip off you and stood over you while you moved it back.'

It's no wonder people aren't happy about our plans when my father's been antagonising them for years, I think.

My father turns to me. 'I did a proper job, Stevie.'

'I don't care. You shouldn't have done it.'

'Now you can tell us what really happened to the Christmas trees, the ones on the north side of my wood which you chopped down and sold to Fifi for the Garden Centre,' Guy goes on. 'Fifi, come over here,' he adds, calling Fifi and her husband across to join our conversation.

'I never,' says my father, but I no longer know if he's telling the truth. 'I never sold any trees to you, Fifi.'

'You sold some to me,' says her husband. 'There were about—'

'Let me guess,' Guy cuts in. 'There were about ten of them, all around so high.' He holds out his hand to demonstrate the height, about five foot.

'That's right. They were good-quality trees, a nice shape with plenty of needles, non-drop. We kept one back for Santa's Grotto.'

'Those trees were on my land. Ray planted them,' says my father.

I push in between Guy and my dad.

'We farmers should stick together. We have enough to contend with without fighting amongst ourselves.' My heart sinks when I see Guy set his mouth in a grim, straight line. This isn't going well and I have the feeling we've made it worse.

'This project will go ahead over my dead body. It's ridiculous.' Guy storms off, taking Jennie with him.

'Sorry, Stevie,' she mouths as she leaves. Everyone stands silent. All you can hear is the grandfather clock in the hall, ticking loud and slow.

'That went well,' I say ironically, trying to make light of it. 'Anyone for more sherry?' I grab a bottle from the side table and carry it around with me, topping up glasses while the guests start looking at the plans.

'For a building that's supposed to be designed by a good architect, it is in reality nothing but an oversized shed. We could do you one much cheaper off the shelf at the Garden Centre,' Fifi says.

'Thank you for the sarcasm, Fifi.'

'I don't think we have anything to worry about. Who is going to want to eat or drink in a shed when they can come to our gorgeous tearoom? You can't get that kind of ambience in a shed,' she adds to emphasise her point. 'The rest of the farm is a mess too. Stevie, you have no sense of reality.'

'It needs a lot of work,' I concede.

'It will take years to turn this place around.'

'It's a tinpot enterprise,' Fifi's husband says.

'And a crackpot one,' Fifi goes on. 'I should stick to dairy farming if I were you, not that you've been making a very good job of that I hear. When are you expecting to open?'

'Easter,' I say.

'You'll be lucky,' laughs Fifi. 'Well, I can see we don't need to stay any longer. The cupcakes are too sweet and the sherry far too dry.'

It's funny how it all disappears though, I think half an hour later, as I check the last bottle, which is empty, and make sure the cupcake I've saved for Leo is safely hidden away. I feel pretty empty too, temporarily drained of energy and enthusiasm, as I watch everyone leave, their opinions – I suspect – unchanged.

'I'm going too,' I tell my father. 'I'm going to leave you to think about how you're going to make it up to me. That was a complete bloody disaster.'

'Where? Where are you going?'

'To get the cows in. What did you think? That I was abandoning the farm, you silly old fool.'

'What did you call me?'

'You heard. Have you any more little secrets?' I ask him. 'Is there anything else I should know about?'

'If there was, I wouldn't tell you, the way you speak to me,' my father says crossly. I don't respond. Whistling for Bear, I walk out.

Chapter Fourteen

Don't Feed the Animals

It's early August when James starts work on building the accommodation for the animals. The plans for the farm haven't been approved, but here's hoping, I think when I leave the dairy, smelling of milk and cleaning chemicals from where I've been scrubbing out the tank. Crossing the drive to the field opposite the house, I greet James, who is already hard at work with a hire truck – his van is away for repairs – and a load of wood and fence panels. On the hard-standing that has set at last – the concrete mix wasn't right the first time and had to be dug out – are the three sides of a long, narrow shed made of breezeblocks.

'Hi there, Stevie.' James is up on a ladder, hammering in tacks to hold the roofing felt to the timber struts. The front of the building isn't finished yet. We're going to have chicken wire and wood frames to divide the shed into four separate areas.

'That's looking great,' I say, shielding my eyes from the sun. 'It looks like five-star accommodation.'

'It's a lot of money and work for what is just a giant rabbit hutch.' James's voice is filled with doubt. 'I could save you a bit by getting rid of those double doors on the plans. Do you really need that kind of security for rabbits and guinea pigs?'

'They're to stop the children escaping,' I say, smiling.

'Would you mind passing me the bigger hammer? It's in the toolbox. No, that's a mallet,' James goes on as I pick up the wrong tool.

'I'm a farmer, not a chippie.'

'By the way, I was wondering about the carnival. I fancy building a float this year and I was wondering if you'd mind if I borrowed a corner of the barn for it.'

'Not at all. You're welcome to, James.'

'If you like, I could enter it in the name of Nettlebed Farm.'

'Well, thank you.'

'And if you wanted to, you could join in.'

I hesitate for a moment, wondering if I can fit it all in. 'That would be great. It sounds like a lot of fun. I'm sure Leo will be up for it.' I notice how a shadow crosses James's eyes at the mention of Leo. 'We could ask Adam, Sophie and Georgia from next door if they'd like to help too.'

'The more the merrier,' James agrees. 'Do you remember how we used to build a float with Young Farmers' every year? Your dad would let us use the end of the barn and we'd get completely ratted on scrumpy.'

'I remember how someone topped up the barrels with lemonade. A dissatisfied customer sent a pair of Trading Standards officers out, but by the time they'd been here half an hour, Ray and I had convinced them we'd done nothing to break the Trades Descriptions Act. I reckon one of them had a pretty severe headache the following day.'

James grins. 'How did you do it?'

'Ray did a swap with Guy – a barrel of Uphill Farm cider in return for a bottle of Dad's whisky. It was a risky strategy, as you can imagine, but although Dad accused Ray of stealing it, he never had any proof.'

'Are you up for giving me a hand today?' James asks.

'Not today, I'm afraid.'

'That's a shame.'

'I'm going to scrape the yard, have another meeting with DJ to discuss his quote for the visitor centre—'

'The Shed, you mean?' James interrupts, amused. 'Just because it's drawn up by an architect doesn't make it less of a shed. I could have designed and built it for you for half the price.'

'You might have to yet – build it, I mean. DJ has put in a ridiculous figure for contingencies.'

'I'm not surprised to hear that. Have you checked his references?'

'I've heard a lot about him.'

'Surely that should be enough to put you off. I'm not sure he finished the job at the Sanctuary for Talyton Animal Rescue.'

'But he's available almost immediately.'

James grins. 'Really, Stevie, where's your common sense? DJ makes a pig's ear of whatever he does. I could do so much better for you.'

'But you're a one-man band. This is a big undertaking – even if it is just a shed,' I add wryly.

'I have a cousin who's in the building trade. He'll help me out.'

'Let me see what DJ has to say for himself, then if you want to give me a quote for the work, I'll look at it.'

'Thanks, Stevie. Much appreciated.'

'Anything for some peace and quiet.'

I meet with DJ who is intransigent over the contingency fund. It makes me wonder if he has another building project in the pipeline or whether he's booked an extended holiday, because he isn't exactly putting himself out. I drop in to Jennie's to talk it through with her.

'What would you do?' I ask her.

'I'd take a risk and go with James if he can match the quote,' she says. 'That's if you want to guarantee it's ready for the spring.'

'I have to say he got me worried when I asked him how long he thought he'd take to complete the build and all he could confirm was that it would take as long as it took.' I pause, recalling what James said about the carnival. 'James and I thought we'd build a float for the carnival in September,' I continue.

'You're a glutton for punishment, Stevie. Are you sure you aren't taking on too much?'

'James will do most of the hard work. I'll be creative

director and supervise. Are you interested in joining in? As James says, the more the merrier.'

'Can we do a float with you?' asks Sophie, coming into the kitchen. 'It sounds fun,' but when Jennie raises the idea with Guy as he comes indoors, he isn't impressed.

'No way. Share with Nettlebed Farm? Absolutely not.'

'But Guy—' says Sophie.

'We are not fraternising with the enemy.'

'Well, I'm going to join in,' says Sophie.

'You can choose to do what you like, but I'm not getting involved. Anyway, carnival is so passé.'

'You run the tar barrels,' Jennie points out. 'That's a pretty ancient tradition too.'

'It's different,' says Guy. 'You don't have to dress up and look like a complete prat.'

Jennie apologises for her husband, not for the first time.

'I don't know what's got into him,' she says as he leaves the kitchen with a mug of coffee and hunk of fruitcake. 'I know he's worried about me and the baby, just like any other first-time father.'

'He really doesn't like the idea of the petting farm.'

'I've told him he'll have to get used to it – he will in the end.'

'I'm going upstairs,' Sophie says.

'You should be outside,' Jennie says. 'It's a lovely day. You could pop Bracken over a couple of jumps to keep her hoof in, so to speak. The final selection for the Pony Club showjumping team is this week. Sophia

258

Fox-Gifford, the district commissioner, is choosing the final four. You and Georgia have a very good chance.'

'Oh Mum, I don't want to go.'

'Well, we're going and that's that.'

As Sophie ignores her mum's advice, I pick up a gingerbread farmer from the plate on the kitchen table and nibble the icing from his foot – he's wearing green wellies.

'To think I could be bringing another Sophie into the world,' Jennie sighs as Sophie stomps off upstairs.

'I doubt it,' I say wryly. 'I think she's a one-off. Didn't you want to know the sex of the baby?'

'I want it to be a surprise.'

'How much longer have you got?'

'Another month or so,' Jennie says. 'I'm as big as a house this time.'

'If there's anything I can do to help you out, just shout.'

'Thank you, but I'm already very spoilt. The girls are taking it in turns to make breakfast, Adam's been helping decorate the nursery – he's moved his bedroom downstairs – and Guy's been doing the shopping.' She smiles. 'I love being pregnant.'

'I don't envy you,' I say, yawning as I rest my elbows on the table. 'I think I got up too early.'

'You look tired,' Jennie observes.

'I'm exhausted.'

'I know it's none of my business, but have you considered you might be pregnant?' At first I think she's joking, but her expression is serious. 'I mean it, Stevie. I was going to say something before, but I didn't feel I

259

knew you well enough. I can usually tell these things –
you have a certain look about you.'

'There's no way, unless it was an immaculate
conception.'

'I'm sorry,' Jennie says. 'My mistake. Forget it.'

The trouble is, now Jennie's brought the subject up,
I can't. I lost weight and developed some muscle when
I started working back on the farm, but I've started
having to loosen the belt on my jeans.

'I'd be pretty far gone if I was pregnant,' I mutter.

'You'd just finished with your ex when I first met
you,' Jennie says.

'That was ages ago and Nick and I hardly ever . . .' I
pause and think.

Jennie raises one eyebrow. 'You didn't fancy him all
that much then? Guy and I couldn't keep our hands off
each other.'

Jennie, too much information, I groan inwardly.

'What about Leo?' Jennie asks. 'Have you and him . . .
you know, been intimate?'

'Not that intimate. Not yet,' I say bashfully.

'How long were you and Nick together?'

'Eighteen months.'

'So there was plenty of time to make a baby.'

'I was on contraception.' Something clicks in my
brain as I bite the gingerbread farmer in half with a
loud snap. 'I put the odd bout of sickness and other
changes down to stress. It didn't occur to me . . .' I
glance down at my stomach. It's impressively hard,
but not entirely flat.

'It isn't impossible,' Jennie says. 'Some women don't

know they're pregnant until they're in labour. If you ignored the early signs or put them down to another cause . . . Oh look, I'm being daft. Let's talk about something else.'

I look at the gingerbread farmer, afraid that I've bitten off more than I can chew in more ways than one.

That evening, I walk slowly back across the yard in my vest top, shorts and wellies, having fed the calves one last time. The sun has already slipped behind the hills above the house, the upstairs windows are gleaming with persimmon light and the front door is lost in shadow. Across the yard, a cow bellows for her friends – it's either Poppet or China. I kept them indoors after milking because they're both due to calve and I like to keep an eye on them, even though they'd probably manage perfectly well out in the field without me as midwife.

'Hi, Stevie. Is that you?' My heart misses a beat at the sound of Leo's voice emerging from the dusk. Bats flit about overhead. 'Do you want to come in for a coffee?'

'I'd love to,' I say. I could do with a break from Dad, Cecil and Mary. The conversation at teatime ranged from the price of wheat to the best way to treat corns, with all three of them opting for calling Mrs Wall, the woman who wishes away not only warts but corns and other blemishes for a small fee. More than that, though, I could do with a break from the nagging worry Jennie has implanted in my head. 'Would you like me to fetch you some cider?' I ask, sorely tempted to drink myself senseless.

'No thank you,' he says quickly. 'That stuff is too rough for me. I haven't the stomach for it.'

It's odd, but neither have I at the moment. Since I've been back, I've lost my taste for it.

By the light of a single lantern, Leo makes coffee – decaff – and cuts up one of Jennie's cakes, a chocolate sponge, into slices to share before he sits down beside me on the sofa.

'How was your day?' I ask, snuggling up against him.

'Not so bad. Busy . . .' He wraps his arm around my shoulders.

'So this isn't the best time to talk about animals? I need to pick your brain.'

'It is my specialist subject, so fire away, unless it's about one of the cows, in which case I can stick my boots on and come and have a look.'

'It's about the project. I thought you might be able to give me some advice on the mix of animals on my list and about sourcing them.' I flash him a smile. 'I have to keep my vet bills down any way I can.'

'You could have some meerkats – they're popular at the moment,' Leo says.

'They're zoo, not farm animals.' I give him a nudge. 'Call yourself a vet?'

'Well, why not have some exotics? You've already said you want rabbits and guinea pigs. They don't fit in terribly well on a farm. You farmers are usually out shooting rabbits.'

'I'm concentrating on having a small flock of ewes, goats and a pair of pigs, preferably unusual or rare breed, like Gloucester Old Spot or Tamworth.' I continue, 'Whatever we choose, I need to make sure the animals are healthy, aren't carrying any diseases that could harm the visitors – and I'd like to offer a home to as many rescues as possible.'

'The public will like the idea of you taking on preloved animals.'

'I thought I could use their stories as part of the displays outside their pens.'

'So you need animals that are suitable for handling – individuals that have been handled before or are at least tractable with a good temperament,' Leo says. 'Much like me.'

'And they should be photogenic and personable,' I add.

'Much like me too. How do you decide a sheep is personable?' He chuckles. 'What are you going to do? Interview them all?'

'I thought you could assess them for me. I'll pay you, as part of your vet duties.' The words I've been trying to hold back come tumbling from my mouth. 'If you're still here . . .'

'If I'm still here,' he echoes.

His expression is soft, yet there is a hunger in his eyes that undermines me. There's something about Leo that gets right under my skin.

'Do you think you'll ever settle down?' I ask tentatively.

'One day. I almost did once.'

'You mentioned you had a fiancée.'

'As soon as I bought the engagement ring, she

changed her mind. I can see now it was right, what she did,' he says gruffly. 'I hated her for it, but if she hadn't, I wouldn't be here now.'

I wonder if he's running away from the memories of his ex-fiancée as well as his nephew.

'I find it hard to trust anyone now. She was carrying on behind my back with someone I thought was a friend of mine.'

'Why did she agree to get engaged in the first place?'

'He was married already. I think she thought that she could make him jealous and see what he was missing so he'd divorce his wife.'

'Did it work?'

'Oh, he got divorced, but he didn't marry her. He married someone else.' Leo shrugs. 'Being with you, Stevie, has made me realise I'm over her at last. I've fallen for you –' he presses his lips to my hair – 'in a big way. I really, really like you . . .'

A flush of heat spreads up my neck. 'I kind of guessed that.'

I can see everything is falling into place and I think of how resentful I will feel if it turns out that Nick has made me pregnant.

'Will you stay this time? I mean, stay over? Stevie, I want to make love to you.' Leo massages my thigh.

'I feel the same,' I say, almost breathless with desire for him. 'Leo, I can't stop thinking about you, but—'

'You're still worried about me leaving at the end of the summer?'

Leo nuzzles my shoulder – we both seem to have lost some of our clothes, the top half at least. I stroke Leo's chest, feeling the hard muscle beneath and tangling my fingers in his dark curly hair as I enjoy his scent of the outdoors, musk and aftershave.

'Of course I am.' It will break my heart. 'I'll miss you.'

'Would it make a difference if I said I'd been thinking about changing my plans?'

I gaze up into his eyes, hardly daring to hope. He touches his forehead to mine.

'Would you stay especially for me?' I ask, my voice husky with emotion.

'Yes, for you, darling.'

'Really?' Do I believe him, I ask myself.

'I mean it,' he insists. 'I'll stay. I'll ask Alex if he can keep me on during the winter. If not, I'll find another position, locum or permanent, as close as possible to Talyton St George.' He smiles. 'I never expected to settle down here of all places, but you're worth it.'

'Oh, Leo, that's the best news ever.'

'I'm not saying it just to get you into bed, although that would be lovely. I'm saying that we can continue to see each other and be a proper couple without you worrying about when I'm going to up sticks and move away at any minute. I'm not stupid. I know it's been bothering you.'

As the darkness presses in on us, an almost overwhelming rush of lust and adoration crushes my chest, paralysing my breathing. Leo has to be the perfect boyfriend. He hasn't said so in so many words, but I know he must love me, if he's prepared to give up his carefree lifestyle for me.

I catch his hand and slip my fingers between his.

'Let's go to bed,' I murmur.

The next morning I wake in Leo's arms to the sound of the cockerel crowing and Cecil calling the cows into the parlour.

'Leo, I've overslept.' I slide out of bed and search frantically for my clothes.

'Hey, come back,' he says, peering out from beneath the duvet. 'Cecil can cope – he's always boasting about how he can do the milking by himself.'

'He struggles sometimes.' I smile ruefully. 'Don't tell him I said that.'

'Well, if you won't come back to bed now, how about tonight? I'm on call, but I can always hope it's quiet.'

I lean down and kiss him several times. I'm sorely tempted to stay, but I can't.

'Tonight,' I say before I dress, run into the house to fetch my overalls and head back across the yard to the parlour to help Cecil.

'Did you stay over with the vet?' Cecil asks slyly.

'Maybe.' I turn away, concentrating on cleaning the next cow's teats, to hide my blushes.

'You will be careful, won't you?'

'I don't know what you mean,' I say archly.

'I'd hate to see you get hurt.'

'I won't get hurt,' I say. 'I know Leo and I know what I'm doing.'

'I hope so,' Cecil mutters and, as I continue with the milking, listening to the sound of the milking machine and inhaling the scent of the cows' soft, sweet breath, I find myself hoping so too. I have the most amazing boyfriend and it would be really bad luck now to discover I was pregnant by somebody else.

I know I should make an attempt to reassure myself that I'm not pregnant, but I can't quite bring myself to. If I was pregnant, it would turn my life upside down, and that's the last thing I want when I'm so happy with Leo. I stay over in the mobile home on most nights, except for the occasions when he's called during the evening, when I return to the house and brave my father's comments about dirty stop-outs. I feel guilty about Bear – he is ecstatic when I come back to sleep in my room and he can join me, lying across my feet at the end of the bed.

The heat becomes oppressive as we drift on through August. The cows are looking sleek and well, out in the fields with their heads down and flicking the flies from their flanks with their tails. The milk yields are up and I'm beginning to wonder if I'm doing the right thing in planning to downsize the herd and diversify, but then I look at the income from the milk and the amount of time and effort and sacrifice we put into producing it, and I know there has to be a better way of securing the farm's future.

I only hope I can persuade the council to give us the go-ahead to create the visitor attraction. If they refuse to okay the plans, we're stymied, and I'll have to go back to the drawing board.

One morning, I receive a letter saying that a couple of members of the Planning Committee and someone from the Highways Agency wish to come and view the site to clarify some issues and take some photos.

'Is that good or bad news?' my father asks, reading over my shoulder at the breakfast table.

'I'm not sure. They haven't given us much notice.'

'Will they want tea?' Dad says.

'I don't think we should offer them anything. It might be construed as unduly influencing a member of the Planning Committee.'

'When are they coming?'

'Today at noon.'

'Don't they know that's dinnertime?' my father says, appalled at the thought of having his lunch disturbed.

A faint pungency of slurry begins to creep inside the house.

'Guy's muckspreading,' says Cecil, joining us.

'Where?' I ask.

'Close by, just the other side of Steep Acres.'

'I don't know why he's chosen to do it, and there – so close to the house – today of all days.'

'I think I can guess,' I say.

'Will it matter?' Dad asks.

'It'll add weight to the argument that this is agricultural land and should be kept that way.' Even for my stomach, the stench is disgusting, as if Guy's mixed it up with chicken and pig manure for extra strength.

'Guy can't know about the visit, can he?' Dad says. 'We've only just received the letter ourselves.'

'Oh dear, I forgot to mention it.' Cecil's mouth turns down at the corners and his shoulders slump further than ever. 'I'm so sorry. Jennie told Adam to find me so that I could tell you, Stevie.'

'Tell me what?'

'That the planners were coming to Nettlebed Farm, but it completely slipped my mind. I hope I haven't ruined everything.'

'You probably have,' my father says unhelpfully, at the same time as I say, 'I'm sure you haven't. What did Adam say?'

Cecil rubs his temple, leaving a grubby mark.

'I don't rightly recall, but it was something about how Fifi had dropped by to speak to Guy about tactics. Tactics, that's what Adam said. Jennie overheard and she thought you needed to know there were tactics afoot.'

'Don't worry.' I pour Cecil a mug of tea. 'I'm going to make sure the yard's tidy before they turn up. I don't think there's anything else we can do.'

Our visitors, two men in a Mercedes and a third in a Highways Agency van roll up an hour late. They apologise, hoping they haven't held me up.

'It's all right,' I say. 'I'm Stevie Dunsford. Can I show you the site?'

'The traffic was appalling – is it usually that busy along the lane?'

'Busy?'

'We got caught behind a couple of horse-riders, a tractor towing a muckspreader and several cars. A second tractor had broken down in the lay-by, so there was nowhere to pass. We had to reverse most of the way back to Talyton.'

'What kind of tractor?' I ask.

'I'm no expert, but it did have a sticker reading "British Beef" in the cab. I remember that. It made me smile because there was a pretty beefy farmer leaning against it, waiting for the AA, or RAC, or the equivalent organisation for tractors.'

'I don't think there is one,' I say, wondering to whom the tractor belongs.

'There was a third tractor left beside the tree at the entrance to your drive, a vintage one. It made it extremely awkward to turn in to the farm.'

So Guy is deliberately sabotaging our plans. He's hired his friends to make the traffic look bad and prove the access to Nettlebed Farm is no good. I am furious, but I try not to show it.

'Usually the only tractors that use the lane are the vehicles belonging to us and our neighbour's. I promise you this is a one-off. You really need to come back several times to get a true reflection of the amount of traffic. I'll do a traffic census, if it will help . . . anything.'

'There's no need for that when we've already experienced it for ourselves,' one of the visitors says.

My heart sinking, I show them the site. They don't give anything away and I have no idea what their decision will be when they leave half an hour later. I decide not to confront Guy. I will never admit defeat, but I have to confess it's much harder than I imagined it would be. I'm exhausted, but I haven't been sleeping at night, either because I've been staying over with Leo, or worrying about the possibility I'm carrying my ex-boyfriend's baby.

After breakfast the following day – when there is no traffic in the lane – I excuse myself and head into Talyton in the Land Rover to pick up a few bits and pieces. I have never been so nervous about a shopping trip. When I enter the pharmacy, the bell chinks as the door closes behind me, making me jump. I take a deep breath of lavender and eucalyptus, trying to calm down, but I'm in a cold sweat by the time I reach the counter. I clear my throat and ask for a pregnancy test.

'Which kind would you like?' the pharmacy assistant asks. 'We stock two: a budget test, and a slightly more expensive brand, which can diagnose pregnancy from the day you missed—'

'I'll have one of each, please,' I say, aware of at least two sets of eyes on me, like hyenas prowling the aisles to scavenge any stray titbits of gossip.

'As you wish.' The assistant seems to take an age to pack the tests in a bag and ring up the prices on the till.

'Thank you,' I say, praying she'll hurry up.

'Hello, Stevie, how wonderful to see you.' Fifi bobs up from behind a display of incontinence products. 'I suppose you'll be putting your project on hold for a while.' Her eyes are fixed on the white paper bag I have in my hand. 'I'm a great believer that mothers should put their babies first.'

'I'm not pregnant,' I stammer. 'I'm buying the tests for someone else.'

'It can't be for Mary or Jennie,' she probes. 'So who are they for? Do tell.'

'I'm bound to secrecy,' I say.

'Oh, you are such a spoilsport.' Fifi shrugs. 'Never

mind, I'm sure we'll find out soon enough. Perhaps it's for young Adam's girlfriend.'

'I didn't know he had one.'

'I believe he has – I've seen him on the Green with a young lady.'

'Goodbye, Fifi.' I turn and walk away as quickly as I can, and go back to the Land Rover. I drive back home via Jennie's. Jennie is in her kitchen, icing the tiers of a wedding cake.

'I'm sorry to disturb you when you're in the middle of something,' I say when she lets me in, wiping her hands on a tea towel.

'I've almost finished this layer, and I need to let it dry before I can do anything else,' she says. 'I could do with a break. I'm sorry about Guy and his ridiculous behaviour when those people came to see you yesterday. I've told him he has to ring the Planning Department and talk to someone to apologise. I'm so angry with him and he knows it. He's made himself scarce today – I've told him there's no cake for him for at least a month.' She pauses, reading my distress, because I am really scared now.

I show her the paper bag from the chemist.

'I can't do this on my own. Do you mind?'

'Of course not,' she says gently. 'I offered, didn't I?'

'You're a real friend, Jennie.'

'The children are out. Adam's out with Lucky and his girlfriend and the girls have gone for a ride. Would you like tea and cake before or after?'

'I couldn't eat a thing,' I say. 'I'm petrified.'

'Let's wait and see, shall we? Go upstairs to the

bathroom and let me know the result straight away.'

'So you can console or celebrate with me.' I walk upstairs, heavy-hearted. My stomach is bloated yet my body is trim and well-muscled, but I can't believe there's anyone in there. It's impossible. I feel giddy, nauseous – I blame it on the slope of the floor. I lock myself inside the bathroom, do the test, wash my hands and wait the allotted time, sitting on the edge of the white wicker laundry basket. I can hardly bear to look as the sky darkens and rain begins to patter against the panes of glass. There's a flash of lightning and a clap of thunder, hardly auspicious.

The alarm goes on my mobile. I squint at the wand through half-closed eyes, trying to blur and obliterate the line that appears in the window. If only I could magic away the past few months and start again. There's another crashing rumble of thunder, as if there's a team of giants playing at tenpin bowling in the loft above my head.

'Well?' Jennie says from outside the bathroom.

'It's positive.' I push the door open.

'Well, that's no great surprise.' Jennie looks at me, her belly thrust out and her feet splayed like a waddling duck. She holds out her arms. 'Congratulations, Stevie. Welcome to the club.'

'Don't. It's the worst news in the world.' I burst into tears.

'There, there.' Jennie hugs me and pats my back as if I'm a child.

'What am I going to do? It's a complete disaster.'

'Let's keep calm and carry on, as they say.' Jennie

guides me to the window-seat on the landing and sits me down amongst the floral cushions while she squats on the floor with her hands flat across her bump, her finger-tips touching. 'First things first. You do want this baby?'

'No, I don't want it.' It's like a parasite growing inside me. 'I can't have a termination though – I'm too far gone.' Why does the word termination sound less brutal than abortion, I wonder, as I blow my nose on a tatty piece of tissue I find in my trouser pocket. 'It would be the easy way out, but I like the idea of not having it less than the idea of having it.'

'It's all right, I understand. It must be a terrible shock when you're not expecting to find you're expecting, so to speak.'

I'm wracked with shudders of fear of the unknown, and devastation at the thought that I'm about to lose my freedom, because that's what it feels like. I want to cry and rant over my bad luck, but not in front of Jennie, not when she's so close to having her much-wanted child.

'I do want children one day, just not now.' I bury my head in my hands. 'I suppose I could give the baby up. There are thousands of infertile couples desperate for a child. Oh, Jennie, you must think I'm a heartless bitch.'

'I can help you look into the possibility of adoption, but I warn you, I couldn't have given any of mine up. Once they're born and you hold them in your arms, you can't help falling in love with them.' Jennie hesitates. 'What about the father? You haven't mentioned him. He's bound to want to have a say in the baby's future.'

I sit frozen, keeping my face covered. My heart is

hammering like a train. A cold sweat breaks out across my back.

'You haven't spoken to him about the possibility yet?'

I shake my head.

'You are sure?'

I nod.

'It is Nick's,' I say with difficulty. I thought I'd moved on, but our relationship has come back to haunt me, big time.

'Your ex, the one with the Aston Martin.'

'Yes, the one with the Aston Martin,' I echo stupidly.

'So you have been pregnant without realising it for some time,' Jennie says.

'Since March, which means it's due –' I look up as I do a quick calculation – 'sometime in the New Year.'

'You must be twenty weeks at least then,' Jennie observes.

'I'm such an idiot. I blamed the occasional bout of sickness and nausea on being stressed coming back to the farm, and the kicks and flutters on wind.' I dab my eyes with shreds of tissue. 'Oh my god, do I *have* to tell Nick?'

'Of course you do . . .'

How I wish we hadn't slept together that one last time, because I'm pretty sure that's when it happened. 'He's going to hate me for this.'

'It isn't entirely your fault. He's fifty per cent responsible.'

I gaze out of the window, watching Jennie's daughters riding back on their ponies, a bay Exmoor pony and a big chestnut part-thoroughbred, in the rain.

'He'll be pretty pissed off.'

'He'll come round eventually.'

'I doubt it very much.'

'At least he has the money to help you out.'

'I don't need his money.'

'You know what I mean. He can do his bit to support the baby. It'll take the pressure off you.'

'How on earth am I going to tell him?' I pick up a cushion from the window-seat and hug it tightly to my chest for comfort.

'You should go and speak to him face to face. Guy can help out with the milking – he'll lend you Adam.'

'At a cost. His rates are pretty high,' I say with a rueful smile.

'You know there are some positives to this situation. We'll be able to help each other out and talk nappies and cradle cap.' Jennie sighs happily. 'There are some topics of conversation that can only be shared with another mum.'

'Fantastic,' I say with sarcasm. 'I can't imagine anything more dull than thinking about nappies.'

'You'll be surprised how important it is to have the right ones when the time comes.' Jennie grins before growing serious again. 'I wonder what kind of father Nick will want to be. Long-distance or hands-on?'

'How can he be hands-on when we live so far apart?' My brain hurts. It's all too much to think about. I can't get my head around the fact I am going to have a baby, let alone what will happen once it's born. 'I don't know what he'll want,' I say miserably. 'I thought we'd made a clean break, but now I'm going to have to see him again.'

To my horror and shame, I notice I've been crying into Jennie's cushion.

'I'm so sorry,' I exclaim. I'll have it dry-cleaned. I'll buy you a new one.'

'Don't worry. It'll go in the wash. I'm not house-proud, not with four kids running around the place.'

'Four?' I look up through the lank fronds of my hair.

'I include Guy – he's still a child at heart, even though he's about to become a dad for the first time.'

'What is my dad going to think? He's bound to give me a lecture.'

Jennie stands up slowly from the floor and touches my shoulder.

'You have to ignore everyone else and concentrate on you and the baby. Anyway, I'm sure your dad will love it.'

'Only if it's a boy to inherit the farm,' I say sharply. 'In his opinion, girls aren't worth anything.'

'That's a very old-fashioned and bigoted outlook.'

'Because he's old-fashioned and bigoted,' I say glumly.

'Stevie, come downstairs and have some cake. It might make you feel better.' When I open my mouth to argue that I'm not hungry, Jennie continues, 'You're eating for two now. You can't think of any advantages of being pregnant yet, but there are some, and having an excuse to eat as much as you like is one of them.'

She's right. Back down in the kitchen, I eat two

vanilla and chocolate cupcakes. Jennie helps herself to three.

'You won't say anything to anyone, will you?' I ask her before I leave Jennie's Folly, taking advantage of a gap in the thundery showers to walk back.

'You're going to have to tell Leo too, aren't you?' she says as if reading my mind. 'It's all right, Stevie. I'll keep my mouth shut. I promise. And if you ever want to talk, you know where I am.'

'Thank you, Jennie.'

I can't help thinking, as I make my way back to the farm, that if I'd accepted Nick's proposal and returned to London, we would have bought our house near Wimbledon Common by now and be about to become a family. I would never have grown close to Leo. What am I going to do about Leo? I'm doubly distraught because I can't possibly continue my relationship with him when I'm pregnant with Nick's child. It isn't fair, not just because it isn't Leo's baby, but because I know how he feels about children and how he couldn't bear any reminder of his nephew's short life. It isn't right for me to remain his girlfriend and lover, but the idea of pulling back from Leo now is heartbreaking.

How I wish I hadn't slept with him now. It's made everything so much more difficult.

In fact, I'm relieved when Leo's on duty this evening, and is so busy he has to prioritise his emergency visits and ask Alex to cover one of them.

'I'm going to do some work on the project,' I tell him. 'I've got plenty of admin to catch up with.'

'That sounds incredibly dull,' Leo says, smiling.

'It has to be done.' I pause. 'By the way, I'm going to have to pop up to London this weekend.'

'Oh? I'm off this weekend. Why don't we go together?'

'No, you'd be bored witless,' I say quickly. 'I'm going to fetch my car and some of my stuff from the flat and catch up with India.'

'I thought you'd got it all. Why do you want your car all of a sudden?'

'I thought the car would be useful, and there are a couple of things I forgot and, anyway, India's having one of her usual crises. I haven't seen her for ages and she could do with a shoulder to cry on.'

'So you don't need me in the way,' Leo says wistfully. 'Next time maybe?'

'That would be fun,' I say, but I don't feel excited over the prospect of going on a weekend trip to London with Leo in the future, when I'm lying to him about my reasons for going this time. I'm delaying the terrible moment for as long as I can, using the excuse that I have to let Nick know that I'm pregnant first.

Tonight, I can't sleep. After midnight, I sit in my old bed with a joyful Bear at my feet and stare across at the window, the curtains open, at the hills beyond, the stars and the milky luminescence of the galaxy. It is so quiet, the air is bursting with silence – that's the only way I can describe it – and a lump catches in my throat and a tear falls onto Bear's silky coat. Why? Why did it have to happen to me? Bear turns and gazes at me, his eyes gleaming softly in the dark. He raises his head and licks my face.

'Bear,' I say, smiling. He wags his tail and rests his head across my legs. 'You're a good boy.'

He raises his lip as if smiling back, rolling over to expose his belly, asking for a stroke, knowing full well that I won't send him back to sleep on his old chair in the lean-to.

In spite of the test, I can't believe there is anyone inside me. I want to scream and scream. Why me? Why us? Why now? What terrible timing! I've always known I want children, just not now, not this minute and not with Nick. I've got myself into a terrible muddle.

I used to think people who fell pregnant unintentionally were just plain stupid or careless, and it would never happen to me, but it has and here I am. If I was merely pregnant, that would be bearable, but I'm pregnant with my ex's baby and I'm in love with Leo.

Chapter Fifteen

The Cow Jumped Over the Moon

'You're very quiet this morning,' Cecil says as I drop a set of clusters on the floor for the third time. 'You seem out of sorts.'

'I have a lot on my mind. I'm going to London tomorrow. I hope you don't mind doing the milking, but I need to pick up some more of my things – my car, for example.'

'Don't you worry, my lover. I keep telling you I can do it by myself.'

'I know you're perfectly capable, but I like to feel I'm doing my bit. Cecil, isn't it time you slowed down?'

'No, Stevie,' he says, and I feel a pang of anxiety when I notice his eyes watering with tears whenever the possibility of retirement is broached. 'It's all right. It had to come. There's no need to beat around the bush out of kindness. You don't want us any more.'

'What do you mean? I've said nothing of the sort.'

'What I feared has come to pass. I expect we'll find a little place in town, or Mary's cousin might be able to put us up for a while.' He utters a grating sigh. 'You need the cottage for the new staff, the young ones.'

'I've said before I wouldn't dream of making you and Mary homeless after all you've done for the farm. You're part of it. No, I wouldn't entertain it.'

'I've been lucky, but I'm not going to be able to work for ever and neither is Mary.'

'You can't afford to buy a house of your own and you'd be pushed to find the rent for a place in Talyton.'

'Ah, but that's our problem, not yours. I reckon you have enough problems of your own.'

Immediately, my mind returns to the baby – little does Cecil know exactly how many problems I'm grappling with. I try to push thoughts of my pregnancy predicament to the back of my brain to concentrate on putting Cecil's mind at rest. I feel rather ashamed that it is my father who unintentionally put Cecil and Mary in a precarious financial position. They have had the cottage rent-free for years, along with a certain amount of food, cider, wood for the fire, use of a vehicle and – at one time – red diesel from the pump we used to have on the farm to fuel the tractor. They have hardly lived like kings and I feel as if we've taken advantage of their loyalty.

'I'm not asking you to retire, Cecil. It would be nice to think you could have a rest, that's all.'

'I couldn't retire. It would drive me mad if I had to stay indoors, and Mary wouldn't want me under her feet all day.'

'When we open the visitor attraction, we'll need your help. There'll still be some cows on the farm that need milking. It will be up to you how much or how little you want to do. There's the garden too – Dad can't do it, and I don't want to. I won't have the time . . .' I glance down at my belly involuntarily and hope Cecil hasn't noticed.

'Are you sure you haven't taken on too much? It's an enormous project.'

'I'm going to give it a go. Nothing ventured, nothing gained and all that,' I go on brightly. Losing my mother, realising my father is mortal and that life is not a rehearsal, has made me stronger and more determined to go for what I want. How am I going to meet the deadline for the project when I'm having a baby in the middle of it all? I feel trapped because there's no way I can give up now, even if I wanted to, because I'll have someone entirely dependent on me for everything: food, clothes, nappies – I grimace at the thought – and attention.

'I'll drive you to the station,' Cecil offers.

'Thank you.' There isn't a station in Talyton St George. 'That would be perfect.' I've told India I'll be dropping by at the flat to collect the last of my bits and pieces – a few clothes and the car keys. I haven't told her I've arranged to meet Nick at lunchtime. I plucked up the courage to call him on the phone last night.

'I need to see you about something,' I said.

'That sounds mysterious,' he responded. 'Aren't you going to tell me what it's about? Only I'm too busy to play games.'

'I wanted a word . . .'

'Really, Stevie, I don't think it's a good idea for us to see each other again, not for me at least.'

'Oh, I see. I don't want to catch up for old times' sake. I have something I need to talk to you about.'

'I'm your ex-boyfriend. I hardly think that qualifies me as your therapist.'

'I don't need therapy.'

'So what is it?'

'I can't say on the phone.'

'Don't rake up the past, Stevie. You can't imagine how much you've hurt me. I don't want to go through that again. I'm trying to move on.'

'I never wanted to hurt you, Nick.'

'Is it work? Don't tell me – you've had enough of the muck and mud and the early starts and you want your job back?'

'No,' I say, but he blunders on.

'That's impossible now. We've taken on a new member of staff.'

'Listen, I'm coming up tomorrow to pick up my car. How about lunch? This won't take long.'

'Lunch,' he agrees eventually. 'One o'clock at the pub. I can't afford to leave the office for long.'

'On a Saturday?' I ask.

'I'm very busy,' he says with pride, and I wonder if he's trying to show me what I could have had if I'd stayed with him in London.

The next day, I take the train back to Wimbledon, wishing the journey would never end, but all too soon I'm at the pub. Nick is already there at a table in the corner – our table, the one where we used to meet when we were trying to hide the fact we were dating from our colleagues – and I feel a pang of regret when I see him that I couldn't make it work. Dressed in shirtsleeves and a tie, he sits with a white wine spritzer, his laptop open and his mobile phone vibrating in front of him. He looks slimmer than when I last saw him, though not anorexic with misery. He doesn't appear to have done the heartbreak diet.

He looks up with a half-smile, quickly converted to a frown as he stands up. 'Stevie, what can I get you?'

'An orange juice, please.'

'You don't like oranges.'

'My tastes have changed.'

'So I hear.'

'What have you heard?'

'India mentioned you'd been seeing the vet. It appears you've been sleeping with the enemy – after all, he did try to convince the Animal Welfare officer to close down your precious farm.'

That stings me. 'For one, Leo's okay as a person, and two, it's none of your business if I'm seeing him or not. Anyway, how come you've spoken to India?' I feel hurt that she's been talking to Nick behind my back. What I tell her is supposed to be confidential. 'I thought you'd collected your things from the flat.'

'She's still finding bits and pieces – it's obviously taken me longer to disentangle myself from this relationship than it has you.'

Nick orders orange juice at the bar before we choose

beef and horseradish sandwiches. I wasn't hungry before, but I am now.

'So what is this all about?' Nick asks as we return to our table. 'I can't see we have anything left to say to each other.'

I pull out a chair and sit down opposite him.

'I hope you don't mind,' I say, closing his laptop.

'I do mind. You've put it into hibernate mode.'

'Nick, I'm pregnant.'

The laptop forgotten, he stares at me. 'Why tell me?'

'Because it's your baby,' I say quietly.

'What the . . .?' He swears aloud. There's the sound of a clattering fork from the adjacent table and the pub falls silent. 'How can it be? I don't believe you.'

'I'm one hundred and one per cent sure. It's your baby,' I repeat. I'm genuinely shocked, because for all my imagining how Nick was going to take the news, I never dreamed he'd doubt me.

'There'll have to be a DNA test. Can you do them before the baby's born?'

'I don't know. If you want a test to confirm, you can do the legwork and let me know what you need me to do. There is no doubt it's yours. I haven't slept with anyone . . . I mean, I wasn't sleeping with anyone else when I was with you . . .'

'So you are sleeping with the vet?'

'All right, yes, I am now, but the dates don't tie up,' I insist. 'I'm more than twenty weeks gone.' I glance around the pub. Two well-dressed men in their twenties – estate agents, I suspect – are watching with interest from the adjacent table.

'Don't stop on our account,' one says. 'This is just like being on *The Jeremy Kyle Show*.'

I glare back at them.

'Ignore them,' Nick says. 'You'll have to explain,' he goes on, lowering his voice to a harsh whisper. 'How on earth did it happen?'

'In the usual way, I guess. Do you want me to give you a biology lesson?'

'You were on the Pill!'

'Yes, but it isn't one hundred per cent failsafe.'

'You didn't take it properly?' Nick rubs his forehead, leaving a red mark. 'Did you miss a day or something?'

'Don't you think I've gone over it again and again already? I don't know why it didn't work.' I pull myself together. 'Don't go heaping the blame on me. You had just as much to do with this as I did. It's half yours.'

Nick buries his head in his hands and I wonder as time passes if he's ever going to face up to his responsibilities. The sandwiches look as if they're beginning to curl at the edges and the bubbles have disappeared from Nick's spritzer. The energy has drained from me too. Nick and I can hardly bear to speak to each other, let alone be in the same room. How can we possibly raise a child together?

'I've always wondered if they would work, if I would end up finding out I was firing blanks,' Nick begins eventually. 'It's pretty bad luck then to get caught out like this. How many weeks did you say you were again?'

I tell him.

'Does that mean it happened when we were on holiday?'

'I think it was that last time, at the farm.'

'What are you going to do?'

'I was hoping you'd say, "what are *we* going to do?" but if you want to wash your hands of it, it might make life easier.'

'More straightforward, you mean. I don't think your life is going to be easy.' Nick looks me up and down. 'Are you absolutely sure? You don't look pregnant.'

'It's in there, all right. I've done a pregnancy test – four, in fact, since I did the first one at Jennie's – and I've felt the baby move. I'm going to get in touch with the doctor and midwife this week.'

'So you're keeping it?'

I nod. 'I don't believe in termination.'

'I want to play a part in the baby's life and be a proper dad,' Nick says.

'How can you do that when we live so far apart?'

'Stevie –' Nick places his hand on mine and cages it with his fingers – 'can we start again? You, me and the baby?'

It's something I hadn't considered and he's taken me by surprise. The tang of horseradish rasps at the back of my throat.

'It's like this was meant to be. Come back and live here. We can be a proper family.'

'No, Nick.'

'I want to be a good dad, not some bloke who lives over a hundred miles away and sends presents twice a year.'

'I hadn't thought you'd want to be so involved,' I stammer.

'Of course I want to be involved. This is my baby.' Half smiling, yet on the verge of tears, he pauses before blundering on. 'I know what you're going to say, that it isn't at all romantic, moving in with me because you're pregnant, but that's life. We have to face up to the commitment and responsibility of bringing a child into the world.'

I try to pull away, but he won't let go.

'It won't work, Nick. Having your baby isn't going to change how I feel about you.'

'Love can grow,' he says, the sinews in his neck taut with desperation. 'It does happen.'

'Not to me.' I shake my head. 'Not to us. I'm sorry.'

'This is fate. Can't you see there's something conspiring to bring us back together? That's the only explanation.'

'There's no such thing as fate, or the supernatural. There's no higher being who's suddenly decided they fancy doing a bit of matchmaking. We had sex and created a baby. It's as simple as that.' Feeling rotten as hell for being so abrupt with him, I wrench my hands from his grip.

'Stevie, will you marry me, please?'

'I really can't marry you. It's kind of you to offer, but—'

'There's nothing kind about it. I'm very fond of you. I've missed you. It makes perfect sense.'

I stand up. 'Nothing makes sense any more. It can't work, Nick. I'm in love with Leo,' I tell him and I burst into tears. 'I'll be in touch to talk some more. I've got to go.'

'Stevie, don't . . .' Nick begs, but I grab my bag and run outside. Nick doesn't follow me. He texts to check I'm okay and apologises for coming on too strong. I text him back, promising I'll meet him again later to talk through a few practicalities, before I spend the next hour pounding the pavement, railing against the baby for just being, and Nick for not being a complete bastard about it because life would be so much easier if he was.

Nick and I talk again in the afternoon, but we fail to resolve anything. I'm torn over his involvement. I know he means well and he's desperate to care for his child – he's always wanted children and I guess he thinks this could be his one chance. Not only that, he's a responsible and thoughtful person – in many ways, the ideal dad.

I fetch my car and belongings from the flat, having a brief chat with India who seems unhappy about me being there.

'You should have let me know you were staying the night,' she says as she offers me tea in the kitchen. 'I've got a date.'

'That's all right. I don't expect you to cancel. Who is he?'

'I don't want to jinx it by talking about him,' India says mysteriously.

'Oh?' I feel hurt.

'It's nothing personal, Stevie,' she goes on.

'I'll stay over and go home in the morning, if you don't mind, that is.'

'You can do as you wish. It's your flat,' she says.

'India, is there some problem?' I ask, hands on my hips.

'I'm not sure. Have you seen Nick?'

I decide not to lie to India. 'I had lunch with him . . . It's all right. I thought it would be nice to catch up, seeing I was here,' I add when I notice her brow furrow with suspicion.

'Was that a good idea?'

'It was only two friends having a drink and a sandwich, that's all.'

'I can't believe you did that, considering how you parted. Poor Nick.'

'Well, I won't be seeing him again for a while.'

India hands me a mug of tea and excuses herself, saying she needs to shower and change before she goes out. I lean against the units, looking out over the communal gardens, sipping my tea and wondering at how life has changed. I call the doctor's surgery which is open all day on Saturdays and speak to Nicci, one of the GPs, about contacting the midwife on Monday.

I drive home the following morning without seeing India again because she stays out all night. I send her a text to say goodbye. On the way back, Jennie texts me to ask how the meeting with Nick has gone. When I arrive at Nettlebed Farm, Leo is out – which is a relief, because it means I can avoid telling him about the baby for a little while longer. Instead I call Jennie to ask her if she'd like to come round for coffee.

'Can you come round to mine?' she says. 'I have a wedding cake in the Aga. I don't like to leave it.'

'I'll be there in five minutes.'

Jennie's kitchen is in chaos, with dirty mixing bowls stacked up in the butler sink, packets of cocoa and dried fruit strewn across the table and a laptop open with a list of orders and customer details.

'I like to do the wedding cakes here rather than in the bakery. It means I have complete control and I can have a break when I want one. I'm beginning to feel like an elephant.' She offers me cake. I decline. 'Have you contacted the doctor to arrange your scan and midwife appointments?'

'Yes, that's all under control, but I'm not sure how I'm going to deal with Nick.'

Jennie sits down opposite me at the table. 'How did it go? Tell me everything.'

'It was a shock, of course, but after he had a bit of a wobbly about whether or not he was definitely the father, he calmed down.'

'And?'

'He wants to be part of the baby's life.'

'That's good. There are men who would have preferred to walk away.'

I pick at a scab on the back of my hand – I caught it on a rusty nail in the cowshed. 'He wants to be part of my life too. He thinks we can make a fresh start.'

'What, and be a couple again?' Jennie shakes her head. 'Not for the sake of the baby. You mustn't do that. Anyway, what about Leo? Everyone knows you're an item.'

I bite my lip. I adore Leo.

'You haven't told Leo yet?' Jennie says.

'I can't. When he finds out, he'll hate me.'

'Oh, Stevie, what a mess,' Jennie sighs. 'But Leo's an intelligent man. He might be a little annoyed and upset at first, but I'm sure he'll come round. He loves you.'

'I think he loves me, or the person he thought I was.'

'You're having a baby. These things happen.'

'Leo doesn't want children,' I say.

'What, never?' Jennie's eyebrows shoot up under her hair. 'I can't believe that.'

'He's told me.' I explain about Jonas, and his fear of getting close to and losing another child. 'So, you see, he'll run a mile when he finds out I'm pregnant.'

'I can't really understand that,' Jennie says. 'There's no reason why history should repeat itself, and one day he'll want children of his own, surely?'

'He says not, and I believe him.' I pause. 'It isn't only that, I lied to him about why I was going to London. I've deceived him.'

'People make mistakes,' Jennie says. 'I made a mistake coming here to Devon after my divorce. David, my ex-husband, and I used to drive back and forth to London every other weekend, or meet halfway. Whatever we tried was never quite satisfactory. David was shattered after a long week at work, and I was struggling to get my business off the ground, and working on updating the house and garden.'

'Does he still see the children now?'

'They tend to go and stay less often, but for longer each time, so they might go and see him for half term, or a couple of weeks in the summer. It's interesting juggling their activities, especially Pony Club camp and the other horsey events. Adam works here and there, and now he has this girlfriend, so he isn't as keen to see his dad as he was.'

'Does David have other children?'

'Two little ones who are unbearably spoiled.'

'Is he okay about not seeing so much of your kids?'

'He's rented a holiday cottage locally before – that works well. I didn't realise how much it would affect everyone when I moved down here. It was a reaction to the divorce, I suppose. I had a dream and it worked out in the end. And we live happily ever after – almost happily – ' Jennie corrects herself. 'We have our ups and downs like any other married couple . . . I didn't care about how David felt at first. He didn't deserve any consideration after the way he'd treated me, cheating on me with a younger woman, but it has affected him. He misses our children, and they miss him.'

'He's still with the same woman?' I ask.

'Oh yes. It's funny really – he thought he was going to live this high life with a racy young girlfriend, travelling the world and going out to the best places, when in reality he's ended up remarried to someone who's actually quite staid, had children and got stuck in the same rut he tried so hard to get out of. Basically, he went from driving a people-carrier to driving a sports car and back to the people-carrier again. You have to laugh,' she adds rather wistfully. 'We had some good times together. My only regret is how the split affected our children, especially Adam.'

It occurs to me that all families have their complications.

'Listen to me going on,' Jennie says. 'We're supposed to be talking about you and Leo.'

'I'll pick my moment. I'll suggest we go out for a walk on the beach tomorrow night.'

'Why not tonight?' Jennie asks.

I shrug. 'I'm tired.'

'You can't put off telling him for much longer.'

'I know,' I say. I thank Jennie for the chat and return across the fields to Nettlebed Farm, where I run into Leo who's getting out of his four-by-four, laden down with bags of shopping.

'Hi, Stevie,' he mutters, his keyring between his teeth. Smiling, in spite of everything, I take his keys from him and unlock the caravan to let him in. 'Thanks. I'm glad you're back.' He drops the shopping onto the table in the living area and gives me a hug and a kiss. 'You should have texted to let know you were back.'

'I'm sorry.'

'Never mind,' he says. 'Would you like some lunch?'

We eat together and I wash the plates in the sink before excusing myself to go and help Cecil with the milking.

'Come over afterwards,' Leo says, moving up and pinching my bottom. 'I've bought a couple of DVDs to watch later – the latest James Bond and a comedy.'

'Can we catch up tomorrow night instead?' I say, watching his face and hoping I'm not hurting his feelings. 'I could do with catching up on some sleep.'

Leo grins. 'I get it. You stayed up all last night with India.'

I nod. 'I thought we could go and walk along the

seafront at Talymouth if it's a fine evening. We could buy some fish and chips.'

'That sounds great, a date at the beach,' he says, kissing the back of my neck as I wipe down the draining board. 'It'll give me something to look forward to when I'm TB-testing goodness knows how many cattle tomorrow.'

'I'll see you then,' I say.

'If not before,' Leo adds, and a quiver of guilt runs right through me when I see how happy he is. I lean up and give him the briefest kiss on the lips before I make a rapid escape.

Having done the milking and contacted the midwife to make appointments for an initial checkup and a scan, I walk across the yard on Monday morning, my hands in the pockets of my gilet (which I can no longer fasten across my front), telling myself that I have to calm down and stop railing against my bad luck. It's all very well, but this inconvenience is a baby and another human being. I recall my father rejecting me when I wanted to stay on the farm and my blood runs cold. It was the worst feeling in the world, and I would hate my baby to feel unloved and unwanted. It isn't fair. It didn't ask to be conceived.

'There's someone to see you, Stevie,' Leo says, putting his head around the door of the calves' shed where I'm mixing up more milk replacer for them. 'I've given him a coffee and biscuits.'

I pause, frowning. I'm not expecting anyone.

'It's me,' says Nick, pushing past Leo.

'Um, this is a surprise.' I can hardly believe my eyes. 'Nick? What are you doing here? Aren't you supposed to be at work?'

'There are more important things than accounts, Stevie. I've come to talk. It's all right. I won't stay and I'm not going to make a scene,' he says quickly. 'Is there anywhere we can go, in private?'

'You'll be all right, Stevie?' Leo says protectively, but I can see the muscle in his cheek tautening and relaxing and the tightness in his shoulders. Nick's presence appears to have put his back up, or is Leo upset with me about something? Does it have something to do with the other night, or with me rushing off to London, or with my ex-boyfriend turning up out of the blue when all along I've claimed Nick is no longer part of my life in any way whatsoever?

'I'm fine thanks, Leo. I'll see you later.'

'You haven't forgotten I'm doing the PD visit this afternoon?'

'Thanks for reminding me.'

'I should be back here at about one-thirty, if the TB testing goes smoothly and if that's okay with you.'

'Yes, I'll have the cows ready for your examination.' I look from Leo to Nick and back, and try to hurry Leo away before Nick starts talking. 'Bye, Leo.'

'What's a PD visit?' Nick asks after Leo has gone.

'PD stands for pregnancy diagnosis.'

'That's ironic,' Nick says icily. 'So you've moved the vet in.'

'Into the mobile home – he needed somewhere to stay.' I pause, trying to keep my cool when I'm actually

297

really annoyed at Nick for turning up unannounced. 'Nick, why are you here? Why didn't you tell me you were coming?'

'I thought I'd surprise you in return. India said I should come and talk to you face to face.'

'India? You've told India?'

'Well, yes, I assumed you would have talked to her before me. She always was your first port of call in a storm.'

'I didn't because you had to know first, seeing as you're the baby's father. It feels like you've adopted my best friend as your own.'

'She's been good to me since you dumped me.' Nick taps his lip with his forefinger. 'I really don't want our baby being brought up by another man.'

I worry the baby will already hear its parents at loggerheads. I don't want it born into a state of tension and mutual resentment.

'Do you want to go inside?' I ask, pointing to the house.

'Can we go for a walk?'

I take him through Steep Acres right to the very top, gratified to hear his laboured breathing – in spite of his gym membership – as we ascend the slope.

'Do you still go to the gym?' I ask him when we get to the pond.

'Can we sit down?' he says, and I show him to a stack of logs Cecil must have chopped up a while ago when one of the trees came down. The trees struggle to grow along the ridge – only the strongest survive. There are various saplings along with three fully grown oaks and three elms, and a couple of these don't look too healthy, their foliage sparse and turning brown at the tips. I scramble onto the stack and sit there, swinging my legs, whereas Nick examines the logs for any dirt that might rub off onto his designer jeans.

'Here, you can sit on my gilet,' I say, slipping it off.

'You won't be too cold?'

'I couldn't be bothered to take it off earlier. I'm quite warm.'

He takes it and spreads it out before perching himself carefully in the middle of it, keeping his feet on the ground. I wonder if the baby will take after Nick or me; if it will be a country child or a townie?

I gaze around me at the blue sky and green fields that sweep down towards the house and farm buildings. The sun is shining on the ripening corn and the blackberries in the hedgerow, like the baby growing and ripening inside me.

'Let's talk,' says Nick.

'Yes, let's,' I say, heavy-hearted.

'I've been thinking – in fact, I can't stop thinking about it. You're obviously in a very hormonal place—'

'Don't say that. That's incredibly sexist of you.' I wish I'd let him get his jeans dirty now. 'I'm perfectly rational.'

'I'm sorry. I apologise,' he repeats. 'I know you won't accept my offer of marriage at the moment, but I will leave it open so if you should change your mind at any time—'

'I won't change my mind, Nick, and that's the end of it.'

He holds up his hands. 'All right, I won't keep going on about it.'

'Is that all you came here for, only I'm pretty busy—'

'Stevie, this is important,' he cuts in. 'I want some reassurances from you that I can come with you to the hospital for the first scan and be present at the birth of our baby.' His eyes are wide, his expression hopeful, and I realise he has feelings for our child already, as have I. How can I deny him the opportunity to make a relationship with him, or her, no matter how difficult it will be?

'You can come for the scan,' I say.

'And the birth,' he says firmly.

'I'm not so sure about that.' It's a bit too intimate for me, the idea of Nick seeing me semi-naked, if not fully exposed, but the first moments are supposed to be very precious. 'How about you being available so you can see the baby immediately after the birth? Nick, I'm not sure how to deal with the situation, but I really don't think I could cope with you actually being there while I'm in labour.'

'We don't have to decide straight away, as long as you agree to it in principle,' Nick says. 'However we work it out, I promise I won't make things difficult. I just want to meet our baby as soon as she enters the world.'

'She?'

Nick smiles. 'I have an inkling already that she's a girl. I don't know why. How about you?'

I touch my stomach. 'I haven't a clue. It's pretty active so I wondered if it might be a boy.'

'Now who's being sexist?' Nick says wryly, and I have to laugh at myself for making assumptions when I've railed at my father so often for being sexist.

Nick doesn't stay for long once I've promised him I'll let him know the date and time of my first scan, and when he leaves, I watch him from the house. He has a brief chat with Leo outside the caravan, which is odd because I thought Leo had gone off on his rounds, and drives away in the Aston Martin.

'Why was that bloke here again, turning up like a bad penny?' I turn to find my father breathing down my neck.

'Have you had a shave recently?' I ask, noticing the whiskers growing on his chin.

'Stop distracting me, Stevie. I asked you a question.'

'I didn't want to have to tell you this, but it's inevitable.' I bite my lip. 'I'm pregnant.'

'Up the duff?' The eyebrow on Dad's good side shoots up under his hair. 'You aren't married.'

'You don't have to be married to have a baby. Look, I don't want to discuss it. I don't want any recriminations. I'm having this baby and that's all there is to it.'

'Whose is it? Leo's?'

'No, Dad. It's Nick's, of course. That's why he was here.'

'I'll drag him down to the church and make sure he marries you.'

'I am not going to marry him.'

'In that case I'll have to bloody well shoot the bastard.'

'Don't be silly, Dad. You haven't got a gun anymore.'

At least I hope he hasn't got any more hidden away. 'Please don't go on about it.'

'How are you going to carry on here on your own with a baby?'

'I'll just have to get on with it.' I notice Leo exiting the mobile home. 'Dad, I've got to go. Leo's doing the PD visit this afternoon. I'm going to give him a hand.'

'You can't. You're pregnant.'

'Dad! Don't go on about it. I'm perfectly capable of carrying on as normal.' I look at him, half cross, half smiling. 'Promise me you won't go shooting anyone.'

'Can I tell Cecil and Mary?' he asks.

'Not yet.'

'Are you worried about what people will think?'

'I really don't care,' I say emphatically, but I do care. I care what Leo thinks of me and I realise I'm going to have to tell him as soon as possible before somebody else does.

Leo is late back from TB testing and I join him in the collecting yard at three o'clock with the five cows Cecil and I kept back for him to check. I send Domino into the crush while Leo slips a glove over his arm and squirts it with lubricant before feeling around inside the cow, searching for signs she is pregnant. I watch his expression, waiting nervously, because I'd love Domino to be pregnant again so she can remain with us, doing her job. Leo looks sombre, almost angry.

'Well?' I ask.

Withdrawing his arm, he shakes his head. 'Not this time.'

'I'll give her a couple more chances.' I let Domino out of the crush. Not surprisingly, she's in a hurry. I know the longer she stays barren, the less economic it is to keep her, but I'm fond of her. I'm not ready to let her go. I drive the next cow into the crush, but before he examines her, Leo turns to me.

'You didn't tell me you were pregnant.' he says.

'H-h-how do you know?' I stammer.

'Your ex told me. Didn't you think it was something I should know about, considering you were supposed to be my girlfriend?'

'Were?'

'Obviously "were". You have lied to me and betrayed my trust.'

'I'm not like your ex-fiancée,' I say, shocked. 'What do you mean?'

'You withheld the fact you were pregnant when you decided to sleep with me—'

'When *we* decided to sleep together,' I correct him. 'It was a mutual decision.'

'Which I wouldn't have made if I'd known you were carrying a child.' He's annoyed and upset at me and I'm livid with Nick for revealing our secret before I've had a chance to talk to Leo about it. 'Don't you see how it looks? For all I know, you could have been trying to trap me. Luckily, with your ex turning up as he did and telling me himself, it meant I had a lucky escape.'

'I wasn't. I'm too far gone, Leo.'

'How far?'

'About twenty weeks.'

Leo whistles through his teeth. 'You don't look it . . .

I can't believe that.' His voice falters as I pick up on what he's just said.

'So you can understand how I missed it? Jennie suggested I might be pregnant and I did a test last week.'

'You didn't suspect a thing before that?'

'I put it down to stress.' A silence falls between us, and it's as if we're drifting apart on different ships, Leo to one end of the earth, me to the other. 'Leo, please don't be angry with me.' I'm close to tears. 'I don't think I can bear it.'

'I'm not just *angry* with you, Stevie. I'm absolutely *livid*. This isn't just about the pregnancy. If you *really* didn't know, then it's unfortunate, considering how I feel about children and babies . . . But it isn't just that, is it? You didn't tell me the truth about why you were going to London at the weekend. You said you were going to see India, not Nick.' Leo seems to tower over me, his eyes flashing with fury. 'I'll never trust you again.'

'Leo, please. I had to tell Nick first, can't you see that? Can't you?' I begin. 'Can't we carry on as we were?' Even as I say it, I know it's impossible. 'I'll never do it again.'

'You won't because I won't give you the chance. I've been there before, remember.'

'I'm sorry.' I reach out to hold him, but he pushes me away. 'Leo . . .' His name catches in my throat.

He swears and, for a moment, I think he's going to soften and change his mind, but he backs off.

'I don't want to talk about this again. Let me get on with my job,' he says curtly, and he puts on a fresh disposable glove, twisting the fingers as if he wishes he was twisting my neck.

Crying, I wait for him to examine the next cow.

'Positive, about forty-five days,' he says.

I release the cow from the crush and send the next one in. She's pregnant too and normally I'd be over the moon, but I'm devastated. Even if I hadn't lied to Leo about going to see Nick, and told him about the baby as soon as I'd found out, the consequences would have been the same.

I want to fight for him, to win him back, but I can see there's no way forward. The damage has been done and there's no way to return to those nights in the caravan, lying in Leo's arms with the light of the moon falling across our faces and listening to the screech of the barn owl. The problem, I think, as I watch him check the last cow, is not only that I'm carrying another man's child, but that Leo doesn't want children.

Chapter Sixteen

White Rabbits

Leo keeps his distance and I keep mine, but two days later, as I'm crossing the yard in the middle of the afternoon to get the cows in for milking, I find him carrying a rucksack and holdall out of the mobile home and heading for his four-by-four.

'Are you going somewhere?' I call.

He hesitates as he places the holdall in the back of the vehicle.

'I suppose I should have told you,' he begins. He looks exhausted, with dark rings around his eyes, his hair even more tousled than usual and his mouth turned down at the corners. I want to comfort him. Most of all, I want him to hold me in his arms and tell me everything will be all right. 'I'm moving out,' he goes on.

'Where will you go?'

He shrugs. 'I'll find somewhere. I can always get a room at the Barnscote – anywhere but here.'

'Leo, don't!'

'I can't bear to look at you.'

'I'll keep out of your way. Please, stay at least until the end of the summer.'

'I've made my mind up,' he says.

'Wait there.' I run across the yard, past the house and to the cottage where Cecil is putting on his boots outside the front door. 'Cecil, Leo's leaving. Can you make him stay? Please, he might listen to you.'

'What can I do? He's a grown man.'

'Just try. I feel so guilty about what's happened and now he's moving out with nowhere to go because of me.' I bundle a protesting Cecil towards the caravan and leave him with Leo. 'I'll get the cows in.'

When I get back with Bear and the rest of the herd, the first thing I notice is that Leo's four-by-four is still in the yard. I duck inside the parlour to see if Cecil's ready for the first batch of cows.

'What did he say?' I ask. 'Is he staying?'

'He's very upset,' Cecil says. 'You've treated him harshly. I'm surprised at you, Stevie.'

I wince at Cecil's justified criticism of my behaviour.

'Oh dear,' Cecil goes on. 'You have got yourself in a muddle. What are we going to do with you?'

'I don't know,' I wail.

Cecil pats my shoulder. 'Don't worry, my lover. It'll all come out in the wash. All you have to do is look after yourself and this baby.' He smiles. 'And help me get these cows milked. Come on. Let's get a move on.'

Later the same evening, when I'm feeding the calves, I hesitate at the door to the nursery. Leo is singing and playing his guitar. Tears stream down my face because I so very nearly had it all, everything I always wanted, and now I've lost him. I touch my belly where the baby stirs beneath my fingertips. Instead, I have a new responsibility, a renewed involvement with my faraway ex and the continuing uncertainty about the project to save Nettlebed Farm.

I feed the calves and retire early to bed.

News spreads fast and my pregnancy triggers a flurry of knitting. Within a week, Mary has presented me with a tiny white cardigan with rocking horse buttons, two hats and a pair of bootees. The appointment for my twenty-week scan is not for another week after that, which makes it twenty-two weeks in reality. I wake up at the usual time in the morning, even though I could have had a lie-in because Adam is helping Cecil with the milking.

Nick is meeting me at the hospital and, although I'm pleased to have his support, I'm dreading seeing him again. It's a strange situation, almost businesslike.

'Hello, Stevie,' Nick says when I meet him outside the café at the hospital. He looks pale and fraught.

'Hi, Nick. How are you?'

'Okay. I didn't think I was going to make it because of the traffic on the M3.' He switches his mobile off. 'We'd better find out where we're going. How are you?'

'Are you asking after me or the baby?'

He frowns briefly. 'Both, of course.' He guides me along the corridor, his hand on my back. I walk a little faster. 'Are you nervous?' he asks. 'I'm excited and nervous at the same time. Do you want to know the sex of the baby?'

'I haven't really thought about it.' I have, but it hasn't been uppermost in my mind. I've been more preoccupied with grieving for the end of my relationship with Leo, his presence at the farm being a constant reminder. I'm grateful to Cecil for persuading him to stay on though.

'Oh?' says Nick, as if he's thought of nothing else. 'Stevie, I'm so sorry about this. I can see what a struggle this is for you and I wish this hadn't happened, but it's hard for me to . . . to see you not caring about this baby, our baby, not wanting it.' He hesitates as I stop in the corridor, my heart beating fast, sweat pricking in my palms, because I want to run away and forget about the baby, put its existence out of my mind, but I can't go anywhere. I'm on a conveyor belt with no way of getting off.

'Nick, I do care,' I say. 'How can you think that? You aren't building this up into something it isn't are you? You aren't going to make a case for . . .' I look at him, really look at him. 'You wouldn't, would you?'

'I might.'

'You bastard!' I walk smartly away towards the antenatal clinic.

'Stevie, you're taking it the wrong way. I didn't mean . . .' I'm aware of the sound of Nick's feet squeaking along the lino behind me. ' . . . Stevie!' I turn left into the clinic and stop at the reception desk.

'Stephanie Dunsford for a scan.'

'I'm coming in with you,' Nick says beside me.

'I'd rather you didn't,' I say, angry with him. 'How can I trust you when you're angling to get custody of our child?'

'I didn't say that. What I'm saying is that if you really can't cope with bringing it up, if you can't love it, I'll be a full-time dad—'

'And I'll see it every other weekend, or whatever the court decides, because I'll fight you tooth and nail, Nick.'

'Is this man being a nuisance?' the receptionist interrupts anxiously. 'Only I can call security if he is.'

'No, it's okay.' I head into the waiting area with Nick following me. As I make to sit down, he sits down beside me. 'Will you push off and leave me alone?' I hiss.

'Stevie, I haven't said I'm taking the baby away from you. Please be reasonable.'

That expression 'Please be reasonable' is like a red rag to a bull: a rural expression with a lot of truth in it. I'm too upset to speak.

'I didn't come here to fight. I came to support you while you have the scan and see the baby for the first time. I'm not stupid, although you treat me that way at times. Babies should be with their mothers.' Nick leans close to me, fire in his eyes. I've never seen him like this before. 'You know me. All I want is to do the right thing.'

I sit back, overtaken by a wave of exhaustion. I haven't got the energy for a fight. I look up at Nick's face. He's calm, cool even, and I believe he means what he says. I'm grateful that he has our baby's best interests at heart, but he's given me this niggling concern that he might put up a fight for custody after the baby is born.

'Stephanie Dunsford.' The sonographer calls us through. 'Are you dad?' she asks Nick, who blushes and nods. She chats us through the procedure, squeezes a blob of cold gel onto my naked bump and presses a probe against my skin, and there it is in shades of grey: proof that there really is a baby in there.

'Oh,' I gasp. It's real and, although I wasn't sure before, I find myself smiling as I glance at Nick and back to the screen again. 'Hello there, Baby.'

'It's a miracle,' Nick says softly, clearing his throat.

'There's Baby's head,' the sonographer says.

'Can you tell if it's a boy or a girl?' Nick asks.

'You want to know?'

Nick looks at me. I nod.

'She's a girl,' says the sonographer.

'I knew it. That's wonderful. Amazing.' Smiling, Nick reaches out and squeezes my hand. 'Is she right for the dates? Is she twenty-two weeks?'

Nick, why did you have to go and ask that, I think. Does he really have doubts? Does he not believe me?

'All the measurements point to that – she's a bonny baby.'

'I'm sorry, Stevie. I had to ask, for my own peace of mind,' Nick explains when we're walking back along the corridor towards the hospital entrance. 'Can I get you a coffee to make up for it?' When I hesitate, he continues, 'If this is going to work, we're going to have to ditch all our baggage for the baby's sake.'

311

'You're right,' I say eventually, and we head for the café for drinks and pastries. Nick sits opposite me.

'How's India?' I ask.

'How would I know?' he says quickly.

'I just thought . . . She said she'd seen you a couple of times.'

'She's okay, as far as I know. I thought you'd have kept in touch with her.'

'I have, but you've seen her in the flesh. Talking on the phone isn't the same.'

'Well, if you want me to tell you she has a new hair-style, I'm not the man to ask. She always looks . . . she takes care of herself.' Nick sips at a latte. I drink orange juice. 'India misses you.'

'I miss her too.'

'Have you thought any more about the flat? Have you changed your mind about keeping it, only I'll make you an offer if you want to sell?'

'You want to buy it?'

'I have money to invest and, as you've said before, it's a sound investment.' Nick clears his throat. 'I'm not trying to buy my way back into your favour. I know you won't stand for that, but I'm not a bad man. I'm sure you could do with releasing the money, especially now – what with the farm project and the baby.'

I thank him, saying I'll think about his offer, because it is tempting, considering the potential costs of the project are snowballing, but I can't help wondering if Nick has an ulterior motive in making it. Is he hoping that I'll eventually see what a wonderful guy he is, and marry him so we can play happy families with the

312

baby? I'm not sure it's fair of me to think that way, but I can understand how he feels. I'm the same with Leo, hoping and praying that if he stays on the farm, and catches sight of me now and again, he'll be reminded that I'm not all bad, and, just maybe, he'll stop avoiding me and we'll get back together again. It's a long shot, but I live in hope.

I take advantage of a sunny early evening after milking to join James in the barn, where he's sawing wood to create a frame that we can attach to the trailer on the float.

'I thought you'd be putting your feet up,' he says, looking up from his workbench. He's dressed in chainsaw gloves and trousers, and an orange helmet.

'I'm not ill, James. And anyway, I'm creative director of this tableau, so I need to keep an eye on things.' I'm teasing and James knows it.

He chuckles. 'Are you here to crack the whip?'

'We haven't got long to get this finished and it has to be perfect if we're going to beat the competition.'

'I thought that was part of the charm of carnival – the mock-ups and imperfections.' James smiles.

'I hope you're doing a proper job because I want to ask you if you'll take on the building project.'

'Have you got the planning permission?' James's eyes light up.

'Not yet. I'm still hoping. No, DJ won't budge on his budget, so I've said I'll find someone else. So if your offer still stands, I'd like to take you up on it. If the planning does go through, we'll start building the

Shed in January. Any time after that and it will be too late.'

'My cousin will be made up,' says James, 'and it'll give me a good start to the year.'

'Let's hope we get good news soon then.'

'I'd better get on with the float. Stand back, Stevie. I don't want any accidents.'

He slips his visor down over his eyes and touches the chainsaw blade to the wood, the teeth bind and there's an enormous clattering sound and swearing as the chain snaps away, flying into the air, followed by a scream and the sound of horses' hooves thundering away into the distance.

'Ohmigod,' I shout, glancing back to check James is okay as I run to the side of the barn, pull up a barrel and climb onto it so I can scramble over the wall and see what's going on outside on the footpath. Sophie is lying on the floor, sobbing and gasping for breath, while Georgia is clinging to her horse for dear life as it rears and tosses its head repeatedly, trying to follow its friend Bracken as she gallops off away from home.

'That noise,' says Georgia. 'It spooked the ponies.'

'I'm so sorry. James, come quickly. I'll look after Sophie,' I say as he vaults over the wall. 'You go and catch the pony.'

'If I can,' he says, grimacing as it disappears into the distance. 'It looks more like a bloody racehorse.'

I join Sophie on the floor, putting my arm around her and telling her to breathe slowly. She's conscious, but winded, and I worry she's broken something.

'Can you take your horse over there?' I ask Georgia, who's clearly worried for her sister too. 'I don't feel terribly safe with those horseshoes flashing about so close to my ears.'

Georgia tightens her calves against the horse's sides and it springs forwards, taking a hold of the bit and dancing on the spot. Bracken is the bay-brown creature with the mealy muzzle and bug-eyes, while Georgia's mount is a big chestnut horse, part thoroughbred with long legs and pricked ears.

'Stop being such an idiot, Chester,' she tells him, smacking him on the neck with her crop at the same time.

Gradually, Sophie catches her breath and begins to calm down. I start to relax a little. I don't think we need an ambulance.

'Are you hurt?'

'My bottom hurts and my leg.'

'I'll call your mum and let her know what's happened,' I tell her.

'She's at the bakery.'

'I'll go and get her,' says Georgia and she rides Chester past. In the meantime, while we're waiting for Jennie, James appears with Bracken. She is mooching along on the end of the reins as if nothing has happened.

'Are you going to get back on?' James asks.

'I don't think so,' Sophie says as Bracken stops and snatches mouthfuls of grass from along the side of the path. 'I don't want that pony any more. She hates me. She's always bucking me off.'

315

'It wasn't the pony's fault,' I say, helping Sophie up. 'James was working in the barn and the chain snapped on the chainsaw. It went with a terrific bang.'

Sophie seems a little disappointed that she hasn't broken a bone.

'Georgia broke her arm when she fell off Bracken. She couldn't ride for ages.' Sophie hobbles along, holding on to my hand, and I wonder what it will be like, having a daughter of my own. 'I don't really like riding much. I prefer mucking out. In fact, I don't think I'll ride any more. Georgia makes me go out for hours and she's mean to me.'

'Oh, I doubt that.'

'She is. She makes me go out in the rain until I get soaked. She was the one who decided to go this way today. I told her we should have gone down the lane. I hate my stupid sister! I don't know why Mum won't put her in a foster home.'

I try not to laugh, but I'm concerned about Sophie's opinion of riding. Isn't it every girl's dream? We used to have a pony on the farm and I did ride him on and off for a couple of years, but he was often lame and my father didn't want to waste any grazing on ponies, so we weren't allowed to have another one, plus my mum wasn't horsey like some of the Pony Club mums. It seems such a shame that Sophie has a pony but she doesn't really want to ride.

Jennie comes waddling as fast as she can along the track towards us. She waves frantically.

'It's all right,' I call. 'She's still in one piece.'

By the time she reaches her mum, Sophie is hardly

limping. She has a sandy patch on her jodhpurs and her face is smeary with dust and dried tears.

'Are you going to jump back on?' Jennie asks. 'I think you should get back in the saddle at least to walk back to the stable. I don't want you losing your confidence over a tiny little tumble.'

'It wasn't that tiny,' I say. 'Bracken shied and cantered off.'

'Well, no harm done,' Jennie says brightly. 'You'll still be all right for the showjumping team competition next weekend.'

'I don't wanna do it,' Sophie says.

'But you've been training all summer.' Jennie glances at me. 'I feel as if we've all been focused on it. You've been selected for the team – it's a great honour. I don't think Guy would be very pleased if you back out now after we've spent all that money on the ponies. We spend a fortune keeping you in jodhpurs.' Jennie has the bearing of an over-competitive mother and I wonder if I'll be the same with my daughter.

'I'm sorry, but I think it was our fault,' I say. 'James was working on the float.'

'How is it going? I'd forgotten I was supposed to be making some costumes for the girls.'

'Haven't you got enough to do? Isn't the baby due around carnival time?'

'Any time in the next two weeks. I was late with the others.' Jennie looks down as she stretches her smock across her bump.

'Why don't I look for a couple of those all-in-one

suits – there's bound to be a cow or a pig onesie available online.'

'Ah, they both want to be ponies,' Jennie says. 'A pig is a complete no-no. They might come round to the cow with some bribery and corruption.'

'I'll have a look,' I say.

'Guy was telling me about how Uphill Farm and Nettlebed Farm were fierce rivals at carnival time.'

'Just at carnival time?' I cut in, amused.

'Good point,' Jennie says.

'Did he tell you about the time when he and his brother sabotaged our float?' They were a lot older than us and should have known better, but they wanted to win by fair means or foul.

Jennie hesitates for a fraction of a second too long, making me doubt her.

'No, I don't believe so,' she says. Is she protecting her husband?

'We were creating a round-the-world theme and they stole our globe. In return, Ray and I let the tyres down on their trailer at the last minute. Okay, I'm not proud of it either, but it was war.'

'Guy told me you let down their tyres before they stole the globe,' Jennie says.

'So they did do it,' I say. 'I could never prove it – until now!'

Jennie's hand flies to her mouth. 'Perhaps I shouldn't have said anything.'

'I knew you weren't telling the truth,' I say lightly. 'Jennie, you give yourself away.'

'So you aren't cross with me?'

I shake my head. 'I've always wondered.'

She breaks into peals of laughter. 'Guy will kill me.'

'He won't, Mummy,' says Sophie. 'He loves you too much.' She turns to me. 'He brought Mummy breakfast in bed before he did the milking this morning.'

'It was lovely, but too early,' Jennie smiles.

'Let me know if you need me – when the baby's on its way,' I say.

'Thank you, Stevie.' Jennie looks down the footpath where the two girls are heading back towards Uphill Farm, Georgia on horseback, Sophie hobbling alongside Bracken.

'I hope she's going to be all right,' I observe.

'She's fine,' Jennie says. 'She'll stop limping as soon as she gets round the corner. Oh, I know, I'm not terribly sympathetic at the moment. Sophie's being very difficult – I think she's worried about the baby and how it's going to impact her. You have all this to look forward to, Stevie. How is Leo? What did he say when you told him?'

'It's over,' I say. 'I assumed everyone knew.'

'I heard rumours, of course, but I saw he was still living at the farm so I wasn't sure. I'm sorry. I know you liked him a lot.'

'I probably shouldn't because I expect I'll be disappointed, but I live in hope that we might at least be friends again one day.'

Leo did wave to me this morning as if he wanted to speak to me, but he seemed to change his mind and walked away in the opposite direction. I fold my arms across my chest, trying to check my emotions. 'I'd better get back to the float. I'll see you around.'

'Take care, Stevie,' Jennie says before she follows the girls back along the footpath.

'Panic over,' James says when we return to the barn. 'There's never a dull moment around here. Are you going to make a start on the painting?'

'I'm not sure my artistic talents are up to it. I did Art GCSE and scraped a pass.'

'I'm sure you can manage a couple of animals – a donkey and a rabbit, maybe. They can be cartoon characters.'

'Well, they aren't going to be fine art.'

'Go for it, Stevie. There are some brushes over in the corner and I found some old part-used tins of paint at home. They're in the van.'

'What are you going to do about the chainsaw?' I ask as I pick out the paintbrush with the most bristles from the bucket James has brought with him.

'I can fix it. I have a spare chain.'

'You're really getting into this, aren't you?'

'I love it,' he grins.

'You're in a very good mood.' I perch on a bale of straw. I'm putting off the moment when I have to apply paint to the vast expanse of board that is leaning against the wall behind the plough. 'Are you going to stay for tea and cider? Mary's made a ham salad and fresh bread. There's plenty of it.'

'Thanks, but I'm not staying late tonight.'

'Oh?'

'In fact, I need to get going. I have a date,' James says, blushing.

'Who is she?'

'No one you know. She lives in Talysands – she runs the go-karts down on the seafront there. I did some gardening for her.' He has a twinkle in his eye when he goes on, 'I mowed her lawn and dabbled in her flowerbeds.'

'What's she like?'

'Divorced with two kids, quite tall, nice smile . . .'

'Have a good evening then,' I say, pleased for him.

When James has gone, leaving the paint with me, I turn the lights on in the barn and have a go at drawing a rabbit, using a piece of chalk to do a rough sketch on the board.

'Hi, Stevie. I heard noises and thought I'd come and investigate.'

I turn at the sound of Leo's voice as he approaches, his shirtsleeves rolled up and his hands in his pockets.

'Where's the dog? He hasn't barked.'

'He's over there.' Bear's made himself a bed out of the dustsheets and can't be bothered to move. 'What do you want?' I ask. My mouth is dry, my knees weak. Why is Leo here? Why this sudden change of heart, seeking me out so he can talk to me? I don't believe he came just because he heard noises . . .

'I came to see what you and James have been up to,' Leo says.

'What do you think?' I say, taking a step back to show him my artwork.

'It's a rabbit,' he says after a moment's hesitation. 'Shouldn't the ears be a bit bigger?'

I hand him the chalk. 'You have a go.'

321

Leo moves up close to me.

'You have chalk on your face. Here. And here.' He touches my cheek, and smiles, making my heart lurch with longing, but the expression in his eyes is one of deep sadness.

'How's the float going?' he asks, moving away.

'Slowly, as you can see. We could do with some extra pairs of hands.' I hardly dare ask. 'Would you like to join us? It's good fun.'

'I don't think I've been to a carnival before.'

'Then you can come with us and see what you've been missing,' I say, hoping that, if Leo and I can spend time together, he'll see that we are meant for each other, in spite of the baby, and he'll forgive me.

'When is it?'

'Late September. You have plenty of time to swap your on-call.'

'I'm afraid I'll have to pass,' Leo says awkwardly, shifting from one foot to the other. 'I probably won't be here.'

'Why? Where will you be?'

'I've got a new job.'

A chill descends on the barn and it is as if I am standing outside myself. I see myself press my fingers to my lips to suppress a cry of distress at the thought of Leo not being here at Nettlebed Farm, of not being even a small part of my life any more. I hear the sob that catches in my throat and see myself turning away from him, pretending I'm chasing a stray eyelash. I see Leo at my side, putting his arm around my shoulders.

'Why are you so upset?' he asks quietly. 'You knew I

wasn't staying for longer than the summer.'

'But you said you would consider staying on,' I say, the words choking me.

'That was when we were together. We aren't together any more,' he says to emphasise the point. 'You didn't think I'd stay on when there's nothing to stay for?'

'Of course I didn't,' I say, but I'm lying. I've thought about Leo staying for good, dreamed it and hoped for it. 'This is so stupid,' I sniff. 'It's my hormones making me cry all the time. I'll miss having you around.'

'I know things have been bad between us recently, but I'd like you to know that, in spite of everything, I think you're a wonderful person, Stevie, and I'd like to count you as my –' he corrects himself – 'one of my best friends.'

You are my best friend, I want to say, but I don't want to let myself sound desperate because the last thing I want is for him to feel guilty. It's better that Leo remains in ignorance about the depths of my love for him. I glance down at the small swell of my stomach. I resent the fact I'm pregnant. Sometimes I hate this baby, this parasite growing inside me. I glance towards Bear. He's listening to the conversation, one ear cocked, and I sigh. I made my bed, as my father would say, and now I have to lie in it.

'So, when do you leave?' I ask him, more in control of my emotions.

'I fly out at the end of September or the beginning of October. I'm waiting for confirmation of my flight.'

'So soon?'

He nods.

'I couldn't turn it down, Stevie. It's what I've been looking for since I qualified.'

'The dream of working with your friend? New Zealand?' Any tiny hope I had that he might at least be staying in the UK is dashed, swatted down like a fly. 'Don't you need immigration papers to work there?'

'It's all in hand,' Leo says. 'I've done my homework.'

'Well,' I say bravely, 'I won't say I'm glad you're leaving. I wish you all the luck in the world.'

'Thank you,' he says, and he dives forward and kisses me briefly on the cheek. 'Can we be friends?'

I nod. 'Friends,' I confirm, my heart screwed up with love, sorrow and confusion. I'm lucky I have my dad, Cecil and Mary, James and Jennie, and the float and the project to work on, but when Leo finally leaves Nettlebed Farm, it will feel like the end of all my dreams.

Chapter Seventeen

Carnival of the Animals

'Why don't we have *Carnival of the Animals* as our theme?' I recall my brilliant idea and wish I hadn't gone into this on such a grand scale. Carnival of the animal, singular, would have been better, more manageable. I am finishing painting a cow on the boards at the back of the float, a smiley cow that looks more like a hippopotamus, with black and white patches and a flower sticking out of her mouth. It isn't right. I'd like to paint over her and start again, but – I glance at my watch – it's too late. The carnival is tonight and we need to get going.

I'm glad in a way. It gives me something to take my mind – if anything can – off the fact that Leo is leaving soon, having had his flight confirmed for the end of September, just after the carnival.

James turns up, along with Jennie, Adam, Georgia and Sophie, and Leo texts me to say he'll be along later because he's delivering a calf on a farm up near Talyford. We're on friendly terms again, but there are no more cosy evenings curled up together in the caravan.

'What happened with the date?' I ask James who's pulling on his furry onesie. He's supposed to be a yellow dog, but he looks more like a Teletubby. 'I forgot to ask.'

'It didn't work out. She wasn't my type and I reckon all she wanted was some free landscaping.'

'I'm sorry.'

'It doesn't matter. By the way, I've found out who's judging the carnival this year,' James says. 'It's Fifi.'

'Oh no . . .'

'I was wondering about lodging an objection.'

'This is supposed to be fun,' I point out.

James stares at me as if I'm slightly touched.

'Stevie, we're in it to win it. We haven't put all this work into the float to come last.'

'I'm ready with the face paints,' says Jennie, her make-up laid out along the trestle table with brushes and wipes. Perched on the edge of a canvas chair, she looks enormous.

'Are you sure you should be doing this?' I ask.

'I'm fine,' she says, smiling. 'In fact, I've never felt better. And I wouldn't miss this for the world. I've never been part of a carnival. Guy's such an old stick-in-the-mud when it comes to these kinds of events. He's happy enough to run around the streets with a burning tar barrel on his back, but when it comes to dressing up, he won't do it.'

'Isn't he coming then?'

'He'll be in the pub. He'll come out and watch us. He won't be able to resist. Adam, have you got the bucket for the collection?'

'I've got it, Mum.' He rattles the small change in the bottom. He's dressed as a farmer in wellies, jeans, waxed jacket and hat. Georgia is a cat and Sophie a rabbit.

'What are you supposed to be, Stevie?' Georgia asks.

'What do you think?' I put the paintbrush down and rest my hands on my hips.

'Another rabbit?' she says.

'I'm a donkey. Can't you tell by the ears?'

'They're a bit floppy for a donkey. You look more like a brown rabbit to me.'

'It's the overall effect that counts. If you're all ready, I'll fetch the tractor so we can hook up the generator for the music and lights.' I head out across the yard, climb into the cab and turn the key in the ignition, but the engine remains stubbornly silent. 'Come on, Bertha.' Unfortunately, Bertha has no concept of the importance of the occasion and she fails to rise to it. There's nothing, neither a cough nor a splutter. 'Oh bugger!' I clamber out – I'm beginning to move with the agility of a long-toed sloth.

'Did I hear somebody swearing?' Georgia calls.

'No,' I call back.

'I think I did.'

'Georgia, it wasn't a swear word,' says Sophie. 'Mum says bugger all the time.'

'Never mind what Stevie said,' Jennie says, somewhat impatiently. 'The tractor's broken down.'

'And we need it to tow the trailer,' says James.

'Yes, I know that, thank you,' I say. 'What are we going to do now?'

'Guy has a tractor,' says Georgia.

'Two tractors,' adds Sophie, 'but the old one doesn't work very well.'

I turn to Jennie. 'Do you think . . . ?'

'I'll ask him,' she says, getting up from the face-painting station and fetching her mobile from her bag. 'Better still, I'll tell him.'

It seems Guy wouldn't lend us a tractor, even if he had a hundred of them.

'Come on, love,' Jennie says. 'You know how much the children have been looking forward to this. It would be a shame to let them down because of your stupid pride. And besides, you've been worrying about me going out without you tonight. This is the perfect opportunity for you to be with me in case I should –' she touches her stomach – 'go into labour.'

I can hear his exclamation of shock.

'I've been having a few aches and pains today, nothing much, but you never know.' Jennie turns and winks at me. She's winding him up. I smile back. 'Oh, thank you, darling. You are such a wonderful man. The children will be so happy. Yes, we'll see you in ten minutes.' She pauses and adds, 'No, we're not expecting you to dress up. You don't need to. Everyone knows you're an old bear.' She switches off the mobile.

'I do love my husband. He's a sweetie really. He'll do anything for me.'

I look away, suddenly tearful. I wish I had someone who would do anything for me.

Guy brings his tractor up to the farm and hitches it to the trailer, hardly speaking, and we travel slowly along the lane to join the procession of floats and performers at the bottom of Talyton St George, near the Dog and Duck. There's a party atmosphere, the scent of sausages and fried onions in the air, and even a fine drizzle can't put a dampener on the proceedings. Sophie, Georgia and James are dancing to the music playing from the loudspeakers that James rigged up on the float, while Adam walks alongside, rattling the loose change in a bucket to encourage the onlookers to contribute to charity. Jennie and I sit on a bench, taking up the rear, waving and smiling. Jennie is dressed up as an elephant in a grey cloak and big ears. She's removed her trunk.

'Stevie.' She grabs my arm as we travel towards Market Square, holding it in a vice-like grip.

'Jennie, what's wrong?'

'My waters have broken.' OMG, I think, as she goes on, 'The baby's on its way. I can't move.'

'Can't you hang on for an hour or so?' I ask, looking at the length of the carnival procession. It's slowed right down because the longer trucks in front of ours are having to reverse back up two or three times each to make the corner by Mr Rock's fish-and-chip shop. 'We could be stuck in this queue for a while.'

'This baby isn't going to wait.' Jennie bites her lip.

'Babies aren't usually in such a hurry are they?' I say, nervously.

'This is my fourth. It might pop out at any time.'

'How long do you think it will be?' My voice rises to a squeak with panic.

'I don't know, do I?' she exclaims. 'I'm not a midwife. It could be a couple of hours or twenty minutes.' She starts to rock back and forth, moaning and clutching her stomach.

'I'll talk to Guy,' I say, moving to the front of the float and leaning up over the boards to yell at Guy who's driving the tractor.

'Guy. Guy!' He can't hear me. 'Adam, get your stepdad to stop the tractor!' I yell, and eventually the float jerks to a stop, unseating Jennie and sending the rest of us flying. The music stops.

'What is it?' Guy says crossly over the sound of the engine.

'Guy! Jennie's having the baby,' I shout.

'I know she's having a baby,' he says, sounding faintly irritated. 'I was there at the conception.'

'No, she is having *the* baby. She's in labour.'

'Guy, keep driving.' Jennie's screams run right through me, making me dread the thought of going into labour. 'I need to get to the hospital.'

'You can't take the tractor,' I say. 'It'll take too long. Let's see if we can beg a lift from the St John's ambulance. They're over there outside the Co-op.'

Guy stares at me. 'What about the tractor?'

'I can drive it,' I offer.

'What? You drive my tractor? Do you know how much this beauty cost?'

'I have a fair idea.' I've been looking at one like it in the brochures. This will make a good test drive. I glance towards Jennie. Her brow is damp with sweat and her face contorted with pain. 'Guy, forget about the tractor and get your wife to hospital, otherwise she's going to give birth on the spot.'

A pair of clowns performs cartwheels past the float. A horn sounds, and another, until there's a cacophony of hooting and tooting coming from behind us.

'Please, Guy,' Jennie begs.

'All right. Let's go, darling,' Guy says, making his mind up.

'Mummy, don't go,' calls Sophie.

'I have to. You know that. The next time I see the three of you, the baby will be here. Now, stay with Stevie and she'll look after you.'

'But, Mummy . . .'

'You have to collect our prize,' Jennie says as Guy helps her down and carries her through the crowd towards the Co-op. 'Go on now. You have to catch up.'

Relieved that I'm not going to have to deliver the baby by applying my knowledge of delivering calves, I jump into the tractor and drive on, trying to catch up with the majorettes and the Brownies. The procession stops at the top end of the town where Fifi as lady mayor presents the awards. We are given second place for the medium-sized float with a natural theme, a blue rosette and a voucher for tea for six at the garden centre.

'So you can see what a real tearoom looks like,' Fifi says.

'Thank you,' I say, sorry that Leo hasn't made it in time to see any of the carnival.

'Was it worth doing all that work for that?' Adam asks James.

'Of course it was. It's the taking part, not the winning that counts.' James lowers his voice, but I can still hear him. 'I've got a few beers behind the generator.'

'James, no,' I say. 'I'm responsible for Adam at the moment. I don't think he should be drinking.'

'I can speak for myself,' Adam says. 'Mum lets me drink. In fact, she encourages it.'

'Does she? I don't quite believe it.'

'She says I should learn to drink in moderation. Apparently, it will reduce my desire to binge-drink later. It's a proven scientific fact, isn't it, James?'

'Indeed, it is,' James says with a straight face.

'I don't believe either of you,' I tell them. 'Now, Adam, Georgia and Sophie, would you like to stay at Nettlebed Farm tonight while we're waiting for your new brother or sister to arrive?'

'Will the scary old man with the gun be there?' Sophie asks.

'That's my dad you're talking about.'

'Oh, I'm sorry.' She blushes beneath the streetlight.

'I'd like to stay, Stevie,' Georgia says.

'So would I,' Sophie says.

'I'd like to, but I can't,' Adam says, and I wonder if he's cross with me about the beers. 'Someone has to let Lucky out. It's all right, Stevie. I have a key.'

332

'You don't,' Sophie says. 'That's just what Mum says to tell everyone because she doesn't want the whole town knowing we keep our doors unlocked.'

'Lucky would bite a burglar on the bum,' Georgia says.

'I'll take you all back to the farm,' I say. 'Adam can walk home from there.'

'Or I can drive the tractor,' he says. 'Guy lets me. I have a provisional licence and I'm almost ready to take my test.'

'In a car, not a tractor,' Georgia says scathingly, their skirmish reminding me of me and my brother.

When we get back, I check my mobile. No one has heard anything from Jennie and Guy yet and I wonder if they made it to the hospital in time.

Jennie texts at eight in the morning to announce the arrival of a baby son, a brother for Adam, Georgia and Sophie, at 3 a.m., weighing in at a massive ten pounds. I text back my congratulations, only for Jennie to ring me a few moments later.

'How are you?' I ask her.

'Not too bad, although I felt as though I was giving birth to a watermelon. I could have stayed for the rest of the carnival – the travelling slowed everything down.' I can tell she's smiling when she continues. 'I won't give you all the gory details because I don't want to put you off.'

'The girls would love to come and see you,' I say as they jump up and down beside me. 'I can bring them. Or are you coming home soon?'

333

'I'm staying here for as long as I can.'

'Don't you want to come home?'

'Oh no, not yet.' She giggles. 'I'm looking forward to having a break – don't tell anyone.'

'How is Guy?'

'He's so happy I reckon he'd give your project his blessing if you asked him about it now.' Jennie pauses. 'Have you seen Adam, only I can't get hold of him? I would send Guy, but he's completely overwhelmed by his new son. He can hardly put him down.'

'I'll go and look for him.'

'Guy has a relief herdsman in doing the milking – I expect Adam's showing him where to find everything.'

I drive up to Uphill Farm. There are lights on in the parlour, and the herdsman is halfway through the morning milking, but there's no sign of Adam.

'Have you seen him?' I ask.

'Not so far.'

'Okay, I'll try the house.'

The tractor is parked outside Jennie's Folly with its front wheels on top of Jennie's car. The car is crushed.

'What the—?' I swear aloud. 'Adam, where are you?' I yell. 'What have you done?' I'm furious with him because I reckon Guy will hold me responsible just as he's begun to come round to the idea of talking to us (his idea of the neighbours from hell}. I can't get in through the front of the house because the tractor is in the way of the gate, so I rush around to the back, wondering where Adam is and what I'll find next.

Lucky comes trotting out to greet me. I enter the

kitchen via the utility room, stepping over boots, dog bowls and horsey grooming kits. In the kitchen there's evidence of a midnight fry-up, and as I walk on through to the hallway, there's a strong smell of beer.

'Adam?' I check the living room and perform a quick bottle count – there are eight, all empty, and the dregs of malt whisky in a glass. 'Adam?'

With Lucky at my side, I follow a trail of strewn clothing back across the hallway – T-shirts, sweatshirts and a purple thong that appears to have come from the lingerie section in the back of Aurora's Cave. Lucky stops outside a door, sniffling excitedly and wagging his tail so fast that it blurs. Very quietly, I push the door open. Lucky scampers inside and leaps onto the bed at which a girl sits up and screams.

'It's just the dog,' I hear Adam mutter from underneath the sheets.

The girl catches sight of me and screams again, making me cover my ears. 'No, it's, it's, look, it's—'

'It's me, Stevie from next door,' I say calmly, although I feel as if I have a nest of angry hornets trying to escape from my chest. 'Adam, aren't you going to introduce me?'

'This is Rosie, my girlfriend.'

'Nice to meet you,' I say. She's a pretty girl with a sleek, pixie-style haircut that suits her elfin features. She also appears to be naked. I bend down, pick a dressing gown off the floor and throw it in her direction. 'Adam, what happened to the tractor last night?'

'Um, I took it for a bit of a drive—'

'After I told you not to,' I interrupt. 'How could you? Guy's going to be furious. What am I going to say to him?'

'Guy?' Adam peers out from the sheets. 'Please don't say anything at all. He'll kill me.'

'He's going to find out you double parked the tractor on top of your mum's car at least.'

'Did I?' Adam stammers.

'You took me out for a ride in it, don't you remember?' Rosie says.

'You need to get dressed, both of you. You can clear up this mess before I take Adam and his sisters to the hospital to meet their new baby brother. Yes, Adam, he's arrived.'

'I can't move,' Adam groans, burying his face in his hands. 'I've got brain ache.'

I have brain ache too, I think, by the time we get to the hospital, but the pain soon disappears when we find Jennie and Guy on the ward with Reuben, who's dressed in a blue babygro with a tractor motif, as if Guy's starting as he means to go on, inducting his son into life as a farmer. He's cute and chubby but I don't feel a rush of longing to hold my baby in my arms, just a curiosity to see what she looks like.

Sophie and Georgia are over the moon to see their new brother, giving him a teddy bear and a rattle, which he has absolutely no interest in yet, whereas Adam hangs back, looking pale and queasy. In fact, he looks so rough I almost feel sorry for him.

I decide not to say anything to Jennie and Guy in order not to ruin the moment, but Adam is uncomfortable. It won't hurt him to sweat it out for a while, I think, as he watches Guy and Jennie kissing.

'Ugh, you two are so embarrassing,' Adam grimaces.

'There are times, Adam,' I say, 'when passion over-whelms all sense of reason and propriety. I'm surprised you don't know that yet.'

He blushes at the sarcasm in my voice.

'You're so lucky, Jennie,' I add. 'I imagine Adam will be offering to do lots of free babysitting for you.'

'Will you?' she says, raising her eyebrows.

He nods sheepishly.

'Is there something we should know?' she asks.

'Are you sickening for something?' Guy says.

'Um, I had a bit of an accident last night . . .'

'I'll make myself scarce for a while,' I say quickly. 'I'm going for a coffee – I'll be back in half an hour.'

On the last day of September the leaves are on the turn, the mist swirls around the apple trees and the sloes are full and ripe in the hedgerows. The mornings are cold; if I had central heating I'd switch it on. I'm begin-ning to enjoy my pregnancy, aware of the baby kicking and moving around. I would be happy, if it weren't for Leo leaving. I join him in the morning to wish him farewell, finding him packing the last of his belong-ings into the four-by-four. I did offer him a lift, but he's driving up to Talyton Manor where Justin, Alex's per-manent assistant, is taking him to the mainline station in Exeter.

'I've just been to see Jennie and the baby again,' I say when he sees me. 'You should have come along too and said goodbye.'

'Oh no, I've told you before – babies and children are not really my thing.' He smiles ruefully.

'You can be honorary uncle to my baby,' I say, touching my bump and immediately wishing I hadn't used the word 'uncle'. 'I'm sorry. That was insensitive of me.'

'No, Stevie. I'd like that very much.'

'Would you like some help?'

'I'm all packed,' he says.

'Have you got everything?'

'You can have a look if you like.' He shows me up the steps into the mobile home. 'I've left the throws. I hope you don't mind, but I'm travelling light.'

Inside, I notice the two mugs on the draining board beside the sink. I try to stay strong like a pillar of salt, but inside I'm dissolving into a pool of hopelessness.

'I've got you a present,' Leo says, proffering a small box-shaped package in a bag.

'What's that for?'

'To say thank you . . .' he falters. 'For being a friend. I've had some great times here, Stevie, and I'll take those memories with me. Open it,' he adds softly.

It's a necklace, a silver chain with an iridescent butterfly pendant. It reminds me of the butterflies that danced in the fields when we were turning the hay.

'Thank you.' I can hardly speak, choked up by his generosity and thoughtfulness.

'I hope you'll wear it sometimes and think of me –' Leo clears his throat – 'as I will think of you.'

'Can you . . .?' I hold it out to him, dropping it into

his palm. I turn away, bundling up my hair, exposing the back of my neck. Leo, standing behind me, puts the necklace over my head and fastens the chain at my nape. He's so close I can hear the rough catch of his breathing and feel the heat of his body and I want him more than I've ever wanted anything. Letting my hair down, I touch the butterfly and swing round to face him.

'What do you think?' I say, trying to break the tension between us.

Leo steps back, bumping into the sofa. He recovers himself and answers, 'I think you look absolutely beautiful.'

'I wish you were staying,' I say, bursting into tears.

'Please don't cry, Stevie,' he says awkwardly. 'I never meant to make you cry.'

'It isn't you,' I mutter. 'It's me. Leo, I love you . . .'

Leo's face contorts with pain as he grapples for my hands, squeezing them tight as if he'll never let them go.

'Let's sit down and talk,' he says. 'I've got half an hour before I'm due at the manor. I think this is something we should have done before.'

We sit side by side, Leo gently massaging my hand.

'I wish I hadn't said it now,' I begin.

'I'm glad you did. I love you too, Stevie. There, I've said it. I love you.' He leans in and kisses the tracks of my tears from my cheek down to the curve of my chin. 'I've been a complete idiot. I should never have ended it with you. It was a terrible mistake, the worst one I've ever made.'

'I understand. You've loved and lost before – first your fiancée and then your nephew. I should have been straight with you.'

Leo clears his throat. 'It wasn't just about what you said and did, Stevie. One of the reasons I backed out was because of Nick.'

'Nick? What has he got to do with it?'

'When he turned up to see you, I gave him coffee and biscuits because he came straight to the caravan and knocked on my door, wanting to talk to me. I was trawling through some job ads, looking for somewhere close to Talyton St George.'

'So you were going to stay?'

'Yes, but then Nick asked me to leave you alone because you and he were hoping to make a go of it, to get back together for the baby. He seemed pretty optimistic.'

'How dare he do that!' I stand up and move towards the window, hugging my arms around my chest. 'How could he interfere?' I turn to face Leo once more. 'I'd already told him I wouldn't consider it. I didn't love him, Leo, and I really don't like Nick very much now. The bastard!'

'Come back here,' Leo says, patting the sofa. 'Let's not waste the last few minutes.' I fall into his arms and we hold each other close until it's time for him to leave.

'I don't want you to go,' I say.

'I know, but it's all decided.' Leo nuzzles my hair and kisses my ear. 'I have my passport and my ticket. My friend's expecting me.'

'I'll never forget you.'

'I hope not. You're going to promise me you'll keep in touch. I want to know when the baby arrives that you're both safe and well.'

'Isn't it better to make a complete break?' I murmur, but I know as I say it that I can't.

'At least I know you'll never be alone,' Leo says. 'You'll find someone else.'

'I don't want someone else . . . I want you . . .'

'You could always come with me,' he says lightly.

'Do you mean that?' I stare at him, my heart beating a chaotic rhythm. 'How?'

'By the usual means – I've heard travelling by air is quicker than by sea, so I'd recommend a plane ticket.'

'Oh, Leo.' Even now, he can make me smile. 'I can't leave the farm.'

'You see, I knew you'd say that.' He grows serious again. 'You know, it could run without you. You could install James as manager – he's a very capable guy.'

I think about it for a moment. I couldn't possibly leave Nettlebed Farm right now when I've invested so much time and energy – not to mention money – in the new visitor attraction. I can't leave it unfinished and nor can I go running across to the other side of the world after Leo for love, because love is so fragile, so tenuous, and who knows how Leo would react after the baby was born.

Leo gives me one last kiss before he disentangles himself from my embrace. 'I'll be in touch. Goodbye, Stevie.'

I watch him go, tears streaming down my face, my

heart empty, and wonder if I'll ever see him again.

I stay in the mobile home for a while, gathering myself together before I phone Nick.

'Stevie, I wasn't expecting—'

'This isn't a social call. I wanted to ask you what right you think you have to interfere in my life, warning Leo off like that?'

'What are you talking about?'

'You know very well. You told Leo to back off. How *dare* you! Thanks to you, my chance of happiness has gone.' I'm hot with rage.

'I'm sorry,' Nick says. 'Now please calm down – the baby . . . '

'What do you care?' I snap. I'm being unreasonable, but I've had a terrible day so far.

'Of course I care,' Nick blunders on.

I cut him off. I don't want to listen to him any more, but two seconds later my mobile's ringing again. He calls three times before I answer it.

'I didn't realise Leo meant that much to you, Stevie,' Nick says quickly. 'I thought I was doing the right thing. He was only a locum, after all.'

'Only?' I swear out loud. 'I loved him, Nick, and now he's gone.'

'Sh, please don't let yourself get wound up. What can I do to make it up to you?' I blow my nose when he continues, 'Let me be the best dad I can to our daughter. Please don't shut me out as some kind of revenge. Promise me, Stevie.' Nick sounds close to tears too and I soften slightly.

'All right,' I say, 'but don't you ever do anything like

that to me ever again.'

'I won't.' Nick hesitates. 'Do I dare ask you how you are?'

'I wouldn't if I were you.' I sniff into my tissue.

'What can I say then? Have you been playing those tracks I suggested to the baby?'

'That makes you sound rather controlling. She likes listening to the radio in the parlour.'

'It's better for babies in the womb to listen to classical music,' Nick persists. 'It's more educational.'

'There'll be plenty of time for her to get an education.' In spite of the situation, I can't help smiling.

'I don't want her to have a Devon accent either.'

'You're doing it again,' I exclaim.

'You have booked those antenatal classes?'

'I've been for all my check-ups and I've decided I'm having the baby at home.'

'I don't like that idea.'

'I've talked it through with Kelly, the midwife at the surgery, and she sees no reason why not.'

'I can think of plenty of reasons,' he says gloomily.

'Nick, you are not a midwife.'

'Stevie, where are you?' I hear the sound of James's voice calling for me.

'I'm in here,' I call back. 'I've got to go. We'll talk again soon.'

'What do you want, James?' I ask as he puts his head around the door of the mobile home.

'I wanted to check you were all right,' he says.

'I'm fine,' I say, my tone curt.

'It's just that I saw Leo was gone – I thought you

might be upset.'

'Yes, I am.' I notice how James's expression changes, how the shy smile disappears to be replaced by a frown. 'I'm sorry, this isn't a good time,' I tell him.

'I'm a bit of a prat, aren't I?' he says.

'Sometimes,' I agree. 'Like giving Adam that beer after the carnival.'

'He had a bit of a skinful. I thought he'd be fine.'

'He's having to work for Guy to pay him back for the damage to the tractor and Jennie's car.'

'Stevie, can I just say I'm here for you if you need me?' James says.

'Thank you, James,' I say, touched at his concern.

'I'll see you later.'

I watch James head back across the yard where he's assembling the fixings for a new gate for the farm entrance, wondering when Leo will contact me. I don't have to wait for long because he texts me from the airport, saying he'll Skype me as soon as he can. Two nights later, he gets in touch.

'What's it like out there?' I ask him.

'It's brilliant. The practice and the scenery are perfect and I'm renting a proper house with furniture. There is one thing missing, though, and that's you, Stevie.'

'Oh, Leo, don't make me start.' I cover my mouth to stifle a sob.

'I'll keep in touch, I promise. You can come out for a holiday.'

'That won't be for a while,' I say, imagining travelling by plane with a small baby.

'In that case, I'll have to come over to you for a break.'

Do I believe him? I do, but it won't be for a long time and it doesn't alter the fact that even for the world's greatest optimist, maintaining a successful long-distance relationship when you're half a world away seems impossible.

The first frost comes a few mornings after Leo has left. Having done the milking and picked a tub of sloes from the hedges, I return to find my father searching for something in the lean-to.

'Stevie, have you seen my winter sweater?' he asks.

'No . . . ? Which one?'

'My special one, the one I've had for years.'

Oh dear, I think. What was Cecil's expression? That he would have my guts for garters. I decide a little economy with the truth is a good tactic, although it hasn't done me much good in the past. 'I thought I saw it one of the drawers.' I pretend to search through the cupboards, pulling it out. 'Is this it?'

'Ah yes, that's it.'

I hand it over and he opens it up. 'It's full of holes . . .'

'I expect we have moths out here. It's made of wool, isn't it, and moths like wool.'

'They must be ruddy great moths.' My father struggles to put it on. I give him a hand to pull it over his head. 'I'll have to use it as a waistcoat,' he grumbles. I'm worried he's going to complain about the smell of cows, but he doesn't. I help him put a coat over the top so he can wander out into the yard to see the calves.

'Leo went off just like that, without a word?' my father says, frowning. 'He didn't say anything?'

'Dad, he did. He said goodbye to me.'

'I thought with you being so fond of him and him of you . . . I thought he might stay and make an honest woman of you.'

'That's really old-fashioned. Why should he? This isn't his baby.'

'I am of a different generation, but these things happened. Men married women who were carrying other men's children. It just wasn't talked about like it is today. People didn't expose their private lives willingly like they do today on those dreadful television shows.'

'The ones you like to watch,' I say lightly.

'It's quite interesting what kinds of scrapes people get themselves into. It's opened my eyes.'

'Well, if you're referring to me, I'm not going on telly to talk about it.'

'I wasn't suggesting you did,' he says. 'You can talk to me,' he goes on. 'I admit I haven't always been an easy person to confide in, but now, well, it's just us two and the baby, isn't it? We have to stick together now.'

I walk away, tears pricking my eyes at his sensitivity, heading upstairs where I lie on the bed for a while feeling sorry for myself. The baby kicks, reminding me I have other priorities now, and that it's going to be an independent human being with its own routine, desires and dislikes.

'I hope we aren't going to clash, Baby,' I tell her as I wonder what life will be like. Jennie says you can't imagine it until it happens.

Later, I go to babysit Reuben for a couple of hours, so

Jennie can go out with Guy. I'm doing this for Jennie, though, not her husband – although Guy seems more mellow since the baby was born. I arrive at Jennie's Folly at six with my tub of sloes.

'Come in,' Jennie says, dressed in maternity leggings and a casual jacket. 'I know Reuben's only two weeks old, but I'm determined to start as I mean to go on this time, so he's used to being left with a trusted friend. I didn't leave Adam and he became really clingy, so when I did go out, I would sit there waiting for the babysitter to call and tell me to come home, which they invariably did because Adam did nothing but scream. I'm so excited to be going out on a date – it's ages since Guy and I have had time to ourselves.' She takes me through to the living room where the fire is burning in the grate behind a huge fireguard. Reuben is in a Moses basket, awake but quiet, watching the shadows of the flames flickering on the wall.

'How am I going to cope?' I say. 'What do I do with him? He seems so little.'

Jennie is laughing so hard she can hardly speak. In fact I think she's been on the wine already. 'You can handle a herd of ninety cattle yet you're worried about looking after a single tiny baby!' She glances down to my hands. 'What have you got there?'

'Sloes. I'm going to sit and prick them for the sloe gin.'

'It always seems a shame to adulterate good gin with sloes.'

'It makes it palatable,' I say.

'Well, good luck,' Jennie says. 'And thank you,

Stevie. Adam is out with his girlfriend and the girls are in the kitchen doing their homework. I felt they were too young to look after Reuben yet. Don't look so worried. It'll be good practice for when you have your baby, and a distraction, I hope.'

Guy puts his head around the door.

'Have you two stopped twittering yet?' he asks. He's dressed in a shirt and tie.

'I've just got to fetch my shoes,' Jennie says.

'Fetch or choose?' Guy says with mock weariness. 'Why does it take you so long to get ready to go out?'

'Where are you going?' I ask, a little stiffly, when Jennie has disappeared off upstairs.

'The Barnscote.' Guy lowers his voice. 'Don't say anything – I've told her we're going to Mr Rock's to eat in.'

'Well, I hope the traffic's all right,' I say, having a dig at him.

'Oh that,' he says, rubbing his chin. 'I'm sorry, I've been a bit of an idiot.'

'Are you growing soft in your old age?'

'It's Reuben,' he says. 'Since he's been here, I've realised there's more to life than farming and neighbourly spats.'

'It was a bit more than a spat,' I say. 'You've been trying to prevent what is a perfectly legitimate business.'

'I know. I have withdrawn my objections to your plans – I saw the new application, the most recent one with the new building with the larger footprint and lower roof, and I think I can live with that.'

I'm gobsmacked. I don't know what to say.

'I can't say that it will make any difference to the outcome of the decision – you'll have to wait and see.' Guy pauses. 'I really appreciate your kindness to Jennie and the children—'

'Even if I didn't do a terribly good job of keeping an eye on Adam,' I cut in.

'It was only the car that was a write-off. At least the tractor was all right.' He smiles before calling for Jennie. When she returns downstairs, he kisses her on the lips and says gruffly, 'Come on, love. Let's go.'

As soon as they leave, Reuben starts to snuffle and cry; needless to say, I don't get to prick the sloes.

I do get around to making sloe gin for Christmas eventually. Dad agrees to scrap the mobile home to make the farmyard look more appealing. He also talks of my mother and how I'll be a good mum like her, and suggests we decorate my brother's old room as a nursery, sending Cecil up into the loft to find the old cot used for my brother and me, which he and Mum had kept.

I throw myself into life on the farm while we continue to wait for planning permission, having tweaked and resubmitted the application. Domino remains barren so I retire her, turning her out over the winter with the heifers to enjoy the remaining years of her life. Leo and I talk on Skype every other day, and the bump grows steadily larger until I think it can't possibly grow any more. I could do with a set of maternity overalls, but Tony at Overdown Farmers doesn't see a market for them.

Chapter Eighteen

Welcome to the World!

My father and I are invited to attend the Fox-Giffords'
party up at Talyton Manor on New Year's Eve. I used to
go with my parents and brother every year, and it was
pretty deadly for a teenager partying with the hunting,
shooting and fishing set. They are here tonight, along
with the local farmers and tradespeople, including
Jennie and Guy and their family, Mr Lacey from
Lacey's Fine Wines, the Dyers from the butcher's shop,
the Pitts of Barton Farm and Tony from Overdown
Farmers.

I've been hoping the baby might arrive beforehand
so I would have a really good excuse not to go, but it
isn't to be. The baby doesn't oblige and I feel I have to
accompany my father who is determined to be there.

This year, Alex Fox-Gifford and Sophia, his mother,
host the party. Alex is in his forties and pretty fit for his
age, while his mother is slender and wiry, her grey hair

stiff with hairspray or setting lotion, and I'm pretty certain she's wearing the same outfit she wore to the last party I came to when I was eighteen years old. It's definitely the same moth-eaten fox fur with glassy eyes wrapped around her neck.

Talyton Manor hasn't changed much either. It sounds incredibly grand, but it's falling down; the Axminster in the drawing room is threadbare and the sofas shabby. The paintings of the Fox-Gifford family through the ages, attired in pink hunting coats and breeches, are dark with dirt, and the electric chandelier is dusty and missing a few bulbs. There's a pack of labradors and spaniels scrapping for a place in front of the fire, which burns in a marble fireplace adorned with holly and ivy and priceless antiques.

There is mulled wine, Buck's Fizz or orange juice to drink and the customary chicken and mushroom vol-au-vents.

What's missing is Old Fox-Gifford, Alex's father, who died a couple of years ago in shocking circumstances. He reminded me a lot of my dad.

'Good evening, Stevie.' Fifi, who is a vision in pink, greets me, making me feel decidedly underdressed in my maternity clothes.

'Hi, Fifi. How are you?' I say, as she leans in and kisses me on both cheeks.

'Very well, although this is the busiest time of year for me with all the functions I'm obliged to attend. Now, I hate to talk shop on an occasion such as this, but have you thought about where you're going to source your landscaping materials? Only—'

'Hang on a minute, Fifi. What are you saying? I haven't had a decision on the planning application yet. Do you know something I don't?' I pause, waiting for her to respond. She appears to be having some difficulty.

'Oh dear, I think you should really hear this through the proper channels . . .' She looks around as if she's checking for spies. 'I don't suppose anyone will mind. You'll know soon enough.'

'And?' My heart misses a beat. Does this mean we have planning permission to develop the farm at long last?

'It will be granted,' she whispers 'Within the week at the next meeting of the committee.'

'That's fantastic.' I can hardly contain my excitement. I want to clap my hands and announce it to the whole of Talyton St George. 'So we can go ahead with the new building . . .' I grab Fifi and give her a big kiss. 'Thank you. What made you change your mind?'

'It isn't just me,' she says rather stiffly. 'I'm not solely responsible, although I do have an influence. On careful consideration, we can see there's no reason to oppose it, not one that would stand up to an appeal, at least.'

'Thank goodness for that. If only you realised what kind of stress you've put me and my father under. It's been almost intolerable.'

'I'm very sorry for that now, Stevie. Let me make it up to you,' Fifi says.

'I'm not sure.'

'I can do a good deal on materials and plants, and beat everyone else's prices. I assume that the visitor centre alone will cost you an awful lot of money.'

'Well, yes, you're right. I'll consider your offer, Fifi. Thank you.'

'You know where I am.' Fifi gazes down at my bump. 'When is this baby due?'

'Yesterday,' I say, relaxing a little, as Jennie strolls up to rescue me.

'Thanks, Jennie,' I say when we escape from the throng into the hallway, crossing the tiled floor to the foot of an imposing oak staircase.

'Are you all right?' she asks.

'Fifi's just let on that the project can go ahead. The planning application will be granted within the week.'

'That's wonderful news,' Jennie says, 'but I'm asking about you.'

'Not you as well,' I groan. 'Everyone keeps asking me if I'm all right.'

'That's one of the side effects of being in your condition. I'd make the most of it,' Jennie says, grinning, 'because, from the look of you, you aren't going to be pregnant for much longer.'

'I've been getting the odd pain now and again; my back aches sometimes and I can't see my feet.' Although I'm excited about seeing the baby, I am happy to delay the moment for as long as possible, even though I have a wonderful midwife and I'm prepared for a home birth, fingers crossed.

'The sooner it gets going, the sooner it's over,' Jennie says. 'Have you tried some brisk exercise?'

'I'm still milking the cows twice a day. I've tried a curry – Mary cooked a rather interesting fusion meal of curried chicken and potatoes for dinner last night, but all it's done is leave me with a touch of heartburn. I've tried the raspberry leaf tea, which tastes disgusting.'

'Sophia would tell you to go and have a good gallop after hounds.' Jennie glances up towards the staircase. 'You could try and shift it by sliding down the banisters. That would be fun.'

'I couldn't,' I say.

'It's easy.'

'Jennie!'

'It's all right. I've done it before. Last year, I had a little too much to drink. Guy egged me on and we both had a go.'

'It's all right. I'd prefer to remain pregnant,' I say, smiling at last. 'Have you seen my dad?'

'He's regaling his old cronies with tales of the good old days when all farmers were men and ploughs were drawn by horses.' Jennie chuckles. 'Are you staying for "Auld Lang Syne"?'

'I doubt I have a choice. James is driving me and Dad home. How about you?'

'Guy's asleep.'

'Are you sure?'

'He's snoring on the sofa by the fire. I've prodded him a couple of times but he's well gone. It's all this getting up in early the mornings that does it. He can barely stay awake past nine.'

The remainder of the evening passes quickly and we join the traditional singing of 'Auld Lang Syne' at midnight when the baby decides it's time to wake up. In fact she's probably been woken up by the sound of everyone's voices joining in. She doesn't so much kick now as press so hard on my bellybutton that it feels as if it will pop inside out. There can't be much room left in there for her, I think as I look down at my enormous bump.

'Come on, Stevie, let's get you and Tom home,' James says, appearing with my coat.

'We've as good as got the go-ahead, James. We can start building.'

'You mean it?' James frowns. 'I can start on the Shed. That's fantastic. If you weren't so heavily pregnant, I'd pick you up and whirl you around like they do on *Strictly*.'

'Where is Dad?' I ask as he drops my coat around my shoulders.

'I've parked him in the car ready to go.' James guides me across to the front door, but before we get there, he stops. 'How about a quick kiss?' he says gently, pointing to the mistletoe suspended above our heads.

'I'm a pregnant woman,' I say, trying to make light of it. Kiss James? Not after Leo.

'It suits you. You're one hot mama.'

'Oh James.' Smiling, I push him away.

'One little kiss to wish each other a "Happy New Year", that's all.'

I turn my cheek towards him, but he aims for my lips. I pull back abruptly.

'James!'

'I'm sorry. Too close . . .'

'It was,' I confirm, at least as embarrassed as James appears to be. He stares down at his hands as if gathering himself together before looking me straight in the eye.

'Stevie, I know your heart is elsewhere for now, but I'd like to hope that one day you'll move on, and when you do, I'll be there waiting.'

'It isn't possible. You're a great friend and I'm very fond of you, but I'm in love with Leo and that will never change, no matter how far away he is.'

'I understand,' James says gruffly. 'Let's not speak of this again.'

'Thank you,' I say. 'Happy New Year, James.'

'Happy New Year,' he says. He changes the subject. 'You look as though you're about ready to drop this baby – I hope you're going to wait until I get you home.'

'She isn't ready yet. I've been having these practice twinges for a while now and I feel really good.'

I'm not even tired when I get up at five in the morning to milk the cows with Cecil. Wrapped in many layers of thermals, a hat and scarf, I join him in the parlour where he's already got the first batch of cows in from the collecting yard.

'Shouldn't you be resting or something?' Cecil asks as I follow behind him, drying each udder off – gently because I understand now how it feels. As I slip the first set of cups on one of the cows, I feel a twinge, a dull ache in my belly that stops me short.

'Are you all right, my lover?'

'I'm fine.' I bite my lip. 'I'll be all right in a minute.'

'Are you sure you should be out here?' Cecil asks again. 'Why don't you go indoors and sit down for a while?'

'Cecil, stop fussing.' The rhythm of the milking machine helps me relax until a second wave of pain passes right through me, followed within a couple of minutes by another. I grab the railing, catching my breath.

'Stevie, I said you can let this lot go now,' Cecil says, his voice cutting into my consciousness. 'Stevie?'

I reach up for the lever and pull, releasing the catch on the door so it slides open to let the cows out. They stroll past me, a blur of black and white. I let the cords of pain in my thighs relax, then return the lever to the closed position.

'Come on, girls,' I call as Cecil lets the next batch in.

'Why don't you phone the midwife to make sure – put your mind at ease?'

'Put your mind at ease, you mean,' I say sternly. I take the hose to clean the first cow's teats.

'That's my job,' Cecil says, taking it back from me as another wave of pain cramps through me. If these are merely the practice contractions, I'm dreading the real thing.

'You look like a cow that's about to drop,' Cecil says, alarmed. He takes me by the arm. 'Trust me when I say I've seen enough animals give birth to know when they're in labour. Come on, these can wait here a minute while I take you to the house.'

I don't argue anymore. I can't. I walk across the yard with Cecil, pausing to focus on a small patch of mud to get me through the next contraction.

'I'm sorry.' I release my grip on his arm. 'I'm hurting you.'

'Never mind,' he says gently. 'You can always lean on me. You know that.' He waits until the pain passes and leads me through into the kitchen. 'Sit there while I fetch Mary. She'll know what to do.'

I can't sit down. I can only stand, holding on to the edge of the table. My father potters in using his stick to join us, while Cecil looks on, uncertainty etched in his expression.

'Tom, Stevie's about to drop,' Cecil says. 'What shall we do?'

'I would say to call the vet because they know what they're doing,' my father says brightly, and I wish I did have the vet here – specifically Leo. I wish he was at my side, his voice calm and reassuring and his hand on mine. If only he could have been my birth partner. I feel so alone in the company of two old men who might have some idea of what to do, extrapolated from calving many cows over the years, but I'd really rather not let them anywhere near me.

'We could fetch Bertha and the calving ropes just in case we need to pull it out,' Dad jokes.

'It isn't funny,' I say, cut short by another contraction, which feels like a coiled python crushing me around the belly. I bite my lip so hard I can taste the metallic warmth of fresh blood. I fumble for my mobile and hand it to Cecil. 'Call the midwife, please. Look in "Contacts" – she's called Kelly.'

I listen as he speaks to her immensely slowly to give her a full description of my activities throughout the morning and a blow-by-blow account of his opinion of how I looked when he first saw me come into the parlour at milking time.

'Give it to me,' I say, snatching the phone. 'Kelly? It's Stevie.'

'How are you?' she asks.

'I'm in pain.' I begin to sob. 'It hurts soooo much.'

'How often are the contractions coming?'

'I don't know. Every two or three minutes? I can't talk long.'

'I'll be right with you. I'm in Talyton so it'll take me five minutes. Get someone to run a bath and try to keep moving if you can. And remember to breathe.'

'Thanks for that,' I say, but she's gone, already on her way.

'Nick. I must get hold of Nick.' I dial his number. He answers straight away, as if he knows. 'She's on her way. I'm in labour.'

'I'll leave in ten minutes. Hold on for me, won't you?'

'I don't think it's going to be long now,' I mutter.

'I'm going to fetch Mary,' Cecil says as Nick continues talking. I'm not sure what he's saying anymore.

'I'll stay here,' says Dad as I slump forwards over the table, waiting for the next killer pain. I thought I was organised and ready, but it seems I'm not. All I want is for it to stop.

'Stevie? Stevie, are you still there?' The mobile slips from my grasp and clatters across the floor, the battery and cover flying in different directions.

'I'll see to that, my lover.' Dad guides the pieces close together with his stick so he can pick them up. 'Where are you going?' he asks when I make a move.

'Upstairs.' On the way, my waters break, and I'm on my knees at the top step when Mary rescues me, helping me to the bedroom.

'Sit there quietly on the edge of the bed, Stevie. Hold my hand and give it a good hard squeeze if you need to.' She smiles, but she can't disguise her concern. 'I was in the house when your mother gave birth to Ray and you, and when my sister had her three boys, but I can't claim I know what to do.'

I take her hand.

'There, there. We'll have help here soon. You and the baby will be fine. All will be well, you'll see . . . That must be the midwife,' she adds when a car drives into the yard and Bear starts barking.

Kelly appears in the room soon after, wearing her uniform and a smile.

'Hello, Stevie. Let's see how you're progressing.'

'Kelly, I've changed my mind – I want to go to hospital.'

I'm aware of the glances that pass between Kelly and Mary.

'I'm here now, and from the look of you this baby isn't going to wait for an ambulance. She's going to be born at Nettlebed Farm just as you planned.'

'Like Stevie and her father before her,' Mary adds.

'Where's your bag, the one you packed in case you went to hospital?' Kelly asks. 'Is dad on his way? At what time did you have the first contraction?'

I'm losing my grip on reality. I can't be bothered

360

with all these questions. I can't think. I'm tired, confused and retreating into myself.

'I don't know where the bag is, and as for Nick, I don't care. He's the one who got me into this mess in the first place.'

'Hey,' soothes Kelly. 'Let's get you out of those clothes and into a nightie.'

I grab an oversized T-shirt from the chest of drawers.

'Stevie, you're putting it over your day things – not such a good idea when you've been out milking cows.'

'I don't want to get changed. Ohmigod.' The pain takes my breath away. It's like nothing I've experienced before and I can't take it. I can't go through with it. 'I can't do this.'

'You have to,' Kelly says. 'It's too late to back out now.'

'Don't laugh at me,' I snap. 'This isn't funny.'

'I know, I know. I'm sure you don't want to know this now, but you're in transition.' It vaguely rings a bell, I think, as she continues. 'It won't be much longer. Now, do you want to stay on your feet or . . . ?'

'I don't know what I was thinking. I want an epidural, a Caesarean, anything . . . Just get this baby out of me.'

'You wanted as natural a birth as possible when we wrote your plan together. Have you taken your Arnica?'

'Arnica? What good are a couple of sugar pills going to do?'

There's a box of latex gloves on the dressing table, a gas canister and a TENS machine on the blanket box. Following my gaze, Kelly sets me up with gas and air, and the TENs machine – anything and everything, including the music Jennie and I chose, thinking it would be soothing, but the only music I want to listen to is the sound of Leo singing and playing his guitar . . .

'How much longer?' I ask between contractions.

'Baby isn't coming as quickly as I thought, but she's perfectly happy in there.'

'I want an epidural,' I say, when a couple more hours have passed and I'm leaning over the bed, sucking for all I'm worth on the gas and air and keeping the button on the TENs machine pressed down, but Kelly is determined that I have a home birth as planned.

'You can't hurry some of these little ones. This one's a proper Devonian, taking life in the slow lane, but it's looking promising,' she says eventually. 'It won't be long now. The baby's crowning. You can push, Stevie.'

In spite of my exhaustion, I push, bearing down hard.

'Here she comes,' says Kelly.

'Push. Breathe. Breathe. Pant lightly, Stevie. Now push with everything you've got. Push . . . You aren't pushing.'

'I am!'

'Push!'

There's a strange sensation between my legs and sudden relief, followed by a high-pitched cry, and I drag myself onto the bed. Kelly wraps the baby in a towel and rests her on my chest.

'Congratulations, Stevie. You're a star.'

I hardly hear her, my attention focused on my daughter.

'Hello, Baby.' With one finger I pull the corner of the towel away from her face while Kelly cuts the cord. 'Welcome to the world.'

'She's beautiful, isn't she?'

'Amazing.' I press my nose to the top of her head, breathing in her unfamiliar, egg-like scent, and my heart floods with love and adoration mixed with worry over the sudden responsibility I've taken on. Is she too hot or too cold? Is she hungry? How do I tell?

'Is everything all right?' I hear Mary calling from downstairs. 'Can we come up? Are you decent?'

Kelly gives me a sheet to cover my modesty. I'm sure I look completely wrecked, but I don't care.

'Dad, you should have waited for me to come down,' I tell him when he appears at the bedroom door, struggling along with his stick.

'You kept us waiting long enough, Stevie.' He is smiling like I've never seen him smile before. 'Let's see my lovely new granddaughter.'

'Oh, isn't she lovely?' coos Mary, as the three of them crowd inside.

'I don't see how you can tell with her being so tiny,' Cecil says. 'She's all hair.'

She does have a lot of hair for a newborn, a damp mop of light brown hair. She has milk spots across her nose, and tiny fingernails.

'When you've all met Baby, you can go and make some tea,' says Kelly. 'I have things to do here. Go on.'

They leave reluctantly and Kelly weighs the baby – at

seven pounds five ounces in old money, as she says. She measures her too, and checks her temperature before handing her back.

'I wish my mum was here to meet her,' I say quietly, choking up.

'Where's dad? I thought he wanted to be here.'

'He's on his way. I should call him, but my mobile's downstairs.'

'You stay there. I'll get it.'

Someone has pieced my phone back together, so I can call Nick to let him know his daughter has arrived safely. It's a strange conversation and I wish it wasn't happening.

'I wish you'd given me more warning,' Nick says quietly. I picture him on his hands-free, driving down the A303. 'I would have liked to have been there at the birth.'

'I didn't have much warning. I'm sorry, really I am, but events somehow overtook me.'

'You could have called, or got someone else to call, Stevie, but maybe that's what you want, to shut me out.'

He's making me feel guilty because maybe subconsciously he's right.

'You're okay?'

'Yes, thank you for asking. That's kind of you . . .' I bite back a sob as my normal self disappears into a whirlpool of irrational sadness. I'm drowning in hormones. 'You can stay at the farm, if you like.'

'It's a nice offer, but I think I'd prefer to find a B and B,' he says.

'I'll call Lynsey up at Barton Farm to ask her if she has a room.'

'India is here with me,' Nick adds, and I feel a small stab of guilt that I didn't get in touch with her straight away myself. 'We'll see you soon.' When he cuts the call, I realise I haven't asked him if he wants one room or two.

'How do you feel about seeing Nick?' Kelly asks.

'Resigned, I suppose.' I bite my lip, then worry that stress might curdle my milk. 'It's important for her to know her dad, but – oh, this sounds selfish – I want her to myself.' Nick is being reasonable at the moment, but I'm scared that he'll fall in love with our daughter like I have and take her away from me. 'Do you think he'll try for custody? I don't think I could bear it.'

'A tiny baby should be with its mum,' Kelly says. 'I'm sure you can come to some kind of agreement that works for everyone. Now, Stevie, you haven't delivered the afterbirth yet and we need to make sure—'

'I know it's important to make sure it's all out – I've seen it with the cows.'

Kelly smiles and says, 'I almost forgot you're a farmer,' before she gives me an injection and helps me attach the baby to my breast to suckle, but nothing happens. 'I'm sorry, Stevie, we're going to have to get you to hospital. I'll call an ambulance.'

'Can't we give it a little longer? I don't want to go anywhere now.'

'You're going to have to leave Baby here. Shall we ask Mary to look after her, or is there someone else?'

'I don't want to leave her.' I start to cry at this unexpected turn of events.

'I'm afraid you aren't allowed to transfer in the ambulance with your baby on this occasion in case you require urgent medical attention on the way. It's a common-sense precaution, that's all,' she goes on, as if she's trying not to worry me, but it's too late.

'What sort of attention? What's going to happen to me?'

'I'm not saying anything is going to happen. There's a slight risk of post-partum bleeding, that's all, and I'd rather be on the safe side.'

'I'm not sure about leaving her with Mary. She isn't experienced with babies. I'll call Jennie next door. Kelly, isn't there any way . . . ?' As I gaze at my daughter, unable to take my eyes off her, I notice a change in the colour of her skin. My heart stops. 'She isn't breathing.'

Kelly whisks her away from me and starts to resuscitate her, calling for a second ambulance at the same time while tears stream down my cheeks.

Please be all right. Please, I beg silently. I'll give up everything – the farm, the project – as long as my baby is fit and healthy.

I watch as Kelly sucks fluid from her throat and administers oxygen, and gradually the colour returns to Baby's face. Although Kelly reassures me that my daughter will be fine now, she wants her to go to hospital too as a precaution, so my daughter travels in one ambulance and Jennie – who's turned up in a hurry – and I travel in another.

'Everything will be all right,' Jennie says, but I can't bring myself to believe her. I've never been so frightened in all my life.

Chapter Nineteen

A Twenty-First Century Girl

'What's happened to Nick?' Jennie asks. 'I thought he was supposed to be here.'

'He's on his way with India – I left it too late. I didn't realise how quickly it would happen. I suppose I thought, as she was my first, it would take ages for her to arrive.' I start to panic again. 'What if he doesn't get here in time to see her? I'll never forgive myself.'

'The baby will be fine,' says Jennie. 'That's what Kelly said.'

'She's in an ambulance on her way to the hospital – how can she be fine?'

'She will be,' Jennie says firmly. 'When we get to the hospital, we can let Nick know where we are.'

'I need to let Leo know too. I promised him . . .'

'There's no hurry.' Jennie hesitates. 'I don't see why you have to rush to contact Leo of all people. Stevie, you have to look forward now, not back. This is like a new beginning. Make the most of it.'

'Are you telling me to forget him?'

'Not forget, but move on with your life. It's what I did after my divorce. Don't go wasting all your energy on a man who's on the other side of the world.' She pauses. 'Perhaps now is a good time to break contact with him, put him out of sight and out of mind.'

'Jennie, I know you mean well, but I couldn't. I . . .' I swallow hard, choking up at the thought of Leo, and him being so far away when I need him here with me. 'I love him.'

'I know you do, Stevie, but you have to remember that Leo is in New Zealand through choice, not because you were torn apart like Romeo and Juliet. You're completely besotted with a man who isn't here.'

'You're a practical person, so I can see where you're coming from,' I say, 'but I'm a romantic. I believe in true love, the one and only.'

'I'm sorry to have upset you, but it's the truth. You can't spend the rest of your life dreaming of what might have been.' Jennie's tone is soft, but the idea of never speaking to Leo again is too much for me to bear. 'Come on,' Jennie continues, 'let's concentrate on making sure you're well enough to care for your baby. I can't wait to introduce her to Reuben. They'll be able to play together. It's wonderful.'

I smile weakly. I'm feeling nauseous and faint in the back of the ambulance and I'm relieved when the journey's over, but my hopes of meeting up with my daughter fade when I find she's been taken to the special care baby unit for observation and tests, and I'm expected to undergo treatment on the maternity ward without seeing her first.

I meet the doctor who recommends manual removal of the placenta under general anaesthetic, which will delay me seeing my daughter by a few hours. I'm devastated, but it's essential to avoid infections and bleeding.

'You have to have it done, Stevie,' Jennie says. 'Trust me, you need to be well to look after her properly. Let me find out if Nick's arrived yet, and how the baby's doing. I'll be back.'

I'm taken down to theatre for the anaesthetic. I don't know how long it takes, but I'm soon back on the ward, groggily asking for my daughter.

'She's doing well, Stevie,' Jennie says from my bedside. She's brought me a bottle of energy drink and a sandwich, but I'm not hungry.

'Jennie? Are you still here?'

'Yes, of course.'

'Thanks for coming with me when you have your own family to look after.'

'Don't worry about that. It's what friends are for. And I can understand how scary it is to think of your baby going off to hospital like that.'

'I thought she'd . . . gone.'

'Hey, don't. She's going to be all right now.' Jennie holds my hand. 'And so are you.'

'When can I see her?'

'The doctor says you must stay here for a few more

hours yet.' She pauses. 'Nick is with her. I know it seems unfair, but at least the baby has one of her parents with her.'

'I wish I was there . . .'

'He'll be here to see you soon. Remember, all this is being done with everyone's best interests at heart. Now, I'm going home to see Reuben. I can come back anytime if you need me, otherwise I'll drop in tomorrow morning to see when you're both ready to come home.' She smiles wryly. 'Your dad, Mary and Cecil are desperate to see you and the baby again, but I've persuaded them to wait. I hope you don't mind.'

During the evening, I fall asleep again, drowsy from the anaesthetic and exhausted from labour, and I'm only vaguely aware of Nick coming to my bedside to reassure me that the baby is doing well and is expected to join me in the morning. He's paid for a private room too, for which I'm grateful.

'I thought you needed a good night's sleep,' he says, patting my hand. 'You know, the baby's beautiful, Stevie. I can't believe she's ours.' His eyes fill with tears. 'I just wish . . . Oh, it's too late for the "if onlys". I'll see you in the morning.'

'Did you find somewhere to stay?'

'Yes, there's no problem. Don't worry, Stevie.'

I struggle to sleep after he's gone, but eventually I drift off, only to be woken early by crying babies. My heart aches and my breasts are heavy with milk.

'Where's my baby?' I ask a nurse I find in the corridor outside my room. 'I'd like to see her now.'

Having ascertained who I am, she contacts the unit to find out what's going on. She returns, beaming.

'Baby's just been with the doctor. She's coming down to the ward in the next half an hour or so.'

I can hardly wait. I bounce up and down on the balls of my feet, which isn't a good idea because the exertion makes me feel giddy and I have to return to bed, where I sit and look at the photo Kelly gave me of the baby before she left me on the ward the previous afternoon. I burst into tears yet again. I have never cried so much in my life.

'Here she comes, Baby Dunsford,' says a nurse, pushing a trolley into my room. 'You stay there, mum. I'll pass her over so you can feed her. Don't worry if it doesn't come naturally at first,' she goes on. She parks the cot beside me, lifts the baby out and hands her to me, and I'm overwhelmed with joy and anxiety, over the moon to find her fit and well, and afraid I'll drop her.

'Babies aren't as fragile as you might imagine.' The nurse chuckles at my ham-fisted attempt to cuddle her without letting her head flop back.

'Hello, Baby.' I press my lips to her forehead, but she's more interested in food than starting a conversation, and it doesn't take long for her to get the idea about latching on to the breast. 'How will I know when she's had enough?'

'She'll decide,' the nurse says.

Nick returns as promised with India in tow, and the nurse makes an excuse and leaves us to it, at the same time as the baby decides she has finished feeding, dropping off the breast with her eyes closed, and every now and then pursing her lips and sucking, as if she's feeding in her sleep.

'How are you, Stevie?' India asks. She looks stunning, dressed in a jacket from Diesel, straight jeans and long boots.

'I'm all right now, thank you,' I say.

'This is so exciting. I feel like an honorary auntie. Here –' she hands me a present – 'I bought some clothes for the baby. I couldn't resist.'

'Can I take her while you open it?' Nick asks.

'Of course.' I'm not sure which of us is the most nervous about the whole manoeuvre of transferring the baby from one parent to the other, but our ridiculous fumbling breaks the ice.

'That looks pretty comical,' India observes. 'You two need some practice. Is there some kind of training class for beginner mums and dads?'

'It isn't that easy, India,' Nick comments as he settles the baby against his shoulder. 'I can't believe she's so small.'

With a tug of regret, I realise he'll make a great dad and I wish it could have been different. How I wish I could have found a way to love him instead of Leo! He gazes at her adoringly. 'You've got such a cute nose.' He looks up to me. 'She looks like you, not me, luckily for her.'

'She has your eyes,' I say as India pushes the present across the bed to remind me to open it.

'Thank you.' I tear the paper. The sight of the baby clothes – a Ralph Lauren and a Moschino romper – makes my heart melt. 'They are so cute, but they must have been expensive.'

'Nick contributed as well. I couldn't buy any old rompers. I'd hate to see her growing up dressed as a country bumpkin,' India grins.

The baby starts to cry and kick her feet as if she's Sir Bradley Wiggins pedalling a bike.

'Oops, I reckon she's hungry again,' Nick says.

'She can't be.'

'You'd better go back to Mummy.'

It's effortless, the way he says it, and it hits me suddenly that I am a mum. He passes her back to me and I try to sort myself out to feed her discreetly. Although Jennie says you don't care who sees what after you've had a baby, l really don't want to expose myself to Nick of all people, even if he has – or maybe *because* he has – seen it all before.

'Is there anything you need, Stevie?' Nick asks. 'I can nip down to the shop to get you a sandwich or coffee. You're looking a bit peaky.'

'Thanks, Nick.'

The baby doesn't really want to feed again. She suckles for a couple of minutes then falls asleep.

'I'll go,' India says, getting up quickly, as if she's pleased to have an excuse to escape. 'I'll buy a selection.'

When she leaves us, Nick wants to take pictures of our daughter, but she won't wake up now. He reaches across and tickles her cheek. She merely yawns, so he snaps her anyway and texts the photos to his mum and dad, and it occurs to me that they'll want to see the baby soon. It occurs to me too that Nick and I should have thrashed all this out before.

'Nick,' I begin, 'have you thought about how often you'll want to see her?'

'As often as possible,' he says, and my heart sinks a little. 'While she's little, I'll come and visit every other week or so, and when she's older, I'd like to have her at weekends – not every weekend, maybe one in three.' He sighs. 'I did consider walking away, and if I'm honest it would have been the easiest and most painless option for everyone, but now I've seen her, I'm glad I didn't.'

'I'm glad too.' I don't hate Nick. In fact, I respect him for how he's made the effort to meet our daughter.

'I believe every child should have the chance to know its parents.' He lowers his voice. 'I was adopted as a baby.'

'I didn't know that. Why didn't you mention it before?'

'I've known for sure since I was twelve, but I've never made a big issue of it because I didn't want to let my mum and dad down by going to look for my birth parents, but now I've seen her, I realise it's something I have to do.' Nick clears his throat. 'Everyone should know where they came from.'

'Oh Nick. That's such a sad story.'

He reaches out and touches my hand. 'Thanks for not making this difficult for me. I'm glad we can be polite to each other. Friends?'

'Friends,' I say. 'You know, I was afraid you might try to take her away from me.'

'No way, Stevie. What do you think I am? I'm not a monster. I'm an ordinary bloke.'

'And a very special dad,' I say, catching his fingers and giving them a squeeze. 'How are you and India?' Even in my muzzy postnatal state, I recognise there is something going on between them.

'Why don't you ask her? I thought she would have given you all the gory details. You two share everything.'

'We used to.' There is an awkwardness between us when I've always thought she was one of those friends I'd be able to pick up with again after a break without ever feeling different, but, to my sadness, it isn't to be.

'I hope you don't mind, but India and I have grown close and we've decided to make a go of it. It sounds weird when we're so different, but I think it's truly a case of opposites attract.'

'I see.' Do I mind? I suppose I would have liked to have known before, but it's none of my business. I wonder if she fancied him when Nick and I were together. 'That's wonderful news, Nick,' I say after a moment's thought. 'I'm very happy for both of you.'

'Have you decided about the flat? The offer's still open. It's probably not the best time to discuss it, but . . . '

'I'd like to sell it now the project has the go-ahead. I'll never come back to London, whatever happens. The farm will always be home to me now. Let me know the details sometime. There's no great hurry.' I pause. 'Would you like to hold Baby again?'

'We can't keep calling our daughter Baby,' Nick says. 'I'd like to register her birth. She needs a name and I'm happy to let her take your surname – for her sake. Have you any ideas?'

'I like Holly or Poppy.'

'Oh?' Nick grimaces. 'I was thinking of Rosemary after my mother, or Tara. I like Tara.'

'After one of your ex-girlfriends? I think not.'

'How will she feel when she's my age and everyone's calling her Holly? It isn't a classy name and she wasn't even born at Christmas.'

'That's your opinion.' I move the blanket away from Baby's face. 'She looks like a Holly.'

'How can you say that? What does a Holly look like?'

'Look, Nick.'

He peers at the baby and shakes his head. 'I can't see it, Stevie.'

'Say cheese.' The sound of India's voice announces her return. I look up to the flash of a camera. 'Ah, that's beautiful. Mummy, Daddy and . . .'

'Holly,' I say.

'Holly?' Nick murmurs. 'Holly Dunsford. HD, High Definition.'

'HRD for Holly Rosemary Dunsford,' I suggest, determined to have my way.

'That has a nice ring to it. Yes, I think I can go with that.' Nick repeats the name several times.

'Make sure you get it right when you register the birth,' I say, smiling.

'She'll need her own Facebook page,' India says. 'I want to upload this piccie to her timeline.'

'No, India,' I say protectively. 'She's far too young for that.'

Much as I appreciate Nick's presence, and his willingness to run out for more nappies and a bottle of champagne to wet the baby's head, I can't wait to spend some time alone with Holly . . . and sleep . . . and contact Leo to tell him my news and show him the new addition to my family on Skype. For all my father's determination to keep Nettlebed Farm in the dark ages, his granddaughter is going to be a twenty-first-century girl.

When I take the baby home a couple of days later, the first thing I do is rush up to my bedroom – with Holly, of course – to Skype Leo.

'I've missed you,' he says. 'I thought you'd forgotten about me.'

'How could I forget you?' I say, cheerful now I've seen him and spoken to him again. I show him the baby in my arms, moving her close to the camera to show him her face. 'Meet Holly.'

'Hello, Holly,' he says, gradually moving closer to the camera at his end. 'She's very cute,' he says eventually, 'like you, Stevie.'

'I love her to bits,' I say. 'I can't believe how she's taken over my life in such a very short time.'

'That's what babies do,' Leo says, his voice catching. I glance from Holly to Leo's face on the laptop.

'You're upset,' I say. 'I'm sorry, I shouldn't have done that. I feel as if I've forced her upon you when you probably would have preferred me not to.'

'Don't be silly. I know what I said about feeling

uncomfortable around babies and kids, but Holly's your baby. It's different.' He changes the subject. 'Motherhood suits you. You look more beautiful than ever.'

'Oh, Leo.' I'm blushing, touched by his compliment. 'I wish you were here,' I say, my heart aching for his touch.

'I wish I was there with you too,' he says gruffly. 'I miss you.'

Holly starts to cry. 'I'll have to go for now.'

'Keep in touch, Stevie,' Leo says.

'I will.' I recall what Jennie advised me in the ambulance, to break contact and move on, but I know, deep in my heart, that I can't.

I cut the call and head back downstairs to join my father, Cecil and Mary for a small party with champagne and cake to celebrate the baby's arrival at Nettlebed Farm. I invited Ray and his family but, although he sent a card, chocolates and some personalised bibs with Holly's name on them, he doesn't come. I don't blame him – it was a long shot, considering his relationship with Dad.

My dad is completely smitten with his new granddaughter.

'She looks just like you when you were a baby, Stephanie.' As I'm slipping into my overalls in the hallway the following morning, he holds her in his arms while I hover, afraid she'll open her eyes and cry at the sight of his grey whiskers and razor cuts.

'I expect you wish she was a boy.'

'Not at all. I've learned my lesson on that one,' he confesses; a small victory, I think with a smile. 'I regret not spending more time with you and Ray when you were babies. I let your mother do it all while I worked on the farm. I wish we'd been more like the modern kids, and shared the load.' Soon my father is crying, not the baby.

He's very emotional and I don't like it because it isn't like him. He needs something to keep him occupied, so I encourage him to look things up and contribute to decisions about the farm. I suggest he starts pottering about in the yard, sorting through the rusting farm implements to decide which ones he can bear to throw away. His face lights up.

'I can store some of it in the shed behind the cottage,' he says brightly.

'I know what you're thinking, that it will give you an excuse to start driving again, so the answer to that idea is no. Promise me you won't get behind the wheel. Promise?' I repeat.

'Here's Jennie come to see you,' is my father's response, before he makes a rapid escape to the living room where he puts the television on.

Jennie brings Reuben with her.

'Excuse me, but where do you think you're going?' she asks as I stand up.

'Out to feed the calves and scrape the yard for Cecil. I can't sit around here all day.'

'Oh no you don't. Adam's offered to help him out.'

'That's very kind of him.'

'I did give his arm a little twist. We haven't

forgotten about his minor accident with the tractor.' Jennie smiles. 'How are you today? And how's baby Holly?'

'She's all right, I think. Actually, Jennie, I'm worried she isn't getting enough milk. To be honest, I feel rubbish.'

'That's all the more reason for you to stay indoors.'

'I'd rather be up and about. You know, I envy you having Guy around.'

'He's a great dad. He's been a wonderful stepdad to my three older ones and he adores Reuben.'

'How do you manage to keep baking?'

'I have Jane working in the bakery. Adam and the girls babysit when I'm creating wedding cakes.' Jennie pauses. 'If you're going to stay well and sane, you need to learn to accept all the help you're offered, so you can start practising now. Stevie, I'm here to help. What can I do? Have you given Holly a bath yet?'

'Kelly showed me yesterday, but I haven't done it on my own. I've topped and tailed her.' I smile at the reference to topping and tailing because it reminds me of my mother preparing blackcurrants and goose-berries for preserving.

'Reuben can sit in his car seat and watch. I'll tell him to keep his eyes averted when you're taking Holly's clothes off.'

'Is it warm enough?' I really don't feel confident in what I'm doing; my nipples are cracked, my breasts are throbbing and I wonder if I'm coming out in sympathy with some of the cows. 'Shall I put her in the big bath, or what?'

'You can bath them in a bucket at this age. Mind you, Reuben never was a tiny baby like Holly.'

I fill the baby bath, find a towel and some bubbles, and sit splashing water over Holly's tummy. I don't think she's going to be a water baby the way she screams in the bath, I muse when I'm drying her. Jennie and I drink coffee and eat cake while I talk about making a start on building the Shed, looking for suitable staff and animals and selecting some of Jennie's bakery products to sell in the tearoom. Someone from Petals, the florist in Talyton, delivers what I can only describe as a *mahussive* bouquet of flowers. Jennie assumes they are from Nick and I leave it that way – in fact they're from Leo.

Chapter Twenty

Little Donkeys

February passes in a blur as I look after Holly and supervise the building work on the farm. I do what I can with the milking, although Holly – more often than not – demands to be fed just as I'm dressed and ready to go out and join Cecil in the parlour. She has perfect timing.

In the middle of the day, I give her a bottle before I get ready to go into Talyton. My father hovers, worrying about whether she's having enough milk and if she's growing properly, and demanding to know when I last took her in to the doctor's surgery to have her weighed.

'Dad, stop it. Holly's fine. In fact she'd put on half a kilo last time.' I pause. 'Would you mind looking after her for me until I get back? She shouldn't need anything while I'm out.'

'Of course, I'll look after her.' He looks down at his

granddaughter in my arms. 'We'll have a lovely time, won't we?'

'You won't disturb her if she falls asleep, will you? I'd rather she slept now. Please don't poke her or pull funny faces again or you'll wind her up. She needs her sleep – she was awake at two, three and four in the morning, and so was I.' I wipe a dribble of milk from the corner of Holly's mouth before placing her in the Moses basket where she lies gazing up at the donkey on the mobile. I wind up the music. The repetitive tune of 'Old McDonald Had a Farm' – Jennie's idea of a joke, drives me to distraction, but Holly finds it sooth-ing, and within a couple of verses she's fast asleep. I bend down and touch my lips to her forehead. She looks so delicious with her soft brown hair and peachy complexion, I could eat her.

'Mummy will be back soon,' I whisper. 'I promise.'

'Stevie, will you or Cecil have time to take the tractor to the top of Steep Acres before it gets dark?' My father prods at the fire in the grate with a poker, making a burning log collapse into itself with a soft, shimmering sound. An orange fragment of ash lands on the floor. My father treads on it, leaving a blackened scar in the carpet and the smell of singed wool in the air.

'I don't know. What's the problem?'

'Guy phoned to say there's a tree come down across the fence.'

'Well, there's no hurry to fix it,' I say. 'All the cows are indoors.'

'But his sheep are at pasture in the field next door. I don't want them rampaging across our grass.'

'Dad, since when do sheep rampage?' I say, trying not to laugh because my father is being serious.

'They'll be everywhere,' he insists. 'And Guy's threatening to cut up the tree for firewood. Well, that's our tree – it's our boundary so it belongs to us.'

'Don't worry about it. I'll sort it out tomorrow.' A thought occurs to me. 'Perhaps we should let Guy have the firewood – he can chop it up and take it away for us.'

'We'll need that firewood to get through the rest of the winter if it carries on as cold as this. Waste not, want not.'

'Leave it with me. I'll do it, but not today. The ground was frozen solid earlier and now the rain's fallen on top of it – it's too risky to take the tractor up there. If necessary, I'll walk up there with Bear in the morning. At this rate it'll be dark anyway by the time I get back from town.'

'It seems ridiculous to me. You haven't got time while I'm sitting here twiddling my thumbs.'

'I'll deal with it.'

'If you let young Holly sleep all day, she'll be awake all night,' my father says, changing the subject.

'You won't forget she's here, will you?' I say, hovering anxiously.

'I won't let him forget.' I overhear Mary coming into the room, wearing her scarf wrapped around her head and carrying a basket of brown eggs she's collected from the hens.

'Thank you. I won't be long.'

'You know you must make time for yourself, my

lover,' Mary says. 'All this dashing around so soon after you've had a baby isn't good for you. You must look after your health. You've had a hard time of it, remember.'

It's strange, but I've almost forgotten the pain and fear of being in labour. I suppose if nature didn't wipe out the bad memories, no one would ever have a second child, let alone a third or fourth like Jennie.

'You're as bad as your father,' Mary scolds. 'I can see you aren't going to take a blind bit of notice of me.'

I smile to myself because she's right.

Waving to James, who's clearing the topsoil from the ground that will become the new car park as I leave, I drive into Talyton to pick up nappies and a few groceries, and pop into Overdown Farmers to buy food for Bear. I choose a new jumper for my dad – it's his birthday in a couple of days and – belatedly – I need to replace the one I used for Pearl the calf. I take my time, relishing the chance to be me, not just Holly's mum, until – within about half an hour – I'm overwhelmed by a wave of maternal guilt and can't stay away from her a moment longer. I drive back along the lane under a dark sky with a wintry shower slamming against the windscreen, so hard the Land Rover's rather sluggish wipers can't keep it clear.

I park in the farmyard. As I walk across to the house with my bags, I notice the tractor is missing, and there's no sign of the dog, which is odd, because Bear always comes running to greet me. I let myself in to the front of the house where the sound of Holly bawling sends a dart of guilt right through me for taking too long in town. I find Mary walking up and down the kitchen, rocking Holly in her arms with rather more vigour than I can cope with.

'I'll take her,' I say quickly.

'She's been looking for her mummy,' Mary says, her expression one of relief. 'She wants feeding.'

'And changing, I expect.' I cradle Holly in my arms. She's a feisty bundle, all arms, legs and lungs.

'I'll get a bottle out of the fridge,' Mary offers. 'You go on inside and make yourself comfortable. I'll bring you a nice cup of tea and some cake.'

'Thanks, Mary.' I'm about to sit down on the end of the sofa when, in my befuddled, post-baby state, I remember the tractor. 'Where's Dad?'

'He's gone out.'

'He was supposed to be minding Holly for me.'

'I said I'd take over. He said he wouldn't be long, but it was a while ago.' She checks her watch. 'I don't know where he was going – he didn't say.'

'Where's Cecil?'

'There was a problem with the milking machine, so he's a bit behind. I imagine he's in the parlour if you want him.'

I don't know what to do first, feed a screaming baby or find my father. I try his mobile. It rings from inside the house, from right beside me in fact, having fallen between the cushions of the sofa.

'How many times do I have to tell the old boys to keep their mobiles with them? Oh, never mind.'

'He's probably with Cecil.'

'Someone's taken the tractor out. He isn't supposed

to be driving. He can hardly control his crutches let alone a vehicle. I asked him to stay with the baby. I bet he's taken that tractor and the dog up to the top of Steep Acres – I told him not to.'

'Yes, and we all know how unreliable Bertha is. She'll have broken down halfway up the hill.'

'I'd better go and look for him. Mary?' I look up. She nods and takes Holly and the bottle from me.

'Take James with you, Stevie. I'm sure he won't mind.'

I don't hesitate because I'm thinking of the possible consequences of a man who's recovering from a stroke taking a dodgy tractor out on the steepest slope on the farm in the ice and rain. I run outside with a torch, calling for James who's packing up for the day as darkness falls.

'James,' I yell across the drive. 'Have you seen my dad?'

'Stevie? I noticed the tractor go out a while back, but I assumed it was you or Cecil driving.'

My heart is pounding with apprehension.

'James, would you come and help me find him?'

'Anything for you,' he says lightly. 'You're worried about him?'

'Yes, he isn't supposed to be anywhere near it. What am I going to do with him?'

'Let's go. I'll drive.'

I don't argue when James takes over and drives the Land Rover to the bottom of Steep Acres where the lower part of the field glistens wet under a cold silver moon.

'Can you see anything?' James asks.

I lean out of the window because the inside of the Land Rover is steaming up. The light from the headlamps catches a glint of metal partway across the field. 'Just over there,' I say urgently.

James drives further in and there's Bertha lying on her side at the bottom of the steepest part of the slope with evidence of her having skidded a long distance down the hill, leaving the scars of her tyre marks in the ground behind her.

'Oh my God.' I touch my throat, stifling panic at the sight of a dark hump of a body lying with its face upturned some distance away from the stricken tractor, and with the dog standing over it. 'Dad!'

'Stay there,' James warns, but I'm already out of the vehicle and running to my father's side, falling to my knees.

'Dad, wake up. James, call an ambulance.' I check my father's pulse and breathing. He's breathing, but his heartbeat is very slow and faint, and there's blood coming from somewhere at the back of his head. He's freezing, his hands grey in the light of my torch.

'Stevie, let me take over.' James gives me his phone. 'I've done a first-aid course. I want you to talk to the ambulance control centre to explain exactly where we are.'

There is talk of sending the air ambulance, but the weather conditions aren't great and there's nowhere suitable to land close by. My instinct is to scoop my father up and put him in the Land Rover, but James

389

says it's a bad idea and to wait for the land ambulance to turn up.

I run and grab one of Bear's old blankets out of the back of the Land Rover, and wrap it gently over the casualty. Kneeling down, almost oblivious to the cold and mud, I apply pressure to the wound on his head, and wait. Bear lies down alongside my father's legs, as if he's trying to keep him warm.

'How long are they going to be?' I mutter. Time is still, as if the world has stopped turning. 'Come on . . .'

'They'll be here,' James says.

'What if they can't find us?'

'They will.'

'You stupid man, I told you not to go out.' What happened? Did my father have another stroke, which made him lose control of the tractor? Or did it simply slide down the slope where the ice was partially thawed? He couldn't have checked the ground conditions before he came out. He must have slid forty or fifty metres out of control, the tractor then bounced and overturned, throwing him out where he hit his head against a loose stone. He wasn't wearing a seatbelt, which is typical of him. I can hear his voice in my head, saying, 'We never had seatbelts in my day.'

I'm beginning to freeze. My body aches from shivering. James fetches more blankets and places one over my shoulders.

'It won't be long,' he says when I thank him, but I cannot be reassured. I wonder if my father will make it or if his luck has run out this time.

'Hang on in there,' I pray, 'for Holly's sake if not mine. You have so much to live for.'

'I can hear something,' James says. 'Look, there are blue lights on the horizon. I'll stick the dog in the Land Rover.'

The last thing I need is for Bear to attack the paramedics, but Bear has other ideas. He will not be parted from his master; in the end I have to hang on to him with a rope around his neck so he can see what is going on, and check that the paramedics are not harming him. I can see his body tense and hear the low growls in his throat.

Once my father is stabilised and in the ambulance, the paramedics say they can take me with him.

'What about Holly?' I say.

'I'll look after her,' James says gamely. 'Don't you worry, I don't see why I shouldn't be able to, as long as Mary's around to advise me.'

'Can you ask Jennie? Please, James, if you go round to see her, I'm sure she'll agree to help out.'

The next few hours pass in confusion. My father regains consciousness in the hospital. He has a scan of his head and various other tests, after which the doctor pronounces that there is no evidence of a further stroke or bleeding to his brain, and concurs with the patient that he has a skull as hard as granite. He has his hair shaved from the back of his head and six stitches put in his scalp to close the wound. He's even feeling bright enough to flirt with the nurses.

'You should be ashamed of yourself,' I tell him, 'putting us through this. You could have been killed. If

James and I hadn't found you when we did, they say you'd have died of hypothermia.'

'That's rubbish. Look at me. I'm as strong as an ox.'

'You don't look it,' I say as he lies back on the trolley, his face almost the same shade of pale as the pillow. 'Can I get you a drink?'

'A whisky would be nice,' he says.

'You'll be lucky.' I pause. 'You know there'll be an investigation into the accident.'

'More bloody officialdom! I never did set much store by health and safety.'

'So I've noticed,' I say dryly. He wasn't impressed when I attended a health-and-safety seminar at our local agricultural college earlier in the month to learn how to create risk assessments aimed at controlling or preventing ill-health through contact with animals at visitor attractions. 'Now, I'm going outside to call James. Can I trust you to stay there?'

He nods sheepishly.

'Don't move a muscle.' I contact James who tells me Jennie has Holly. It's late, but I call her anyway.

'Holly's fine. How is your dad?' Jennie says as soon as she answers the phone.

'He's conscious.' I go on to explain what happened. 'I'm hoping he has learned his lesson. I told him not to go out.'

'Do you know when you'll be home? I'm not saying that because I want to get rid of Holly, by the way. She and Reuben are having a lovely time, gurgling at each other. I wish I knew what they were talking about.'

'Is she still awake?'

'I'm afraid so. It's all too exciting going out for your very first sleepover. Please don't worry, Stevie. I know you'd do the same for us.'

'Can I come and get her?'

'Any time. I know you can't bear to be without her.'

'Thank you.' I cut the call and stand outside the hospital, looking from the outside in, feeling completely bereft without my baby. I check the time. I haven't spoken to Leo today either and I miss him. I collect Holly on the way back to Nettlebed Farm, and she sleeps the rest of the night and well into the next morning.

'I'm sorry for being such a fool,' Dad says when I bring him home to the farm a couple of days later and help him into the house. I run out and fetch Holly, who's fallen asleep in her car seat on the journey back from the hospital. Once in the sitting room, I transfer Holly into the Moses basket.

'You don't have to say anything,' I tell my father when he starts talking again.

'Let me speak, Stevie.' He reaches out and touches my hand, wincing at the same time. I'm surprised because he isn't a tactile person. I can't remember him ever giving me a hug. All I have is a vague memory of him carrying me on his shoulders through the fields when he was fetching the cows in for milking. 'Now, you might think I've had a knock on the head, going soft like this in my old age, but I did a lot of thinking while I was lying outside that tractor and I want to tell you before it's too late and I'm dead and gone—'

'Oh, Dad, don't,' I interrupt with a sigh.

'I've had some lucky escapes recently and you're right that I should have listened to you and not taken the tractor out, but you and Cecil needed help and you have to spend time with the baby, so I did what I thought was right. I wanted to get back out there on the farm. It was now or never. Turns out it was never,' he goes on sadly. 'I'm too old and useless for anything.'

'Dad, you look after Holly for me and you answer the phone.'

'It's nothing compared with what I used to do.'

I gaze at him softly. It must be hard when you've been so active and capable to go from running a farm to being virtually housebound, but that's life. I wish he could accept his lot, but I doubt he ever will.

'Will you ever forgive me for what I did when you were eighteen?'

'Dad, all is forgiven.' I forgave him everything when I found him lying unconscious in the field. All I wanted was to have him back.

'If you hadn't come back I'd have gone to prison.'

'I doubt a judge would have had you locked up.'

'They would have done, because I'd have shot anyone who'd tried to take them there cows off me.' My father begins to sob. 'I'd have been forced to sell up. There would have been nothing left.'

'Please don't cry . . .'

'I'm not crying,' he says gruffly, turning away to blow his nose.

'You are,' I say, infuriated that he still insists on pretending and putting up a front for me, his daughter.

'After I've gone and you're the lady farmer and sole owner of Nettlebed Farm, you'll need a husband to take care of you.'

'That's ridiculous. I don't need a husband.'

'I don't like the idea of you being alone in this big old house.'

I'm touched. 'I won't be alone. You're going to be around for a very long time, along with Cecil and Mary.'

'And James?' Dad asks.

'James?'

'You know he's soft on you. Always has been.'

'Aside from the many other girls he's been out with,' I point out lightly.

'He's single at the moment and so are you. It seems like fate.'

'Dad, please stop it. James and I have discussed the situation. He knows the score and he's totally accepted that we are just friends. Now, if you don't mind, I need to get on. I have a baby and a deadline to open the farm to the public by Easter.'

'I thought that Nick might have offered when he saw Holly, but I can see that was wishful thinking.'

'He did, but it was over between us, and it would never have worked. You didn't like him anyway.'

'I know. He was a right townie, but you would have thought he would do anything to be with his baby, especially when she's so beautiful.' My father gazes proudly at Holly, who is lying in her Moses basket, fast asleep.

*

The work is daunting, even without programming in looking after a baby. Mary takes care of Holly for some of the time, more than I'd anticipated.

'I never had a baby of my own, which is a deep regret to me,' she says when I apologise for handing Holly over to her for another half-day. 'Cecil and I weren't blessed with children. You're like our family now and I wouldn't change it.' She rocks Holly in her arms rather violently, as if she's making a cocktail. Mary smiles when I stare at her. 'Don't worry about us, Stevie. I won't put her down until you come back. Where are you going?'

'With James, Dad and Jennie's girls. We're going to choose rabbits from the Sanctuary and collect two miniature donkeys from Delphi at the Equestrian Centre.'

'Ah, I love a donkey. Your granddad used to have one in the orchard. It takes me right back. Cecil, my lover, Stevie was just saying they're going to collect the donkeys.'

'I know, I know,' Cecil says, kicking the mud from his boots as he enters the kitchen.

'Don't you go bringing any dirt in here.'

'It's good for the little one to have a bit of dirt,' he argues. 'Isn't that right, Stevie?'

'I've heard experts say the presence of germs helps reduce the risk of developing allergies, but Holly's probably met enough of them already.'

'We're on the map at last. There's a new sign for Nettlebed Farm up along the lane,' Cecil says. 'Some man from the council was putting it up this morning.

It looks pretty impressive.'

'All we need now is our own signage at the entrance to the drive.' My father wanted me to hand-paint one, but I didn't want to give potential visitors the impression they were coming to pet a couple of sad-looking half-bald sheep. It's got to look amazing, so people want to come and pay to get in; and then the experience has to be so wonderful they want to return or stay all day. I think of the frame for the Shed that has yet to be assembled and the path for the nature trail that needs to be laid. There's so much to do I can't believe we'll ever be ready in time.

I take Jennie's girls, my dad, who is still recovering from his tractor accident, and James.

I drive, trying to ignore my father's backseat driving, which becomes more extreme when we reach the particularly narrow and twisty lane up to the Sanctuary. Buttercross Cottage, a quaint cob-and-thatch house with diamond leaded windows and flowers around the outside, is gone, destroyed in a fire one night some years ago. In its place stands an unprepossessing modern box of a bungalow, with holly growing up around its large windows to disguise the slate-grey render. The few remaining berries on the holly match the red front door. Jack's Animal Welfare van is parked in one of the bays in the tarmacked car park. To our left is the wood, Longdogs Copse, and to the right is a small paddock divided into two with electric fencing tape. One side is empty while the other contains a black-and-white billy goat and two fawn nannies. Beyond, there are some outbuildings, a barn open at one end, a cattery and a kennel block.

James, the girls, my father and I get out of the Land Rover and make our way across the car park. The dogs in the kennels bark and howl.

'They're noisy,' Sophie observes. She's dressed in a skirt, coat and long boots, while her sister is wearing a Puffa jacket and jodhpurs.

'Can we choose a dog?' Georgia asks.

'We're looking for rabbits today,' I say, concerned that I've made a mistake coming here when I realise I'll want to take them all home.

'I thought we were choosing guinea pigs,' Sophie says.

'You're my guinea pigs.' I smile at the misunderstanding. 'I've brought you along to interview the rabbits to see if they're good with children and suitable for handling.' I notice that I appear to have offended Georgia with my reference to children. 'Of course, you're teenagers, not little kids.'

'Sophie is eleven,' Georgia says. 'She is not a teenager.'

'I'm almost a teenager,' Sophie says.

'You have two years to go yet.'

'Let's go and see the rabbits.' James gives me a wink.

'Welcome to the Sanctuary,' Jack says, emerging from the barn with a woman I assume is Tessa. She's tall and slim with dark, almost black hair, full lips and sculpted cheekbones, reminding me of a Bond girl.

'Hi,' she says, smiling. 'Let's go and choose some

rabbits – it's like rabbit city here.' Sophie and Georgia warm to her immediately.

We pick out fifteen altogether.

'How many did you want?' Tessa asks.

'I was told ten,' James says.

'We can't leave those two giant rabbits behind,' Georgia says. 'The little kids will love them.'

'And I like all the fluffy ones,' Sophie says.

'When do you want to pick them up?' Jack asks.

'Tomorrow?' I say. 'I know it's early, but we're opening the farm in April, so we'll have a couple of months to give them time to settle, to get them health-checked by one of the vets at Otter House, and let Georgia and Sophie play with them to get them completely familiar with being handled. Jack, you can advise us on food and bedding. I'll pay you. I don't want anything to go wrong.' I pause. 'I'd like the goats as well. They seem perfect.'

We make the arrangements before we drive over to collect the donkeys, taking the road south towards Talysands and catching the first glimpse of the sea at the top of the hill where the water reflects the light of the pale winter's sun. I turn off the main road into a drive-way, passing a sign reading 'Letherington Equestrian Centre', and a small, warehouse-style building that houses the shop, Tack 'n' Hack, on one side, and pad-docks on the other, where a couple of horses dressed in their winter woollies are sharing an enormous round bale of hay.

I continue past a modern barn and into a car park that faces onto a yard of breezeblock-and-tile stables.

Beyond is a second yard of older higgledy-piggledy part-brick and part-cob buildings, where we find Delphi and the donkeys.

Slightly unkempt, with dirty nails and weathered skin, Delphi is in her mid-to-late forties. Dressed in a long riding mac, breeches and long boots, she exudes an air of horse, Chanel and superiority. I don't know her very well, having met her only briefly at various New Year parties held at Talyton Manor, where she used to throw herself at Alex Fox-Gifford when he wasn't attached to either his ex-wife, who ran off with a footballer, or his current wife, Maz. I recall her cut-glass accent and horse-like laugh.

She shows us to where she has the miniature donkeys in an equally miniature stable. There are two geldings, one a grey dun with sorrel highlights and one black, and they stand less than a metre tall at the withers. My heart melts when I see them together with their head-collars on, one blue and one red.

'Guy says you could have had Bracken and Chester and stuck some false ears on them instead,' Georgia jokes.

'Hey, you can't get rid of my pony,' Sophie says in a sulky tone.

'My mum bought Bracken from here,' Georgia says.

'How is Bracken?' Delphi asks.

'Well, she was a very naughty pony when we got her, but she's a good girl now.'

'She can jump three foot six,' Sophie pipes up.

'She threw me off and broke my arm,' Georgia says. 'Mum was really cross when you wouldn't take her back at first, but then she said it was a good thing you wouldn't because you'd only have gone and sold her to another mug.'

'Did your mum really describe herself as a mug?' I ask.

I wonder if Delphi is feeling a little awkward, but I'm not sure.

'That's what comes of letting novices take on a pony,' she sniffs. 'Anyway, do you want these little chaps or not? They have the sweetest temperaments. They've never been seen to bite or kick, and they always come running for a carrot.'

'Where did they come from?' James asks.

'A friend of mine has had them standing out in a field at Bottom End for the past couple of years. Their pasture flooded over Christmas and the poor things nearly drowned.'

'Aah,' Georgia sighs.

'All I'm asking is that they go to a good home and a small contribution to cover the cost of feeding them for the past month,' Delphi goes on. She mentions a figure that my father thinks is far too much.

'How much does a pair of miniature donkeys eat?' he complains. 'That's bloody extortionate.'

'I have a couple of other people interested in them,' Delphi counters.

'Dad, please. I want these donkeys,' I say.

'They are good to handle?' my father asks.

'Go in and see for yourself.' Delphi unlatches the stable door and lets the girls inside. The donkeys are peculiarly quiet. I'm impressed and, having overridden my father's doubts, I agree on a slightly reduced sum of money. I pay in cash, we load them – they're called Sneezy and Grumpy – into the trailer and take them back in triumph to Nettlebed Farm, where I let them out into the paddock we've made for them alongside the car park. They stand in the field shelter for a while, falling asleep on their feet as if they've had a very long day.

The following morning the rabbits arrive. After we've settled them in their mansions, I decide that Georgia and I should catch the donkeys and give them a brush to get them into a routine. I fetch two carrots from Mary's store in the larder and, armed with the head-collars, we enter the paddock. As soon as the donkeys see us, they trot away to the furthest corner and wait for us to trudge across in our wellies.

'Come here, Sneezy,' Georgia calls softly.

Sneezy turns his bottom towards her and kicks out.

Luckily, she is just out of his reach.

'Come back, Georgia,' I warn. 'I don't trust these little guys.'

'You have to act confident, even if you aren't,' she says. 'We used to have trouble catching Bracken.'

Is this history repeating itself? My heart sinks because I think I've made a terrible mistake.

I fetch a longer rope and manage to lasso Grumpy, who walks alongside me with Sneezy following behind until we reach the gate, when he takes umbrage and digs his heels in, refusing to budge. He grinds his teeth and swishes his tail. When Georgia tries to shoo him through he kicks out again, catching her on the knee.

'Ouch,' she squeals.

'Are you all right?' I say, panicking.

'I'll be okay.' She grimaces as she touches her toe to the ground. 'He hasn't broken it.'

'What are we going to do?'

'I don't think he's suitable for small children,' Georgia observes, 'or large ones for that matter.'

As I'm focusing on Georgia, the donkey takes advantage and nips at my arm, tearing the sleeve of my waterproof jacket.

'Don't do that!' My automatic reaction is to swipe the offender around the nose, but before I make contact, he's pulled the rope from my hands and cantered back across the paddock with his partner in crime.

'They are evil,' says Georgia.

I scratch my head, unsure what to do. 'Do I call Delphi and demand she takes them back?'

'She wouldn't take Bracken back. She said it was our fault.'

'We could just load them up and leave them there?'

'We couldn't do that. Look at them. They like it here.'

Now they know we're nowhere near them, the donkeys have their heads down grazing.

'Perhaps they have something wrong with them,' says Georgia.

'What sort of thing?'

'A mental health issue.'

'Where did you get that idea from?'

'We decided that was what was wrong with Bracken.' Georgia leans on the gate.

'I'll call the vet.' It's a pity Leo isn't here, I think sadly.

Two days later, Alex Fox-Gifford calls in to assess the donkeys – we catch them up in the morning before he arrives, using Bear, James, Cecil and Mary as reinforcements, and putting them in the nursery in a pen so that they are trapped in as small a space as possible.

'So what's the problem?' Alex asks.

'They're vicious,' says James. 'Georgia thinks they have mental health issues, whereas Cecil believes they have a shortage of lead in their brains.'

'You mean he wants them to take the bullet,' Alex says. 'They're handsome little donkeys. Are they really that bad?'

'They bite and kick. They're wild.'

'They were very calm when we picked them up from Delphi's,' Georgia says. 'Do you think they were sedated, Alex?'

Alex shrugs. He's hardly likely to comment on that, I think.

'There's no way of proving or disproving that theory now. Let me examine them.' He checks them all over while they stand looking disgruntled at the attention. I don't know what it is about Alex, but he seems to inspire respect in even the most wilful donkey. 'There's nothing much wrong with these two,' he pronounces, 'apart from the fact they have a few visitors. Look.' He parts the hair on Grumpy's neck. 'They have lice, which we can easily treat with a pour-on product. I wouldn't advise you to use them in the petting farm until they're clear.'

'I'm not sure I'll be able to use them anyway. They're a health and safety hazard and this whole project is a nightmare. I hope I don't make the same mistakes when I'm interviewing for staff.'

'It's all right, Stevie,' James says gently. 'Keep the faith. It'll come together in the end.'

'I hope you're right,' I say.

'I'm always right – you can rely on me,' he says cheerfully.

I'm afraid that I do rely on James rather too much. The project is moving along, one step forward and two steps back, but will it ever come together in time?

Chapter Twenty-One

Pulling the Rabbit out of the Hat

'Does Leo still Skype you?' Jennie asks me one day in February. I'm having coffee at her house. For some reason I'm missing Leo more than ever, and it seems Jennie can tell what's on my mind.

'Almost every day.' Given how affectionate he is when we talk, I harbour secret hopes that we will find a way to be together one day.

'So you're still pining for him?'

'It's probably my hormones,' I say, half expecting another lecture about how I should break contact with Leo.

'You can't keep using them as an excuse.' Jennie smiles. 'How old is Holly?'

'I suppose I can't be post-natal for ever,' I smile back ruefully.

'Let's face it, if Leo had loved you that much, he

wouldn't have gone away. I wouldn't have. In fact, I didn't.'

'What do you mean?' I cast a glance at Jennie. Holly and Reuben have been lying on the floor, kicking and gurgling at each other, but now Holly begins to whinge, apparently bored with Reuben's company. She sticks her fist in her mouth, meaning she's hungry again.

'When I moved to Devon with the children, after my divorce from my first husband, Adam was struggling to cope with leaving his friends and settling down in the country. He went missing one day.'

'Goodness, that must have been so scary for you.'

'I thought he'd run away to London – I had visions of him being taken advantage of on the streets, mugged or drugged and worse. He hadn't though – we found him almost frozen to death at the edge of our pond.' She shakes her head. 'I thought I'd lost him – my baby.'

'So did you actually pack up and go?' I ask.

'I put the house on the market – I was all ready to leave when Guy and Adam between them persuaded me it would be a huge mistake. And here we are, as one very happy family.'

My mind flits back to Leo.

'So I firmly believe that if Leo loved you, he would have stayed.'

'But it's his dream job.'

'It's only a job. There's plenty of work much closer to home.' Jennie picks Reuben up from the floor and checks his nappy, sniffing at it, and I can't help laughing at what motherhood has brought us to.

'Nappy days,' Jennie grins.

'How do you feel about being back to nappies and sleepless nights?'

'Well,' she tips her head to one side, 'the sleepless nights don't worry me. I haven't the same energy as I did when the others were babies, but everyone helps out, including Guy. He's amazing. He'll do a long day on the farm and come indoors to bath Reuben while I finish dinner.'

It makes me feel sad that I haven't got someone to lean on too. I'm lucky I have my dad, who does what he can, and Mary who adores Holly, but it isn't the same.

'Didn't you and Leo ever talk about you going out to New Zealand with him?'

'He asked me to go on the day he left, but it was all too last-minute and I wasn't sure if he was serious, and I was pregnant. Oh, it's all about the wrong timing. In another universe, Leo and I are together.'

'Stop fretting about him, Stevie. Just be patient and love will come along when you least expect it. It did for me. When I moved here, the last thing I wanted was to fall in love with someone else after my divorce, but along came Guy . . .'

'Is that somebody taking my name in vain?' booms Guy's voice from the hallway.

'Hi, darling.' Jennie gets up from her chair with Reuben in her arms. 'There's coffee in the pot.'

'I'm not stopping,' he says, dodging into the living room and kissing his son and his wife. 'Hello, Stevie. How's life in the zoo?'

'It isn't a zoo,' Jennie says lightly.

'I hope we're going to be ready for Easter.'

'You have doubts.'

'A few,' I say. 'James and his cousin are working flat out on the new building and I've been sourcing suitable animals, but there's still so much to do on the landscaping and final touches, signage and taking on staff.'

'I think you're mad,' Guy says. 'I haven't changed my opinion.'

'Wait and see.'

I'm determined to prove Guy and Fifi and all the others wrong. Nettlebed Farm's new venture *will* be a success.

After another week of intense organisation, opening the petting farm on time begins to look more feasible and, on a chilly morning at the beginning of March, when the daffodils are beginning to bloom along the drive, I'm walking around the farm with James, running through a list of last-minute things to be done. The Shed is finished and we have our hygiene certificate for the tearoom kitchen.

'You did check the rabbits properly?' James asks.

'They've been examined by Maz or Emma and had the jabs they need. Animal welfare is at the forefront of what we are doing, after all. The animals are here for the children, but not at the expense of their health.'

'The male of the pair of giant rabbits got me this morning. He savaged me. Look.' James rolls up his sleeves to show me a set of giant scratch marks.

'Oh? That isn't good. Have you written it in the accident book?'

'No,' he says.

'Well, I think you should.'

'I'd rather not. It's embarrassing. Anyway, I don't know what you want to do with him. I think he's being protective over his girlfriend and it comes out as aggression. He's called Boris and she's Nibbles, but it should be the other way round.'

'He's been neutered,' I say. 'It cost me a fortune.'

'Did they remove the right bits?' James says dryly.

'I don't know what to do. We can't have the children going in with him if he's like that. He'll put them off rabbits for life, and there'll be hell to pay with the parents. If anyone hurt Holly I'd be furious.'

'You'll have to sack him then,' James says.

'I can't afford to be sentimental, but I know I'll keep him because I can't bear the thought of sending him back to the rescue centre.'

'We could make him into bunny burgers.'

'No way!' I start laughing. 'Give me some good news.'

'The ewes are ready to lamb at any moment, so there'll be some lambs to stroke and maybe feed. I think that will go down well.' He pauses. 'I'm going take the trailer to pick up the tables and chairs you ordered.'

'Thanks, James. I'll go and check on the heifers.'

Domino doesn't come up to the field gate with them. I find her in the ditch under the hedge, cold and trembling. I call Talyton Manor vets with a sinking sensation in my heart and Alex Fox-Gifford turns up half an hour later, but all he can do is confirm that this is the end of the line for poor Domino and help her along into the next world, whatever or wherever that may be, which is how I find myself on my knees in the mud, my arms around a dead cow's neck, sobbing my eyes out while I wait for the knackerman to collect her.

My father used to threaten me with the knackerman if I misbehaved when I was a child, and I still dread his visits to the farm.

'It's the way it is,' I say to Leo later on Skype, 'but it doesn't make it feel any better.'

'I reckon Domino was like a cat – she had nine lives, but eventually they ran out.'

'I wish you were here,' I say.

'Stevie, are you crying?'

'It must be the signal, the picture quality . . .'

'Don't try to tell me you've dropped your laptop in the bath,' Leo says wryly. 'I can see tears.'

'I want you to have the best life. Don't worry about me – I'm all over the place what with the post-baby blues and Domino dying. I kept the switch from the end of her tail as a keepsake. Does that seem macabre?'

'It's a little odd. I wish I was with you too,' he goes on softly. 'You need a friend. If I was there, I'd put my arms around you, hold you close and never let you go.'

'Leo, I can't bear it.'

'I'm sending you a virtual hug. I'll call you tomorrow, same time, same place,' he says lightly. 'Good day, Stevie.'

'Goodnight, Leo.' I switch off the laptop and walk

across to Holly's cot. She's asleep, twitching and smiling as if she's dreaming.

'I love you,' I whisper. And I love Leo too, so much that I'm beginning to consider whether I could tear myself away from Nettlebed Farm and move with Holly to New Zealand, temporarily at least, to see if Leo's love for me could possibly overcome his fear of getting close to a child – my baby.

We open two weeks before we'd planned, in the middle of March. I don't sleep the night before the grand opening of Nettlebed Farm. We've invited all the locals and advertised in the press, and I've spoken to Ray to let him know he and his family are welcome. I'm too excited to sleep and the rain patters against the bedroom window; my father shouts out in his dreams and the cockerel starts crowing well before dawn, which makes me wonder if we've ended up with a dud cockerel with a body-clock problem as well.

'Some of this is down to you,' I say, looking down at Holly, who is lying fast asleep with her thumb in her mouth, her skin smooth and pale in the morning light. An urge to wake her washes through me, falling away again when I contemplate the consequences. Let sleeping babies lie, I tell myself. My heart clenching with love, I lean over and plant a kiss on her cheek. She yawns and stretches, curling and uncurling her fingers around her soft yellow blanket. Her light-brown hair forms a downy halo against the undersheet. 'My angel,' I whisper.

I decide to risk leaving her to sleep while I grab a quick shower, and it works. I really think I'm getting the hang of looking after a baby at last, because I manage to both dress and check my phone for messages without waking her. There's one from Leo.

Good luck for today. Wish I cd b there. Miss u xxx

I text back, promising I'll attach some photos later, at which point Holly starts to cry.

'Hey there.' I lift her out of the cot and cradle her against my chest. 'Let's go down for breakfast.' I can smell bacon – Mary's beaten me to it and Dad is up too, dressed in what looks like his Sunday best, a tweed suit, yellow shirt and brown tie. He walks up to me and smiles at his granddaughter in my arms.

'Good morning,' he says, and Holly stares at him, going cross-eyed before she gives him a smile back.

'She smiled at me,' he says, as she stuffs her fist into her mouth, as if to say, feed me. 'That wasn't wind that time. Ah, she's hungry. She needs her bottle, Stevie.'

'Dad, I know that.' He's like a mother hen. I can't imagine he was like this when Ray and I were babies.

'Am I late?' I ask, going over to the fridge to grab a bottle to warm up for her.

'I'm early,' Dad says. 'I wanted to be sure I was ready.'

'Thanks, Dad. You're looking very handsome,' I say lightly.

'I thought I'd make an effort,' he says, looking a fraction embarrassed.

'He scrubs up well, does Tom,' says Cecil, joining

us in the kitchen with Bear and the aroma of cow and sheep. 'We've had triplets arrive safe and well in the night.'

'That's great,' I say. 'The visitors will love seeing the newborn lambs. I can't believe everything is going to plan, apart from the weather. It wasn't supposed to rain today. I hope it doesn't put people off.'

'Rain before seven, fine before eleven,' says Cecil. 'The clouds are clearing from the southwest.'

I feed Holly and run through the plan for the day, the timings and the allocation of duties, before I wash and dress her, put her in the pram and meet the others in the visitor centre. We are joined by James who is here to help out, along with Adam from Uphill Farm and Adam's girlfriend Rosie, and one of her friends Maddie, who is true to her name, being as mad as a hatter, but warm and friendly, and, I hope, hardworking. I check that everyone who needs them has a functioning radio.

'Is everyone ready?' I ask. 'Does everyone know what they're doing?'

'We'll muddle through, Stevie,' says Cecil.

'The whole point of a plan is not to muddle through,' I point out with a smile. 'It's ten o'clock. Good luck and let's go.'

'Let's get this party started,' Adam says.

Cecil is in charge of the cows and keeping the rest of the farm running. I'm troubleshooting for the day and my father is responsible for taking the money at the gate. I worry about his people skills, that he might frighten small children, but when I check up on him in

414

his sentry box along the drive, which is bordered by hundreds of daffodils that James and I planted in the autumn, he's in his element, using his gift of the gab, as he calls it, to schmooze and sweet-talk our first paying guests.

'Where are the elephants?' asks one girl, who walks in with her teddy bear under her arm.

'This is a farm,' Dad says. 'We aren't allowed to keep elephants here because we haven't got room for any more animals. We have chickens, sheep, cows, ducks, geese and rabbits. And you'll love stroking the guinea pigs.'

'Anyway, elephants should be left in the wild where they can roam free,' says the little girl's mum who's struggling with a buggy. 'Come on, Ella, let's go and find the animals.'

'You're managing okay here, Dad?' I ask as the next car draws up.

'Leave it with me, Stevie.' He smiles. 'I can do this.'

'Radio me when you want a break.' I glance along the queue of traffic lining up along the drive and the lane. I have to admit Fifi and her supporters might have been right about the extra cars – it's gratifying but I hadn't expected so many people to turn up to Nettlebed Farm. I only hope they love what they see.

'Go on, Stevie. Don't you worry about me,' Dad says, shooing me away. 'I've got work to do. I can see Fifi in the queue – I don't want to keep her waiting.'

I decide to check up on Adam – in a nonchalant, not-really-checking-up-on-him kind of way, because he is a little sensitive and I don't want to put him off. I find him with the goats, talking about them, telling people their names and where they came from.

One of the little boys in the assembled crowd screams as the billy goat puts his head over the top of his door and looks at him in an apparently threatening manner.

'He's just being friendly,' Adam says, but the little boy is unconvinced.

'It's got butters,' he cries.

'Butters?' Adam scratches his head.

'I think he means horns. He doesn't like the horns,' the boy's mum says.

'I don't like amamules.'

'He means animals,' his mum explains, but her translation gets lost in more screaming.

'You'd better take him away,' Adam says, 'you're frightening the goats.'

'Adam,' I warn him. I wish he'd be more tactful, otherwise it's going to be him, not my dad, who's going to frighten the visitors. 'Where's Rosie?'

'She and Maddie are with the rabbits.'

'Together? I've asked them not to work together – they'll only chat.'

'There's quite a crowd. The rabbits and guinea pigs are very popular,' Adam says brightly. 'In fact, you might want to get rid of the goats in future and concentrate on the small furry animals.'

When I reach the rabbits, there are lots of visitors queuing up to pet them. I suggest to some people that they move on to do the Nature Trail while the weather's better and come back to the rabbits later. I wonder if there's going to be a welfare issue with some of the animals having to work harder than others. I can't help smiling to myself at the thought of the rabbits working to rule, but I soon lose my sense of humour when an irritated parent accosts me to complain their child has been savaged by one of the guinea pigs.

'It was Bernie,' says Maddie. 'She scratched the boy because he was rough with her.'

'That is rubbish,' the father says. 'She was squeaking and struggling to get away – clearly she isn't suitable for handling by children. She's dangerous.'

She's a guinea pig and she's been chosen especially for her temperament and been trained, I want to say. I bite my tongue. Isn't it the case that the customer is always right?

'I'll radio for our trained first-aider,' I say, calling for James.

'Code blue,' I say, using our pre-planned code so as not to cause alarm among our guests.

'I'll be right there. Over and out.'

James arrives within half a minute, screaming up on the quad bike with a first-aid kit, a beaming smile and a cock-and-bull story of how he was once bitten by a crocodile.

I touch his shoulder as he squats down beside the boy and chats to the dad. 'Thanks, James. I don't know what I'd do without you.' I move on to the far end of the rabbit housing – I used to call them the small furries but today small furies would be more appropriate. In the end pen, two of the rabbits are mounting each other.

'Granny, those rabbits are gay.'

'They are just playing, darling.'

'They are mating with each other. I've seen it on a nature programme.'

'Sh, Hannah, not in front of your grandmother,' her mum says.

'Don't you worry about me,' says the older woman. 'I'm seventy-eight and I've seen it all before.'

'Well, I don't think it should be allowed. It's so embarrassing and awkward trying to explain it to the children.' The mum directs her complaint to me. 'It isn't appropriate in front of young children, especially when it's two boy rabbits. I mean, it isn't natural, is it?'

I don't apologise. 'Far from going into the nature versus nurture debate, it's what animals do. I want to show life down on the farm as it is, not some sanitised version that doesn't reflect reality. I don't see what I can do, apart from offer to separate the offending animals, but they're friends. They need company of their own kind.' I pause. 'Why don't you come along and see the chickens?' Inwardly I'm hoping they're not squawking and pecking each other as they were the day before, maintaining their social hierarchy.

I escort them to the chicken coop where, to my surprise, I find my brother and his two girls.

'You came,' I say, as Ray and I kiss each other's cheeks. 'What do you think?'

'It's so cool,' says the younger girl, Christiane, who's come prepared in spotty wellies and a matching fleece. 'I've stroked a sheep and a rabbit.'

Alisiana wrinkles her nose. 'It's all a bit smelly,' she says.

'I'm sorry, it's her age,' says Ray. 'She's hit puberty early.'

'Please don't talk about me like that, Ray,' she says. 'I shall tell Mummy.'

'Why don't I buy you an ice cream?' I say, finding some cash. 'Mary is selling ice creams in the Shed.'

'Go on, girls,' says Ray. 'I'll catch you up. You've done well, Stevie. I can't believe you did it.'

'Thanks,' I respond. 'Have you spoken to Dad?'

'He made me pay full price for our tickets,' Ray says with a rueful smile. 'Stevie, I know what you're doing, trying to get us all together again, but it won't work. I'll be civil to the old sod, but that's as far as it goes.'

'Well, that's great because that's more than I expected, Ray.' I pause. 'Have you seen your baby niece yet?'

He shakes his head.

'Come with me. She's with Mary.'

'What's that saying again?' I ask Mary, once Ray and the girls have cooed over Holly – and Christiane has tried to feed her ice cream – and they've returned outside to see the rest of the farm, Ray promising to make more effort to keep in touch.

Mary looks up from where she's supervising Georgia, who's doing some waitressing during the school holidays. 'What was that, my lover?'

'What's that saying,' I repeat, 'the one about never working with children or animals? There's a lot of truth in it.'

She smiles. 'Sit down, Stevie. I'll fetch Holly's bottle and a cup of tea.' She lowers her voice. 'Don't look

419

round, but Fifi is here – she's eating Jennie's cider cake. Can you believe it after all she said?'

The rest of the day runs smoothly. I spend the last half an hour topping up the soap and paper towels for hand-washing and reuniting a family who managed to get themselves separated somewhere along the Nature Trail. We have signs everywhere, reading, 'Children, if you lose your parents, ask the nearest member of staff and we'll put out a message to find them.'

By four-thirty, the last of the visitors go home, and we have a small celebration for the staff in the tearoom, with food and drinks – a chance to say thank you and relax. I hold Holly in my arms, making up for the time we missed out on during the day.

My father raises a glass of bubbly and makes a speech that touches my heart.

'A toast to my daughter and lady farmer, Stevie. I doubted her, but she didn't give up. Thank you for bringing the farm back to life.'

'Thank you, Dad, for letting me get on with it in the end.' I walk up to him and kiss him on the cheek, waiting for the applause to die down before continuing. 'Thank you for everyone's help today and over the past few months. I couldn't have done this without you.'

'Let me have my granddaughter,' Dad says, and I willingly hand her over.

'We've enjoyed every minute,' says Cecil, joining in. 'Almost every minute.' I wonder if he's a little tipsy when he continues. 'It isn't what you've done in life that you regret. It's what you didn't do. And our Stevie will have no regrets. Cheers, Stevie.'

'Thank you, Cecil.' I give him a hug. 'I owe you so much. You're a very special man.'

'We've got something for you,' Adam says, interrupting. He hands me a package. I open it to find a sweatshirt with 'Nettlebed Farm, The Boss' embroidered on it. I put it on straight away.

'Perhaps you'll all listen to me now,' I tease.

It's been a brilliant day, exceeding all expectations, and I reckon with the takings as they are and the fact that Nick has finalised the purchase of my London flat, it won't be very long until we can afford to buy that new tractor I've had my eye on, but there is never a moment when my thoughts are not with Leo. I miss him more than ever.

Chapter Twenty-Two

Home Is Where the Heart Is

I wrap Holly up in layers of vests, babygros and a furry onesie with floppy rabbit ears attached to the hood – we sell them in the gift shop – before I tuck her into the sling, hugging her to my chest and wrapping my coat around her. She's three-and-a-half months old now, yet I feel as if I've known her all my life.

'You'll be as snug as a bug in a rug,' I tell her as she wriggles to find the most comfortable position and then I begin to worry that she'll overheat. 'I have never worried about anything so much in my life,' I tell Mary, who's slaving over a hot Aga. 'It's all-consuming.'

'Where are you going?' Dad asks. He is up and dressed and shaved, with a bloody nick on his chin.

'You've cut yourself.' I hand him a tissue from the box on the dresser. He takes it and sticks it in his jacket pocket more intent on protecting his granddaughter from the perils of the great outdoors.

'You aren't taking Holly out in this weather? It isn't right. She'll get pneumonia.'

'She'll be fine with me.'

'What are you doing, though? Cecil's milking the cows.'

'I'm hiding the eggs for the Easter egg hunt.'

'Can't somebody else do that?'

'I want to do it.' I smile. 'I know all the best hiding places.'

'You don't have to do everything. You'll wear yourself out, Stevie.'

'I want everything to be perfect. I don't want to disappoint anyone.' I pause, stroking the top of Holly's head. 'I wish Holly was old enough to be excited about an Easter egg hunt.'

'Don't wish her life away, my lover,' Dad says. 'She'll be grown up soon enough and then you'll wonder where the years went.'

I leave the house, crossing the yard to watch the last batch of cows enter the parlour, looking happy and healthy. I head for the beautiful new building which will forever be known as the Shed, unlock the door and go inside to fetch the box of Easter eggs, putting them on a trolley so I can move them while carrying Holly at the same time.

As I walk back outside, James and Adam appear in the doorway, ready for work.

'Hey!' I say, as James snatches a creme egg from the top of the box. 'Go on, Adam, you can have one too, but no more. Don't go looking for eggs because I want some left for the other little kids.'

I grin. At last I feel confident. I feel like the boss.

'I hope people turn up today,' James says. 'It's pretty cold outside. There's ice on the donkeys' trough and the goats' water buckets.'

'We'll just have to hope it warms up. Thanks for your concern, guys, but I'm supposed to do the worrying around here.' I go outside and start hiding eggs among the bales of hay in the barn. Someone is watching me and, when I turn round, I find Bear standing beside the trolley, sniffing the air for the scent of chocolate.

'Don't you dare,' I tell him, and he slopes off with his tail between his legs, casting me backward glances.

Once I've finished, I return the trolley to the shop, just as Holly decides she's worked up an appetite. I take her to the house to feed her and myself.

'I see your appetite's come back,' Mary observes. 'You look much better.'

I smile to myself. I know she means well and I know what she's trying to do – make me realise I can live without Leo and be happy.

James radios through to me. 'Hi Stevie, one of the ewes is lambing. She needs some assistance and my hands are too big, my father's greatest disappointment,' he says with humour. 'Can you pop straight over?'

'Okay,' I sigh. 'I'm on my way'.

I leave Holly with Mary and join James in the sheep pens. One of the mule ewes – we call her Erica – is lying in the straw, straining to give birth, the water bag hanging from her rear end.

'Have you any idea how long she's been like this?' I ask.

'She's been down for twenty minutes or so. Cecil said she was all right when he checked on the ewes before milking.'

I wash my hands and don a pair of latex gloves. 'Hang on to her for me, will you?'

James moves around to the ewe's front end and kneels in the straw, restraining her in a headlock so I can examine her. I can feel a pair of feet in the birth canal. I slide my fingers gently past them, waiting while the ewe strains before groping for the rest of the lamb.

'I can't feel a head.'

'Is it coming backwards?' James asks.

'It's coming forwards as it should be, but I think its head's turned back and caught on the bones of the ewe's pelvis. Or it could be its rump.'

'Do you think you can sort it?'

'I'll have a go.' I'll have to be careful though. It's a delicate manoeuvre and the last thing I want to do is cause the ewe any pain or, even worse, long-term damage.

'Should I call the vet or fetch the Land Rover? We can put her in the back and rush her over to Talyton Manor.'

'Give me five minutes. If I can straighten the lamb out, we'll be all right. If not . . .' I close my eyes, ignoring James and concentrating on saving mum and baby. Between contractions, I push the lamb back into the womb before I can identify which leg is which. 'I think it's a front leg I've got hold of,' I say, frowning. 'I've got the fetlock, which is connected to the shank which is joined to the knee or wrist.'

James starts singing 'Dem Dry Bones'.

'It is the front leg – I've found the head.' I move it gently to line up with the front legs when the ewe strains again, forcing the lamb back into the birth canal.

'How's it going?' James asks.

'It's on its way, but I don't think it's going to make it.' It won't suck on my finger. 'There's no sign of life.'

'It isn't the best start to the day. It's lucky it arrived before any kids turned up to watch,' James says as the ewe lifts her head to look for her baby as it emerges onto the straw. It's heart-wrenching to watch her sniff and lick at it, trying in vain to revive it. As I wipe a tear from my eye, James hands me a scruffy handkerchief.

'It's clean,' he says, sliding his arm around my back.

'It always gets to me,' I sniffle. 'I'll never make a proper farmer.'

'You wouldn't be a proper farmer if you didn't get upset sometimes. It's gutting to lose any animal.'

'I know,' I say, thinking of Domino.

'Is there another one in there?' James asks, looking down at the ewe.

'I didn't check.'

'I reckon there is.'

We watch the ewe strain again once, twice and three times, and out drops a second lamb onto the straw. The ewe, giving up on the first lamb, turns and licks the membranes from the second lamb's muzzle, at which it lifts and shakes its head, as though surprised at its hasty entrance into the world. The ewe nuzzles it fondly and the lamb bleats. Within minutes, it's on its feet, unstable and shaky, looking for milk.

Smiling through tears of happiness this time, I watch the second lamb sucking from its mother, as I envision a new life beginning for me and Holly. It's time I made some difficult decisions.

As the second lamb continues to nudge at the ewe's udder, she begins to strain again and a third lamb pops out. This one is alive.

'Hooray,' I say, cheering up, but my joy is short-lived when Erica nuzzles it then turns away in favour of the lamb's sibling. I try to encourage her to take an interest in it, holding it in front of her, but she appears more intent on trampling it than nurturing it.

'We'll have to bottle-feed that one. The visitors will like that. It's lucky you're used to getting up through-out the night,' James says. 'I'll deal with the dead one and catch up with you later.'

I take the rejected lamb indoors and stomach-tube him with some of the first milk from the ewe to make sure he gets as much protection from disease as possible. I pop him in a low oven – with the door open – until he begins to warm up and dry out and pick up his head. I make one more attempt at return-ing him to his mum, but she charges at him. I rescue him from a serious head-butting and take him back into the kitchen, where I leave him in a cardboard box filled with straw beside the Aga. He looks up at me and bleats.

'You're going to be okay,' I reassure him. 'You've had a shaky start, but now you have the chance of a new beginning.' I call him Colin. I don't know why. He just looks like one.

I realise it's now or never. I could ask James to act as manager of the farm. I'm sure he wouldn't turn it down. That would leave me free to travel to New Zealand with Holly, but what about my father? He would miss his granddaughter. And what about Nick? He's bound to put up some argument about how I shouldn't go, but how many times has he seen his daughter? For all his promises at the start, he's visited us twice.

I wash my hands and grab a couple of chocolate biscuits.

I have to take a chance. I've put the farm and family first, and I know everything will be all right here now. Dad was right that I can be flighty and impulsive, but this is something I have to do. If it doesn't work out, I'll come home. I'd rather try and fail than not try at all.

Once I've dealt with the lamb, the visitors start to arrive at the gate. Dad is selling tickets and Adam is waving the cars through to the car park. A lump catches in my throat as my dad spots me and waves me across to the sentry box, reminding me how hard it will be to leave all this behind.

'How are you doing?' I ask him.

'They're queuing to get in.'

'Don't sound so surprised.'

'I never thought anyone would pay good money to visit Nettlebed Farm.' Dad reaches out and pats my arm. 'As I said before, I'm very proud of you, my girl. I didn't think it was going to work, if I'm honest.'

'Didn't you? I would never have noticed,' I say, lightly sarcastic. 'You don't need any more change, or a cup of tea?'

'I have my flask.' Dad taps his coat pocket.

'You mustn't be drunk on duty.'

'It's all right. I'm having a small drop in my tea for medicinal purposes only.'

'Since when have you started taking your medicine?'

'When I found I had something to live for,' he says more seriously. 'Now, you get along, Stevie. I have a job to do.'

'So have I,' I smile. 'I've allocated myself my favourite area for the morning and I can't wait.'

'Where are you?'

'At the coop.' We call it the chicken coop, but it's a long shed sectioned off into an area for the incubator, eggs and chicks and an area for the chickens. I love the chicks – some are yellow, some fawny brown, and they don't bite, kick or scratch. They're also very popular. Already, there are two families of five or six crowded around the incubator where the chicks are hatching.

'Look, it's making a hole in the shell,' one of the mums says.

'Which do you think came first, the chicken or the egg?' her friend says.

'Both,' one of the children says.

'Is that possible?' the mum says.

'One of them had to come first.' The friend looks in my direction. 'Perhaps the farmer knows. Let's ask her.'

'I'm afraid I don't know the answer to that question.' I feel a little deficient in front of all the expectant faces. 'I believe it has something to do with evolution, that maybe a chicken-like dinosaur came first.'

'It's still the same problem: which came first, the dinosaur or the egg?' The mum smiles.

'Can I hold a chick?' says one of the children, a girl of about seven.

'What's the magic word?' her mum asks her.

'Yellow. I wanna hold a yellow one.'

'How about please?' her mum says.

'Please, please, please,' the girl says, bouncing on her toes.

I pick one out of the incubator. It's soft, fluffy and warm. I place it very gently into the girl's hands.

'Wow,' she breathes, staring at the chick. 'It's saying *'pip, pip, pip.'*

I watch her fingers tightening around its tiny body.

'Be careful not to squeeze him too tightly,' I say, smiling. It's nerve-wracking to watch.

'I've never held a chick before. Could I hold one?' asks one of the mothers who joins us, along with another, filling the area with toddlers and buggies.

'Of course.' I pick out another one and another. The rest of the chicks cheep and make tiny pipping noises as they huddle together in the incubator, keeping warm. I check on the eggs too, clearing out the empty eggshells.

Time passes quickly and at eleven Cecil appears, pushing Holly in the pram.

'Hey, have you looked at the rota?' I ask lightly. 'You aren't supposed to be here until twelve.'

'Young Holly had other ideas. Mary says she needs her mum, Stevie.'

'She's a girl who knows what she wants.'

430

'Like her mother,' Cecil grins, showing off his new false teeth. 'Actually, Stevie, it would be a good idea for you to take Holly somewhere quieter. I didn't realise it was so busy in here.' His eyes are shining. He seems remarkably upbeat, as if something has fired him up. 'Go and get yourself a cup of tea in the tearoom. The kettle's on.' Cecil shuffles over to the group of visitors and introduces himself as the dairyman. I hesitate for a moment, making sure he isn't going to frighten the kids like my dad can, but they seem to like him and I judge it's safe to leave.

I wash my hands and push Holly across to the Shed, parking the pram outside the tearoom under the awning.

'Come on then, Holly-pops.' I pick her up and carry her inside. It isn't busy yet. Rosie is arranging fresh flowers on the tables and Mary is chatting to a man with his back to me. As the door swings closed behind me, jangling the bell, the man turns to face me and I almost drop the baby. It's Leo.

'Look who's here, Stevie,' Mary says, beaming, 'all the way from New Zealand. Here, let me take Holly. I've got a pot of tea for you and a bottle warming up for her. Go and take the weight off your feet for a while.'

I kiss Holly on the top of her head as I pass her over to Mary.

'Come on there, my little lamb. Come to Mary. Your mummy's got some catching up to do.'

'I don't understand,' I say as Leo moves towards me, lightly tanned, fresh-faced and as gorgeous as ever. 'Has something happened? Is your sister all right?'

'Everything's fine, and even better now I've seen you.' He draws close and kisses my cheek before holding out a chair for me. 'How are you?' He fixes his eyes on my face. 'You look very . . . well, even better than you do via Skype.'

'So what are you doing here?' I ask, sitting down. I feel a sense of shock, as if I've seen a ghost.

'I should have warned you I was coming.' He bites his lip. 'I'm sorry, I'm a bit on edge. When I was on the plane I couldn't wait to see you, but now for some reason I'm really nervous.'

Leo keeps his gaze fixed on my face. Could it be that he's come all the way from New Zealand especially to see me, I wonder, my heart beating fast, like a chick's. Is it really possible?

Holly begins to cry. I overhear Mary trying to soothe her with a bottle and kind words, but Holly isn't having any of it.

'She wants her mum.' Mary brings her to the table and passes her back to me. 'She has a lot to say for herself.'

I hold my screaming bundle close and rub her back, at which she burps and ejects a string of baby sick down my sweatshirt.

'Oops,' I say, smiling.

'She'll feel better now,' Mary says, handing me a tub of baby wipes.

Holly settles down and gives me a beatific smile. I glance at Leo.

'She's cute, isn't she?' he says awkwardly. 'Oh dear, I'm not good at babies.'

'Can you hold her for me?' I ask. 'I'm going to fetch another bottle.'

'I'll fetch it,' he says, jumping up as if I've asked him to hold an unexploded bomb.

I feed Holly and put her back in her pram.

'I'm going to have to get back to work, Leo,' I tell him. 'I can't let everyone down. Will you stay? I know I've told you all about it, but I'd love to show you what we've done.'

He accompanies me around the farm as I point out the difficult donkeys, the ferocious guinea pig and angry rabbit.

'You aren't supposed to find our tribulations funny,' I tell Leo, who can hardly stop laughing.

'I'm glad I came back,' he says suddenly. He looks down at Holly in the pram. 'She looks like you.'

'Except for the lack of worry lines,' I smile.

'Is Nick coming to see her again soon? You've rarely mentioned him in our conversations.'

'He's hardly seen Holly, for all his promises, but I've managed, as you can see, with a lot of help from Mary and Cecil, Dad and Jennie.'

'I think you're amazing,' Leo says as we pause outside the goats' enclosure. He takes my hand and pulls me to him, embracing me and hugging me tight. 'Oh, I've missed you.'

'I've missed you too. I'm so happy you're here.'

'I would have stayed if you'd said something. Why didn't you ever say anything?'

'When I did it was too late. You were about to leave for the airport, remember? You'd set your heart on

New Zealand, and I didn't want to tie you down.' I hesitate. 'Maybe if we'd still been in a relationship at the time I would have asked you to stay, but we'd split up, hadn't we? Knowing what kind of man you are, I wouldn't have wanted you to come to feel I'd trapped you in any way.' I shrug resignedly. 'I think we've made rather a mess of things.'

'I admit that you being pregnant made it easier for me to walk away,' he says. 'It was a gift in a way, the gift of an excuse for me not to have to face up to my feelings.'

'I genuinely didn't know I was pregnant until late on. You know that.'

'But at the time . . .' Leo takes a step back and picks an imaginary piece of fluff from his sweater. 'This might be too soon – you might not be ready – but is there any chance that you and I could start afresh?'

'As a couple, you mean?' My pulse starts to throb with hope and anticipation. 'I'd love to, Leo, but it isn't just about me any longer. Holly and I are a package.'

'I realise that,' Leo says.

'You are lucky to find me here,' I go on. 'Now the petting farm is up and running, I've been planning a trip to New Zealand.'

'You mean you were planning a holiday?'

'An open-ended trip,' I say bravely.

'You were going to sacrifice everything – your friends and the farm – for me?'

'For us: for you, me and Holly.' I take a deep breath. 'So, as far as I can see, you have to make a choice, Leo. Either face up to your fears or walk away.' I turn to push the pram on along the Nature Trail, following the path up through Steep Acres, forcing myself to smile at Holly as she chuckles and coos at me, trying to engage me in some baby talk.

'Stevie.' I hear Leo following behind me. I keep walking right to the top of the hill, stopping beside the pond where the ducks are waddling about at the edge, foraging through the mud for snails and algae. 'Stevie, wait there! I have something to say.'

I stop, remembering to put the brake on the pram, turn and face him, squinting in the midday sunshine.

'I've been on a long journey,' he says. 'It took a flight to New Zealand with the prospect of a new life to make me realise that my life should be here with you.'

I open my mouth to add 'and Holly' but he puts his finger to his lips.

'Sh, let me speak. I'm not great at the touchy-feely stuff, and the self-analysis, but I've learned a lot about myself and how I've wasted a lot of time running away from situations instead of facing up to them. I've learned you can't run away from memories, but you can focus on the good ones, instead of the bad.' He reaches out and takes both my hands. 'I don't want to lose you again, Stevie. I'll go and see Alex – I expect he'll need a locum for the summer at least.'

It's very quiet, apart from the fluttering of a bird, flying down from the trees on the ridge of the hill. I can feel the tension in Leo's fingers, gripping mine.

'Do you need somewhere to stay?' I ask.

'I'll find somewhere. I noticed the mobile home has gone.'

435

'I had it scrapped. It was an eyesore.' And, if I'm honest, it was a painful reminder of Leo and happy times. Whenever I walked past it, I thought of him. 'You can stay here – in the house, if you like.'

'I'm not sure that's such a good idea.'

'There's plenty of room – there's only dad, Holly and me. You can have the spare room, or . . .' I look at him and he holds my gaze for a long time and my mouth goes dry and my heart pumps harder.

'Does the baby share your bed?' he asks quietly.

'Sometimes,' I admit.

'As well as the dog?'

'Well, I'm quite a social sleeper.'

'Is there room for one more?'

I cannot resist any longer. I want him, completely want him. He sets me on fire and makes me forget everything else, apart from Holly, of course.

Somehow, I'm in Leo's arms again, and he's holding me close as if he'll never let me go, his fingers tangling in my hair, stroking the skin at the nape of my neck. 'I love you, Stevie.'

'Oh, Leo,' I sigh. 'I love you too.' I lean up, tilting my face towards his, and he presses his lips to mine and kisses me three, four, five times before drawing back, smiling and keeping his arms around me.

'Cecil made a point of speaking to me one day when I was fitting a heel to one of the cows – they call me the Jimmy Choo of the cow world, don't you know?'

I smile back. I can't stop smiling as Leo continues, 'Anyway, he said to me, "Never forget that home is where the heart is." I dismissed it as an old man's

436

ramblings. You know what he's like. He does come out with some gems sometimes. Anyway, I've thought of what he said many times since, and he was trying to tell me in a roundabout way that I should take a good look at my life – and he was right. Home is where the heart is and –' Leo raises my hand to his lips and my eyes flood with tears of joy and hope for the future – 'my heart is with you, Stevie.'

It's a Vet's Life

Cathy Woodman

Christmas is coming, and life is busy for vet Maz Harwood.

She has a beautiful baby boy, George, and she will soon be marrying fellow vet Alex Fox-Gifford. Frankly, though, life is not as rosy as it looks. Because between arranging the wedding, performing life-saving animal surgery, and taking care of George, Maz doesn't have much time left for Alex, and even if she did, he's working even harder than her so she rarely sees him. And as Alex won't do anything to make life easaier, Maz has decided to take matters into her own hands.

But Maz's solution has truly terrible consequences for them all, and as the wedding approaches, Maz realises that it will take a Christmas miracle to get her and Alex to the altar.

Praise for Cathy Woodman:

'I absolutely love Cathy's books. They are a treat to read.'
Katie Fforde

arrow books

ALSO AVAILABLE IN ARROW

The Village Vet

Cathy Woodman

**In Talyton St George, vet nurse Tessa Wilde
is on the way to her wedding . . .**

It should be the happiest day of her life. But then her car hits a
dog, and though the dog is saved thanks to the Otter House vets,
her wedding is not.

Animal welfare officer and part-time fire-fighter Jack Miller spends
his life saving animals and people. As one of Tessa's oldest
friends, he feels he has the right to interrupt her wedding and
rescue her from a marriage that can only end in tears.

But does he? Tessa is sure she doesn't need rescuing, least of
all by Jack.

When they begin to work together at the Animal Rescue centre,
however, Tessa begins to wonder whether being rescued by Jack
might not be such a bad thing after all.

Praise for *The Village Vet*

'A wonderful story about rescued animals and romance.
I loved it.' Katie Fforde

arrow books

THE POWER OF READING

Visit the Random House website and get connected with information on all our books and authors

EXTRACTS from our recently published books and selected backlist titles

COMPETITIONS AND PRIZE DRAWS Win signed books, audiobooks and more

AUTHOR EVENTS Find out which of our authors are on tour and where you can meet them

LATEST NEWS on bestsellers, awards and new publications

MINISITES with exclusive special features dedicated to our authors and their titles

READING GROUPS Reading guides, special features and all the information you need for your reading group

LISTEN to extracts from the latest audiobook publications

WATCH video clips of interviews and readings with our authors

RANDOM HOUSE INFORMATION including advice for writers, job vacancies and all your general queries answered

Come home to Random House

www.randomhouse.co.uk